NOV 0 4

DATE DUE

DEC 28 '04			
2-9-05			
MAR 23 '05			
APR 08 '05			
FEB 11			
MAY 20			
JUL 12			
NOV 24			
FEB 28 '07			
GAYLORD			PRINTED IN U.S.A.

Junie B., First Grader
Shipwrecked

BARBARA PARK

Junie B., First Grader®
Shipwrecked

illustrated by Denise Brunkus

A STEPPING STONE BOOK™

Random House 🏠 New York

www.randomhouse.com/kids/junieb

Library of Congress Cataloging-in-Publication Data
Park, Barbara.
Junie B., first grader : shipwrecked / by Barbara Park ;
illustrated by Denise Brunkus. — 1st ed.
   p.   cm. — (The Junie B. Jones series ; #23)
"A Stepping Stone Book."
SUMMARY: Junie B.'s journal entries start with Room One's stomach virus
excitement, the first-grade Columbus Day play, and getting the part of
the *Pinta,* the fastest ship.
ISBN 0-375-82804-4 (trade) — ISBN 0-375-92804-9 (lib. bdg.) —
ISBN 0-375-82805-2 (pbk.)
[1. Sick—Fiction. 2. Theater—Fiction. 3. Schools—Fiction.
4. Columbus Day—Fiction. 5. Diaries—Fiction.]
I. Title: Shipwrecked. II. Brunkus, Denise, ill. III. Title.
IV. Series: Park, Barbara. Junie B. Jones series ; v #23.
PZ7.P2197Jsk 2004 [Fic]—dc22 2003018361

Printed in the United States of America   First Edition
10 9 8 7 6 5 4 3 2 1

Contents

1

■ ■ ■ ■ ■ ■ ■ ■ ■

Breathing Germs

Friday

Dear first-grade journal,

Today is the end of the week.

Mr. Scary is taking attendance. Attendance is the school word for who isn't here today.

There are lots of children out sick in Room One.

I am going to count them, I think.

I will be back in a minute.

Okay. Here is a teensy problem
I just ran into.
   'Cause how can I count the
people who aren't here? On
account of they didn't show up,
apparently.
   Taking attendance is ~~dificulter~~ harder
than it looks.
          From,
          Junie B., First Grader

I put down my pencil to think about this
situation.

   Only I didn't even have time to concentrate, hardly. 'Cause, all of a sudden, there was a noise on the other side of the room.

I turned my head to look.

And *SPLAT-O!*

A boy named Roger throwed up on the floor!

It was the disgustingest thing I ever saw. Also, the air did not smell delightful.

I quick held my nose and closed my eyes.

Only too bad for me. 'Cause my dumb-bunny eyes have a brain of their own. And they kept on sneaking peeks of the splat-o.

It was Cheerios, I believe.

Finally, I put my head on my desk. And I covered up with my arms.

Only just then, more trouble happened.

And it's called, a boy named Sheldon couldn't stand the splat-o.

And so he jumped up from his chair!

And he ran straight out of Room One!

And that was a surprise, I tell you!

Mr. Scary ran after him.

He brought Sheldon back in a jiffy.

Then he quick called the school nurse, Mrs. Weller, on the phone. And he told her that we need her help right now.

"Hurry!" he said. *"Fast!"*

And so, Mrs. Weller zoomed to Room One as fast as a speedy rocket.

And then she hurried over to Roger. And she talked to him in a calmy voice. And she said everything is going to be okay.

Roger hanged his head real embarrassed.

I felt sorry for that guy.

Also, he was making me ill.

Finally, Mrs. Weller helped him get up from his chair. And she held his hand. And she took him to her office.

After that, Room One could not do any work. On account of how can you do work with splat-o on the floor?

Only hurray, hurray!

'Cause pretty soon, our janitor named Gus Vallony came rushing through the door.

I jumped right up when I saw him.

"Gus Vallony! It's me! It's me! It's Junie B. Jones!" I hollered out. "Roger throwed up! Roger throwed up!"

Gus Vallony winked at me.

Then he went straight to Roger's desk. And he took out his important janitor equipment. And he sprinkled powder all over the splat-o.

And wowie wow wow!

That stuff sweeped up like a miracle!

We could not believe our eyeballs.

"Whoa!" said my friend named Lennie.

"Sí . . . whoa!" said my other friend José. "That powder is like magic."

I sniffed the air. "Yes! It *is* like magic, José!" I said. "Plus now it smells lemony fresh in here!"

Other children sniffed, too.

"Mmm. It *does* smell lemony fresh," said a girl named Shirley. "I wish I had some of that stuff for my mother. She *loves* to clean up messes."

"Mine does, too," said my bestest friend named Herbert.

Then, all of a sudden, Herb sprang out of his seat very excited.

"Wait! Hold it! My mother's birthday is on Sunday!" he said. "And so *that's* what I'll get her! I'll get her a tub of that magic powder! What's the name of it, Mr.

Vallony? Huh? What's it called? What's it called?"

Gus Vallony's face went kind of funny. He glanced his eyes at Mr. Scary, and then back at Herbert again.

Finally, he ran his fingers through his bald hair. And he said the name of it.

"*Vomit absorbent,*" he said kind of quiet. "It's called *vomit absorbent.*"

At first, Herbert just stood at his desk very frozen. He did not say any words.

Then, after a minute, he did a little shiver. And he sat back down.

"Maybe I'll just draw her a picture," he said.

Gus Vallony nodded.

Then he packed up his stuff. And he waved goodbye to Room One. And Mr. Scary walked him into the hall.

While he was gone, Sheldon put his lunch sack on his head.

As soon as Mr. Scary saw it, he tried to take it off.

But Sheldon held on tight.

"No . . . don't! I need this!" he said. "If I stay in here, I won't catch Roger's germs."

I raised my eyebrows at that remark.

"Yeah, only I don't get it, Sheldon," I said. "How can you catch Roger's germs? 'Cause Gus Vallony just swept them up in his bucket, remember?"

Sheldon talked to me through his bag.

"Roger's germs aren't *just* in the bucket, Junie B.," he said. "Whenever somebody throws up, their germs shoot out in the air all over the place. Then, if somebody else breathes that same air, those germs can get sucked right up their nose nostrils."

I did a little cringe at that information.

Then I looked all around in the air.

And—very slow—I lifted my hand. And I closed my nose nostrils.

Room One watched me.

Then—one by one—they closed their nose nostrils, too.

And so all of us held our noses tight with our fingers.

And we didn't breathe for the whole rest of the morning.

2

Letting Go

It is not easy to hold your nose and eat a sandwich.

You cannot swallow good like that.

Also, you can't actually breathe.

The reason I know this is because Room One kept on holding our noses while we ate lunch.

My ears felt blocked when I chewed.

I tapped on my friend Herbert.

"I am not enjoying my cheese sandwich today," I said.

"Me too," said Herb. "I am not enjoying

my sandwich, too. Plus I don't even know what I'm eating. 'Cause I can't taste what's under my lettuce."

I thought for a minute.

Then I tapped on him again.

"Yeah, only what if you're eating something you hate?" I said.

Herb thought, too.

Then he quick put down his sandwich. And he lifted up the bread so both of us could see.

We leaned our heads in real close.

Lennie and José leaned their heads in, too.

"Hmm," said José. "This is only a guess . . . but I'm thinking tuna salad."

Lennie shook his head. "I'm thinking ham spread."

Herb made a face.

"I'm thinking I'm done," he said.

After that, he got out his apple. And he tried to take a bite. Only he couldn't actually get it in his mouth. On account of he was still holding his nostrils.

Finally, Herbert got frustration in him.

"I give up," he grouched.

Then he let go of his nose. And he breathed in a big sniff of air.

"Mmm . . . ahhh . . . air," he said.

It looked good to do that.

I let go of my nostrils and breathed, too.

"Mmm . . . ahhh . . . air," I said.

Next to me, May's whole mouth came open. She did the cuckoo sign at us.

"You two are *crazy* to do that," she said. "Dirty, nasty germs are getting sucked right up your nose this very minute, I bet."

I looked surprised at that news.

"Really, May?" I said. "Thank you for telling me that."

Then I leaned over next to her. And I breathed out my nose air on her shoulder.

"There. All gone," I said.

May did a gasp.

"EW! EW! EW!" she hollered real loud.

Then she jumped right up. And she tattle-taled to Mr. Scary at the front of the table.

"Mr. Scary! Mr. Scary! Junie Jones breathed nose air on my shoulder! And now I've got germs on me!" she yelled.

Mr. Scary kept on eating his lunch.

He was pretending May was not there, I believe.

May kept on tapping on his arm. And she wiped her shoulder.

"Nose air! Nose air! Nose air!" she hollered in his ear.

Finally, Mr. Scary stood up real calm. And he walked May back to her seat.

"Boys and girls, I know that many of you are still worried about what happened to Roger this morning," he said. "And I promise that we'll talk more about this after recess, okay? But right now, I want all of you to release your nostrils. And eat your lunch."

He stood there and waited.

One by one, all of us let go of our nostrils.

Only not Sheldon.

Instead, Sheldon ducked his head under the lunch table. And he said he was looking for his pickle.

I peeked at him under there.

He was hiding under his napkin holding his nose.

When the bell finally rang for recess, Room One was the first class out the door.

"FRESH AIR! FRESH AIR! FRESH AIR!" we shouted very joyful.

Then all of us breathed big snorts of breath. Because Roger couldn't have shot his germs all the way outside, probably.

After that, we skipped and jumped and clapped and played.

Except for not Sheldon.

And not May.

Sheldon sat down and held his nostrils some more.

May went to the water fountain and washed her shoulder.

3

V-I-R-U-S

It is still Friday.

Dear first-grade journal,

We just came in from recess.

We are waiting for Mrs. Weller to talk to us about germs.

May started holding her nose again.

Also Sheldon put another paper bag on his head.

                          interesting

_Today is an ~~intersting~~ day in
Room One._
         From,
         Junie B., First Grader

Just then, there was a knock at our door.
And Mrs. Weller came in.

Mr. Scary went to meet her.

"Mrs. Weller, I'm very glad you could
come back," he said. "Room One is still
worried about what happened to Roger this
morning. And we need some advice about
how to stay healthy."

Mrs. Weller's eyes glanced over to Sheldon's bag head.

Mr. Scary's eyes glanced there, too.

"Some of us are a little more worried

than others," he said kind of soft.

Mrs. Weller went to the board. And she printed some big letters:

V-I-R-U-S

"Virus," she said. "These letters spell the word *virus*, children. Have any of you ever heard the word *virus* before?"

Lucille jumped right up.

"I have! I have!" she said real excited. "My nanna grows viruses all over the place! You should see our house, Nurse! Sometimes we have fresh viruses in every single room, almost!"

For a second, Mrs. Weller's face went funny. Then, all of a sudden, a light bulb came on in her head, I think.

"Ohhhhh. I think you mean *irises*, Lucille," she said. "Irises are very beautiful flowers, aren't they? But *viruses* are tiny little germs that can make people sick."

Lucille started fluffing her hair very embarrassed.

Then she fluffed and fluffed and fluffed.

21

Until finally, she sat down again.

Mrs. Weller kept on talking.

"Boys and girls, there's a stomach virus going around school. And I'm guessing that your classmate Roger has caught it now, too."

May nodded her head and pointed at herself.

"That's why I'm holding my nose," she said. "See me, Mrs. Weller? I'm being smart by not breathing the germy air."

Mrs. Weller looked kind of puzzled.

"Yes, but you're still *breathing*, May," she explained. "The air is simply going in your *mouth* instead of your *nose*."

May looked shocked at that comment.

Mrs. Weller smiled.

"I'm sorry, dear. But I'm afraid it just doesn't help to hold your nose," she said.

"In fact, one of the easiest ways to catch a virus is to touch your nose with germy hands."

May didn't move a muscle. She just kept on sitting there looking surprised.

Finally, I leaned over and tapped on her.

"I think that means you, nose squeezer," I said.

Lennie and Herbert laughed real loud.

They enjoy my humor.

After that, Mrs. Weller printed four rules on the board about how to stay healthy:

1. Do not share straws or glasses or forks or spoons!
2. Do not share food or drinks!
3. Keep your hands away from your mouth, eyes, and nose!
4. Wash your hands—OFTEN—with soap and water!

She put down the chalk and glanced over at Sheldon again.

"Oh, and I'm sorry to have to tell you this . . . but you can't really *hide* from germs, either," she said. "So—for those of you wearing paper bags on your heads—there are probably thousands of germs in there with you."

For a second, Sheldon sat as still as a statue.

Then, all of a sudden, he shouted real loud, "AAUUGGHH!" And he quick pulled off the bag!

Then he zoomed straight to the sink!

And he washed his hands and face with soap! Plus also, he washed his arms and his legs with a paper towel.

After that, he took off his shoes to wash his feet. But Mr. Scary said *no.*

"We're not doing a full-body scrub, son," he said. "Your face and hands are enough."

Sheldon looked upset.

"But germs can get on other places, too," he said. "Like what if someone drools on your arm? Or what if you get burped on? Or what if you fall down on top of a sick person, and he sneezes germs right directly up your nostrils?"

Mr. Scary rolled his eyes. "Come on, Sheldon. Now you're just being silly," he said. "I've been around a long time. And believe me, no one has *ever* sneezed germs directly up my nostrils."

After that, he took Sheldon's hand. And he sat him down again.

Pretty soon, Mrs. Weller had to go back to her office. But before she left, she took us to the sink. And she showed us the right way to wash our hands.

Room One lined up and washed very perfect.

Then we waved goodbye to Mrs. Weller. We were sad to see her go. 'Cause now we had to do schoolwork, probably.

Only here is what we didn't even *know*.

Mr. Scary had a happy announcement! And he'd been waiting all day to tell us!

"Boys and girls, I know we had a pretty rough morning. But I think I have some news that will cheer you up," he said.

He smiled. "In two weeks, our school is having an event called *Parents' Night*. Have any of you ever heard of Parents' Night before?"

Lennie quick raised his hand.

"I have!" he said. "My sister told me all about it. She said Parents' Night is the night when parents come to school and they poke their nose in your business."

Mr. Scary did a little frown.

"Yes, well, I don't really think that's the best way to put it, Lennie," he said. "Your parents don't come to poke their noses in your business. Parents are interested in what we do here in school. So sometimes they like to come to the classroom and—"

"Spy on us," said José.

"Butt in where they don't belong," said Shirley.

"Invade our own personal space," said Sheldon.

Mr. Scary closed his eyes a second.

Then he walked back to his desk real slow. And he sat down in his chair. And he ran his fingers through his tired hair.

"Okay. I'll get right to the point," he said. "This year for Parents' Night, I thought it would be fun to do something special. So I was wondering how you would feel about putting on a *play*."

My ears perked up at that word.

"A play?" I said kind of thrilled.

"A play?" said Herbert and Shirley.

"A play?" said May.

Then, all at once, Room One started clapping and clapping.

"A PLAY! A PLAY! A PLAY!" we shouted. "YAY! YAY! A PLAY!"

I springed out of my chair.

"I know a *lot* about plays, Mr. Scary!" I said. "On account of last summer I went to a real, actual children's theater. And I saw a play about a mouse. And that thing was a hoot, I tell you! And so maybe *we* can do a mouse play, too!"

Mr. Scary smiled. "Yes, well, I'm sure a mouse play would be fun, Junie B. But since it's October, our play is going to be about Christopher Columbus," he said. "We celebrate Columbus Day this month, remember? So Parents' Night will be perfect timing."

I thought it over a second.

Then I shook my head no.

"Nope, sorry. I think a mouse play is still the way to go here," I said.

Mr. Scary said *thank you* for my opinion and *please sit down*.

I tapped my foot kind of annoyed. Then I gazed my eyes around the room.

"Okay. Who would rather do a mouse play? Please raise your hands," I said.

Mr. Scary snapped his fingers at me.

Snapping means the conversation is over, I believe.

I sat down.

4

Finding Facts

That day when I got home from school, Mother was already back from work.

I like it when that happens.

She was in the kitchen with my dog named Tickle.

I gave her a paper Mr. Scary sent home about the play.

Her face smiled when she read it.

"Oh boy! Your class is going to do a play for Parents' Night, huh?" she said. "How fun!"

I shrugged my shoulders.

"Yeah, only it would be funner if it was a mouse play," I said. "But Mr. Scary says it has to be about dumb old Columbus Day."

Mother kept on reading.

"Oh, and look at *this,*" she said. "It says that over the weekend you're supposed to look up facts about Columbus and his ships. And whoever has the most facts will get to choose their part first."

I rolled my eyes.

"Fact number one," I said. "Columbus is not a mouse. And so I don't even care about being in this dumb play."

After that, I turned around. And I clomped out of the kitchen kind of grumpy.

Tickle clomped with me.

We were almost to my room when my mother called after me.

"I just don't *get* it, Junie B.," she hollered. "I thought you always wanted to be a *star*!"

I stopped clomping.

Tickle stopped clomping, too.

"A *star*?" I said. "Whoa. I never even thought about *that* situation."

I quick turned around and zoomed back to the kitchen.

"A *star*?" I asked. "I could really be a star, do you think? Like the one and only star of the whole entire production, you mean?"

Mother grinned.

"Well . . . maybe not the one and *only* star," she said. "But still, if you bring in the most facts about Columbus, you'll be able to choose any part you want."

Just then, my legs jumped all around very excited.

"The *star* part, Mother!" I said. "I am going to choose the *star* part!"

I quick grabbed her hand.

"Let's go! Hurry! Hurry! We have to go to the library to get my facts straight!"

Mother undid my hand.

"Sorry, honey. But we can't go now," she said. "Ollie's right in the middle of his nap. And I don't have a babysitter."

I slumped my shoulders very glum.

"Darn it," I said. "Darn it, darn it, darn it. That dumb old baby ruins everything."

Mother wrinkled her eyebrows at me.

"Ollie's not dumb, Junie B.," she said. "And besides, you and I can go to the library tomorrow. Tomorrow will be plenty of time for you to collect your facts."

She stood there for a minute.

"*Or*," she said, "if you want to do it right now . . . we can look up some Columbus facts on the computer. How does that sound?"

I grabbed her hand again and pulled her to her desk.

"Perfect!" I said real squealy. "That sounds perfect!"

And so me and Mother sat down at her desk. And she typed the name of *Christopher Columbus* on her computer.

And wowie wow wow!

A jillion pages came up about that guy! 'Cause he was famouser than I thought!

There were easy pages. And hard pages. And shortie pages. And longie pages. And picture pages. And poem pages. And there were even song pages!

Me and Mother read the pages out loud together. I read the easy pages. And she read the hard ones.

Then I wrote down lots of important facts we found out. And before I even knew it, I had *eighteen* whole facts printed on my paper!

I jumped down from my chair very thrilled.

"Eighteen! Eighteen! I have eighteen whole facts! And eighteen is more than my wildest dreams!" I said.

Then I hugged Mother real joyful.
And me and Tickle skipped to and fro.
And far and wide.
And round and round and round.

5

■ ■ ■ ■ ■ ■ ■ ■ ■ ■

The Winner(s)!

Monday morning

Dear first-grade journal,

18 FACTS!

I GOT 18 FACTS!

I can't wait to choose my part in the play!

This is going to be the time of my life, I tell you!

From,

Junie B., First Grader

P.S. Two more kids are sick from school today. Plus Lennie just went to the nurse.

P.S. (again) Sheldon is wearing sandwich bags on his hands today. It is to keep germs off, I ~~beleeve~~ believe.

Just then, Mr. Scary finished taking attendance. And he said to please put our journals away.

"As you can see, we're missing three more classmates today," he said kind of frustrated. "It's going to be hard to do a play with so many people absent. But we'll keep our fingers crossed that our classmates will be back in time to participate."

Just then, we heard a rustly sound.

Sheldon was crossing his fingers inside his sandwich bags.

After he got done, he waved to Mr. Scary very pleasant.

Mr. Scary looked at him for a real long time. Then he waved back.

Finally, he stood up and walked to the board.

"Boys and girls, I thought it would be fun to base our play on the facts you gathered for homework," he said.

He picked up the chalk. "If you have a fact you'd like to share, raise your hand and I'll write it on the board. Then—when we've listed all our facts—we can choose our play parts," he said. "Now who would like to go first?"

José shot his hand in the air speedy fast.

"I would! I would! I have a *poem*!" he said.

Then he jumped right up, and he started to read.

In fourteen hundred ninety-two,
Columbus sailed the ocean blue.
He had three ships and left from Spain;
He sailed through sunshine, wind, and rain.

Mr. Scary smiled.

"Nice, José. That's a great poem you found," he said. "Let's see how many facts we can find there."

He wrote them down.

1. Columbus was a sailor.
2. He had three ships.
3. He sailed from Spain.
4. The year was 1492.

Just then, Sheldon started waving his plastic hands very urgent.

"I know the names of the ships! I know the names of the ships!" he called out. "They're the *Niña,* the *Pinta,* and the *Santa María.*"

"Excellent job, Sheldon," said Mr. Scary.

He printed the names on the board.

5. Niña, Pinta, Santa María

Then Mr. Scary started to call on someone else. But Sheldon stood up and read more from his paper.

"Columbus sailed across the Atlantic Ocean. He landed on some islands near America," he read.

Mr. Scary added the new facts to the list.

6. Sailed the Atlantic Ocean.

7. Arrived in islands near America.

"Okay. Well, thank you *again,* Sheldon,"

he said. "Now I think we should let someone else have a—"

Sheldon interrupted. "My uncle Vern
sailed to an island once," he said. "He
came back with a woman named Bunny."

Sheldon kept on standing there. "Aunt
Bunny has tattoos," he said.

After that, Mr. Scary hurried to Sheldon's desk. And he put him back in his
chair.

May went next.

"My fact is about the *Mayflower*," she
said. "The *Mayflower* is the ship that
brought the Pilgrims to America. And so I
am going to be the *Mayflower* in our
Columbus play. Because both of our names
start with *May*."

Mr. Scary looked curious at her. "Yes,
but the *Mayflower* didn't sail to America

until over a hundred years *after* Columbus," he said.

"I know it," she said. "But both of our names still start with *May.* Don't you *get* it?"

"Yes, May. I *get* it," said Mr. Scary. "But we can't change history. So I'm afraid the *Mayflower* won't be sailing in our Columbus play."

May sat down in a huff.

Lucille stood right up.

"My fact is about the richie queen of Spain," she said. "The richie queen of Spain was named Isabella. And she gave Chris the money for the trip. So I am going to be richie Queen Isabella in the play. Because if there's one thing I know, it's how to be rich."

José raised his hand.

"You shouldn't call him *Chris*, Lucille," he said. "In Spain, they called him *Cristóbal Colón.*"

Lucille made squinty eyes at him.

"Chris . . . Crystal Ball . . . whatever," she said. "A queen can call you whatever she wants to."

She fluffed her hair and sat down.

That's when I springed up. And I waved my paper all around.

"Eighteen facts! I have eighteen facts!" I said real happy. "And so listen to this, people! The *Niña* was the *smallest* ship. And the *Pinta* was the *fastest* ship. And the *Santa María* was a big old tub."

Mr. Scary winked at me.

"Those are outstanding ship facts, Junie B.," said Mr. Scary. "Great job."

He printed them on the board.

And guess what?

After that, Shirley told him even *more* ship facts.

And so that's how the whole rest of the morning kept going.

Room One kept on telling him facts. And Mr. Scary kept on writing them down. Until finally, we'd told him every fact in the book!

Then ha! That's when the funnest part of all happened.

'Cause Mr. Scary walked around the room. And he counted how many facts each of us had listed on our papers.

And wait till you hear this!

He said, "We have a *tie*!"

Because me and my friend José *both* had EIGHTEEN FACTS!

We jumped out of our seats and gave each other a high five!

Then I skipped around my desk very joyful. Plus also, I skipped to the pencil sharpener and back.

Mr. Scary came back and shook our hands.

He said we would choose our play parts when we come back from lunch. And so meanwhile we should be thinking about what parts we want.

"Yeah, only I already *know* what part I want!" I said real thrilled. "And it is the bestest part I can think of. Only I'm going to keep it a secret till after lunch. And so nobody ask me. And I *mean* it."

After that, I pretended to lock my lips with a make-believe key.

Herb turned around. "You mean you're not even going to tell me?" he said kind of disappointed.

I got out my key and unlocked my lips.

"Okay . . . except for I will just tell Herb, and that's all," I said.

I locked my lips again.

José frowned at me.

I unlocked my lips one more time.

"Plus also, I will tell José. But that is my final offer. And I mean it."

Just then, Shirley did a big huffy.

"Okay, fine . . . and Shirley," I said.

That's when Sheldon raised his hand and pointed to himself.

Then all of the other children pointed to theirselves, too.

And so that day at lunch, I whispered my secret to everybody in Room One.

But that was all.

6

Teamwork

After we got back from recess, Mr. Scary went back to the board.

"Okay, everyone. It's time for the big event," he said. "We're going to begin choosing our play parts now. We'll start with Junie B. and José. Are you two ready to go?"

"Ready!" hollered José.

"Ready!" I hollered. "And guess what *else*, Mr. Scary? I'm even going to let José go first. 'Cause that will be very polite of me. Plus José already told me that he wants to be Columbus. And I don't. So being polite will work out beautifully this time."

I pointed at José.

"Okay, go," I said.

José looked annoyed at me. "But you already *told* him, Junie B. I want to be Columbus."

I clapped my hands real delighted.

"I knew it!" I said. "I knew being polite would work out good this time! On account of I want to be the *Pinta*! 'Cause the *Pinta* was the fastest ship! And the fastest ship is the winner ship. And the winner ship is the *star* ship!"

I skipped to the pencil sharpener and back again.

Mr. Scary said *please stop doing that.*

"Being the *Pinta* is fine, Junie B.," he said. "But you *do* understand that our ships will not be *racing,* right? All three of our ships will be arriving *together.*"

I did a little frown.

"Yeah, only that's not how I actually had it pictured in my head," I said. "'Cause a race will be more exciting, I think. And so maybe I will just arrive a *little bit* first. Like by an inch, or a foot . . . or half an hour, possibly."

Mr. Scary shook his head no.

"This play is not about stars or winners. It's about *teamwork,*" he said. "You are more than welcome to be the *Pinta,* Junie B. But you can't arrive before the other ships. Got it?"

I did a big sigh.

"Got it," I said kind of glum.

Mr. Scary wrote my name next to the *Pinta.*

Then he called on the other children to choose their play parts, too.

Lucille chose richie Queen Isabella.

And Camille and Chenille chose the Atlantic Ocean.

Then my bestest friend Herbert chose to be Land. And that is the importantest role of all, almost. 'Cause without Land, you can't actually land, probably.

After Herb, lots of other children picked their parts, too.

Then finally, it was May's turn.

May had to go last because all her facts were about the dumb *Mayflower,* and not about Columbus.

She stood up very grouchy. "All the good roles are already taken. So I guess I'll have to be the tubby old *Santa María,*" she grumped.

Mr. Scary wrote her name on the board.

"The *Santa María* is an excellent choice, May," he said. "The *Santa María* was the biggest ship. And it carried Columbus, you know."

May sat up a little straighter.

"It *did*?" she said. "It really *did*? It carried Columbus? Nobody told me that before."

She reached over and tapped on me.

"I bet *you* didn't know that, either. Did you, Junie Jones? If you knew that, I bet *you'd* be the *Santa María*," she said.

I rolled my eyeballs at her.

"Of *course* I knew that, you silly-head May," I said. "The whole entire world knew that except for you, probably."

May looked disappointed.

She turned her head back around.

I waited for a second to make sure she wasn't looking.

Then I slumped down in my chair. And tapped my fingers very annoyed.

'Cause guess what?

I didn't know that.

7

Ship Building

Friday morning

Dear first-grade journal,

   We have been working on our play for the whole entire week.
   We ~~aredy~~ already wrote some of our words.

   And ha!

   I am going to say, Land! Land! We landed on Land!

   Only bad news. On account of

Herbert is Land. And today
Herbert got sick with the virus.
   And so, NOW what am I
supposed
~~sposed~~ to do? Just sail around
and around the whole livelong
day?
                    explorers
   Without Land, ~~xplorers~~ are
nothing.
              From,
         Junie B., First Grader

Just then, the bell rang for school to start.
And so I quick put away my journal. And I
got ready to work on the play some more!

'Cause hurray, hurray!

Today we were making our costumes!

Mr. Scary got out costume supplies from boxes he brought from home.

He gave me and May cardboard to make our ships. Plus also, he gave us ship patterns!

He gave Sheldon a ship pattern, too.

Because guess what?

Sheldon was going to be the *Niña*!

He said he didn't even care that the *Niña* was the smallest ship. On account of he liked the little squiggle over the *n*!

"The little squiggle makes the Niña look special," he said. "It looks like a little bird."

Mr. Scary smiled at that comment.

Then he told us how to tape our ship pieces together. Plus he showed us how to make banners and sails.

"I'm going to color my ship banner red. 'Cause red is my favorite color," I said.

May looked down her nose at me.

"I'm going to color *my* ship banner *gold,*" she said. "'Cause gold means you're the golden best. And the *Santa María* had to be the best. Or else why would Columbus choose it?"

I tapped on my chin very thinking. Then I did a little grin.

"Maybe he liked big old tubs," I said.

After that, I laughed and laughed at my own joke.

I see nothing wrong with that.

Pretty soon, Mr. Scary went to help Lucille.

She was not working on her costume.

"My richie nanna is going to hire her sewing lady to make my costume," she said. "Plus she's also going to buy me a crown of fake jewels."

Mr. Scary said *no.* "We're *all* making our costumes in class, Lucille," he said. "It's part of the project."

After that, he got an encyclopedia from the shelf. And he found a picture of Queen Isabella.

Lucille did a loud screech.

"Eeeesh! She's not even *cute*!" she said. "And what is that ugly hat thing on her head? Look! It has ear flaps!"

Sheldon ran over to see the ugly hat thing.

"Maybe she just got back from snowboarding," he said.

Lucille started to cry.

Mr. Scary said to please calm down.

Then he brought her a fake velvet towel she could use for a robe. And he gave her gold glitter to make a paper crown.

Lucille stopped crying. "Glitter?" she said a little perkier. "I get to use glitter?"

After that, she got right to work on her golden crown.

A little glitter can turn your whole day around.

At the end of the afternoon, our costumes were almost done.

Mr. Scary let us go to the front of the room and show the other children what we made.

And what do you know?

Lucille's crown turned out very beautiful! She looked like a real alive queen in that thing.

Plus also, I liked Camille and Chenille's ocean costume. They cut roly-poly waves at the top of a long roll of blue paper. Then—when they held it near the floor—it looked like the real ocean, sort of.

Me and Sheldon and May went last.

We sailed to the front of the room in our ship costumes. And we introduced ourselves.

"I am the *Pinta*. And I'm the *fastest* ship," I told them.

"I am the *Santa María*. And I am the *biggest* ship," said May.

"I am the *Niña*. And I have a little bird on my *n*!" said Sheldon.

Then all of the children laughed and clapped. And me and Sheldon and May sailed back to our seats.

Only too bad for me. On account of May sailed way too speedy. And she got to her desk before I did.

She looked very smuggy at me.

"What took you so long?" she said. "Are you the poky little *Pinta*?"

Then she laughed and laughed at her own joke.

That is not good taste.

8

Practicing

That weekend was the longest day of my life.

I kept on wanting to get back to school so I could work on the play some more!

That's how come on Monday morning, I ran to my desk as fast as I could. Only I couldn't even stay in my chair that good. 'Cause I had excitement in my seat, that's why!

Finally, the bell rang for school.

And then wowie wow wow!

Mr. Scary took us to the auditorium to

practice on a real, actual stage! And that is a dream come true!

My heart was thumping and pumping when I walked up the steps.

Then all of us sat down on the stage floor. And Mr. Scary got us started.

"Boys and girls, we're going to begin with the very first scene, where Queen Isabella meets Columbus," he said. "Lucille and José? Will you come here, please?"

José and Lucille hurried to the front. Then Mr. Scary stood them on separate sides of the stage. And they walked toward each other until they met in the middle.

They said their lines.

"Hello, sailor. My name is richie Queen Isabella," said Lucille.

José did a bow.

"Hola, Queen Isabella. My name is

Cristóbal Colón," he said. "I would like to look for a new trade route to China. Can I please have some money to sail the ocean blue?"

Lucille pretended to think for a second. Then she fluffed her fluffy hair. And she pulled fake money out of her purse.

"Okay. Here's some money," she said. "But please bring back the change."

Mr. Scary quick raised his hand and hollered, "Hold it!"

"I don't really remember the line about bringing back the change, Lucille," he said. "Is that something new you've added?"

Lucille nodded. "Yes. My nanna and I thought of it over the weekend," she explained. "Nanna says that rich people *always* ask for the change. Or else how do you think they got rich?"

Mr. Scary stared at Lucille a real long time.

Then finally, he said, "Let's move on." And he called for the actors in Scene Two.

Scene Two is where Columbus picks out the sailors for his trip.

All of the sailors ran speedy quick to the front of the stage.

Then José stood on a box in front of them. And he said his next line.

"Who would like to sail the ocean blue with me? Please call out your names," he said.

And so the sailors called out their names. And guess what?

One was named Sinbad! And one was named Popeye! And another one was named Captain Hook!

I clapped my hands very happy.

"This play is turning out better than I thought!" I said.

After that, it was time for the three ships.

I quick grabbed Sheldon's hand. And I pulled him behind me to the front of the stage.

And what do you know?

I got there first!

And Sheldon got there second!

And May was last!

I skipped all around her very springy. And I sang a happy ship song.

It was to the tune of "The Farmer in the Dell."

> The *Pinta* got here first!
> The *Pinta* got here first!
> Hi-ho, the derry-o,
> The *Pinta* got here first!

Mr. Scary made a mad face.

"Junie B., that's enough," he said. "For the very last time . . . this is *not* a race."

May stuck her nose in my face.

"Yeah, Junie Jones. This is *not* a race," she said. "Not, not, not a race!"

Mr. Scary bent down between us.

"I'm talking to you, too, May," he said. "If you two can't get along, I'll find someone else to do your parts. Do you both understand?"

May kept looking at me.

"*I* understand. Do *you* understand, Junie Jones? Huh? Do you? Do you? Do you?"

Mr. Scary stood back up.

Then—very silent—he took May to the back of the stage. And he made her sit down.

I laughed and pointed and waved to her back there.

Then bad news.

I had to sit down, too.

9

Shipwrecked

Thursday

Dear first-grade journal,

TONIGHT IS PARENTS NIGHT!
TONIGHT IS PARENTS NIGHT!

And good news!

Roger came back to school today! Only now he has a little bit of a cold. Only who even cares?

'Cause YAY! He's going to be Land!

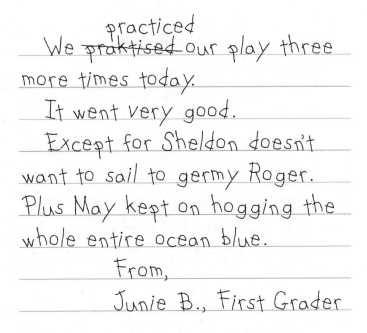

practiced
We ~~praktised~~ our play three
more times today.
   It went very good.
   Except for Sheldon doesn't
want to sail to germy Roger.
Plus May kept on hogging the
whole entire ocean blue.
                From,
            Junie B., First Grader

As soon as I finished writing, the bell rang
to go home.

   I quick put away my journal. And I
skipped out of Room One very gleeful.

   Only ha! That night, after I ate dinner,
Mother and Daddy drove me right back

there. And I skipped back in again!

And guess what?

There were parents snooping every-where!

They were snooping at our bulletin boards. And snooping in our desks. And they were even snooping in our test papers!

All of the children had tension in us.

'Cause every test can't be a gem, you know.

Then finally, Mr. Scary saved the day.

He clapped his loud hands together. And he said it was time for the play!

Then whew! All of us got relief on our faces. And we hurried to the auditorium as fast as we could go. And we quick put on our costumes.

I tapped on Sheldon very giggly.

"My stomach has flutterflies in it," I

said. "Does yours, Sheldon? Does your stomach have flutterflies in it?"

Just then, Roger sneezed real loud near Sheldon's ear.

Sheldon made a sick face. Then he quick held his nose nostrils again. And he whispered the word *germy boy*.

Pretty soon, Mr. Scary made the shush sign. Then he smiled at us in our costumes.

"Okay, people. It's *showtime!*" he whispered very excited.

He did a happy thumbs-up.

We did a happy thumbs-up back.

Then, very slow . . .

Mr. Scary opened the curtains . . .

And our Columbus play began!

Lucille and José walked to the middle of the stage.

"Hello, sailor. My name is richie Queen Isabella," said Lucille.

José did a bow.

"Hola, Queen Isabella. My name is Cristóbal Colón. I would like to look for a new trade route to China. Can I please have some money to sail the ocean blue?"

Lucille reached into her purse.

"Okay. Here's some money," she said. "But please bring back the change."

After that, José bowed to Lucille again. And Lucille curtsied to José. And they walked off the stage.

The sailors hurried to their places.

My heart pounded and pounded inside me. On account of after the sailors came . . . *the ships!*

Mr. Scary lined us up to go onstage.

"Good luck, you three!" he whispered.

THEN WOWIE WOW WOW!
IT WAS TIME!
I swallowed very hard.
Then me and May and Sheldon sailed

right onto the stage. And we started to say our lines.

"I am the *Pinta*. And I am the *fastest* ship," I said.

"I am the *Santa María*. And I'm the *biggest* ship," said May.

Then Sheldon started to say his line, too. Only too bad for him. 'Cause just then, Roger did another loud sneeze. And you could hear it everywhere.

Sheldon scrunched his face very disgusted and looked back at him.

"I am the *Niña*. And Roger should wash his hands," he said.

Me and May looked surprised at that line. But Mr. Scary whispered to *keep on going*.

José walked out and said his next words.

"Ah! Three fine ships! Just what I need

to sail the ocean blue. Tomorrow we will begin our journey."

After that, Shirley walked out with a big sign. It said:

OKAY . . . NOW IT'S TOMORROW.

The audience did a chuckle. Only I don't know why.

Then Camille and Chenille stretched their ocean waves across the floor.

And hurray, hurray!

All of us ships began to sail to Roger!

There was a curvy line on the floor of the stage for us to follow.

We were supposed to sail side by side very perfect.

Only just as I thought!

Pretty soon, May tried to squeeze in front of me!

And that was just plain wrong. On

account of the *Santa María* was *not* the fastest ship. And you *can't change history*!

That is how come I had to speed up a teensy bit.

Only too bad for me.

Because when I speeded up, I accidentally nudged May's ship in her side.

And then *BAM!*

She nudged me back . . . *hard*. On purpose, I mean!

And *CRASH!*

The *Pinta* fell right off my shoulders! And I tripped over my ship! And I fell right smack on the floor!

Then OH NO! OH NO!

May tripped over my feet! And she fell down right on top of me!

And so Sheldon almost fell, too!

Only he quick did a swervy! And he crashed into Land instead!

And then *KABOOM!*

Both of *them* fell on the floor across from us!

And *that's* when the worstest thing of all happened!

Because, all of a sudden, *AH—AH—AH—CHOOOOO!*

Roger sneezed in Sheldon's face!

And it went *right directly up his nostrils*!

"AAUUGGHH!" yelled Sheldon.

Then he quick tried to get up. But he just kept falling down again.

And so Mr. Scary rushed onto the stage.

And he stood Sheldon up on his feet.

Only more bad news!

Because Sheldon pulled away from him.

And then *VAROOM!*

Fast as a race car, he sailed straight back to Spain!

And down the steps!

And off the stage!

And right out the auditorium door!

I did a gasp at that sight.

Then I sat there sickish and frozen. And May sat sickish and frozen, too.

'Cause now Columbus would *never* get to America.

And it was all our fault!

10

■ ■ ■ ■ ■ ■ ■ ■ ■ ■

Surprise!!!

It was the terriblest moment of my life.

I looked at the side of the stage.

All of the children had shock in their faces. Plus Mr. Scary had shock in his face, too.

He quick hurried over to close the stage curtain.

Only that's when a miracle happened!

'Cause just at that exact same minute, José hollered, "WAIT!"

Then, zippedy fast . . .

He jumped right into the ocean . . .

AND CHRISTOPHER COLUMBUS
SWAM TO AMERICA!

He did! He did! He *really* did!

He swam like the wind, I tell you!

And he landed right on Roger!

And all of the audience clapped and
clapped!

Because Columbus got to America after all!

And that is not all the happy news, either!

'Cause the play was last night. And so today Mr. Scary brought a delicious cake to school! And we are going to have a *YAY, JOSÉ!* party!

Only there is still one teensy problem. On account of some of the children aren't actually speaking to me and May because of what happened in the play.

And so lucky for me that my bestest friend named Herbert got back from the virus today. 'Cause he already helped me write a 'pology to Room One.

I am going to read it after we have cake. On account of children are in better moods if they have sugar in them.

Here are the words I wrote to say:

Dear Room One (except for not actually May),

I am sorry I fell down at the play.

I am going to take all of the blame for what happened. 'Cause that will be big of me, I think. And so I am not going to ~~menshun~~ mention about how I got rammed in the side by another ship. Real hard, I mean. Like an iceberg.

Thank you for not being mad at me.

You are a delightful bunch.
Your friend,
Junie B., First Grader
P.S. In the next play, I will be
a mouse. On account of ships
can sink. But mice just float,
usually. And so a mouse play is
still the way to go, I think!

Squeak! Ha! Squeak!

Ha!

People! People!
Read this next book
about my fun in first grade!

Coming in
August 2004

THE
DARLINGTON
JAUNT

THE
DARLINGTON
JAUNT

Angus Ross

WALKER AND COMPANY ✸ NEW YORK

First published in the United States of America
in 1984 by the Walker Publishing Company, Inc.

ISBN: 0-8027-5585-2

Library of Congress Catalog Card Number: 83-40399

Printed in the United States of America

10 9 8 7 6 5 4 3 2 1

Saturday

It was a wet grey morning, bleak and miserable, but I began that weekend as I did any other with a resolve to make the most of it. Finish laying the floor tiles in the kitchen, a couple of pints before lunch, then an afternoon spent filling the bookshelves because the white paint was now bone-dry and the house was beginning at last to look ship-shape. Another two or three months, say around the middle of August, and I should be able to make a start on the riotous jungle outside. That, I was not looking forward to.

I was lying in bed, thinking about these things and mustering the will to rise, when the dogs began to bark. I got up quickly and looked out of the bedroom window. All I could see was rain, but I heard the muted crunch of tyres on the drive by the gable end. I put on slippers and dressing-gown and padded across the landing into the spare room at the back and looked down onto the old farmyard. A peat-brown Rover eased around the corner and nosed up to one of the barns, and Charlie stepped out and my guts turned cold.

When I hurried downstairs to let him in the dogs milled around my legs, doing their best to trip me up. I opened the kitchen door and Charlie pushed in past me, shaking water off his coat. He eyed me upwards, starting at the slippers, and:

'What's going on?' he said, 'You poorly, or something?'

'Well, I am now.'

'Shift these bloody dogs.'

'Go on boys,' I said, 'lie down on your beds.'

They backed off reluctantly and Charlie shed his wet Burberry. 'How come you're not dressed yet?' he said. 'It's half past eight, for God's sake.'

5

'It's Saturday, Charlie,' I said, 'and I had a pretty late night last night.'

'On the piss, I suppose.'

'You're right, for once. So what about it?'

'Get the kettle on.'

'Get it on yourself, you know where it is. I'm off for a bath,' I said.

'Never mind bath-ing, get washed and dressed — '

'And you get knotted,' I said.

' — and pack a bag.' He was filling the kettle.

'Listen, Charlie . . ' I said.

'Got any bacon?'

'In the fridge. Listen — '

'Where's the frying-pan, then?'

'Bottom left-hand cupboard, but look — '

'What you hanging about for?' he said, 'Soon as we've had some breakfast, we're leaving.'

'Leaving for where?' I said.

'"Tell you later. Where are the plates?'

'Oh, look for the buggers!' I said.

Back upstairs, I lay in the bath and cursed my luck. Gone were all my plans for the weekend and, if past experience was anything to go by, most of the following week. Just when things at the office were moving nicely, as well. I'd been asked to act as a minder for a twice-robbed jewellry salesman on a five-day tour of the north, at seventy-five a day plus expenses, and a job like that was not to be sniffed at. Now, I'd have to farm it out, and there probably would not be a next time. I cursed my luck again and tried to think of a valid excuse for saying "no" to the Man.

But I knew that even if I thought of a beauty, Charlie would brush it aside. So, shaved and dressed in my second-best dark grey worsted, I packed a small suitcase, then used my bedside extension to phone old Mrs Tidy and ask her to see to the dogs. She assured me that she would, that it would be no bother at all, and how long did I think I would be away. I

6

told her about a week, because five or six days was part of the course. One good point in Charlie's favour, he did not mess about.

Just before I went downstairs to rejoin my unwelcome guest, I unlocked the little steel-lined hidy-hole let into the bottom of one of my fitted wardrobes and lifted out the Smith & Wesson. I reassured myself that it was fully loaded, checked the action and clipped the open holster snugly over waistband and belt. I hoped that I wasn't going to need it, but I knew the hope was probably forlorn.

Dogs can sense when people are anti-. They were lying on their bellies, on their beds, watching Charlie eat his breakfast without attempting to beg. There was a lingering smell of fried bacon.

'Enjoying that, Charlie?' I said.

He looked up. 'Yours is in the oven.'

'Did you do me a slice of fried bread?'

'No, I didn't. Just get it down you.'

Charlie resented the ritual of eating. He considered it a sheer waste of time, a necessary nuisance to be handled with dispatch. Not the least of the things which made working with him an ongoing battle of wills. He had put my plate in the Aga's top oven and the bacon was hardened to the texture of biltong. I could have soled my shoes with the eggs and he'd left the teapot without its cosy. The pale, weak tea was lukewarm. We were starting out in the time-honoured manner.

'God Almighty,' I said, 'am I supposed to *eat* this?'

'Look, don't start,' he said. 'Get it scoffed, we're running late.'

'Late for what?' I said.

'A little jaunt up to Darlington — I take it you know where that is?'

'Of course I do. But what's there, for us?'

'There was a mugging last night,' he said, 'and the mugger got more than he ever expected.'

7

'Like what?'

'Like ten thousand quid. He was carrying it when the local cops nicked him.'

'So where do we come in?'

'The mugger didn't know his own strength. The bloke he clobbered is dead. He died at quarter past three this morning, in Darlington hospital.'

'I still can't see — '

'Don't stop eating, just stop interrupting,' he said.

'Gawd, this tea's like maidens' water!'

'And give over moaning,' he said, 'I'm trying to tell you about the late-lamented.'

'Get on with it, then,' I said.

He shot me one of his warning looks, which I studiously ignored, and began to tell me about Josef Peltz as he pushed his empty plate aside. Peltz had been with a party of West Germans over here on an exchange visit from Mulheim, Darlington's twin town in the Ruhr, and one of the items of entertainment laid on for them had taken the form of a piano recital in the fine old manor-house recently converted into an arts centre. Herr Peltz had excused himself at some time during the buffet supper which followed the recital and, pleading a headache, had announced his intention to walk back to the King's Head hotel. He was mugged around half an hour later in an alley on the far side of North Road railway station, more than a mile away in the opposite direction.

The attack was witnessed by a civic-minded motorist driving home with what was probably a belly full of beer, because, having stopped at a handy phone box to report the incident to the police, he declined to give his name or to wait around and have his breath smelled. No matter, there was a panda car roving the area and its two-man team were very quickly on the job. They picked up a running youth, found his pockets all bulging with wads of used tenners and, after having seen Peltz into the ambulance, hauled

8

the youth down to the nick. A very smart detective sergeant had properly sensed something odd and had initiated a Report through Channels, which report had filtered down to us. The unsung firm of McGowan and Farrow, the Section's northern mob.

'This Peltz bloke,' I asked, 'is there anything known?'

'Don't talk wet,' Charlie said. 'If there was, he'd never have been sent here, would he?'

'Sent here? Sent here by whom?'

'Christ, if we knew that, Farrow, we wouldn't —'

'All right, all right,' I said.

'The BfV are running a trace.'

'He could be one of their own.'

'Don't think that hasn't occurred already.'

'On the other hand,' I said, 'he could be an innocent civilian who happened to have ten thousand quid.'

'And I could be the ghost of Chiang Kai-shek. Come on, shake it up!' he said.

Detective Sergeant Harry Royston looked to be in his mid- or late thirties and was rather short, for a policeman, but chunky as a whole tin of pineapples. He had a bristling thatch of coarse blond hair and his very bright china-blue eyes, deeply set under thick wiry brows, were like two little cornflowers in a tangle of wheat. He ushered us into a windowless cubicle furnished with one small regulation desk, an extra couple of straight metal-and-canvas chairs, and not much more of anything else. Just the three of us made the room seem overcrowded, which fact brought on Charlie's only known weakness. Claustrophobia. When Royston made to close the door:

'Leave it open,' Charlie said.

'What? Oh, yes — ' Royston made a little more space for us by squeezing in behind the desk' — it does get rather stuffy in here.' He indicated the chairs. 'Have a seat.'

'No thanks, we're not stopping. We just want to

talk to the yob.'

'I don't think you'll get much out of him.'

'We can but try,' Charlie said.

That modest, dead-pan comment drew a hard blue stare from Royston, and if he didn't then begin to suspect that Charlie McGowan could get *anybody* to tell him *anything*, he was a lot less shrewd than I thought he was. He reached for the phone which stood on a little shelf attached to the side of the desk, made a brief internal call and looked across at Charlie as he cradled the receiver.

'They're bringing him up right away. You can talk to him in the interview room.'

'Has he got any form?' Charlie said.

Royston nodded. 'Two lots of Borstal, six months' porridge. For thieving, and assault.'

'What's his name?'

'Darren Mooney.'

'This chap he mugged,' Charlie said. 'Little feller, was he?'

'No, not at all,' Royston said. 'Five-ten or -eleven, around fourteen stone.'

'Was he, now?' Charlie said. 'Right, then, let's go see Darren.'

The interview room, not much bigger than Royston's office, boasted a plastic-topped table and two wooden chairs. Mooney was sitting on one, the upper half of his body sprawled across the table top, left hand supporting the side of his face. Boredom personified. I looked at the spectacle he presented, thought about others of his age down there in the South Atlantic and was saddened yet again by the miasmal atavism of *Homo sapiens.*

His skull had been shaved at the sides to leave a bushy Mohican scalp-lock made stiff and spiky by alternate daubs of red, white and blue paint, and the sleeves of his denim battledress blouse had been torn off at the shoulders in order to display arms and hands disfigured overall by crude and ugly do-it-

yourself tattoos. The lobe of one ear was pierced by a large common safety-pin; from the other hung a little gold cross. The battledress blouse, and his ragged jeans, were stiff with layers of dirt and he stank like a mangy old polecat. Charlie wrinkled his nose.

'You filthy little bastard.'

'Hey — watch it!' Mooney said.

Royston nodded at the uniformed constable standing by the door. 'All right, Booth, I'll call you when we're ready.'

The constable left the room. Charlie stood with his hands in his raincoat pockets, looking down at the youth. I put my back against the door. Royston moved to one side.

'You,' said Charlie, 'sit up straight!'

I thought for a moment it was going to start there and then, but there was something about Charlie which made the youth choose discretion. He took his sweet time about it, but he did raise himself up off the table to hook an arm over the back of the chair and lift his gaze to look Charlie over. I wondered if what he saw was anything beyond the surface image: just a fairly tall, fairly well-built old geezer, excessively neat and clean, shiny rimless spectacles. Fair hair whose tight little waves were beginning to glint with threads of silver. Calm cold eyes the colour of pond-water seen through the sides of a jar, devoid of any expression. Short straight nose and a wide, thin-lipped mouth; skin as soft as a girl's.

My speculation was answered by Mooney's insolent sneer because obviously, what he didn't see — or, rather, failed to perceive — was the awful and terrible menace inherent in the man. No reflection on Mooney. People of far superior intellect had made the same bad mistake. I almost felt sorry for the stupid young sod.

'That's better,' Charlie went on. 'Now then, tell us all about it.'

11

'All about wot?' Mooney said.

'You know, about the murder. How you killed a man,' Charlie said.

'Give over! It was a naccident!'

'Oh, I see,' Charlie said. 'He fell, and his head hit your bovver boots.'

'I'm sayin' no more,' Mooney said. 'I've got my rights!'

'Is that a fact? You horrible stinking turd! Ever hear of a book called the Bible?'

'O' course I 'ave!' Mooney said.

'An eye for an eye, and a tooth for a tooth?'

'Wot's that supposed to mean?'

'It means scum like you ought to be put down. Like vermin,' Charlie said. 'You're a festering scab on the arse of humanity.'

'Hey, lissen — !' Mooney said.

'I'm listening already, so just start talking.'

'Piss off!' Mooney said.

Charlie sighed. 'You heard him, gents. Better do as he says.'

Royston and I swapped glances. For me, it was *déjà vu* time. We had been here on more than one occasion. Royston caught on fast and even Mooney sensed what was coming. He stared open-mouthed at Charlie, then swivelled round on his chair to look first at Royston, then at me. I shrugged and shook my head. Royston coughed and cleared his throat.

'Ah, now, wait,' he said. 'He's not supposed to be left unaccompanied.'

'He won't be,' Charlie said. 'I'll accompany him for you.'

'Well . . I *do* need to take a pee . . . '

'Remember to wash your hands. Give me three minutes. Farrow — '

'Yes, I need one, too, Chas,' I said.

'Here! 'ang on a minute!' cried Mooney.

'— and shut the door,' Charlie said.

When we were back in his tiny office and I was

12

packing a pipe, Royston expressed a touch of disquiet.

'Listen, er . .'

'Farrow,' I said.

'I hope your mate doesn't mark young Mooney.'

'*Mark* him? What on earth do you mean?'

'Well, you know . . .' he said.

'No, I don't know — and neither do you. And don't forget that,' I said.

'Who *are* you people, anyway?'

'Inland Revenue.'

'Look, come on, I'm not stupid.'

'You could have fooled me, chum,' I said. 'Wise men know when not to ask questions.'

'Not if they're coppers,' he said. 'Are you from Special Branch, or what?'

'Ask my gaffer,' I said.

'He strikes me as being a dangerous bugger.'

'Rubbish. He wouldn't harm a fly.'

'Well, okay, if that's your story.'

'It is — and listen,' I said, 'don't get nattering to your mates. If you're assigned to help on this job, just do your thing and keep your mouth shut and before you know where you are, they'll be making you up to detective inspector.'

'Big deal,' Royston said, 'seeing as I've already passed the exams.'

'You're home and dry, then,' I said. 'You're a teed ball, Royston, you're laughing.'

'I bloody well won't be,' he said, 'if Mooney's lawyer starts screaming brutality.'

'He hasn't got a lawyer,' I said.

'No, but he damn' soon will have. When the social workers get wind, they'll be falling over one another to provide him with legal aid. They'll try to get him off with three months suspended.'

'I'd suspend him for about three minutes — at the end of a rope,' I said.

'Keep your voice down. One of 'em might hear you.'

13

'I don't give a monkeys,' I said. 'What about a coffee?'

Royston reached for his phone. 'How do you like it?'

'Black, with sugar, please.'

'Shall I order one for your buddy?'

'He's not my buddy,' I said, 'and he thinks that coffee is only for pufters.'

'I think I'll have tea, then,' he said. 'I wouldn't want to give him the wrong impression.'

'That's very prudent,' I said.

A pretty little WPC brough in two plastic cups of something hot and the stuff she gave to me tasked like Oxo with saccharin. As I was forcing it down, the door swung open and Charlie breezed in, dry-washing his pale, freckled hands. Royston set down his cup and jumped to his feet.

'You haven't left Mooney alone!'

'Relax,' said Charlie, 'he's sitting quietly. He's not going to leap away.'

'Well, maybe, but Jesus!'

Royston hurried out. Charlie scowled at the reek from my pipe.

'God, what a stench!' he said. 'I thought you'd stopped smoking that bloody thing?'

'I did, but I started again.'

'You stupid, weak-kneed pillock!'

'I knew you'd sympathise. Anyway, what about Mooney? Confide in you, did he?'

'No sweat.'

'Tell you something we didn't already know?'

'Nothing I hadn't guessed. Peltz was a hefty specimen, and Mooney's just a lousy yob.'

'No stomach for single combat?'

'You've cottoned on,' Charlie said, 'there were five of the bastards. A real bloody rat-pack — grab that pad, and write down these names.'

I was scribbling the fourth and last one when Royston returned to the room, his manner grimly

14

thoughtful. He flicked a sideways glance at Charlie in passing, sat behind his desk and ran a hand through his straw-coloured hair. I passed him the list of names, which he looked at without even seeing.

'Good God — he can't even walk!'

'Serves him right,' said Charlie. 'Maybe next time, he won't be so rude.'

'What the hell did you do to him?'

'I just chatted him up,' Charlie said, 'asked him to tell me which of his pals were out with him last night.'

'With him? Last night?'

'Yes. Those are their names. You'd better round 'em up, before they spend all the money.'

'What money?'

'Forty thousand quid. It was fifty, counting Mooney's share.'

'Jeee-zus!' Royston said.

'Royston seems like a useful bloke.'

'Useful, my arse,' Charlie said. 'Mooney had him believing that he tackled Peltz on his own.'

'Be fair, Chas. He hasn't had much time — '

'Five minutes,' Charlie said, 'that's all it takes. Five minutes.'

'Maybe, for us,' I said, 'but Royston's a cop. He's to go by the book.'

'Look, just drive,' Charlie said.

I wasn't too familiar with Darlington, but I did know my way around enough to get us out of Park Place and up to the King's Head hotel, the entrance to which is in Priestgate. I nudged the car in behind a big mobile compressor, the shuddering roar of whose diesel engine was almost drowned by the iron clatter of heavy pneumatic drills as a gang of council road-men went about their business of tearing up the tarmac surface. The hotel front seemed hunched defensively between what must over the years have been a creeping encroachment of divers shop facades.

15

As we approached the double glass doors the road-gang gaffer, distinguished by his badge of office in the form of a collar and tie, bellowed at us above the hideous din.

'Oy! You can't park there!'

Charlie left my side to step off the pavement and move up close to the man. I wasn't able to hear what it was he said, but although it could not have been more than a few words, Collar-and-Tie fell back a couple of paces with an expression of shock and dismay. Charlie turned his back on the man and nodded me forward into the hotel. Inside, the head-splitting racket from the drills was muted, but not very much. Fortunately, however, the old King's head premises are considerably more extensive than the Priestgate entrance might suggest and Herr Wagner's big pleasant room was located in the wing which overlooks Prebend Row. Royston had phoned from the police station and Wagner was expecting our call. I suspected that the third armchair in the twin-bedded room had been brought in especially for us. After the preliminaries:

'Please,' Wagner said, 'sit down.'

His accent was as fat as the rest of him. I would have said he was a chap who liked his sausage and saurkraut, and plenty of both, with spuds. It was toss-up whether his fast wheezy breathing was due to all that excess weight he was carrying around, or asthma, or just plain nerves. Possibly a touch of all three. Like Charlie, the head of the German delegation wore rimless spectacles, but the lenses of his were fogged with perspiration and with grease from his bushy white eyebrows. He looked to be about sixty-two or -three, but could have been several years younger. According to information from Royston, he was the owner of a fair-sized engineering works, and a prominent member of Mulheim town council.

Charlie perched on the edge of the chair beside

16

the dressing-table in the large bay window, with his back against the light, and adjusted his clothing to preclude any creases. He scrutinised his fingernails and checked the knot in his tie, and only then looked up at Wagner to establish his command. The German was fussing around us like an agitated old hen.

'Sit yourself down, Mr Wagner.' He pronounced it with a "W".

'Yes, yes, of course, Herr Farrow.'

'McGowan,' Charlie said.

'*Bitte*?'

'He's Farrow, I'm McGowan.'

'*Ach*!' Pardon!'

'That's okay. Now tell us how well you knew this chap Peltz.'

Wagner lowered his bulk into the remaining chair, shaking his big bald head. '*Ja*,' he said, 'so terrible — terrible!'

'Friend of yours, was he?'

'*Nein* — no. He was . . how do you say . . an acquaintance only. From business, you understand? And now is he dead!'

Charlie nodded. 'As a doornail,' he said.

'Please? I do not know what this means.'

'It means that's a fact,' Charlie said. 'So what do you know about his movements since you got here yesterday?'

What Wagner knew about Peltz's movements was virtually nothing at all. His party of twenty-three people — the odd number being due, perhaps significantly, to the fact that Peltz was the only one not to have brought along a wife or a secretary — had arrived at Teeside airport at half past ten the previous morning, where a bus had been waiting to take them directly to the King's Head. There, they had an hour or so to relax and freshen up before boarding the bus again for the run out to a lunch at the Europa Hotel as guests of a local firm, Teesco Engineering Ltd. When, at about ten to twelve,

17

Wagner had begun to round up his flock and hustle them into the transport, Peltz had been conspicuous by his absence. He had, however, turned up outside to join his anxious comrades on the waiting bus just minutes before it was due to depart.

'Did he not say where he'd been?' asked Charlie.

Wagner shook his pouch-like jowls. 'Only that he had looked at the town.'

'Hadn't he been here before, then?'

'*Nein*. For Josef, it was the first time.'

'What about the rest of the day?'

'I will tell you . . . ' Wagner said.

The programme devised for the Mulheim visitors was a fairly restful one. They were "free", after the Teesco lunch until half past seven that evening when their bus would be waiting, again, to take them this time to Darlinton Arts Centre. Most of them had opted to spent the afternoon just wandering around the town but Peltz, it seemed, had other ideas. The Europa Hotel happened to be situated highly adjacent to a first-class golf-club and, having made known his love of the game, Peltz was invited by his hosts to stay on and play a round with one of the Teesco directors who was a member of Blackwell Grange. It appeared to have taken the twosome over four hours to complete the course, and the Teesco man had returned Peltz to the King's Head with barely time enough for the visitor to wash and change before leaving for the piano recital.

About the rest, we knew as much as Wagner: Peltz's headache, and his having left the buffet supper early, never to be seen alive again. Not by his compatriots, anyway.

Towards the end of Charlie's grilling of him, Wagner kept glancing at his watch. His buddies were already disporting themselves at a civic reception in the mayor's parlour, up at the splendid new town hall, and he was patently anxious to get in amongst the action. I took advantage of a lull in the chat to

try and let him off the hook.

'Well, that seems to be it, then,' I said. The first and only words I got in.

'Listen,' said Charlie, 'I'll meet you in the lobby. You know what you've got to do.'

I took my cue and left them to it and tramped along corridors and down two flights of stairs, and found my way back to the desk at Reception. There, the little old lass who had directed us to Wagner's apartment looked up from her *Woman's Own*.

'Now then,' she said, 'can I help you?'

She must have been well past retiring age, a perky sparrow-like biddy with eyes as bright and sharp as a youngster's. Twin-set, fat string of beads, hair in a bun at the back of her neck.

'I hope so, Mrs .. er ...?'

'Hornby, Gladys Hornby. And it's Miss, not Mrs,' she said. 'I'm what they call a spinster.'

'Ah, yes, thank you,' I said.

'What for?' she grinned. 'Being a spinster?'

'We'll get to that later,' I said. 'Were you on duty yesterday?'

'I was, all day,' she said. 'From ten in the morning, to eight in the evening.'

'Your union know about that?'

'Unions? You can stick 'em!' she snorted.

'Tut tut, Miss Hornby,' I said. 'I mean, I *could* be your local convenor.'

She laughed. 'Fiddlesticks!' she said. 'I know very well what *you* are, young man.'

'Thanks for the "young",' I said. 'But cast your mind back to yesterday morning — '

'Five past eleven,' she said. 'He left here at just about five past.'

'Who did?'

'That poor Mr Peltz, of course. I checked the party in at a quarter to, and at five past, he went out.'

'What makes you so sure it was Peltz who went out?'

19

'Because he was the only one who did, and they were looking for him later on.'

Miss Hornby was very much on the ball. 'You're a real smart lady,' I said. 'you'll be telling me next where he went to.'

'Oh, that's easy,' she said, 'he went to the library.'

'Are you sure?'

'Well, I can't be certain,' she said, 'but he did ask me how to get there.'

'One more question,' I said, 'and if you can answer, I'll give you a kiss.'

'Oh, that's what they all say,' she said. 'But all right, then, what is it?'

'Did he make any telephone calls?'

'Just one, a local,' she said. 'I know because Joan — she's our girl on the switchboard — had to go to the ladies' room, and I was doubling for her.'

'Ah, I see,' I said. 'I don't suppose you remember the number?'

'I knew you'd welsh on me! You said just one more question, then you go and make it two.'

'You mean you can't tell me?'

'I mean I don't know. I was busy. He asked for a line, and I plugged him one in and left him to it.'

'If he dialled the number himself, how could you tell the call was a local?'

'Must have been,' she said. 'He'd hung up again in less than two minutes.'

'How do you know he got through?'

'Because when he came down, I asked him.' She smiled. 'Besides, I checked in the log.'

'Gladys,' I said, 'you're a little cracker.'

'Get away with you, cheeky!' she said.

At that moment, our ears were assailed by the sudden eruption of a thunderous racket coming from the street outside. I'd forgotten about the road gang. They must have been having a tea-break or something. Miss Hornby grimaced at me and covered her ears with her neat little hands. The noise of

20

the clattering drills drowned out the sigh of the lift doors opening and the first I knew of Charlie's return was a hard finger stuck into my ribs. When I turned he jerked his head, a signal that we were to leave, and I winked goodbye to Miss Hornby before tagging along behind. Out in the car, with the windows all closed, we could just about make ourselves heard. When I told Charlie what I had learned from Miss Hornby:

'Right, get yourself down there,' he said.

'Down where?'

'The *library* — Jesus!'

'All right, keep your hair on,' I said. 'Where do I meet you, afterwards?'

'Back at the nick,' he said. 'By that time, Royston should have got what we want.'

'I hardly think so,' I said.

'Never mind what you hardly think — and what are you waiting for?'

I thrust my door open and as I stepped out, 'Knickers, Charlie,' I said.

The Darlington central library is housed, along with the town's information centre, in a large and handsome red-brick building on the low side of Crown Street, not far from the King's Head hotel. It's lofty interior is redolent of that grand inky smell of books and its long service counter is staffed by that very rare and lucky breed — people who love their jobs. My own good fortune was almost unbelievable, because although the first two eager and helpful assistants to whom I talked could actually help not at all, they passed me on to a veritable treasure. She was filing cards at the Fiction index, a merry-faced slip of a lass whose dark eyes shone with intelligence. A much younger version of my lovely Miss Hornby. I described Josef Peltz, and his clothes, and asked if she remembered any such person.

'Do you know, I think I do!'

21

'Yesterday morning, about ten past eleven?'

'Yes, that's right,' she said. 'I noticed him particularly 'cos he didn't return any books, and he didn't take any out with him, either. He just walked in, and wandered around.'

'How long did he stay?'

'Oh, not very long. About five minutes or so.'

'Did he talk to anybody?'

The girl bit her plump lower lip, frowning as she pondered. Then, slowly, she shook her head. 'Er . . no . . at least, I don't think so. Not that I noticed,' she said.

'But you weren't watching him all the time?'

'Well, that's the point,' she said. 'He was walking around between the stacks.'

'So it's possible he did meet someone?'

'Yes, but it's like I said. He could have, but I don't think he did. There were very few in at the time, no more than five or six people — that's how I noticed him. That and the fact that he looked, well . . . *foreign.*'

'You've got good sharp eyes, miss,' I said.

She blushed very prettily. 'Thank you.'

'Now, I want you to think hard,' I said, 'and tell me exactly what he did.'

'Oh, I'm sorry, but that's all,' she said. 'He just strolled — no, wait! He looked at some books.'

'Go on, luv,' I said, 'you're doing just fine. *How* did he look at 'em?'

'Well, you know, he just took them off the shelves as people normally do . . . looked at the cover, and the photo of the author . . . glanced at a page or two . . .'

'You mean as though he were choosing a book to take out?'

'That's it exactly,' she said.

'But he wasn't choosing one, was he? Do you think he stole one?'

'No.'

22

'What makes you so certain?'

'It's part of my job.'

'And you do it damned well, lass,' I said.

I said the same thing again, to Charlie, when I met him down at the nick.

'But it's still not a positive identification.'

'Look, that kid was mustard,' I said. 'What more do you want, for God's sake?'

'I want her to look at the sketch.'

'Is it ready, then? Where's Royston?'

'He's taken it away,' Charlie said. 'He's making photocopies.'

'Christ, that was quick!' I said. 'He had to collect his tame artist, whip him down to the morgue — '

'All right, we'll get him a medal.'

'You're kindness itself, Chas,' I said.

We were sitting in Royston's dog-kennel and Charlie, being Charlie, was desperate to get away. 'Jesus!' he fumed. 'Where the hell has he got to?'

'How long have you been here?' I said.

'Too bloody long!'

'Did you come straight away, after we left the hotel?'

'No, I didn't.'

'Where did you go, then?'

'That door's open, Farrow,' he said.

'The fuzz is on our side, Charlie.'

'Side? What side? he said. 'We don't *have* a side, we're on our own.'

'Royston's detailed to help us,' I said.

'Listen — don't go shooting your mouth off! *I'll* tell you what I want him to know, and *you* will tell him nothing. You got that?'

'As you've put it so nicely,' I said, 'I'll try to remember.'

'You better remember.'

'Remember what?' Royston said, as he bustled in with a sheaf of folios.

'Nothing,' Charlie said. 'Are those the photo-

23

copies?'

'Yes — what d'you think?' Royston said.

He handed a sample to each of us and I studied the boldly-drawn face. The artist, working of course from the corpse, appeared to have done a good job. He'd contrived to animate the features, investing them with the bloom of life. Far better, for identification purposes, than a photograph could ever be. Detailed in small, precise lettering along the bottom of the A4 sheet were the subject's physical characteristics. Height, 5' 10"; weight, 178 lbs; muscle tone; average for age (43); hair, dark; eyes, brown; complexion, swarthy; no identifying marks or scars (other than those inflicted at time of death) or tattoos.

'He was quite a handsome feller.'

'Never mind his looks,' Charlie said. 'Get yourself back to the library.'

'Hang on a minute,' I said. 'That's a fair old walk — and it's pissing down.'

'Take the car — ' he tossed me the keys — 'then come back here and pick me up.'

'Why the library?' Royston said.

'Because that's where they keep the books,' said Charlie.

'What sort of answer is that?'

'It's the sort you might as well get used to.'

'Now listen — ' Royston said.

'Farrow — are you going, or not?'

'On my way, Charlie,' I said.

My admirable young librarian was in no doubt at all and I was back at Park Place in record time. Charlie was waiting for me and I wondered what had passed between him and Royston. I parked in a slot marked MAGISTRATES ONLY and as I stepped out of the car, himself came dashing up through the rain.

'Open the bloody door!' I ducked back inside to lean across and manipulate the lock and he jumped in quickly. 'Well, how did it go?'

24

'She was right first time,' I said. 'She recognised Herr Peltz immediately.'

'That's what I thought,' he said. 'They used the library as a message drop.'

'We don't *know* that, Charlie,' I said. 'We don't even *know* that Peltz was a baddie.'

'Christ, use your loaf!' he said, 'The sod was a paymaster, wasn't he? Sent here with some brass for the boys!'

'Well, I must admit it's a fairish assumption.'

'Thanks for the vote,' he said. 'You don't know what a comfort it is. I mean, good grief, what would I do —'

'There's no call for sarcasm, Charlie.'

'Get your finger out, then.'

'I will, when I know where we're going.'

'Take the A66. We're heading for a place called Sadberge.'

'Ah — The Hill of Pleas.'

'What the hell are you talking about?'

'That's what they call it,' I said. 'Don't you know your local history?'

'It's not my local history,' he said, 'and what's more, I don't give a tosser — get *moving*!'

'Balls, it *my* licence,' I said.

The ancient Wapentake of Sadberge lies about four or five miles to the east of Darlington town centre, and the cluster of mostly white-painted houses which now forms the old Saxon village huddle around the crown of a hill. Once vastly important as the seat of Prince Bishops, the last half dozen or so centuries have seen it reduced to the status of upper-class dormitory for the bourgeois industrialists from the town in whose borough it lies. Its spruced-up cottages are fronted in the main by steep-sloping lawns, few of which are fenced in, and the free open aspect is cleanly attractive. As we drew into the hamlet:

'Stop by the pub,' Charlie said, 'and I'll nip in to

25

ask for directions.'

'I'll nip in, if you like.'

'Oh no you won't, I'll do it myself. I don't want you stinking of beer.'

'Not beer, Charlie, Scotch. I never rush beer.'

'You're not rushing anything,' he said. He was back in the car in a couple of minutes. 'First left, then left again, then start to take it easy. We're looking for a place called Stag's End.'

The house appeared to have originally been a row of three small flat-fronted cottages and someone had spent a lot of money knocking them into one. The usual tiny square windows had been replaced by bottle-glassed bow fronts painted black-on-white, and neatly pleasing. The wide central porch must have been added a good many years ago because now it was decked overall by old-established roses. As we pulled up onto the sharp gravel drive, the front door opened inwards and a short, stocky man stepped outside. His iron-gray hair was thick and wavy and he had the fresh-faced look of an outdoors type. His corduroy slacks were baggy at the knees and he stood there watching us climb out of the Rover with both of his hands thrust deep in the pockets of his knobbly fisher-knit cardigan. He spoke to us between his teeth, which were clamped around the stem of a bulldog pipe.

'Mr McGowan?'

'That's right,' said Charlie.

'I'm Bill Newby — come in.'

He did not offer to shake hands, which was just as well because Charlie never shook hands with anybody. Including, even, the Man. He saw no need for such foppish behaviour. Newby led us into a large chintzy sitting-room to the left of the long narrow hall and turned to ask if he might take our coats. Predictably, Charlie said no.

'Well . . sit yourselves down. Can I get you a drink?'

Charlie declined for both of us, as invariably was

26

his wont, and got right down to the heart of the matter. 'Now, Mr Newby, about Josef Peltz . . .'

'Dreadful,' Newby said. 'A shocking, ghastly business.'

'Yes, quite,' Charlie agreed. 'I understand you played golf with him yesterday afternoon?'

'You understand correctly.'

'Good player, was he?'

'Lord, no! One doesn't wish to sound condescending, of course, but frankly, it was a waste of my time. Especially as I'd some work to do. . .'

Newby made no bones about the fact that he had used his Blackwell Grange membership to organise a game for Peltz only because his chairman, Teesco boss Norman Branston, had more or less ordered him. He'd had appointments at his office that afternoon and was put out at having to cancel them.

'What about gear?' Charlie said.

'Gear?' said Newby.

'Yes, you know, the stuff you play with. Did Mr Peltz have his own?'

'Oh, no, but that was no problem. I hired a set of clubs from the pro.'

'What about clothing?'

'He just took off his jacket. It was a warm enough day,' Newby said. 'In any case, I lent him a sweater — although it didn't half clash with his cap!' He chuckled and put a match to his pipe. 'Where he got the thing, Lord only knows.'

'Cap? What cap? said Charlie.'

'One of those baseball jobs. That horrible day-glo yellow colour, neb about half a yard long.'

'He wasn't wearing it at lunch, I hope?'

Newby chuckled again. 'No, no, he had it stuffed in his briefcase.'

'Was he carrying a briefcase, then?'

'Not on the course. He left it in my locker — but see here,' Newby said, 'might one ask what this is all about?'

27

'Certainly,' Charlie said, 'we're investigating Peltz's movements.'

'Yes, that I can understand, but I don't see how this can help you.'

'It's helping just fine,' Charlie said.

'But all I did was play golf with the man!'

'Tell us about the game.'

'Well, it was hardly a *game*. I'm afraid he was hopeless. He must have lost a dozen new balls. It took us four hours to get round nine holes!'

'Are you saying he'd never played before?'

'No, no, he knew the form, all right. I mean, just occasionally, he hit a really good one.'

'Beginner's luck?'

'Oh no, but I'd say he hadn't played for years.'

'What did you talk about?'

'Nothing much. As a matter of fact, I was bored to tears.'

'You didn't talk shop?'

'Well, no. I couldn't, really, anyway. I'm the firm's accountant, you see. I know very little about the nuts and bolts. I look after the finance.'

'I see. Did he talk to anyone else, then?'

Newby puffed on his pipe, then nodded. 'Yes — but only for a minute or two. A chap who was helping him find a lost ball. We'd let this chap play through — '

'Play through?'

'That's right. He'd come from behind us, and our slow play was holding him up, so I waved him on to overtake. Peltz was lost in the rough, and the chap stopped to help him look for his lie.'

'And where were you at this time?'

'I was up near the green.'

'How far away?'

'About a hundred and twenty yards. I was going to back and lend a hand, but they signalled they were okay.'

'This chap — do you know him?'

'No,' said Newby, 'I never saw him before.'

'Can you describe him?'

'Middle twenties, good-looking lad, couple of inches taller than me, reddish hair, and rather slim — not *thin*, though.'

'That's good,' Charlie said. 'Would you say he was a member of the club?'

'He would have to be,' Newby said. 'We don't allow visitors on Fridays and weekends.'

'What a splendid rule,' Charlie said.

'I reckon friend Newby's quite genuine, Chas.'

'Watch that motor-bike,' he said.

'I'm watching it. Well, don't you agree?'

'Any damn fool could see that.'

'Must be our mysterious young golfer, then.'

'Brilliant.'

'So all we need to do now is weed him out and have a natter.'

'First things first,' Charlie said.

'Ah — you mean lunch.'

'No, I *don't* mean lunch, and *watch that motor-bike!*'

'Listen,' I said, 'who's driving this thing?'

'A bloody good question,' he said.

We were pulling into Darlington. I swung around the big traffic island and onto the dual carriageway and, after that, I had to ask.

'Where are we going, then?' I said.

'Park as near as you can to the library.'

'It'll be closed now, Charlie,' I said.

'Don't argue, just do it.'

'Mind telling me why?'

'You're not thinking, Farrow,' he said. 'What time yesterday did Peltz leave the library?'

'About twenty past eleven,' I said.

'And what time did he get back to the hotel?'

'Just on noon,' I said.

'How long does it take to walk that distance?'

'Okay, five minutes.'

'Okay. So where did he go in the meantime?'

29

'Hold it right there, mate!' I said. 'It's now half past one.'

'What about it?'

'Just this — I'm hungry,' I said.

'You're always bloody hungry.'

'Only when I'm working with you.' I was easing the car into a space by the kerb. 'If we don't get something soon, all the restaurants will have packed up serving.'

'We'll grab a sandwich, then.'

'Bollocks, I want a good hot dinner.'

'You've got a job to do.'

'All right, I'll do it afterwards.'

'Like hell you will,' he said.

'You want to bet?'

'You'll do it now!'

'Look, are you *betting*, I said.

But dealing with Charlie, you just can't win. He fretted all through the meal, pestering the waitress to hurry it up. He was finished long before I was and the chop, chips and peas did me no good at all. They lay on my belly like lead and a cup of coffee was out of the question. Even as I was paying the bill, he was up and away and heading for the door. One small consolation, the rain had almost stopped. Charlie looked up at the watery sky, buttoning up his dark-blue raincoat.

'Half an hour wasted,' he said. 'Do you think you're strong enough to get on with it, now?'

'Yeah, me and my heartburn,' I said. 'Ask me, Charlie, I don't see the point.'

'I'm not asking you, am I?' he said.

We had eaten in a little greasy-spoon caff, for the very simple reason it was the first place we had come across. After leaving Charlie, I nipped back down to the library because if his theory was correct, and Peltz had in fact bought the yellow baseball cap upon instruction from the letter drop, that was the

obvious point of departure. I put myself in Peltz's place, a stranger in a strange environment, and began to quarter the surrounding streets in search of any likely shop.

Just under half an hour later, and after visiting seven or eight stores, I finally struck lucky. One of those ubiquitous Army & Navy Surplus outfits which stock just about everything except that which they purport to sell. A sad-eyed and shabby old assistant left a prospective customer agonising over the choice between a cheap and an even cheaper anorak and asked without really meaning it if he could help me. When I told him I was looking for one of them there American baseball caps, he nodded listlessly and asked what size. When I told him I wanted first to have a look at what he'd got, he sighed wearily and set a short wooden ladder against a rack of shelves. He lifted down a large cardboard box, dumped it on the counter and shuffled off without another word. When he came back from the anorak lady, having failed to make a sale, he dashed a dewdrop off the end of his nose.

'They're £3.95,' he said.

I pretended to rummage around in the box. 'I'm not struck on these colours,' I said. 'Haven't you got anything in yellow?'

'You're too late, mister,' he said. 'We sold the last one just yesterday.'

'Did you, now?' I said. I hauled out my likeness of Josef Peltz and held it up in front of his eyes. 'This the fellow who bought it?'

The old man barely glanced at the sketch. 'Who remembers faces?' he said. 'They come, they go, they're all the same.'

'Wake up, you old bugger,' I said, 'or I'll have you down to the Station!'

He blinked. 'Hey — what is this?' he said.

'Look at this properly, and answer the question.'

'I've told you, I don't know,' he said. 'All I know is

31

he sounded foreign.'

'Why the hell didn't you say so!' I said.

I found a phone box and rang the nick. Royston came on the line and passed me over to Charlie, who, when I told him my good news, sounded not in the least appreciative.

'Took half an hour,' he said. 'You must have followed in Peltz's footsteps.'

'That's what I figured,' I said. 'It accounts for the missing time just nicely.'

'All right, listen,' he said. 'Got your street map with you?'

'Yes.'

'Hang on a minute, then —' there was a pause as, presumably, he consulted his own map — 'start walking towards Grange Road, and I'll pick you up along the way.'

'Will do, but don't linger,' I said. 'It looks as though it's going to piss down.'

'Make your hair curl,' he said.

As it happened, the Rover drew up alongside me just as the first big fat drops began to spatter the sidewalk. I ducked very smartly inside and Charlie let the clutch slam out before I could close my door. I made a wild grab at the handle as the car lurched fast away, and almost toppled out in the process.

'Christ, take it easy!' I said.

Charlie flicked out the wipers as he shot up into third gear and turned his head to flash me a look. 'What d'you mean take it easy?' he said. 'Take it easy, my left knacker!'

'Why? What's the hurry?' I said.

'We've got competition, Farrow. Nigel Stone's on his way.'

'Nigel Stone? Who s he, then?'

'Ex-bloody-D15, seconded to Military Intelligence. One of Toby Marshall's chums.'

'How the hell did that lot get into it, Charlie?'

'They're not saying, are they?' he said. 'As per

32

sodding usual!' He gunned us past a small convoy of cars all tailing each other in the rain, bunched together like bananas. He was grimly silent for a couple of minutes, then, 'That's all we need,' he went on, 'that shower of twats getting under our feet!'

I prudently held my tongue. Any response I might have made would only exacerbate his ire. We in the Section had no ostensible link with any of the various arms of Intelligence and none was inclined to acknowledge our existence. Major Toby Marshall of GCHQ — or the Government Communications Head Quarters, Britain's equivalent of America's National Security Agency — had voiced their collective opinion when, and not so long ago, he had described Section personnel as 'an undiscipled mob of ill-mannered thugs'. Charlie, on the other hand, was equally vehement in his opinion that Marshall and his GCHQ were a dilettante shower of namby-pamby poufters.

The truth, like most truths, lay somewhere in between. I had no real inside knowledge of any other government security agency but I did know, and only too well, that our own particular function was not too unlike that of your friendly neighbourhood garbage-disposal crew: sometimes essential, but always unsavoury. We got the jobs from which the others shrank; the assignments they regarded as too hand-soiling dirty, or too risk-involving 'sensitive'. The Section was deemed to hold no such scruples. If the job was dirty, we were expendable; if it was 'sensitive' and therefore quite likely to generate fuss, our very existence could be blandly denied.

That was — and for all I know still is — the Section. Anyone curious as to how I got involved should read *The Manchester Thing*.

I didn't ask Charlie how he knew about the imminent arrival on our scene of this Stone character because (a) I already had a pretty shrewd idea, and (b) he wouldn't tell me, anyway, unless or until he thought I needed to know. But he had probably been given the information upon making a report to the Man. Or, in the Man's absence, Miss Hetherington.

'How's Miss Hetherington, Charlie?' I said.

'What the hell's *she* got to do with it?'

'Nothing. I just thought —'

'Well, don't. Leave the thinking to me.'

'All right, Einstein. Where are we going, then?'

But he was already braking to make a right-hand turn and a signboard at the entrance to the driveway he was aiming at said

BLACKWELL GRANGE GOLF CLUB — PRIVATE.

The club secretary, who preferred to talk to us at a corner table in the near-empty bar, was about as helpful as a cold in the nose. He did not personally know any member of that description, had certainly not noticed him around the place the previous day, and he radiated the general impression that he would not necessarily tell us, even if he had. I coaxed Charlie away from the crusty old buffer, before he blew his top, by telling him that I had an idea.

'Come on, then, what is it?' he said.

We were walking away from the club-house. 'Let's try the pro's shop,' I said. 'Our chum might have needed to pop in for something.'

It was the second triumph of my day. First the baseball cap, now this. We spoke to the junior pro, his boss having left to go home in disgust at the lack of business due to the rain. The junior was a bright young chap, maybe too bright.

'Just a minute,' he said, 'who are you?'

'Who do we look like?' Charlie said.

'Police?'

'We haven't got all day, son.'

'Well, I don't know,' the youngster said. 'I mean, you could be anybody.'

Charlie wheeled away. 'All right, bring him down to the Station.'

34

'Let's not be too hasty,' I said. I'd been given my cue and was ready for it. I turned to the youth behind the glass-fronted counter with its golfing-gear display. 'Look, lad, do yourself a favour.'

'I was only trying to make sure . . . '

'Okay, so now you've done it. Who was he?'

'Sounds like Tony,' he said, 'Anthony Green. He works at Marsden's.'

'Marsden's? What's Marsden's?' I said.

Marsden's Bearings, out on Yarm Road.'

'What time was it when he came in?'

'After lunch, about a quarter past two. He bought half a dozen used balls.'

'Play here often, does he?'

'No, he hasn't been golfing long.'

'So how do you know him?'

'I've always known him. We were at school together,' he said.

'Where does he live, then?'

'Is Tony in trouble?'

'Not that we know of,' I said.

'Then why — '

'We just want to talk to him. Do you have his address?'

'I don't know the number, but he lives in Barnes Road.'

'Thanks. Now, what's *your* name?' I said.

'William Taylor. But you're not going to tell him — '

'No, no, and neither are you. Don't tell anybody anything. Just forget we were here.'

'Come on,' said Charlie, 'we're wasting time.'

'Now think on, William,' I said.

We left him staring after us and hurried off through the rain, back to the carpark and into the Rover. Charlie opened the door on the passenger side, then handed the keys to me.

'You drive.'

'Where to?'

'Get in — get *in*!'

35

'All right, don't panic,' I said.

The fact that tough little old Edgar Marsden wouldn't even tell us the time of day until Charlie flashed his jotter offered us the first real clue as to what it was all about. But our credentials once established, he offered us chairs in his Spartanly furnished office, went to sit behind his plain bare desk and got in first with a query of his own. He asked us what if any connection we had with a fellow called Nigel Stone.

'Has Stone been here already?' asked Charlie.

'No, not yet,' Marsden said. 'He's supposed to be coming in the late afternoon. Is he a colleague of yours?'

'Not likely,' said Charlie.

'Well, what then?'

'Anthony Green,' Charlie said. 'What's his job here? What does he do?'

'He's a first-class draughtsman and designer.'

'Designing what?' Charlie said.

'We make bearings, mister. I thought you knew that.'

'Look, sir,' Charlie said, 'please just answer the questions.'

'I'm a busy man,' Marsden said.

Soon, however, when Charlie got him talking about the sort of stuff turned out by his factory, Marsden seemed to forget about pressures of business. He was an enthusiast, all right, and it quickly emerged that he really did have something to enthuse over. I can't say I spend a lot of time thinking about bearings, but on those very rare occasions that I do, I think of them as hard-steel balls set in a circlip around an axle to make wheels run smoothly. But the bearings made at Marsdens out on the Yarm Road industrial estate were nothing of that kind. They were to the wheel what the wheel must have seemed like before they invented the wheel.

I rapidly lost track of the technical jargon, but I

could pick up just enough of that which the old man was on about to realise that what we had here was a very hot potato. Marsden's bearings were integrated each with its own sophisticated computer system and, at that time, their entire output was trucked not many miles north to that well-known heavy-armaments company which gave us the Chieftain tank and which now makes its deadly successor, the Challenger. The bearings were designed to operate simultaneously around a multiple of axes, to align and realign the turret and gun with pin-point accuracy. And the firm was unique in its field: no Marsden bearings, no Challenger tank. It was as simple as that.

'. . . yes, I see. That's fascinating,' said Charlie.

'Now it's your turn,' Marsden said.

'Our turn?' said Charlie.

'Yes, your turn. *You* can answer some questions for *me*, and we'll start with young Green.'

'What about him?'

'That's what I want to know. If you people think he's up to something — '

'If he is, we'll find out,' Charlie said.

'What happens to security, in the meantime?'

'Don't worry,' Charlie said. 'I'm sure Mr Stone will have some ideas.'

'And what about you?' Marsden said. 'What's your job, then?'

'Oh, it's mostly routine.'

'Yes — and pigs can fly!' Marsden said.

Charlie did not want to alert anybody on Marsden's staff to the fact that Green was under any sort of cloud, so we got the number of his house by the simple expedient of looking it up in the phone book. Barnes Road, in the attractive white-collar suburb of Mowden Park, climbed the flank of a long steep hill and was lined on both sides by well-kept houses most of which, though not large, were detached. I parked at kerb in front of one of the houses around

the corner from Green's place, to preserve the anonymity of the car. Charlie made no immediate move to get out.

'What's the drill going to be, then?' I said.

'We're going to have a chat with the little woman before her lord and master gets home. Then, when he does, we'll lean on him.'

'Better watch it, Charlie,' I said. 'We've got no proof.'

'Don't give us the squitters.'

'It's all very well,' I said, 'but there could be repercussions.'

'Reperbollocks,' he said. 'Listen, I sometimes worry about you.'

'I worry about me, as well.'

'Quite right. You're getting as soft as — '

'Watch it!'

'Oh, let's go, for Christ's sake,' he said.

The youngish woman who answered our ring at the doorbell wore one of those oilcloth aprons printed with a Union Jack, and a frown which said anything but welcome. She had flour all over hands and was holding them clear of her short pleated skirt. She looked us both up and down, but addressed herself to Charlie.

'Yes?'

'Mrs Green?' he said.

'Maybe. What is it? What do you want?'

'A talk with you,' Charlie said. 'Can we come in?'

'No, you certainly can't. What's it about?' the girl said.

'It's about your husband.'

'Anthony? Why? What's happened to him?'

'Nothing, yet.'

'What the hell do you mean? Who are you, anyway?'

I stood to one side, with my hands in my pockets, and let them get on with it. This young lass — I put her age at something under thirty — was going to be

38

no pushover, even for Charlie. Rather tall and very dark, she had a face full of character. Not a pretty face. The eyes were too hard and the cheekbones too heavy, the black brows too thick and coarse and the lips, though full, too wide and determined. She had square, sturdy shoulders and wide, solid hips. Small breasts carried tight and high and the muscular limbs of an athlete. She was feminine without a doubt, but there was nothing about her soft or curvaceous.

'I think you'd better ask us in,' said Charlie.

'Why? What will you do, if I don't?'

'We'll come back with a warrant, and tear the place apart.'

'You're joking!'

'He's not. He's never been known to.'

'I'll handle this,' Charlie said. He had not taken his eyes off the woman. 'Well?'

She didn't like it one bit, but she stepped back off the threshold to let us step into the hall and closed the door behind us.

'You can wait in the front room,' she said.

'And where will you be waiting?' said Charlie.

'I'll be in the kitchen,' she said. 'In case you haven't noticed, I happen to be cooking.'

'We'll come and keep you company, then. My partner's a scoff-hound — aren't you, partner?'

'Chance'd be a fine thing,' I said.

The kitchen was roomy and well-equipped. There was a corner breakfast nook, a built-in split-level oven and Formica worktops galore. All pervaded by a rich meaty odour. One of the worktops was sprinkled with flour. The woman crossed to it and began to flatten a lump of pastry. She spoke with her back to us, banging away with a rolling-pin.

'All right, so now you're in. Say what you have to say, and get out.'

'Now that's not nice,' Charlie said. He perched, armed folded, on the edge of the table. I leaned

against the jamb of the door. 'Not nice,' he went on, 'where's your husband, missis?'

'Anthony's at work,' she said.

'What — on a Saturday?'

'Yes, on a Saturday. His firm works a split-hours rota across a seven-day week.'

'Very busy, are they?'

'Christ! As if you don't know!'

'Does he have to bring work home with him, then?'

'No.'

'Never?'

'You heard me,' she said.

'I hope you're not telling fibs, Mrs Green.'

'Now, look — ' she turned around, and pointed at Charlie with her rolling-pin — 'I don't know what it is you're after, but I will not answer any more questions.'

'Yes, you will,' Charlie said, 'one way or another.'

'What exactly does that mean?'

'Your husband's got himself into trouble, and if you want to help him get out, you can do it best by co-operating with us.'

Her explosive snort conveyed derision. 'What a load of rubbish!' she said, 'Tony's not in any trouble, because if he was, I'd know.'

'You sure about that?'

'Of course I'm sure. We don't have secrets here.'

'Oh yes you do, lady,' Charlie said mildly. 'Where was he yesterday?'

'Where was who?'

'Come on — your husband. Yesterday afternoon.'

'Tony was playing golf.'

'Who with?'

'With no-one. He went round on his own — look, I've got to get this pie in the oven.'

'Feel free,' Charlie said. 'In the meantime, I'll just use your telephone.'

'Oh, do. *Feel free*!' she said.

40

As he passed me in the doorway Charlie's pond-water eyes met mine and telegraphed the message. I closed the kitchen door.

'Now see here, lady — '

'Don't you "lady" me!'

She slammed her pie into the oven, wiped her floury hands and began to assemble dishes and plates. Two of everything. As I watched her set the table, the significance dawned on me.

'Ah, you're Jewish, are you?' I said.

'Don't tell me you're anti-Semitic, as well.'

'As well as what?' I said.

'As well as being anti-people in general.'

'Oh, we're not anti-people,' I said, 'we're just anti-some of the tricks they get up to.'

'Why bother us, then?' she said.

'Listen, I'm sorry about the intrusion.'

'So you should be,' she said. 'That friend of yours is a bloody little Hitler!'

'It's just his manner,' I said. 'His ulcers must be playing him up.'

'Are you taking the mickey out of me?' She stopped bustling about and turned on me, glaring.

'No, no, really,' I said, 'he suffers something chronic.'

'Balls! You're as bad as he is!' she said.

My spirited denial of the canard coincided with Charlie's return. He looked from one to the other of us, and, 'Hello, what's up?' he said. 'Been falling out, have you?' He nodded at the woman. 'I'm afraid your phone's on the blink.'

'On the blink?'

'Yes, out of order.'

'It was all right an hour ago!'

'That's British Telecom for you. We'll report it.'

'Oh, thanks a *lot*!'

'Not at all, you're welcome — ah . . . ' Charlie cocked his head at the sound of the front door being opened ' . . sounds like the breadwinner's

41

home.'

Someone called from out in the hallway. *Ruthie? Ruth? Are you there?'*

Green had his back to us, hanging up his coat.

'Had a hard day?' Charlie said.

When he spun round and saw us, his jaw dropped open.

'What the — '

'Shut your gob, lad,' Charlie said. 'You'll catch a chill on the tonsils.'

Green recovered fast. 'Who are you? Where's Ruth?'

'She's in the kitchen cooking your supper, but we've time for a chat,' Charlie said. 'She's only just put the pie in the oven.'

'Look . . are you from the police?'

'You could say that, in a manner of speaking.'

'May I see your warrant cards, please?'

'Farrow, show him your warrant card.'

'I've lost it, Charlie,' I said.

'Hear that, Green?' said Charlie. 'He's lost it. Christ, the help they send you these days.'

Green made a grab for the phone on the window-ledge. 'We'll see — '

'No, you won't,' Charlie said, 'your telephone's knackered. I've just been trying it.'

'Tony!'

I turned my head. Ruth was standing out in the hall, behind us.

'You all right, love?'

'Yes,' she said. 'Talk to them, for God's sake. Then perhaps they might go!'

Green hesitated. Our informant at the golf-club had given us a pretty good description. Perhaps a year or two younger than the woman, he was a couple of inches taller and he carried an extra full stone. I was struck by a certain similarity between them. Apart from the fact that his colouring was that very deep copper bronze, they might readily be taken

42

for brother and sister. They had the same lithe body characteristics and the same hard, deep-set eyes. He was wearing brown slacks and a light tweed jacket over a soft rollneck sweater. Casual slip-on shoes. When he was through appraising us:

'All right, why not?' he said.

He turned to pass through the doorway on his left and we followed into a room which, like my worthy colleague, was obsessively neat and clean. The modern furnishings looked brand-new and expensive. The large-screen colour TV was equipped with a fancy video recorder, and the stereo hi-fi gear appeared to have more controls than Concorde. There was a notable absence of books, although the shelves on either side of the fireplace were stacked with magazines, most of which seemed to be technical. Charlie took a good look around and:

'Very nice,' he said. 'Sit down, Tony.'

'I prefer to stand.'

'Sit down,' Charlie said.

Green frowned, but complied, as most people did when Charlie adopted that tone. We of course remained on our feet, Charlie with his back to the turned-low gas fire and me at my place by the door. Green ought by this time to have been showing signs of nervousness, but nothing of the kind. He looked up at Charlie.

'Now then, what's this all about?'

Charlie clasped his hands behind his back. 'Josef Peltz,' he said.

'Josef Peltz? Who's Josef Peltz?'

'You know damned well who he is. Don't try to bugger us about, lad.'

'I don't know him, and that's the truth,' Green said.

'Truth my left tit,' said Charlie. 'We've been watching you, Tony.'

'You've what?'

'Are you deaf? I said we've been watching you.'

43

Green laughed. 'Give over!' he said.

'Don't tell me to give over. Where were you yesterday?'

Green fished out a hankie and blew his nose. 'I don't have to talk to you.'

'Got something to hide, sonny?'

'No, of course not.'

'Right, get on with it, then.'

'Why should I?'

'Because I say so. Also,' Charlie went on, 'you've signed the Act. You're working on — '

'No! Not yesterday!' Green said. 'Yesterday, I had a day off, and what I do in my own free time is none of your business.'

'Bullshit.'

'Now listen — '

'No, you listen,' Charlie said. 'What do you think you're on, Green? Your daddy's bloody yacht? You'll talk to us here, or we'll take you somewhere else. It's all the same to me, so make up your mind right now.'

Green stared up at Charlie, then shrugged his shoulders. 'Okay, I played golf,' he said.

'Well, if you already know . . .'

'What did you do in the morning?'

'Nothing.'

'Yes, you did,' Charlie said. 'You went down town to the library.'

'Oh, yes.'

'Yes indeed,' Charlie said. 'You went to leave a message for your friend Josef Peltz.'

'That's absolute nonsense!' Green said. 'I've never even heard of the man!'

'Hear that, Farrow?'

'Shocking,' I said. 'He's being less than frank with you, Chas.'

'You think so?'

'I think so,' I said.

Charlie had kept his cold stare on Green through-

44

out our little exchange, but the young man seemed curiously unaffected and this I found rather strange. Not many of his age could stand up to Charlie, including those who'd been trained. It was as though he knew something he *knew* we didn't know. Charlie would see this, too, but he wasn't finished. Not by a long chalk. I didn't think he would use his fearsome hands on Green, not with the woman around. And not at this stage. It was a little too soon.

'It's a pity,' Charlie said.

'Have you finished then?' Green asked.

'Finished?' Charlie said, 'We're just getting started.'

'My meal will be ready.'

'Too bad. What were you and Peltz talking about?'

'Look, I've already told you — '

'Crap! You've already told us a load of crap! It's *us* who've been telling *you*! Do you want us to tell you something else?' Green shrugged. 'You've had it, boy,' Charlie went on, 'you're blown. We're onto you, sunshine. We've been keeping an eye on you.'

'Green shifted his buttocks on the cushion of his chair.

'Really?'

'Too true,' Charlie said. 'What happened to your previous contact?'

'What contact?'

'Well, Peltz is obviously new, or he wouldn't have needed to identify himself with that stupid yellow-cap routine.'

'I still don't know what you're talking about.'

'Of course you do,' Charlie said. 'You set up the meet at the library, used the place as a message drop, arranged to run into Peltz on the golf-course.'

'Oh, *that*!'

'Yes, that,' Charlie said. 'Started remembering now, have you?'

'The man was a stranger,' Green said. "All I did was help him to find a lost ball. As for your library tale, I've never heard such rubbish.'

Charlie heaved a mock sigh. 'Why don't you make a clean breast of it all?'

'You're talking in riddles,' Green said. 'I've nothing to make a clean breast *of*!'

'That your final word?'

'Damned right.'

'That appears to be it, then, Farrow.'

'It would seem so, Charlie,' I said.

'You mean you're actually leaving?'

'For the moment, yes,' Charlie said.

Royston looked at his watch. 'It's nearly half past eight.'

'Ten out of ten,' Charlie said.

'I should have gone off duty a couple of hours ago.'

'Don't let us keep you.'

'I was only wondering — '

'Go on, get off home,' Charlie said. 'Clock-watchers give me the screaming habdabs.'

'By the way, Charlie,' I said.

'Don't you start, Farrow.'

'But Royston's right, there's not much more we can do. We've got Green under surveillance now, and he can't communicate — '

'How d'you know he can't communicate?'

'You buggered up his phone.'

'Green's telephone is out of order.'

'Yes, well, whatever,' I said. 'The fact remains he's incommunicado.'

'Incommuniknackers!' he said. 'Didn't you see those aerials stuck on his chimney?'

'VHF, Charlie,' I said.

'Maybe.'

Royston's telephone rang and Charlie was the first to reach it.

'Hello? Yes, go ahead . . .' he listened for a short while without interrupting, then put the receiver down. 'Farrow, let's go.' Royston got to his feet.

'Not you,' Charlie went on, 'you'd better get home to your fish and chips.'

'That's the general idea,' Royston said.

He sounded annoyed and who could blame him after all the good work he'd done with the organising of a surveillance team, and radio links with our car. When we split up outside in the carpark I said goodnight to him, but he stumped away without responding.

'See what you've done, Chas?' I said, 'Why the hell did you have to go and upset him?'

'Stop waffling, and get in the car.'

It turned out that Charlie's hectoring tactics might have produced a result. His objective in putting the arm on Green was to make our boyo sweat and panic him into taking action. Any kind of action would do, so long as some movement was generated. Charlie hated having to sit still. His method was to jump in and stir it, keep everybody on the go until somebody tired and made a mistake. That this somebody might one day be us was a prospect which never entered his mind. But it often entered mine and was naught, as they say, for my comfort. I eased myself into the car and started its huge, souped-up engine.

'Where are we going, then?' I said.

'I don't know yet, just get rolling.' He was fiddling with the R/T, receiving nothing but mush and crackle. 'Green's on the move,' he said, 'he left the house a few minutes ago heading for the centre of town — what's the *matter* with this bloody thing!'

I drove us slowly along Park Place and turned left into Park Gate, trundling towards the inner ringroad. After two full circuits of the big traffic island, Charlie mastered the dodgy R/T and found the channel for which he'd been searching.

' . . . Bulldog to Fido . . come in.'

'Fido to Bulldog . . are you reading me — over.'

'I'm reading you now,' Charlie said. 'Where the hell

47

are you?'

'Market Place. Subject's looking for a space to park.'

'Listen — don't go and lose the bastard! One of you stay with the car, the other one tail him.'

'Supposing he spots us?'

'I don't give a monkey's chuff. Just stick with him, and his car, till we get there.'

'Roger.'

'Over and out.' Charlie hung up the hand-mike. 'You heard that — get moving.'

'We've just passed the exit,' I said, 'we'll have to go all the way round again.'

'Put your boot down, then!' he said.

I did and we hit the market square in something like two minutes flat, to a chorus of hooting from outraged drivers. Detective Constable Sewart was parked on a double yellow line outside of a pub called the Boot & Shoe. He wound his window down.

'Mr McGowan?'

Charlie nodded. 'Where is he?'

'He's at the King's Head. He's just gone in.'

'I hope your mate's good.'

'Don's okay — ' They were using the powerful new walkie-talkies patched in direct to the cars and, at that moment, Sewart got a beep. 'Hang on a moment,' he said. 'Subject's made contact with a person unknown having dinner in the King's Head bar, and has sat down with person unknown at his table.'

'Beautiful,' Charlie said. 'Farrow, let's go and join 'em.'

'Anything you say, Chas,' I said.

After giving Sewart further instructions Charlie turned away and we set off through the darkening streets towards the King's Head hotel. It wasn't far, just a few hundred yards. The sky was beginning to clear and between the clouds pale stars were appearing. Tomorrow might be a fine day. Weather-wise, if nothing else. In the meantime, I felt shagged

and various of my old wounds were aching. The one in my thigh worst of all and I must, unconsciously, have started to limp.

'Come *on*, Farrow!' Charlie said, 'What's the matter with you, for Christ's sake?'

'It's been a long day,' I said. We turned into Priestgate.

'Bloody rhubarb!'

'Admit it, Charlie,' I said. 'We're getting too old for this sort of lark.'

'Speak for yourself,' he said.

We pushed through the double glass doors and turned to the right past Reception. No Miss Hornby now, just a bored-looking girl with a paperback novel. She gave us a listless glance, then reburied her nose in the Barbara Cartland as we entered the King's Head Bar. The long bar itself ran down to the right. Facing it, over on the left, was s sort-of-separate dining-area. Not cramped, there was plenty of room, although everyone could see everyone else. There was a rich off-stage odour of food, but it didn't obtrude on the good smell of ale. Suddenly, I wanted a beer even more than I wanted something to eat. Charlie touched my arm.

'Over there, in the corner.'

'I'm ahead of you, mate,' I said, 'and you needn't bother to tell me.'

'It's Stone, the *cunt*!' he said.

'It figures, Charlie. Green was too cocky. He's one of theirs,' I said.

The flanges of his nostrils turned white.

'I'll "cocky" the bastards!' he said.

In a way, I was glad. I felt tired. I wanted a couple of drinks and some grub in my belly, and so to bed. Charlie had other ideas.

'I'll tell you what we'll do — '

'Don't bother. Forget it, Charlie,' I said.

We were standing outside on the pavement, in

49

Priestgate. The road gang's equipment still there, resting. Waiting for Monday morning, or Sunday double-time. I was suffering from hunger and disenchantment. Reaction setting in. A shiver of chill and I fastened my raincoat. My leg nagged.

'Look,' Charlie said, 'there's something bloody funny — '

'Oh yes, hilarious,' I said, 'but it's nine o'clock, and we've had no scoff, and we haven't yet fixed anywhere to stay — '

'Anywhere to stay? We can go back to your place!'

I offered him the keys. 'Be my guest, if the dogs will let you.'

'I'm warning you, Farrow!' he said.

A passer-by turned to stare at us.

'Keep your voice down,' I said, 'you're alarming the populace.'

'Bugger the populace!'

'I wouldn't have the strength. Make your mind up, Charlie.'

'All right — but just wait, boy!' he said.

We ended up, after a sad Chinese meal, at a guesthouse on Greenbank Road recommended by one of the CID blokes. We rarely stayed in hotels, because Charlie spent the Section's money about as freely as he spent his own. So long as the accommodation was inexpensive and very, very clean, he was quite content. He would rather, of course, have lived free, but I wasn't about to drive forty miles to get back to my house.

No way.

Sunday.

Somebody was thumping my shoulder, hard. I groaned
and opened my eyes and looked at my watch. It was
half past seven. He was shaved and bathed and dressed
and he smelled of shampoo. I closed my eyes.

'Come on — get up!' he said.

'What for?' I said. 'It's Sunday, they don't serve
breakfast till nine.'

'We're getting ours at eight o'clock. I spoke to the
lady, last night.'

I groaned again. 'Jesus, Charlie!'

'Move, you lazy sod.'

Charlie was one of those infuriating people who
need a lot less sleep than those of us who are normal. The only trouble was, he thought *he* was normal.
I started to get out of bed.

'Why the hell don't you wear pyjamas?'

'Why don't you piss off,' I said.

The big, half-tiled bathroom was full of steam.
Charlie got his money's worth at guest-houses by
his use of hot water alone. He required as much as a
fair-sized laundry. He was the only person I ever
knew who would bathe before going to bed, then
bathe again in the morning. He was constantly
washing his hair, and his white drip-dry shirts, and
his underwear. Not to mention his socks. I have
seen him change his linen three times in a single
day.

But the guest-house in Darlington must have had
a large cistern, because there was plenty of hotters
left for me, and after shaving I wallowed in a bath
until Charlie banged on the door.

'Shake it up, Farrow, breakfast's nearly ready!'

'I'll be down in five minutes!' I said.

We had the pleasant little dining-room all to ourselves, and our landlady dished up a good solid

breakfast of bacon and sausage, two eggs and a grilled tomato. Plenty of toast and a pot of very strong tea which Charlie promptly diluted. He was finished eating before I had broken the yolk of my second egg but for once he didn't start bugging me.

'I'm going out to find a phone.'

'There's a phone in the hall.'

'I know, I'm not blind. Be ready when I get back.'

'Take your time, then.'

'Just you be ready.'

'Are you leaving this sausage?' I said.

I felt a lot better after that big nosh, but the feeling didn't last long. Charlie was back and rarin' to go, as I poured out my fourth cup of tea. He'd been gone about twenty minutes.

'You can leave that. We're on our way.'

'On our way where?'

'To the cop-shop, first. There's some bumf waiting for us down there.'

The bumf, which had been delivered by a courier who had driven up from London overnight, was contained in a stiff legal envelope. Charlie broke the seals and tipped the contents onto Royston's desk. Royston, on duty weekend, was due to come in at nine o'clock. It was ten to. I got out my pipe.

'You're not smoking that thing in here,' Charlie said.

'Okay, then, I'll go outside.'

'Don't get wandering off.'

'Oh, get on with your bumf.'

I sat in the car, with the windows wound down, and enjoyed a soothing pipe. It was lovely, a short spell of perfect peace. Just before nine o'clock, Royston arrived in a grey Ford Cortina. He did not notice me and I called to him as he made his way between the rows of parked cars.

'Harry — over here!'

As he angled across I leaned down sideways to open the nearside door and he stooped to duck in

beside me.

'Good-morning, you're early,' he said.

'This isn't early, this is late. We've done half a day's work,' I said.

He grinned. 'Where's your buddy?'

'Inside, in your office. He's taken it over,' I said.

'How's it going?'

'How's what going?'

'Well, you know, the job.'

'Nobody tells me anything.'

'In other words, don't ask,' he said. 'Anyway, it's a beautiful morning.'

'That's better.'

'Look, er . .'

'Mark,' I said, 'short for Marcus Aurelius.'

'No! Really?'

'Scouts honour,' I said. 'My old man was hooked on the Meditations.'

'Oh, I see,' he said. I don't think he did, but I wasn't going to push it. 'Anyway, what's in a name?'

'You started to say something.'

'What? Oh, yes. About last night,' he said. 'I wasn't mad at *you*, you know.'

'Don't give it another thought.'

'No, it was that bastard partner of yours.'

'Hold it, Harry!' I said. 'If you and I are going to get on, you can cut that out — understand?'

'Listen, you have to agree — '

'I don't have to agree. Remember that.'

'Oh, okay. But how you put up with him, day after day . . .'

'I'm just wafted along on his charm.'

'Gawd, you stick together like shit to a blanket.'

'That's what keeps us alive, boy,' I said.

'Go on — you're kidding.'

'All right, I'm kidding.'

'Christ, you're *not* kidding!'

'Come on, Harry, make up your mind.'

'Sorry, Mark. It's just that — '

'Forget it.'

'I didn't realise.'

'I said, forget it.'

'All right, I will. But listen, I'm sorry,' he said.

There was a little awkward silence. He ran a hand through his wiry blond hair, then shifted to fumble in one of his pockets. He hauled out a packet of fags and used the car lighter to light one. As he pushed the lighter back home, twin streams of blue smoke drifted out of his nostrils.

'Blow it out of the car,' I said. 'His nibs can't stand the smell of tobacco.'

'What other things can't he stand?'

'It would take me too long to tell you. What have you got on for today?'

'We're moving the yobbos up to Durham.' He meant those who had mugged Josef Peltz. 'And incidentally, there could be some trouble.'

'What kind of trouble?' I said.

'The one your mate . . er, *talked* to has lodged an official complaint. He reckons your mate did him over.'

'Good luck to him.'

'Not the point. There'll have to be an inquiry.'

'Good luck to that, as well. Anyway, Harry, you're in the clear.'

'Yes, but mud sticks, chum,' he said. 'Once the sodding do-gooders start howling . . . ' he shook his head in disgust and tossed away his cigarette end '. . . I'd better be getting inside. I haven't signed on yet.'

'Hang on, I'll come with you.'

As we passed through the bare little entrance hall, the desk man was speaking on the phone. He looked up and saw us and waved to Royston, and slid his window back.

'Hey, sarge! You'd better talk to this bloke.'

Royston moved up to the hatch and reached in to take the proffered receiver. 'Detective Sergeant

Royston here . . . yes, sir . . . would you speak slowly, please . . .' he nodded at the man on the desk, who was standing ready with pad and pencil '. . . yes, sir, yes that's fine . . . let's start off with your name and address . . . Mr Gerald Fowler, Barnes Road . . .'

I eavesdropped with rapidly burgeoning interest which culminated in shock. The real significance was lost on Royston, but the substance of the call was that a metaphorical bomb had exploded. A bomb called Green. He was dead.

Green's front room was cluttered with people.

'Get this lot cleared out,' Charlie said.

Royston frowned. 'They've got jobs to do.'

'They can do 'em somewhere else. Send 'em into the kitchen, tell 'em they can make some tea.'

'I'm not in charge here, *Mister* McGowan.'

'Who is, then?'

'Inspector Devine. That's him over yonder, talking to the doctor.'

Devine was a tall, heavy man, with a bristling crew-cut of hard grey stubble. The doctor was dwarfed by him. They were standing close together, over by the telly, talking in undertones. Also in the room were a couple of plain-clothes men, a police photographer and an elderly chap who looked lost and bewildered. There was no sign of Mrs Green.

'Where's the little woman?' asked Charlie.

'She's upstairs,' Royston said, 'in the bedroom.'

'Kipping, is she?'

'As a matter of fact, yes, she is. The doctor says she's been drugged with something.'

'Something like what?' Charlie said.

'Like sleeping-tablets. Enough to knock her out, but not enough to be dangerous.'

The elderly chap was wearing carpet slippers. He approached us timidly and touched the sleeve of Royston's coat.

'Er, I say, excuse me . . . ' he said.

'Yes, Mr Fowler?'

'All right if I leave now?'

'Oh, I think so,' Royston said. 'You're not going anywhere, are you?'

'No, I'll be at home all day.'

'In that case — '

'Hang on a minute,' said Charlie, 'I'd like a quiet word.'

'We've already got Mr Fowler's statement.'

'Do you mind?' Charlie said.

And so it was that we heard it straight from the horse's mouth. Fowler, a retired shop-owner who lived across the road, had risen at eight o'clock that morning to give his wife breakfast in bed. He had eaten his own in the kitchen and then, it being such a fine day, he had popped out front in his slippers to check his roses after yesterday's rain. But he never got around to it, because a happening over the way demanded his immedite attention. Oily blue smoke was seeping out from under the Greens' garage door.

He thought at first that the garage was on fire. He ran across the road and rang the Greens' bell and hammered on the door. All to no effect. It was Sunday, the morning for lying abed, and there wasn't a soul around. Seized by a sense of something far wrong, he had thrown up the garage door, to be almost choked by the dense acrid fumes which filled the interior. But then he could hear the low rumble of an engine and make out the shape of a car. And half a minute later, when the reek had thinned, he could see there was someone inside. Sprawled awry on the passenger seat, his head laid far back on the squab.

Fowler had been a sick-berth attendant in the Navy during the war and he knew what he had to do. He also knew, when he tried to do it, that his effort was far too late. So he dashed back home and did the next best thing, he telephoned the police.

There was patently nothing more he could tell

56

us, so Charlie let him go. By this time, Royston
had disappeared, with the rest of the Incident Squad,
leaving only Devine and the doctor. Then the latter
left the room, to go back upstairs and look at the
woman. The inspector nodded at us.

'Now then,' he said, 'it's McGowan, isn't it?'

'That's right,' Charlie said, 'and this is my colleague, Farrow.'

'How'd y'do,' I said. I like to get a word in, now
and again.

'I've heard about you two.' Devine's tone suggested
that what he'd heard had given him pause for thought.
'What's the connection between this job, and your
lot?'

'We don't rightly know,' Charlie said.

'Is that why you had some of my people tailing
Green last night?'

'*Your* people?'

'*Our* people, then.' Devine forced a smile. 'What
department you from?'

'Social Security.'

'I see. Cloak-and-dagger boys, are you?'

'More like soak and stagger,' Charlie said. 'He is, at
least.'

Devine looked at me. 'He doesn't have much to say
for himself.'

'He's the strong silent type,' Charlie said.

'Well, if that's the way you want to play it . . '

'Listen,' Charlie said, 'how soon will you boys be
finished around here?'

'They're just about finished now. I shall be leaving
a man with Mrs Green — '

'Leave Royston, then,' Charlie said.

'Royston isn't attached to my team. He's supposed
to be working with you.'

'We can do without him this morning.'

The inspector was nobody's fool. He must have
suspected we were up to something but shrewdly,
he didn't want to know. He was probably cruising

57

towards retirement. He stroked his bulldozer chin.

'Well, we're always a bit short-handed on a week-end . . .'

'That's what I thought,' Charlie said. 'We're only trying to be helpful.'

'All right, Sergeant Royston can stay. I'll just go and brief him.'

'Thank you, Inspector — oh, and if the doctor's still there, ask him to come and have a word with us, will you?'

Devine nodded and left the room and a few minutes later we were joined by the doctor.

'Hello, my name's Brownlow,' he said. 'I'm told you wanted to see me?'

'We still do,' Charlie said. 'How's your patient?'

'Mildly comatose, but she'll be all right,' Brownlow said. 'It's best just to let her sleep it off.'

'And how long is that going to take?'

'Oh, two or three hours yet, it's difficult to say. Pulse and breathing quite firm and regular — '

'No stomach-pump, then?'

'Lord, no. There are no signs of *that* kind of overdose.'

'Very fortunate,' Charlie said.

His sarcasm was lost on Brownlow. 'Yes indeed,' he said. 'She must have been given just enough to ensure a long, heavy sleep.'

'Thank you, doctor,' said Charlie.

'That all you want to know?'

'It'll do, for the moment.'

'Ah, well, I'll be off, then.'

The Incident Squad went too, leaving only ourselves and Royston. An ambulance had taken Green's body to the morgue, where an autopsy would be performed as soon as reasonably possible. The theory was that Green had drugged his wife, possibly by dosing a bedtime hot drink, to forestall any interference from her as he did away with himself. The evidence pointing to suicide seemed unassailable. There were no

58

signs of violence and every indication that Green died peacefully. Access to the garage, an integral part of the house, was by way of a door in the kitchen and that Green had used this door appeared to be quite obvious.

'Seems obvious, Charlie,' I said.

'What seems obvious?'

'Well, how he did it.'

'How *who* did it?' Charlie said.

'Young Green, of course.'

'Young Green, your Aunt Fanny!'

'Who else, then?' Royston said.

'You're supposed to be upstairs, watching the woman.'

'She's sleeping,' Royston said.

'Well go upstairs and watch her sleep.'

Royston flushed, but turned away, and we heard him stomping up the steps.

'Bravo, Charlie,' I said. 'That's the way to cement relations.'

'Who with — your Aunt Fanny?' he said. He was taking off his coat and jacket. 'Come on, let's get on with the job. We might as well do this room first.'

I knew what he meant, of course. We started by moving every piece of furniture which was placed against a wall and pulling back the carpet. We couldn't hope to do a proper search, because that would require a team of four men and could take the best part of a week, with every tiny item returned precisely to its place. But Charlie wasn't bothered about that. He wanted a good quick frisk, as thorough as possible without being too fussy. And he didn't care if it showed.

At the end of an hour, I was sweating. The sitting-room was clean. The hi-fi and video were just exactly that which they were supposed to be and we found nothing even remotely suspicious. It was the same with the loo and the hall, and it began to look

the same with the dining-room. We were down on our hands and knees, hauling up the broadloom, when Royston stuck in his head.

'Jesus!' he said, 'What're you doing?'

'Farrow's lost a stud,' Charlie said.

'No, it's a cuff-link, Charlie.'

'Good grief! Hey, wait —!' Royston said.

'We haven't got time. Was there something you wanted?'

'I was going to make a pot of tea, and I wondered if you fancied a cup — but listen,' he went on, 'if it comes out that you blokes turned this place over . . .'

'How can it come out,' Charlie said, 'unless you go and snitch on us?'

'No!'

'We've got no problem, then.'

We had done the upstairs, all except the main bedroom, when someone rang the front door-bell. Royston went down to see who was calling. It was a man from Telecom. Or a man who *said* he was from Telecom, sent to fix the phone. Royston did not believe him and, come to that, neither did I. Not on a Sunday morning, and not in a smart Ford Capri, and especially not in a hundred-quid suit. Charlie believed him, though, so who were we to start raising queries. But Royston prudently put it on record that he had, in fact, expressed doubt.

'Damn funny, the GPO turning out on a Sunday.'

'Oh, I don't know,' Charlie said. 'It's double money, after all.'

They were passing each other on the stairs, as Charlie went down to talk to the newcomer. They kept their voices low and we couldn't hear what they were saying. I beckoned Royston into the back bedroom, and we each sat on one of the beds. Royston lit a cigarette.

'I'm telling you, Mark,' he said, 'I feel like I'm walking a bloody tightrope.'

60

'Oh, relax, Harry,' I said. 'Put it down to experience.'

'Who the hell needs it?' he said, 'If the Police Commission ever gets to hear about this . . .'

'There's no way they're going to,' I said. 'No way at all, so stop worrying.'

Charlie came back upstairs. 'Sergeant, I think you should go get your lunch.'

'Gladly,' Royston said.

'And take your time with it.'

'Likewise.'

After he was gone, we set about the main bedroom. The woman slept through it all, snuffling occasionally and turning over. When we were very nearly done, the phone-fixer called from the bottom of the stairs.

'Mr McGowan?'

'Hang on, be with you in a minute!' Charlie turned to me, 'Keep at it, and check the bottoms of the wardrobes.'

'Indubitably,' I said.

Later, I heard the front door slam and the phone-fixer's car draw away. When Charlie rejoined me, I was almost finished.

'How's it going?'

'Okay. There's only the bed, now.'

'All right, get her shifted.'

'She's sleeping.'

'So wake her up.'

'Hey, steady on, Charlie.'

'Jesus — get out of the bloody way!'

He elbowed me aside and leaned down over the woman and started to pat her cheeks. Backwards and forwards, gently at first. She moaned and opened her eyes, then closed them. He patted harder. She opened her eyes again and her face contorted with shock and terror. Her mouth yawned to utter a scream. Charlie blocked it with the palm of his hand and pushed her back down on the bed as she struggled

61

to heave herself upright.

'Calm down, lady,' he said, 'nobody's going to do you a mischief.'

She made moaning noises through her nasal passages, wildly shaking her head and trying to disentangle her arms from the bedclothes. Charlie held them trapped and I looked on feeling less than happy.

'He's telling you the truth,' I said. 'Take it easy, we're not going to hurt you.'

Her struggles subsided, but she glared up at us with a mixture of resentment and fear. Charlie kept his fist clamped over her mouth.

'Are you going to be good, now?' he said.

She hesitated, then nodded dumbly, hating him with her eyes. He grinned and loosed his grip on her face and released her encumbered arms. She brought her hands out from under the blankets and put them up to her cheeks, where his thumb and fingers had left angry blotches.

'What are you doing here?' she said. 'What's going on? Where's Anthony?'

'He's had a nasty turn. They've taken him away in an ambulance.'

'*Who's* taken him away? What the hell is happening? My head feels funny . . .'

'You've been nobbled,' Charlie said. 'Somebody slipped you a Mickey Finn. We've been waiting for you to come round.'

'Come round? I don't . . it was you, you bastards!'

'Language,' Charlie said.

She rolled her head on the pillow. 'Oh, Christ!' she wailed, 'Oh my God! Where's Anthony? What have you done to us?'

'Not a thing,' Charlie said, 'we're just trying to help you.'

'Rubbish!'

'Hey, listen,' Charlie said, 'there's such a thing as ingratitude.'

'What!'

She thrust herself up on the bed and the straps of her nightgown fell down off her shoulders. She dragged at them angrily, then pulled up the sheet to cover her breasts where the big dark nipples showed through the flimsy stuff of her nightie.

'Get out of this house!' she said.

'Oh, we can't do that,' said Charlie. 'We promised.'

'Promised?'

'To stay with you,' Charlie said.

'Jesus Christ, I must be going mad!' She screwed her eyes up tight and flopped back against the padded headboard. 'This can't be happening to me!'

'Farrow, get the lady a glass of water.'

'Coming up, Charlie,' I said.

I didn't feel easy about his treatment of the woman, but I went along with it because I probably knew him better than any other person on earth. He wouldn't do anything without good reason. He had limitless energy, but I never saw him squander one ounce of it. Every effort he made was channelled in just one direction: the exercise of his job. To this, he was utterly dedicated, even fanatical, but gratuitous cruelty was foreign to his nature. He simply would not waste the time.

'Now then,' he said, as the woman was drinking, 'tell us all about last night.'

As I took the empty glass from her, 'There's nothing to tell,' she said.

'Of course there is,' said Charlie. 'Tony left the house, did he not?'

'Only for an hour. He popped out to have a drink with a friend.'

'Just so. What happened when he got back?'

'Nothing. We went to bed.'

'Have some supper first, did you?'

'Only a glass of hot milk. Anthony got it for me.'

'Did he seem all right?'

'Er .. yes.'

'You don't sound very sure about that.'

'Well, now that you mention it,' she said, 'he did seem a little . . . preoccupied.'

'Something on his mind?'

'Yes, that's it, exactly.'

'Didn't you question him, Mrs Green?'

'Look, let's get one thing straight. My name isn't Green, and I'm not a Mrs.'

'Goodness me,' Charlie said, 'you've been deceiving us, haven't you?'

'Not at all,' she said, 'you deceived yourselves. You made an assumption.'

Thinking back, she was right, and Charlie acknowledged the truth of her statement.

'Fair enough,' he said, 'but why did you not correct us?'

'It was none of your business,' she said. 'And while we're on the subject — what *is* your business? What are you *doing* here?'

'We're just doing a favour for somebody.'

'Who?'

'Sounds like him now,' Charlie said, as we all heard the rattle of the front door being opened.

'Who is it?'

'He'll tell you himself. In the meantime, you'd better rise up.'

'Now wait a minute! Where's Anthony?'

'Just get dressed,' Charlie said.

He gave me the nod and I followed him as he moved towards the door. He pulled up short on the landing and pointed down the stairs.

'Surprise for you, Farrow. Look who's here.'

'If it isn't young Nigel!' I said.

Stone's surprise seemed greater than ours. He stood down there in the hall, gaping blankly up at us as we slowly descended the stairs.

'He barged right in,' said Charlie, 'never even rang the bell.'

'Jolly rude if you ask me, Charles.'

'No, Farrow,' Charlie said, 'not rude, just plain bloody stupid.'

'What the devil's going on?' Stone said.

'Good question that — isn't it, Farrow?'

'It's not bad, Charlie,' I said. 'Maybe Nigel here can help us with it.'

'Now listen, you two!' Stone said, 'Just what the hell do you think you're playing at?'

'He's done burglary,' Charlie said.

'No, no,' I said, 'it's breaking and entering. It's burglary after dark.'

'Bad enough, though, wouldn't you say?'

'A diabolical liberty.'

'Nigel thought the house was empty.'

'No cars outside,' I said.

We had reached the foot of the stairs by this time and were crowding Stone in the hall. He backed off away from us, into the sitting-room.

'Now just hold your horses!' he said. 'I'm warning you —'

'He's warning us, Farrow.'

'I know, I heard him,' I said.

'Cheeky young bugger.'

'Badly brought up.'

'Sticks out a mile,' Charlie said. 'His mother never taught him no manners.'

'All right, I'm laughing,' Stone said. 'Now perhaps you'll tell me what you're doing here.'

'Take a pew,' Charlie said.

Stone complied without thinking. Charlie perched on the arm of a chair and embarked upon another of his regular ablutions. He shook out a crisp white handkerchief, polished the lenses of his rimless spectacles and hooked them back over his ears. Then he produced three clean white tissues and laid them out on his knee. A separate one to ream out each nostril, the third for a final good blow. Stone watched the performance, fascinated. I'd seen it a thousand times. Charlie then re-

arranged the creases of his trousers, fished out a small steel file and began to work on his fingernails. He looked up from time to time, eying Stone ingenuously.

'Nice tie he's wearing, isn't it, Farrow?'

'Old school, Charlie,' I said.

'In point of fact,' said Stone, 'It's Stowe.'

'Ah, that explains everything. Third rank, Farrow. No proper training.'

'We can't all be Old Etonians,' I said. 'Mustn't appear snobbish, Charlie.'

'No, I suppose not,' he said. 'So Green was one of yours, Stone, was he?'

'As you already know that — yes.'

'You must have put the fear of death in the poor sod.'

'What on earth do you mean?'

'Don't you know he took himself out last night?'

'Of course I know.'

'Yes, of course. But *how* did you know?'

'That's *my* bloody business!'

'No need to get cross,' Charlie said. 'It's a sign of immaturity — isn't it, Farrow?'

'Yes, and it's childish, as well.'

Stone was badly out of his depth and he knew it. He was about twenty-eight years old and a smart but conservative dresser. Good blue suit with a narrow chalk stripe, cream silk shirt and his old-school tie. Well-polished black slip-on shoes. He was tall and well-built, the athletic type. I was willing to bet he played squash. His neat brown hair had a healthy sheen and he wore it cut medium short. He had honest-looking hazel eyes and his smooth, unlined features bore the bloom of innocence. A very useful facade.

'When *I* was a child, I spake as a child.'

'Yes, I remember,' I said.

'I didn't go around giving cheek to my elders.'

'Oh, pack it in!' Stone said.

66

Charlie looked up from filing his nails. 'What kind of talk is that?'

'You people ought to be on the telly — on amateur night.'

'Tut, tut! We're professionals, aren't we, Farrow?'

'Yes, not that it pays very much.'

'Understandable, if you're paid what you're worth.'

'Hear that? He's at it again!'

'You've got to make allowances, Charlie.'

'Not on your nelly!' he said. 'I'm not going to sit here and listen to this lot.'

'Why don't you leave, then?' Stone said.

'Oh, you're the one who's leaving, Nigel.'

'No, I'm not. I've a job to do.'

'So have we, and we got here first. Besides, we're bigger than you.'

'Is that your final word, McGowan?'

'*Mister* McGowan, to you. Open the door for him, Farrow.'

'He can open his own bloody door.'

'I'm sorry about that, Nigel. It's because he hasn't had his lunch. He always turns sour when he's hungry.'

Stone pushed himself up on his feet. 'You realise I'm going to report this, don't you?'

'Why, you rotten little sneak,' Charlie said.

Civilised people eat a nice Sunday dinner. Roast beef and Yorkshire pud, with a couple of veg, and horse-raddish sauce. Apple pie and cheese, or custard for those who prefer it. We had Irish stew, because by the time we got back to the guest-house, everything else was "off". In a different sense, the stew was "off", too.

'Christ! If this is what the Irish scoff, it's no wonder they're such vile-tempered bastards.'

'Trouble with you,' Charlie said, 'you're never bloody well satisfied. You moan when you don't get to eat, and you moan when you're stuffing your greedy guts.'

67

We had the dining-room to ourselves and were sitting at the corner table which was furthest from the door. Charlie had brought in his big brown envelope.

'What's in the bumf, then?' I said.

He had finished his reading of it in the car coming back from Green's house. Royston had returned from his lunch break shortly after we had given Stone his marching orders, and we had left him to take a statement from the woman and generally to look after her. Charlie thought that Stone had a contact in the Darlington CID, hence his awareness of Green's demise. But so far as we could tell, he knew nothing about the Peltz connection. That knowledge was ours alone and Charlie meant to keep it that way. Peltz the man remained a mystery. A short report from the BfV was among the papers in Charlie's envelope.

Peltz had been the production manager of an engineering firm which had trade links with one or two Darlington outfits like Teesco. Nothing sinister — nothing to do with Marsdens — mainly domestic stuff and non-strategic industry. He was an inactive, non-arthodox Jew, no Zionist affilations, just an easy-going bachelor with a quiet, modest lifestyle.

'. . . in other words,' Charlie said, 'tailor-made cover for your Institute man.'

He meant the Israeli Institute for Strategic Studies, much more commonly known as MOSSAD, their fierce and highly successful secret service.

'I've a feeling you're not just saying that, Charlie.'

'O' course I'm not,' he said. 'Remember what happened after the Falklands job when the boss-lady finally found out that Begin had been supplying the Argentinians with goodies, including Exocet gear?'

'She stopped all shipments of hardware to Israel.'

'Exactly,' Charlie said. 'And what were our Jewish friends doing at the time?'

68

'The Lebanon.'

'Correct.'

'Air-and-tanks warfare, mainly tanks.'

'There's hope for you yet,' Charlie said. 'Now cast your mind back a little bit further, when the French did much the same thing with regard to supplies of the Mirage jet.'

'The Israelis started to make their own.'

'Just like that.'

'Well, not quite. They stole the blueprints — '

'Three tons of blueprints. *Three bloody tons!*' Charlie said.

'Okay, so you think they're doing a Mirage at Marsdens.'

'I don't think, Farrow, I know. It's the only explanation which makes any sense.'

'In that case, then,' I said, 'Green must have been a double.'

'Oh, sure. Lovely, wasn't it?' he said. 'He was giving Stone a right load of old cods, and laughing up his sleeve all the time.'

'Ah wait now, just hold it a second. What about this?' I said, 'Stone rumbles Green, and has him put down?'

'Why would he do that?' Charlie said. 'Doubles can be very useful. Once you get to know what they are, you can feed 'em with anything you fancy. Balls 'em up.'

'Yes, I agree.'

'And what about Peltz? Stone couldn't have put *him* down, because he didn't even know Peltz was here.'

'But the muggers killed Peltz!'

'Absolutely. But who put them on to him?'

'Nobody, so far as we know.'

'So far as *you* know,' he said.

'You've been holding out on me, Charlie.'

'Oh, not a lot,' he said. 'With what we had, it didn't seem important. This Green job alters things.'

'You realise what you're saying, don't you, mate?' I pushed my greasy plate aside, 'You're saying we have an unknown element.'

'Ah. You've finally tumbled,' he said. 'Unknown element. I like that.'

'Well, *I* don't like it,' I said. 'It means we're back where we started.'

'That's right. So let's get moving,' he said.

When he said let's get moving, he meant up to Durham jail, because by this time the muggers had been transferred. He drove the car himself, whilst I read the dossiers and telexes from his bundle of assorted bumf. It looked as though the boys in Research had done a fairly good job. I started with the screed on Green's sleeping partner, whose name was Ruth Levinson.

She had been born in Leeds, the only child of refugee parents, in 1954. In 1960, when Ruth was six years old, her father had sold his small business in that chill northern city and had taken his little family to live in sunny Israel. Thirteen years later, Ruth had been conscripted along with every other young person of her age, male or female, to do her bit in the Arab/Israeli conflict of 1973.

The forward communications unit in which she eventually found herself was overrun by a Syrian counter-attack and Ruth was taken prisoner. But not as a prisoner of war. She was brought to trial in Damascus on a trumped-up charge of espionage and sentenced to a nine-year term of imprisonment. British diplomatic intervention — Ruth had retained dual citizenship — was of no avail. She served the full nine years, during which time both of her parents died.

Released at last in 1982, Ruth had turned her back on the Middle East, opting instead to return to the somewhat safer environs of her birthplace. She had been sponsored in this by the only people she still knew in England, her parents' old friends and neigh-

70

bours, Mr and Mrs Maurice Green.

It would seem however that cruel fate was not yet finished with Ruth Levinson. The Greens, driving across from Leeds to Manchester to meet Ruth's plane at Ringway airport, were involved in a motor accident. Maurice Green was killed outright and his wife died in hospital five hours later. They were survived by an only son, and the two young people, now both orphans, sought comfort in each other.

That had been just four months ago.

Anthony Green, born in 1956, was a product of Leeds Technical College. After graduation, he had spent a year on a left-bank kibbutz before coming back home to embark upon a career. After working for various engineering companies he had applied for, and been given, a job at Marsden's over in Darlington. At first, he lived in digs, driving home to Leeds on his off-days. But when his parents were killed, he sold the house they had left him there and moved lock, stock and barrel — and Ruth — to the house we knew in Barnes Road. Due to the economic recession, Ruth could not find work, but Anthony earned enough to keep both of them. They shacked up and settled down. Anthony, a good designer, fitted in well with the Marsden team and the couple seemed all set to start a new life.

This was what the Section knew. What it didn't know, until we found out, was that Green had been recruited by Military Intelligence.

What Military Intelligence didn't know was that Green had a previous commitment. If Charlie's deductions were to prove correct, as I rather thought they would, Green's year on the kibbutz had not been spent growing oranges. Not all of it, anyway. That the youth was potential material for MOSSAD was only too obvious. They would certainly have chatted him up and it would seem that he had agreed to play what someone once called The Most Dangerous Game.

The photo-copied telex messages were rather more mundane, mostly referring to routine questions posed by Charlie over the phone. Some of the information might prove useful later on, but at the moment it led us nowhere.

It had taken me less than half an hour to complete my reading, but Charlie had driven fast and we were close enough now to Durham to see the massive cathedral towers looming over the landscape ahead. I looked up at the great pile of medieval architecture as I stowed the papers away, but my mind was not on its grandeur.

'Good God, Charlie,' I said, 'no wonder Ruthie's a tough little cookie. She's had an extremely rough ride. Do you reckon she knew Green was working for MOSSAD?'

'It's a pound to a pinch of shit.'

'But it doesn't make sense.'

'What doesn't make sense?'

'Any of it,' I said. 'Unless he really did take himself out.'

'Leave off, Farrow!' he said. 'Did Green strike *you* as being suicidal?'

'Not really.'

'There you are, then.'

'But wait — why did he drug the woman?'

'To give her an alibi, in case he hit trouble. He was up to a naughty.'

'Who could have topped him, then? There was no sign of any rough stuff. He must have gone out like a lamb.'

'I'm not concerned as to how he went out. I want to know who did it, and why.'

'Sorry, Chas, I can't help you.'

'What's new about *that*?' he said.

Our second interview with he of the patriotic scalp-lock was of even shorter duration than the previous one. They had him ready and waiting for us in the

72

usual sort of room, sitting at the usual bare table on the usual straight wooden chair. Mooney looked up as we entered, and when he saw who his visitors were, a remarkable change came over him. He leaped up onto his feet, toppling the chair over sideways as he backed off against the far wall. When the warder standing in attendance began to move in fast, Mooney pointed wild-eyed at Charlie.

'Keep 'im away from me! Don't you leave 'im with me — you hear?'

'Behave yourself, lad!' the warder barked, 'And get that chair picked up!'

'I'm tellin' you! Keep 'im away from me!'

Perplexed, the warder turned to us.

'He's a nutter,' Charlie said. 'Don't you know his record? He's violent. He kicked a bloke to death.'

'I never!'

'With a little help from his mates, of course. But all the same,' Charlie went on, 'you'd better stay and watch him. He might do us an injury.'

'Right you are, sir,' the warder said. He swung round on Mooney. 'Pick up that chair!'

'Oh, let him stand,' Charlie said. 'This'll only take a couple of minutes.'

'Keep 'im away!' Mooney yelled.

'Stop screeching like a big soft Jessie, and listen,' Charlie said. 'The sooner you answer the questions, the sooner you're back in your cell.'

'I answered all your rotten questions!'

'Yes, all that I had at the time. Now, I've some more.'

'Get on with 'em, then.'

'That's better,' Charlie said. 'Now then — who put you on to the German?'

'Nobody.'

Charlie sighed. 'Oh, dear, Warder, could you fetch us some tea?'

'No! Hang on!' Mooney said.

'I'll hang on just five more seconds, Darren.'

73

'Bridie Keegan,' Mooney said. 'She give us a tip about this geezer. She said he was carryin' bread.'

'Did she say he was carrying fifty thousand?'

'Jesus, no. Just bread.'

'So where do we find this Bridie Keegan?'

'She works in a pub,' Mooney said. 'The Goat's Head, bottom of Coppergate.'

'You're doing fine,' Charlie said. 'So she pointed Peltz out to you, did she?'

'She couldn't 'ave, she wasn't even there. She just told us to watch for a bloke with a briefcase.'

'Leaving the Arts Centre?'

'Right.'

'So when he left, you followed him.'

'I told you that before.'

'You never told me about Bridie Keegan.'

'You never ast,' Mooney said.

'True,' said Charlie, 'very true.' Then, 'Thank you, officer.'

'Is that the lot, then?' Mooney blurted.

'Yes, but don't leave town,' Charlie said.

I have recorded what was said. I have not described the foul and putrid stench which pervaded that small room from the moment Mooney saw us and flattened himself against the wall. As we were leaving the prison I said to Charlie:

'Christ, what did you do to him?'

He looked at me across the car as I got us under way. 'What d'you mean? You saw for yourself.'

'This time, yes,' I said. 'But how's about last time?'

'What's that got to do with it?' he said.

I should have known better than to ask. The big grim gates were thrown open for us at a wave of Charlie's hand and I wondered who had passed the word. Someone with influence, that was for sure. Someone who knew the Man, or who owed the Man a favour. Such people were everywhere. As we came

upon the A1 approach road, I glanced at the dashboard clock. It was only quarter to four. Amazing. I felt like I'd worked a full, hard day and yet barely half of it over. Charlie was quiet throughout most of the drive back down to Darlington, but as we turned off on the A167 for the last few miles into town, he suddenly snapped out of his reveries.

'Damn and blast!' he said, 'I should have asked Mooney what they did with the briefcase!'

'Why? Is it important?' I said.

'Could be something, might be nothing.'

'What about the Keegan bird? Do you think *she's* important?'

'Possibly. We'll find out later,' he said.

'What are we going to do in the meantime?'

'We're going back to Barnes Road. I want to fix something up with Royston.'

'That should delight him,' I said.

Royston did, in fact, seem pleased to see us. 'I'm glad you're back,' he said. 'I've had a bit of trouble with the lady.'

'Why? What's up?' Charlie said. 'Been attacking you, has she?'

'Hysterics,' Royston said. 'When I told her about her husband —'

'When you *what*?' Charlie said. 'Who the hell told you to tell her?'

'Good God, she's a right to know! Besides, she wanted to go and see him. She said you said he was ill.'

All this went on in the hallway. Ruth Levinson was upstairs, apparently distraught at the news of Green's death. Charlie scowled at Royston and pointed to the telephone.

'Get us a woman PC up here.'

'I'm not sure there'll be one available. It's Sunday.'

'Royston,' Charlie said, 'I don't give a bugger if it's Christmas. Just do it.'

'Well, I'll have a go,' Royston said.

We heard him arguing over the phone and when he joined us in the front room he was able to say that he'd managed to fix it.

'Next thing,' Charlie said: 'did your lot ever find Herr Peltz's briefcase?'

'His briefcase? I don't understand.'

'How do you suppose he was carrying all that money?'

'Oh yes, I see,' Royston said. 'No, I never heard of any briefcase being found.'

'Farrow,' Charlie said, 'phone Durham and get them to ask the yobs what they did with the briefcase — okay?'

'They'll probably need to phone me back.'

'They can't if you don't phone them first!'

'Just remarking, Charlie.'

'Christ Almighty!' he said.

Royston made a pot of tea and as we were drinking it, Durham jail returned my call. The yobs said they ditched the empty briefcase in a spot called Brinkburn Dene. Charlie asked Royston where it was.

'It's close to where they mugged him,' he said. 'Surtees Street runs across the Dene.'

'So what's the Dene?' Charlie said.

'It's a big fat pain in the bloody neck. It's a long narrow valley, sort of rough parkland, which stretches about a mile from Woodland Road up to North Road Station. Bracken and bushes and trees, and up to your ankles in old French letters. Kids on motor-bikes. Courting couples and peeping Toms, louts and layabouts. Whores and comic singers —'

'All right,' Charlie said, 'we've got the picture. I want a search made.'

'I don't think you'll get one today.'

'You want to bet?'

'That's *my* line, Charlie.'

'Belt up, Farrow,' he said. He nodded at Royston. 'Get on to your gaffers.'

'Right-oh, one can but try.'

'That's the spirit. Never give up.'

'Where are you going to be?'

'Don't bother to phone us, we'll phone you.'

'I'll hold my breath,' Royston said.

'It's nice to see how the other half lives, Chas.'

'Bloody poufters,' he said.

Stone opened the door of his first-class suite down at the Kings Head Hotel and saw us standing out in the corridor.

'Oh, it's you,' he said.

'Expecting somebody else were you, Nigel?'

'Are you coming in, or not?' Stone said.

'After you, Farrow.'

'No, after you, Charles.'

Stone flashed us a look of disgust and turned on his heel, and we followed him inside. Small hall, sitting-room, bedroom and bathroom.

'Oh, very nice,' Charlie said. 'Cosy — isn't it, Farrow?'

'Extremely posh,' I said. 'We're on the wrong side of the business, Charlie.'

'Look, don't start that bullshit,' Stone said. 'Let's just get this over with.'

'Hark at *that*, Farrow!'

'Oh, ignore it,' I said. 'Nigel's young and impetuous.'

'And I've a train to catch,' Stone said. 'So you've got about fifteen minutes.'

'Can we sit down, then?' I said, 'I'm feeling knackered.'

'You look it.'

'All right for you, son,' I said, 'but wait till you get to be my age.'

'God forbid.'

'Right,' Charlie said. 'I understand you've been told to come clean with us.'

'How the hell did you swing it?' Stone said. 'A shower of ill-disciplined ruffians — '

77

'Watch it! That's hearsay,' Charlie said. 'You've been listening to that berk Marshall.'

'Major Marshall,' Stone said.

'Did *you* know that Marshall was an officer, Farrow?'

'Well, he's certainly not one of us. He hasn't get enough between the ears.'

'Hey — that's very profound,' Charlie said. 'I never looked at it that way.'

'Your act's getting corny,' Stone said.

He sat on a stool at the writing-table. Charlie perched on the arm of a chair and adjusted his clothing to obviate wrinkles. The sofa beckoned me and I seized the chance to make myself comfy.

'Aaah, that's better,' I said. 'Take your time with him, Charlie.'

'Thirteen minutes,' Stone said.

'So exactly how was Green recruited?'

'He wasn't. *He* approached *us*.'

'Told you he'd been tapped up by MOSSAD? Loyal patriot — that sort of thing?'

'Well . . yes. Why not?'

'Why not!' said Charlie, 'And you fell for it? Jesus Christ!'

'There's no evidence,' Stone said stiffly, 'that he was anything but a — '

'What? A stolid British citizen? Allegiance pledged to the Crown?'

'As you choose to put it that way, yes.'

'So you made him welcome and put him on the payroll.'

'Green never did ask to be paid.'

'So what has he given you that he's never asked pay for?'

'Well . . .'

'Come on, now,' Charlie said. 'what has he actually told you that you didn't already know?'

'Well . .'

78

'What sort of a well? An oil well? Riches beyond your dreams?'

'Look, if you're going to be facetious — '

'*Facetious*?' Charlie said. 'You're the ones who're bloody facetious!'

'Are you always this clever?' Stone said.

'Thank Christ somebody's clever. Did he tell you about Josef Peltz?'

'Of course he did.'

'When did he tell you? What time?'

'As soon as Peltz made contact with him yesterday morning,' Stone said.

'I asked you what time.'

'About half past nine.'

'Ah, I see,' Charlie said. 'So Green was a spiritualist, was he?'

'I don't know what you mean.'

'I mean he would have to be, wouldn't he, to communicate with the Other Side? By that time, Peltz had advanced rigor mortis.'

'It was a dead-letter drop,' Stone said.

'Hear that, Farrow? Nigel made a funny.'

'I can't laugh, Charlie,' I said. 'I've got a split lip.'

'Put a sticking plaster on it.'

'Another one!' Charlie said. 'He's got hidden depths, has our young Nigel — but seriously, Nige,' he went on, 'did Green tell his bedmate what he was up to?'

'Certainly not,' Stone said. 'He was under stict instructions.'

'Maybe, but *she* was under *him*.'

'The Major's quite right, you're a crude bunch of oafs.'

'I wish you'd take care what you say. Mister Farrow's a very sensitive person, he's easily hurt.'

'Is that so?'

'Yes it is. However, all of that's by the way. You're completely wrapped up here, now, I take it?'

'For the moment,' Stone said. 'Until we get another man in place.'

'How soon will that be?'

'Who knows?'

'I hope you're not dissembling, Nigel.'

'You should be able to tell, seeing as how you're the experts.'

'Now *that* is a fact,' Charlie said.

Unaware of the dickering going on between our respective lords and masters down there in the Metropolis, and therefore unaware that he was about to be pulled off the job, Stone had booked the Kings Head suite for the weekend.

'Be a pity to waste it,' I said. 'After all, the Sections's not paying.'

'The answer's no,' Charlie said. 'I don't want you acquiring expensive tastes.'

'All right then, bollocks,' I said. 'But we might as well talk here as anywhere else.'

'Talking's different,' he said.

'So what about friend Nigel, then? Do you think he was telling us the truth?'

'Who cares? I don't give a monkey's, just so long as he's out of our way.'

'Well, you certainly did a job on him, Charlie.'

'Stone was no bother,' he said.

'But it hasn't got us any further forward, has it? With Peltz and Green both dead, it would seem that MOSSAD's shot its bolt.'

'If you believe that, Farrow,' he said, 'I suppose you'll believe about anything.'

'All right, so I'm gullible,' I said, 'but let's consider the possibilities. Let's say Peltz *was* MOSSAD —'

'He was.'

' — why Germany, then?' I said, 'Why send a man from Mulheim?'

'Why the hell not?' Charlie said. 'It's ninety minutes flying time, and it's Darlington's twin town, which makes the cover just about perfect.'

'Yes, but hang on,' I said. 'Why send *anybody* over? Why not let Green do the job?'

'If you think that MOSSAD's going to trust a raw and untried agent with fifty thousand quid, not to mention the running of a network . . . no, Green was working on his own, with Peltz as his cut-out.'

'Okay. So he's young, and inexperienced. His only contact is killed, and before he can get over the shock, he's got us down on his neck. We tell him he's blown. He believes us, panics and does himself in. End of story.'

'End of my tool! What the hell are you raving about?'

'Just speculating, Charlie.'

'Well, speculate about this: somebody tipped off the muggers.'

'Nothing to do with us. Peltz merely got unlucky. Villains sussed he was carrying cash and decided to relieve him of it.'

'Rhubarb!' Charlie said.

We had reached the stage at which this sort of sounding-board exchange was a regular exercise, with me in the role of devil's advocate. It helped us to sort ourselves out and perhaps to shed light on the situation.

'Do you *still* think the woman's involved?'

'I can feel it in my water.'

'Well, I don't know,' I said. 'I mean, what could she do? She's had no training. She was nine years in a Syrian nick and when they let her go she promptly came here. We know that for a fact.'

'Maybe.'

'No "maybe" about it, it's straight out of Section files.'

'Well, forget about Ruth for the moment. Bridie Keegan,' he said. 'What does *that* name suggest to you?'

'Oh, no! Give over!' I said.

'Never mind "give over".'

81

'Listen, Charlie,' I said, 'up here in this north-east corner the Irish are thick on the ground. It's a kind of little Liverpool.'

'I'm aware of that, Farrow.'

'Okay, so what's the big deal? If it's Irish names you're after, just look in the phone book, chum. In any case, why would the IRA want to nobble somebody who was nobbling Britain? Jesus — they'd give 'em a hand!'

'But supposing the Paddies had their own ideas about doing a Marsdens job, and the MOSSAD lot were queering the pitch? There's no love lost between 'em, what with the IRA busy teaching the Palestinians how to blow up more and more Jews.'

'Oh come on, now, Charlie. That would pre-suppose that the boyos were onto MOSSAD before *we* even got a smell!'

'Not impossible, Farrow.'

'No, but it's bloody far-fetched. It would mean that one of the best Intelligence services in the world had been penetrated by the Micks, and an Israeli operation clobbered before it got off the gound.'

'Stranger things have happened.'

'Yes, but not lately,' I said, 'and certainly not in this neck of the woods.'

'There's always a first time.'

'True, but I can't see it having happened in this case.'

'What you can see, Farrow,' he said, 'is not much further than your gullet and your guts.'

'And up yours, too,' I said.

Royston's people found Peltz's briefcase after searching for less than an hour. It would seem that the yobs had ducked into the Dene to examine what they'd got, and to divi up the loot before splitting.

'Lovely,' Charlie said. 'Now then, let's have a look at it.'

The heavy leather briefcase was lying on the desk

in Royston's little office. We had just arrived, after getting the news on the Rover's R/T.

'Help yourself,' Royston said. 'It's exactly as we found it, as per your instructions.'

'I should hope so, too,' Charlie said.

The flap was secured by two brass locks, so what the muggers had done was to cut it open across the top. But doubtless stunned by the size of their haul, and rummaging around in the dark, they had overlooked the slim compartment almost concealed at the back. Charlie didn't overlook it, though. He slipped a hand inside and drew out a much-folded sheet of stiff paper. He laid his find on the desk and after quite certain that briefcase contained nothing else, he tucked the paper into his pocket.

'Thank you, Royston,' he said. 'You can get off home, now.'

'Not so fast. What was that you found?'

'You mean you really didn't take a peek?'

'I told you, no,' Royston said. 'I'm not in the habit of lying.'

'Well, you ought to learn,' Charlie said, 'or you'll never get anywhere in your line of business.'

'Christ Almighty!' Royston said.

'Take no notice of him. Go on home, Harry,' I said.

'That's all the bloody thanks you get!'

'What d'you expect?' Charlie said. 'You're getting paid overtime, aren't you?'

'You can stuff it!' Royston said. 'After this, I'm packing up!'

'Isn't that what I've just said? See you in the morning.'

'Not if I can help it, chum. I've had enough of this carry-on.'

'No, no, don't slam the door, leave it open.'

'So long, Mark!'

'Good-night, Harry,' I said.

When he was gone, Charlie hauled out the paper

and began to open its folds. 'You two seem very friendly?'

'Royston's a good bloke,' I said.

'Yes, well, don't get too damned friendly.'

'I'll please myself about that. Anyway, what've we got here?'

Spread out, the sheet of hard greyish paper covered the whole of the top of the desk. It was one of those very large photocopies which architects make of their plans. In this case, the plans of a building or buildings. In a long deep panel at the side details of various alarms systems were interspersed with diagrams, none of which meant much to me. There appeared to be nothing to indicate what the buildings were, or where they were, but Charlie nodded.

'What d'you think now, then?' he said.

'Marsden's?'

'Well, it isn't Woolworth's, I can tell you that for sure.'

'You were right then, Charlie.'

'Naturally.'

'Where was Peltz going, then?' I said.

'He was going to arrange a contract.'

'Worth fifty thousand quid.'

'Oh, that was probably just a down-payment.'

'Down payment to who, though?' I said. 'The MOSSAD boys work for peanuts, everybody knows that. Christ, they don't even make as much as we do!'

'They were farming it out,' Charlie said. 'They were going to use civilians.'

'Why would they want to use civilians?'

'Oh, get with it, Farrow, even you can't be dumb as all that! They're in enough trouble with Maggie already, over the Argentine thing, and they could lose the support of British Jews if they were caught in this sort of lark.'

'So if something goes wrong at Marsden's, it's nothing to do with them.'

'Right. Green does the groundwork, gets hold of

the layout, points Peltz towards some mob, then Peltz the stranger acts as go-between. So if anything goes up the spout, the mob knows nothing and nobody. If everything goes right, the mob nicks the blueprints at one fell swoop, hands them over to Peltz and receives the rest of their lolly for a nice clean job well done.'

'Leaving Green as pure as the driven snow.'

'Absolutely,' Charlie said, 'perhaps to move on to pastures new.'

'I like it, Charlie,' I said.

'I thought you would, when you'd had it spelled out.'

'I spelled it out for myself. I just wanted to hear you say it.'

'You know something, Farrow?' he said. 'For a second there, I almost believed you.'

'Don't give me that crap,' I said, 'you wouldn't believe your own mother if she told you the correct time of day.'

He was folding up the architects drawings. 'Be that as it may be,' he said. 'What's Royston's private number?'

'Oh, for God's sake be reasonable, man! The poor sod's barely had time to get home!'

'Don't wet your knickers,' he said, 'I don't want him back here, I just want to phone him.'

'Yeah, well, count me out,' I said. 'You can get his number from the switchboard.'

'And where d'you think you're going, then?'

'You know that pub on the corner?'

'Hey — !'

'That's where you'll find me, I said.

Darlington, bless its big warm heart, is not a pretty town. Its very few really fine ancient buildings are tucked away out of sight or juxtaposed, incongruously, cheek by jowl with the new. It is, or was, a railway town. In fact, the very first, and its hundred

thousand citizens are quietly proud of this. Their pride is reflected primarily in the social amenities, hospital, and an arts centre which might be the envy of a borough ten times its size. But to descend from the sublime to the ridiculous, too many of its pubs are grim and there appears to be not one fish-- and-chip shop. With Yorkshire — including Whitby — so near, these last two failings seem incredible.

The boozer in which I waited for Charlie had about as much jolly warmth and cheer as a late-Victorian Methodist chapel. The beer was deplorable and when I switched to whisky it was served in a small ugly glass only slightly less thick than a jam-jar. I filled and lit a pipe, but the atmosphere just wasn't con- ducive to an enjoyment of the smoke and my good tobacco was wasted. In almost any other surround- ings I would have cherished that half hour of peace, but I wasn't even sorry when Charlie turned up.

'How many's that?' he said.

'First one, Charlie, cross my heart.'

'Cross the road instead.'

'What for?'

'Because that's where the car's parked.'

I must say I got quite a kick at his tiny flicker of amazement when I complied without a word. No argument, and no back-chat, only:

'Where the hell you been all this time?'

We crossed the road and got into the Rover, but he didn't switch the engine on. We just sat and talked.

'Ever hear of George Kirby?'

'Who's he when he's at home?'

'The big boss villain around these parts, lives in Harrowgate.'

'Not in Harrogate, he doesn't. If he did, I'd have heard of him.'

'I didn't say Harrogate, Farrow, I said *Harrow- gate*. Harrowgate Hill, just about three miles north of here. They call him Mad Geordie.'

'Go on.'

'Nothing big happens without his say-so.'

'Nothing like what?' I said.

'Like what it would take for the Marsden's caper.'

'If the coppers know that,' I said, 'why don't they grab him and slap his wrists?'

'They'd love to,' Charlie said. 'Trouble being, he's too bloody smart .. too smart for *them*, that is.'

'But not too smart for us, eh, Charlie?'

'I knew you'd get the drift.'

'So we just go and drop on him — that what you mean?'

'Yes, but not right now. I want you to check Bridie Keegan out, first.'

'What, all on my ownsome?' I said.

'You don't need to have your hand held, do you? Here, take this — ' he said. He handed me one of the new two-way radios — 'and listen, it's all tuned in, so don't start buggering about with it.'

'Who's on the other end?'

'I am. Just press the beeper tit, and I'll answer as soon as I can.'

'Soon as you can? Where are *you* going to be?'

'Don't worry yourself about that. Just get us a line on this Keegan bird, but don't put her on her guard. Find out where she lives — follow her home, if you have to — see who her buddies are, and try to —'

'For Christ's sake, Charlie, I've got the message!' I said. 'Is there anything else before I go?'

'Before you go where?' he said.

'Well, as long as you're not going to be with me, I'm dining at the King's Head. I'm going to have a bloody great steak, and — '

'Look! Watch the expenses!' he said.

He dropped me off at the top of Northgate only fifty yards from the hotel, at a quarter to eight on that fresh cool evening. First stop the pleasant

King's Bar and a large Glenmorangie with Malvern water to set me up for the feast. The restaurant part was fairly crowded, but they soon found a table for me, and I ate in leisurely comfort and without regard to the cost. Parma ham with slices of melon, a rare steak with everything and a morsel of Stilton with coffee to follow. A half-bottle of burgundy, for which I requested a separate bill because Witherspoon, down in Accounts, was in for a big enough shock as it was. Mustn't plunge too deep, or I'd be answering his queries for weeks on end.

Nine o'clock came all to soon and with it, a return to the toil. I retrieved my coat from the cloakroom, strolled down to Coppergate and found the Goat's Head on the left near the bottom. The pub had a tall thin facade, drab and dingy and unprepossessing. The inside was even worse, a place which attracts the sort of people who would never feel relaxed unless they could throw fag-ends on the floor. The noise was intolerable. People yelling above the din from a juke-box and the mind-jarring stuttering thud of half a dozen one-armed bandits. The one and only bar occupied most of the right-hand side of a long and narrow room, badly lit and hazy with smoke. In a corner by the door, a rowdy foursome was playing at dominoes, banging the pieces down and roaring hoarsely at each new score. Heads turned when I walked in, and there was a marginal drop in the decibel count. But it soon picked up again and I had to shout to make myself heard.

'Bottle o' Guinness, pal.'

He threw me a shifty eye-corners glance and went on pulling pints for a trio of customers standing at the rail. I could smell the suspicion on him. Of my six-foot-two, and the dark blue raincoat draped around fifteen-stone-odd. I stood there waiting patiently while he figured out the change from a limp and filthy fiver. He was a weedly little cove, with lank greasy locks going grey at the temples. He was wearing a

grubby T-shirt with a legend stamped on its front. The legend was calculated to amuse highly, or offend, according to the nature of one's sympathies. It had the latter effect on me, but I wasn't there to take up arms, so:

'When you're ready,' I said.

He affected not to have noticed me there. He turned as though in surprise and hugged himself to scratch both ampits.

'Yer, what was it?'

'I'll have a Guinness, please.'

There was one other person behind the bar, away at the other end, but it certainly wasn't Bridie Keegan. This one had a beard and was built like a Japanese wrestler. He must have weighed twenty-five stone, and a fair amount of its muscle. Thigh-like forearms flat on the bar, he was leaning far across to chat up a lady only a fraction less large than himself and her shrieks of raucous laughter were soaring above the general din to batter at the eardrums like an ambulance siren. My barman took the top off a Guinness bottle and swished a dirty glass in a sink full of even dirtier water.

'Don't decant it, mate,' I said, 'I'll sup it from the bottle.'

'Up to you,' he said. 'Be forty pee, squire.'

'And a drink for yourself.'

He brightened visibly and said he would have a Jamieson's with me. I told him to have what he liked and got one penny change from the pound note I gave him. He poured his own drink straight from the bottle without bothering to measure it out and I noticed he wasn't mean with himself. He took his whiskey neat.

'Cheers now, mister.'

'Cheers,' I said.

'You must be new at Park Place.'

'Park Place?' I said. 'What the hell's Park Place?'

'Well, I mean, aren't you in the p'leece?'

'Whatever gave you that idea?'

'Well . . you know . . hang on — ' he moved away to draw four pints for the crowd playing dominoes and came back wiping the spillage off his hands on the thighs of his faded blue jeans — 'I thought you was one of the lads, like.'

'No, not me,' I said. 'You the landlord here, are you?'

'Wisht I was!' he said. He tossed off the remnants of the malt I'd bought him and filled up his personal pint pot from a pump marked Finest Bitter. I didn't see any money go into the till, so I guessed that free ale was a perk. 'No,' he went on, 'I'm on'y on casual. That's the landlord, down there.'

'Oh, you don't work here all the time, then?'

'No, on'y now an' again. Just when Billy's short-staffed, like.'

'Ah, that explains it,' I said. 'A mate of mine told me Bridie Keegan worked here.'

'She does, but she's off tonight.'

'What, on a busy night like Sunday?'

'Well, she's usually 'ere, but she's got some relations comin' to visit.'

'Have another malt,' I said.

'Awright if I 'ave it later on?'

'Have it whenever you want.'

I gave him a fifty pee and a ten. He dropped the coins in a half-pint jar, along with the meagre rest of his tips. Then he was called away and suddenly I sensed someone watching me. I lifted my bottle of Guinness to take a sup from the neck and half-turned my head just in time to catch the stare of the loud fat lady. She quickly looked away, shifting her hams on the tall wooden stool to lay her huge breasts on the bar as she leaned across it to put her lips close to the landlord's ear. I saw him nod, but he did not look round. Not at once, anyway. My barman was busy drawing ale. I tried to close my ears against the level of noise in the place and mentally reviewed

the situation as I packed and fired a pipe.

I didn't want to go back to Charlie with my tail between my legs but on the other hand, it had begun to seem that there wasn't much more I could do. He had warned me against arousing Suspicion, against putting Bridie on guard, and if I persisted in asking questions that was precisely what I would do. But hell, I had probably done it already. In for a penny, in for a pound. I decided to chat up my barman again, but first, I had to pee.

The gents' was out back, down a short bare passage with a phone box fixed to a wall which was scrawled all over with local numbers. Some were alongside girls' names and appended with lurid testaments as to their individual charms. The light-bulb was missing from the evil urinal. There was ominous wet underfoot and an acid stink assailed the nostrils. I feared for the state of my shoes and resolved to avoid any further visit by drinking nothing more.

Back in the bar my little informant was being run off his feet while his boss, the landlord, took his ease. I leaned on the rail with my hands in my pockets, fingering the ten-pound note I had taken from my wallet and folded small out there in the black-hole loo. When the barman was free again, I put my hand on top of the bar with the tenner almost hidden by the two middle fingers, so that only he could see. He glanced down at it quickly and licked his lips.

'A Jamieson's,' I said, 'and keep the change, and keep the Jamieson's.'

'Wha-?'

'I'm looking for Bridie,' I said.

'I dunno . . . what you want her for?'

'To give her a message,' I said.

He hesitated. 'What sort of a message?' but I'd seen the greed in his eyes.

'Private, and very urgent.'

'You better ask Billy,' he said.

91

'Bugger Billy, I'm asking you.'

'Just 'ang on a minute, then . .' He fumbled underneath the bar top, next to the grimy sink, and came up with a dishcloth. When he started to wipe the bar, the damp rag brushed the tips of my fingers and I let the tenner go to be swallowed up in its sticky folds. His lips were barely moving and I had to strain my ears to catch what he said. 'She's prob'ly in the Gun and Partridge.'

'All right, but where does she live?'

'End 'ouse, Inkerman Road, Skerne Park. But don't tell nobody I said, else I'll end up — Jesus, talk o' the devil!'

'What?'

'Don't look now, but she's just come in.'

A thirsty customer was calling for service. My barman tossed his dishcloth aside but not, I think, my ten-pound note. As he wiped his hands down the seat of his jeans, the note would disappear into one of his brace of back pockets. He moved off to serve more ale and I turned casually towards the door.

The woman had paused beside the dominoes table. She said something to one of the players, and he said something to her, and she threw back her head to roar with laughter. She mock-punched him on the arm and turned away, still laughing, towards the far end of the bar. There, she joined the fat lady, who promptly bought her a drink which was served up by the bearded landlord. Then the three of them put their heads together. Nobody looked towards me, but I felt their interest in the hairs of my nostrils. My ears burned, as they say.

The mental picture I had formed of Bridie could hardly have been more wrong. I had assumed she would be a contemporary of Mooney's, another punk-rock kid with a grotesque hair-do and ghastly make-up, togged out in ridiculous gear. The reality proved quite different. She was verging on middle age and she looked as though she had never been

young, let alone far-out. She was wearing a belted, off-white trench-coat, flat-heeled lace-up shoes and a nigger-brown rollneck sweater. Her dark, grey-streaked hair was cut short and her sharp sallow features were far from attractive. She was just about average height, flat-chested under the trench-coat and hardly any hips at all. The sort of woman to whom Darren Mooney wouldn't have given a light. They had about as much in common as Sheik Yamani and Golda Meir.

As these thoughts ran through my head, she fumbled in her shoulder-bag and laid a large coin on top of the bar. The landlord picked it up and turned around to open his till and give her a shower of small change. She took it and made her way out back. Change for the telephone, then. She was gone a good ten minutes and if I hadn't already checked there was no way out at the rear, I might have assumed she had done a bunk. But eventually she returned and stood at the bar with her back to me, talking to her two fat friends. Presently, Billy the landlord set them up with a new round of drinks and I decided then to get some fresh air.

Outside, the night was asserting itself and the sky was fast growing dark. I moved to the doorway of a newsagent's shop about thirty yards up the road and got out my little two-way radio and pressed the tit. No reply. Nothing but a soft gentle crackling interspersed by a regular beep. *Where are you, Charlie, now that I need you?* If Bridie should have a car, all I could do was take note of the number and watch her drive away.

Time passed. Five minutes, ten minutes, a quarter of an hour. From somewhere uptown came the boom of a clock as it gonged out ten sonorous notes. The beeper beeped on. I waited.

She came out, alone, at five past ten, and swung sharp left to walk towards me on the opposite side

93

of the road. I pressed back into the shadow of my doorway but she never turned her head as she stepped out smartly up the hill in the direction of the centre of town. By the time I had tailed her into Blackwellgate I was pretty sure she didn't have a car, because she seemed to be heading for the bus terminal. I was confident also that she hadn't seen me. There was a goodly number of pedestrians about, the usual switching of pubs in that last half-hour before closing time, for a final change of scene.

Bridie seemed oblivious to everybody and everything, steeped in private thoughts of her own. She walked with her head down, as though trying to spot lost coins, and looked neither left nor right except at those times when she crossed the road. I tailed her to the terminal, where she joined a fair-sized queue waiting for the number 5 bus. I stationed myself nearby, slipping a hand into my raincoat pocket to switch the beeper off.

The bus rolled in and ate up the queue. I nipped forward smartly and boarded it as it started to move away, and spotted the back of Bridie's head. She was sitting on the lower deck, near the front on the side of the driver. I climbed the stairs and took a seat by a window where I could watch the people get off. When the conductor came round I paid the fare to the end of the line, Skerne Park. It would seem that Bridie was going home.

A mixed quartet of loutish teenagers occupying the front seats of the upper deck were making a rowdy nuisance of themselves and their behaviour prompted remonstrance from a middle-aged lady sitting immediately behind. She might as well have saved her breath. Her rebuke served only to encourage them and elicit further abuse. I might in other circumstances have been moved to intervene, but as it was, I held my peace. The bus was making frequent halts and I was busy watching those who alighted.

But most of the stops were well lit and my vigil

presented no difficulty. We trundled on for about fifteen minutes and came, on the southern outskirts of town, to the look-alike streets of shoe-box houses which marked a council estate. There were several stops around the perimeter and at one of them, the conductor called out Inkerman Road. The louts piled off, but Bridie did not. She stayed on to the end of the line, all the way out to the Parkside terminus. I hung back at the top of the stairs until the last of the passengers straggled off, then quit the bus myself.

Bridie was twenty yards ahead, walking down the gloomy road which was flanked on the left by the railings of a park. Most of our fellow travellers veered off to cross over the way towards the lights of the council houses. I was dropping back to keep a reasonable distance when suddenly, Bridie disappeared. It wasn't until I neared the spot at which she'd vanished that I was able to discern the gate. She must have turned in to enter the park. I paused in the deep shadow of a bank of laurels to hold my breath and listen. Out of the darkness came the sound of light footsteps. Apart from these, all was still.

Too damned still. I hesitated, letting my eyes grow accustomed to the almost total dark. Soon I could make out the winding path and the denser mass of trees. I had no idea what might be beckoning Bridie from the other side of the park and instinct told me that nothing was. My pulse rate had started to rise and I felt the old primeval reaction creeping over me. A shrinking of the testicles into a hard protective knot and a quickening surge of the heart-beat. A constriction of the arteries against possible loss of blood, and a drying-up of saliva. A crawling of the spine.

I turned and looked all around me. Nothing. The crowd from the bus had now dispersed and it passed me, empty, on its way back to town. Bridie's footsteps were fading. I followed her into the park,

stopping a dozen yards down the path to listen intently again. The old leg wound was giving off signals as invariably it did when the nervous system was hyperactive. I remembered having told Charlie that we were too old for this sort of thing and was conscious now of the truth of my words. So, what was I going to do?

I was going to call in the cavalry, *that's* what I was going to do. I hauled out my radio and activated the beeper. No murmur of a reply. I set out after Bridie, holding the thing to my ear and willing Charlie to acknowledge the signal. Come on, Charlie, *come on*! The footsteps in front of me definitely slowed. To let me catch up, no doubt. We were deeper into the park now, but my vision had adjusted well and I thought I could make out the shape of my quarry some fifty yards ahead. I slackened my own pace. *Come on, for God's sake!*

Somebody answered my prayer. A sharp click broke through the faint static mush. Then, 'Farrow?'

'Jesus!' I hissed. 'Where the *hell* have you been?'

'Why? What's up?'

'Just listen. I think you'd better get here fast. I'm tailing Bridie, and it smells like trouble. Follow the number 5 bus route right to the end of the line. A hundred yards past the terminus there's an entrance into a park. We're crossing it now, and I've a funny feeling — '

'Stay with it. I'm on my way.'

It would take him at least five minutes, maybe as many as ten. And if nothing happened in the meantime, I was going to look a right fool. I switched off, and pocketed, the radio and loosed the buttons of my coat and eased the Smith & Wesson in its holster. The feel of its checkered grip was solid and reassuring. It would appear unlikely that anyone might need a pistol in a park in Darlington, though stranger things have happened. Yes, and some of them to me.

But for what seemed like ages, nothing did

We had almost traversed the park and Bridie's small figure was now outlined against the pale filtered glow from the street lamps which bordered along its fringe. Confidence began to return. Actually, they had set it up well and if Bridie hadn't jumped the gun, it might have been all over with me. As it was, she made her break too soon because when she started to run I was not yet quite abreast of the spot where her chums lay in wait for me. Even so, they were up and at it almost before I knew. Two of them, one from either side out of the shrubs which bordered the path.

One of them rushed at me ahead of his buddy and that was where he made a mistake. I whirled half-round to meet his attack and blocked his hasty swing, and caught him with a good hard right. I tried to sink it way under the belt, but my block had knocked him aside and my fist hit him smack in the kidneys. The punch had all of my weight behind it and must have hurt him bad, but there was no time at all to check for results. My ear caught the hissing swish of a heavy object displacing air. I jerked away from the blow and felt a stunning pain in my shoulder. The other one, crowding my back, was wielding the old blunt instrument.

White-hot agony made me retch, but I countered instinctively with a backwards slam of the elbow. It thrust him staggering back and gave me time to spin round and face him. He swung the cosh again and I jumped in fast to make him miss and muffle the force of the blow. It skidded off the back of my skull and an enormous bright firework exploded in the blackness. I felt my senses reel and clutched for support at the front of his coat. My grab pulled him onto me, and I aimed a butt at the blur of his face. He saw it coming and dodged, and my forehead smashed into the side of his neck. He was hacking at my head with the cosh, but he didn't have enough elbow-room because I was dragging him in too close.

My mind was racing with the speed of a computer, trying to recall the skills I'd been taught at the big house in Sutherland. I sensed a knee coming up and twisted to take it on the thigh. My bad one. I felt it give way and clung on grimly to bring him down with me, heaving as I did to try and pull him underneath with my crushing bulk falling on top.

All of this happened in a matter of seconds. Now the first man was back in the fray, using the boot like a battering-ram. But his mate and I were grappling like lovers, rolling about on the ground, and he was having trouble in the darkness to distinguish friend from foe. He was grunting and cursing and dodging around us, trying to see which was who, and not all of his kicks found their mark on me. But some of them did and I was taking a pounding. One vicious smash to the ribs felt as though it had cracked a couple. I was engulfed in sickening pain and felt the strength draining out of my body. I let go the front of his coat and, with every ounce of power left in me, slammed in an upwards thrust. It travelled less than eight inches, but as the heel of my open palm connected, the shock ran right up my arm. I caught him under the lower jaw and heard the sharp breaking of bone and knew that for this one the battle was over.

As I flung myself over and off him, the other one identified me and the kick he aimed hit me under the chest and knocked me onto my back. I saw the vast black sole of his boot as he raised it to stomp my face, and God knows how I mustered the speed but muster it, somehow, I did. I threw up both hands to grab at the foot. My left fist took the shock of the heel and my right clamped over the toe, and I heaved and twisted simultaneously. He was taken completely off balance. He toppled with a crash and a grunting snarl of shock and panic. I was moving even as he went down, clawing forwards on hands and knees to pin him before he could rise.

I saw in that tiny fragment of time that the one with the broken jaw was still flaked out, only semi-conscious. He was rolling his head on the ground and making horrible moaning noises. His mate must have realised he was now on his own, and he decided he'd had enough. He was scrambling up on fingers and toes, like a sprinter going off the blocks, and with one last desperate all-out effort I made a sprawling dive to clutch at his hindermost ankle. I caught a fistful of trouser-leg and again he measured his length on the path. I flopped on top of him, one hand fumbling for the Smith & Wesson to drag the pistol clear and slash at his head with the heavy barrel. He uttered a strangled cry and I felt his body go limp underneath me.

I sagged on top of him, sobbing for air, my labouring lungs all afire. My throat was full of acid bile, but I lacked the strength to spit. Every separate part of me was hurting. I don't know how long I lay there but presently, I felt him stir. Wearily, I pushed myself off him. Then, still on my hands and knees, I tugged at his shoulder to roll him over. When I'd struggled him onto his back, he made a weak attempt to come up on his elbows. I pushed him down again and rammed the muzzle of the Smith & Wesson so savagely under his chin that he must have felt it in the roof of his mouth. My thumb hooked the hammer back and the metallic snicking of the action sounded sharp and clear and I knew he would recognise the noise. Our faces less than a foot apart, I could make out the gleam of his eyes and see their dilation even in the darkness.

'One move, you bastard!' I said.

He froze, his breathing harsh and rapid. I shot a glance at his friend and saw that he was still recumbent, apparently unable to rise. As I sat back on my haunches, I heard a new sound in the night. The slap of running footsteps. I swung the Smith around, ready and willing, now, to use it. In the event, I stowed

it away, having seen the small glint of light on his spectacles. As he drew near, he slowed down and then I caught another glint. This one on the barrel of his gun.

'You won't need that, now,' I said. 'It's all over.'

Charlie stepped up close and peered down at my an ~~pro~~tagonists.

'Been fighting, have you?' he said.

I sat on a park bench massaging my thigh and feeling about a hundred years old. I ached and throbbed all over, not least at the back of my head. That, and the muscles in my shoulder just where they connect with the neck, and my lower ribs, and my poorly leg. Jesus, I was one big pain. Something like twenty minutes had passed since Charlie arrived on the scene, and now the park seemed full of people, most of them in uniform. Over on the road, by the exit, I could see the flashing blue lights of police cars and an ambulance. My assailants were being carted away, one of them on a stretcher. I wanted very much to go home, and take a hot bath, and fall into bed.

'Right, then,' Charlie said. He had broken away from the CID man he'd been quietly talking to, raising his voice as he came towards me. 'Time for us to go.'

'Thank God for that, I've just about had it.'

'Aaahh, poor old bugger,' he said. 'Want me to give you a hand then, do you?'

'You're too bloody late, now,' I said. 'I wanted a hand half an hour ago.'

'You must be slowing down. Christ, they're only a couple of sodding bog-Irish.'

'How d'you know they're Irish?' I said.

'Well, they're certainly not Abyssinian. And one of 'em can still talk — not that he's saying very much at the moment. He will, though, later on.' I got up stiffly and limped along beside him down the dark path back to the car. 'How come you let the woman

get away?'

'Look here, Charlie,' I said, 'I'm not in the mood for jokes, mate — all right?'

'What about visiting, then?'

'Visiting?'

'End house, Inkerman Road. Isn't that what you told me?' he said.

'To hell with that a bowl of porridge! Let the blue-bottles handle it,' I said.

'The bluebottles don't have a search-warrant, Farrow.'

'Neither do we,' I said.

'Ah, but we don't use 'em, do we?'

'Have a heart, Chas,' I said. 'Those two bastards hurt me.'

'Not as much as you hurt them. I shouldn't be surprised if they decide to press charges. It's their two words to your one.'

'I told you, I'm not in the mood for funnies.'

'Where's your sense of humour?' he said. 'Where's the old Farrow repartee?'

'It's frayed around the edges, chum.'

'It'll only take us half an hour.'

'What will?'

'Inkerman Road.'

'I've heard that bloody tale before.'

'Just a quick look-see,' he said.

'I'm not humping furniture and pulling up carpets — '

'No, no, nothing like that. They haven't had time to get organised, have they? They've only been here one day . . if, that is, your friendly barman wasn't feeding you a load of duff gen.'

'Of course he wasn't. He fingered Bridie, and he told me where she lived, so why should he lie about the other?'

'How do I know?' Charlie said. 'He might have got tired of telling truth. People sometimes do.'

'Well, *I* believed him.'

101

'Let's prove it, then.'

'Okay, but listen,' I said, 'one fast shufti, then it's back home to beddie-byes.'

'That's my boy,' he said.

There was a light in one of the upstairs rooms, but the rest of the windows were dark. A street lamp on the corner showed up that small patches of garden at front and side were jungles of waist-high weeds, dockings and nettles and rose-bay willow-herb. The gateway was without a gate and the short concrete path was badly pitted. We paused at the glass-panelled door and Charlie signalled wordlessly that I was to go and stand guard at the back. I made my way around the gable, the end of a block of four, and stationed myself by the kitchen window.

As I hauled the pistol clear, I heard the staccato rattle of a knocker. Charlie, at the front door. A couple of minutes of silence, then another iron tattoo. A further couple of minutes and the kitchen light snapped on, and I cocked the Smith as I brought it up level. No more fisticuffs for me. I'd had enough already. Whoever came out of that door was going to behave, or get one in the leg. I flattened against the wall, next to a smelly dustbin, and waited. There was the rattle of a key in the lock and the door creaked open, but no-one stepped out.

'Come on, Farrow. Inside.' Charlie had done the Yale at the front and had run a quick check on the house before coming through to let me in. 'You won't need the shooter,' he said.

I put up the pistol and joined him. The kitchen was a mess. A sink piled high with unwashed dishes and greasy pots and pans. The plastic-topped table bore untidy evidence of a recent meal for three, and a tin tray left on the draining-board held the remnants of another one. There was a heavy stink of dead cooking and it hadn't been cordon bleu.

'Birds all fled have they, Charlie?' I asked.

102

'Just an old crone upstairs, smelling like a brewery and sound asleep.'

'So Bridie didn't come back.'

'Not a chance. She'd watch the action from a good safe distance, and take it on the lam. And she won't be coming back here, now. No way.'

'So we know she's a naughty, then.'

'Let's find out just how naughty.'

We looked at the front room first. It was small and grubby and cheerless. The sofa and easy-chairs were upholstered in ghastly black vynil and the coffee-table-top was powdered with overspill from the two big butt-filled ashtrays. There was an incredibly nasty sideboard, its cupboards full of junk, but the TV set was smart and expensive. Everything else was cheap; the hideous religious figurines, the tatty carpet square and the almost empty china-cabinet. The walls were adorned by three garish prints: a green-faced lady, a grey-faced bull elephant, and J.C. with his red heart laid bare. The tiles which surrounded the little fireplace were a nauseous shade of puce, those on the hearth mostly cracked and broken. Heaped in the cast-iron grate, a screwed-up jumble of inflammable litter and hundreds of stubbed-out fag-ends.

'Not very houseproud, our little Bridie.'

'They're all the same,' Charlie said. 'A shower of filthy bastards.'

This of course was not strictly true, but Charlie's pure hatred of the IRA was awesome, even to me. They had murdered his young soldier nephew in Ulster in a particularly brutal way and Uncle was a vengeful person.

'Well, there's nothing here.'

'Do the hall, and the pantry. I'm going upstairs.'

The pantry was quite well stocked with a wide range of packets and tins and the shelves of an upright freezer were crammed with frozen foods. Jumbo-sized packs of beefburgers, and a fourteen-

pound carton of fish, and big plastic sacks of ready-cut chips. Not much variety there, but plenty of fodder for the quick easy nosh. It was all quite innocent, though, and I moved on through to check the hall cupboard which was fitted under the stairs. As I felt inside the door-frame for a light-switch, Charlie called softly from above.

'Farrow — come and see what I've found.'

I climbed the narrow stairs and followed him into one of the bedrooms which looked out over the back. Lying on one of the two single beds was a large canvas travelling-bag, unzipped and yawning wide open. Charlie nodded down at the bag, as close to smiling as ever I saw him.

'Hit the jackpot, have you?' I said.

He stepped aside to let me see. He had hit the jackpot, all right. About sixty pounds of plastic explosives, detonators galore, four squat dry-cell batteries, timing devices, coils of insulated wire, pistol ammunition in flat greaseproof boxes, and two 9mm guns both of them fitted with silencers.

'Who's a clever boy, then?' I said.

'I bet you're glad you came, now.'

'Wouldn't have missed it,' I said. 'Anything else?'

'Don't you think that's enough?'

'Enough for what?' I said.

'Enough to make a right mess of Marsden's.'

'Just about,' I said, 'if that's what they meant to use it for.'

'It's a pound to — '

'— pinch of shit. Mr Marsden ought to be grateful.'

'He's not going to know,' Charlie said. 'No point in spreading alarm and despondence.'

'That's very thoughtful,' I said. 'So can we go home, now?'

'In a minute. I want a word with the crone.'

The old one was snoring like an asthmatic grampus, really sawing them up. She was lying on her back in a tangle of bedclothes, her mouth a toothless black

hole and her sparse white hair caught up in a hairnet. She was wearing a thick flannel nightgown tied at her scrawny neck and a pink woollen button-up cardigan. The small room was full of used air, close and stuffy with the stench of sweat and semi-digested beer. There was a half-full glass on the bedside table and, lined up beside the bed, a row of empty Guinness bottles.

'The sleeping princess,' Charlie said.

'Whistler's Mother, twenty years on.'

'Whistle in her lug-hole, then.'

I stooped to shake a bony shoulder and the old one came awake in a flurry of snorts and snuffles. She opened her rheumy eyes, slow at first to orientate. She shook her head and belched, squinting up at us with a puzzled frown. When it finally dawned on her, she wriggled up in the bed to prop herself against the off-white pillows.

'Wha — ?'

'Now then,' Charlie said, 'it looks as though they're all gone and left you.'

'Who are yez?'

'you know very well. This your house?'

'It's me daughter's house.'

'It's Darlington council's,' I said. 'They ought to vet their tenants, Charlie.'

'Too bloody right,' he said. 'This lot's probably on Social Security, as well.'

'Spending half of it on postal orders for sending back to the Auld Sod, to help support the boyos.'

'Goodness me!' Charlie said. 'Do you really believe that, Farrow?'

'It's a known fact, Charlie,' I said.

The old girl was fully awake now. 'Get out of here, ye bastats!' she said.

'Hark at that, Farrow. *She's* telling *us*!'

'And we'd better do as she says, or she'll report us to the Race Relations Board.'

'Don't you mean the RSPCA? Isn't that the outfit

which takes care of animals?'

'I stand corrected,' I said.

'Damn right you stand corrected. That was a serious mistake.' He turned to look down at the seething old woman. 'We've got your daughter's boyfriends,' he said, 'and we've going to get your daughter. So where does that leave *you*?'

'Oh, they'll put her in a nice private nursing-home, at the jolly old taxpayer's expense.'

'Not if I've got anything to do with it. The only home she's going to see is the stinking bog she came from — you got that, Mother McCree?'

'F*** off, you dirty English bastat!'

This malodorous ancient calling *Charlie* dirty struck me as funny. I laughed and she turned her venomous glare on me.

'You too you f****** pig!'

'Hasn't she got a lovely vocabulary?' said Charlie.

'Lovely, but limited,' I said.

'Bastats!'

'There, what did I tell you?'

'You can't always be wrong,' Charlie said.

'What are we going to do with her, then?'

'We're doing nothing,' he said. 'We'll rustle up the forces of law and order.'

'Christ, at last,' I said.

The guest-house lady had given us a key and as we let ourselves into the hall the grandfather clock in the corner set up a whirring sound as it gathered itself to announce the hour. Just one gentle resonant boom and then the house was quiet again. The yellow glow from a solitary table lamp lighted our way up-stairs and as I wearily mounted them, Charlie spoke from behind.

'I hope you're not thinking of nabbing the bath-room.'

'It's all yours, buddy,' I sighed. 'I'm not even going to brush my teeth.'

'You can please yourself about that. Just don't start using up the hot water.'

'I've told you, I'm off to bed — and keep your voice down, people are sleeping.'

By the time I was back in my room I had just enough strength left to take off my clothes. As I unlaced my shoes, I heard the sound of gushing water. Charlie, running a bath. Where in *hell* did he get the energy? Ah well, up to him. I hung up my suit then rolled into bed, groaning with blessed relief. It was an effort to reach out and switch off the light.

Somebody tried to open my door.

'Open up,' the somebody said, 'I've just remembered something.'

I snuggled the blankets up around my ears and 'Bugger off, Charlie,' I said.

Monday

Darlington's new Memorial Hospital is a model of its kind and should be used as such all over the country. It is big, but not too big, and I've seen less attractive entrance halls in many a pretentious hotel. Nowhere the dismal gloom which often pervades our places of healing. There is a large and well-stocked shop and an equally well-stocked library. It is a bright and cheerful place, a place in which to recover from an illness rather than suffer from it.

We sat in the pleasant cafeteria and drank a cup of tea whilst waiting to see Harold Dransfield, a name unknown to me until twenty past nine that same morning.

I had been talking with Royston, in his office, and waiting for Charlie to return from a talk he was having with some Special Branch people brought in from Durham to handle the Inkerman Road job. Royston, with nothing to do for us at that moment, was scanning the daily incident sheet. He looked up from it as I filled a pipe.

'Now there's a thing,' he said.

'Where's a thing, Harry?'

'Oh, it's nothing to do with you, it's just a lowlife pub I've been keeping an eye on. Interesting . . .'

'What is?' I said.

'Well, there's this sleazy boozer in Coppergate — '

'Where's Coppergate?' I said.

'Oh, you won't know it, Marcus. It's down at the bottom end of town — and I do mean *bottom*, you know.'

'Why didn't you just say arse-end, then?'

'Because I don't use such language,' he grinned.

'Well, go on, I'm all ears.'

'Seems there was a bit of a disturbance last night, emergency ambulance call. The landlord, a hard case

called Billy Dickens, reported an accident. Part-time barman injured himself.'

'So what's the big deal about that?'

'Spot of doubt up at Darlington Casualty. Doctor up there seems to think that said barman's injuries not consistent with jumped-up story he was told.'

Royston now had my full attention, but I tried not to let it show. 'So the doctor passed his suspicions to your lot?'

'Ah yes, well, you see, it's not the first time by any means that he's had customers from the Goat's Head, and he's getting a bit fed up with it.'

'What's the barman's name?'

'Chap called Harold Dransfield. Innocuous little bloke, bit of a layabout, petty larceny. No real harm in him, though.'

'What time was the accident reported?'

'It was after they'd shut up shop . . ' Royston ran his eye down the incident sheet '. . ah, yes, there it is, the call was timed at 11:17.'

'Is Dransfield badly hurt?'

'Badly enough so he nearly snuffed it. They've had him in intensive care.'

'What's the nature of his injuries?'

'Multiple fractures, broken ribs, possible crushed insides. Doctor thinks he was beaten up.'

'Oh, well, Harry, it's a violent world. So what are you blokes going to do?'

'I suppose we'll go through the motions, when he gets a bit better,' Royston said. 'See if he wants to change his story. But I don't suppose he will. He'll probably be too scared to tell us who put the mockers on him — if he really did get the treatment, that is. We've got some pretty rough characters running around this patch.'

I had changed the subject then and a little later Charlie breezed in with an air of being pleased with himself. He was rubbing his dry-freckled hands together.

'Won the pools have you, Charlie?' I said.

'Come on, Farrow, get on your bike. And you, Royston —'

'What?' Royston said.

'Pull your police lady out of Barnes Road.'

'But you said — '

'I know what I said. Now I'm saying I want the woman left clear. No surveillance, nothing. Okay?'

'Perhaps she's not fit to be left on her own.'

'I don't give a chuff,' Charlie said. 'Farrow . . '

'All right, I'm coming. So long, Harry,' I said.

The day was dry, but overcast. As we went out to get in the car, I told Charlie what had happened to Dransfield.

'Right, let's get up there,' he said.

'They might not let us see him. He might still be in intensive care.'

'Do you know the way to the hospital?'

'I think so.'

'Good,' he gave me the keys, 'you can do the driving.'

So that was how we came to be hanging about the hospital cafeteria waiting for Dransfield's nurse to change his dressings or something. We had been there about a quarter of an hour. Charlie looked at his watch.

'God Almighty!'

'Patience.'

'Never mind "patience"!' he said. 'Go and ask what's happening.'

'I asked five minutes ago. Finish your char.'

'It's like witch-piss.'

'Well, mine tastes all right,' I said. 'Get yourself a chocolate biscuit.'

'Listen — !'

'Hang on, hang on,' I said, 'I think this lady's looking for us.'

A homely ancilliary worker in the uniform yellow smock had appeared at the cafeteria entrance and

111

was standing there peering around. When I lifted a hand to wave, she threaded her way between the tables, smiling as she approached.

'Mr McGowan?'

'Not likely — that's Mr McGowan,' I said.

She turned to Charlie. 'Doctor says you can see Mr Dransfield now, but only for two or three minutes, and he's not to be upset.'

'About time, too,' said Charlie.

'Yes, well, if you'll please come this way . . .'

Dransfield was in a little side-ward. He had the two-bed room to himself and he looked like one of those accident victims depicted in funny cartoons. Left arm and right leg were encased in plaster, the latter up to the thigh and suspended by wire from a pulley. He was wearing a helmet of bandages and he was strapped up from armpits to waist. His face was one big contusion. He had a plastic tube up his nose and another one stuck in his forearm to drip-feed blood from a hanging bottle. There was a pretty young nurse standing by. Charlie nodded dismissively.

'Thank you, miss,' he said.

She hesitated, unsure of herself. Charlie stared at her. She opened her mouth to say something, but then she closed it again and skirted the bed-end to get tp the door. As she closed it behind her:

'Two minutes only,' she said.

Dransfield's eyes were open, but there seemed to be no life in his gaze. He was obviously drugged to the eyeballs. But he recognised me, all the same. It was just that he was somewhere on the far side of caring. Charlie moved up close to the bed.

'Who did you over, Mr Dransfield?'

'Nobody,' Dransfield said. He spoke in a dull flat whisper which was barely audible.

'Come on, somebody duffed you up.'

'I fell down the cellar steps.'

'Don't give us that.'

'I told you.'

'Why did they do it?' Charlie said. 'Was it because you talked to my partner?'

'No.'

'Why, then?' Charlie said.

'S'truth, I fell down the cellar steps.'

'You were thrown down, you mean,' Charlie said. 'It was Billy Dickens, wasn't it?'

'I'm tired. Lea' me alone.'

'We'll leave you alone when you've told us the truth.'

'My head hurts,' Dransfield said.

Charlie leaned down over him. 'Listen, Dransfield,' he said, 'Nobody's going to get back at you, because we're going to put 'em inside. Every last bastard — understand?'

'Go 'way,' Dransfield said.

As it turned out, we had no option because our two minutes were up and a white-coated doctor arrived on the scene to remind us of that fact. He came in as Charlie was bent over Dransfield, and:

'What's going on here?' he said.

Charlie straightened up. 'We're just having a chat.'

'Well, I'm sorry, but that's enough. This man shouldn't be talking at all.'

'Who are you?' Charlie said.

If he hadn't put such an inflection on the "you" we might have gotten away with another couple of minutes.

'I'm Doctor Patterson.'

The accent was Scots and the hair was fiery and he did not look the type to be flannelled or bullied or messed about.

'When will he be fit?' Charlie said.

'Fit for what?'

'For talking to.'

'Depends on what you mean. For anything longer than a very few minutes, maybe the end of the week.'

The doctor eased us out of the ward and walked with us to the lifts, presumably to see us off the

premises.

'Tell me, doc,' Charlie said, 'are you the one who fixed him up last night?'

'No, I'm not,' Patterson said. 'That was my colleague, Dr Shaw.'

'But you'll have seen his report, I suppose?'

'Of course. Mr Dransfield is now my patient.'

'What's the extent of his injuries, then? Could they be caused by falling down stairs?'

Patterson uttered a humourless chuckle. 'Oh yes, they could,' he said, '— provided the stairs were made of iron, and about five hundred feet high.'

'You agree with Doctor Shaw then, I take it, that he was hurt in some other way?'

Patterson eyed the pair of us shrewdly. He thought we were from the police and was wary of committing himself.

'Is this off the record?' he said.

'Bet your boots,' said Charlie.

'Well, ask me,' Patterson said, 'and I'd say he's taken the most terrible beating. He's going to need surgery. We think he's got a ruptured kidney, and there's certain damage to the spleen, and the fractures to his femur and the lower and upper left arm —'

The lift had arrived and the doors sighed open and Charlie stepped inside. 'Okay, doc, no need to go into detail.'

'Take care, now,' Patterson said.

The Goat's Head frontage looked dismal at night-time, but in the cold light of day it looked worse. Peeling paint and unwashed windows and litter on the pavement outside, and black plastic bags full of rubbish heaped beside the door awaiting collection by the dustbin men.

'Give 'em a knock,' Charlie said.

It was twenty minutes to opening time. I hammered on the door and when my hammering evoked no response I hammered, harder, again. This time, there

was a shout from inside.

'Who is it?'

'Open up,' I said.

'We're shut! Come back at eleven o'clock!'

'Open this door!' Charlie said.

'Who is it?'

'Father Christmas.'

'Look — sod off!' the voice said.

Charlie stepped back a couple of paces, lifted his right foot waist-high and slammed at the door with the sole of his shoe. The lock did not give way, but we heard a muffled yell of alarm. Then a bolt snapped back and a chain rattled off and the door fell wide open. Billy Dickens stood in the gap, filling the doorway from side to side, his bearded cheeks scarlet with rage.

'What the bloody 'ell do you think you're doing?'

'William Dickens?' Charlie said.

'That's right — an' who the 'ell are you?'

'Gas Board,' Charlie said. 'We've come to read your meter.'

'Very funny,' Dickens said. Then the sight of me at Charlie's back caused a flicker of alarm in his eyes. 'You're not from Park Place, so what d'you want?'

He was wearing the same yellow T-shirt, even grubbier now, with baggy blue jeans and leather-thong sandals. The huge fist clamped around a broom made the shaft of it look like a matchstick. But big as he was he began to step backwards under Charlie's steady advance, and I followed them in and shut the door. The acrid smell of a harsh disinfectant vied with that of stale beer and old cigarette smoke and the ghosts of sweaty bodies. Table-tops sprouted a forest of legs from a battery of up-ended charis and there was a pile of sweepings in the middle of the room where Dickens had been brushing the floor. The silent one-armed bandits flashed seductive coloured lights, begging for a feed of tenpenny pieces. Dickens backed up against the bar. Charlie

115

stood facing him, hands in raincoat pockets, feet placed slightly apart, attitude one of weary boredom.

'Nice place you got here,' he said.

'Look, I'm busy, so what d'you want?'

'Now that, I like,' Charlie said. 'Straight to the point — eh, Farrow?'

He spoke without turning his head, or taking his eyes off Dickens's face. It was the old familiar routine, the McGowan-Farrow softening-up process. Guaranteed to provoke and Dickens reacted right from the start. He hunched his tremendous shoulders and his leg-of-mutton forearms bulged as he set aside the broom and clenched his fists.

'Only way to be, Chas,' I said.

Dickens snorted. 'Lissen — are you coppers, or not? 'cos if you're not, you can piss off out of it!'

'Dearie me,' Charlie said, 'what's upsetting him, Farrow?'

'Don't ask me,' I said. 'Unless it's a guilty conscience.'

'I think you've hit the nail on the head.'

A rapid succession of mixed emotions tugged at Dickens's red face and I recognised one as apprehension amounting almost to fear. But he forced a laugh and spat on the floor.

'This crap doesn't scare me!'

'You trying to scare this man, Farrow?'

'Wouldn't dream, Charlie,' I said. 'He's talking a lot of nonsense.'

'Oh, it's worse than that,' Charlie said. 'I think he's hiding something.'

'Don't talk wet!' Dickens said.

'All right, then, let's talk about Harold Dransfield.'

'What about him?' Dickens said.

'You don't know your own strength. You damn nearly killed him.'

'You *what*? You must be mad!'

116

'Did you work him over all by yourself, or did you have help?'

'Work him over? You've got to be joking! He fell down the cellar steps!'

'That's not what he told us — is it, Farrow?'

'Nothing like it,' I said.

'Gerraway!' said Dickens, 'You're tryin' to kid me!'

'No, we're not,' Charlie said. 'We never try to kid people — do we, Farrow?'

'Well, very seldom,' I said.

'You saw Dransfield talking to Mr Farrow, and you wanted to know what he'd said, so you beat it out of the poor little devil.'

'Get lost!' Dickens said. 'Come on, let's 'ave you out of 'ere!'

'It'll be better inside,' Charlie said. 'Will you excuse us, Farrow?'

'Sure, I'll wait in the car.'

Dickens was frankly bewildered now and when he heard this last, it brought a wondering smile to his hairy lips. He thought he was home and dry. He was nearly twice the size of Charlie and with me removed from the scene, he thought he had nothing to worry about. I almost wished I could stay and watch Charlie wipe the smile off his face. But he who does not see can in no way be called as a witness. As I turned and made for the door, Charlie said:

'Hold on a minute . .' he slipped his glasses off and folded the side-frames and handed them over '. . take care of these for me.'

'Do you want me to hold your coat, as well?'

'There'll be no need for that,' Charlie said.

I had packed a pipe in Royston's office, so I didn't go and sit in the car, I took a gentle stroll up Coppergate to enjoy a nice quiet smoke. The tobacco induced a reflective mood and I thought of all manner of things. I thought about who was going to open up the pub when the early doors crowd arrived, and

117

what Doctor Shaw was going to think when he got another one, and whether they'd put him in the side ward with Dransfield. Now *there* would be a thing.

I walked a bit further than I'd intended and found myself in the old church-yard of the medieval St Cuthbert's. I would have liked to have looked inside, but I had been away almost ten minutes and that was quite long enough. Men of far stronger character than Dickens had crumbled in half of that time, and his size made very little difference. So I turned around and quickened my step and sure enough, he was waiting for me. I had the keys of the car, so he couldn't get in. He was not best pleased.

'Oh, you're back, are you?' he said.

'Been waiting long, Chas?'

'Come on, open up.'

'What's all the hurry?' I said.

I gave him back his spectacles and as I unlocked the car he slipped them on and smoothed down his hair. Before I closed the door, I leaned out sideways and knocked out my pipe on the edge of the kerbstone.

'*Come on!*'

'Now, now, Charlie, don't get niggly.'

'Suffering Jesus!' he said.

'Did the laddo give you any trouble?'

'That'll be the day.'

I started the engine and got us moving. 'Where are we bound for?' I said.

'Harrowgate Hill. Just head north out of town.'

'Yes, I know, it's straight up North Road.'

'If you know, put your boot down,' he said.

I doubled back onto the ring road and along St Cuthbert's Way, then left at the roundabout to get onto High Northgate. Charlie was putting a shine on his spectacles. He seemed in a pensive mood.

'What did Dickens have to say for himself?' I asked.

'Not a lot,' Charlie said, 'it was nearly a waste of energy.'

Nearly, but not quite, because Dickens wouldn't be hitting people again for some considerable time.

'He must have told you something.'

'Sure. He told me all he knew. But like I said, he's nothing but a thug who likes to use his fists. Our Bridie wanted to know what it was you were asking Dransfield about, and he did her a favour, that's all. Trouble was he thought Dransfield was holding out, and he let himself get carried away.'

'Did the little bloke really fall down the steps?'

'He didn't fall, he was kicked. Dickens should have a guard-rail around that trap-door.'

'Why? Same thing happen again?'

'Accidents always come in threes.'

'Well, don't look at me,' I said. 'I had my bloody share last night.'

'Still moaning, are you?' he said, 'Get past this bus.'

'There's a lorry coming.'

'Go on, there's plenty of room.'

'You want to get there in one piece don't you, Charlie?'

'You're driving like a big Mary Anne.'

'Can't help it,' I said, 'it's the time of the month.'

'Get past *now*, then,' he said.

Harrowgate Hill, a large mixed suburb on the northernmost fringe of the town, has many expensive properties and some which are not so grand. The house we eventually found was in the former category. It stood in an acre of ground and was surrounded by a six-foot stone wall which had a coping of broken glass. The entrance was barred by wide iron gates which looked as though they might be locked. Charlie got out and tried them. They were. There was a bell-push set into the wall and Charlie stuck his thumb on it. As though the ringing had set it off, a furious barking broke out and a big black dober-

man shot through the hedge which flanked the gravel drive and hurled itself, snarling, at the rails of the gate. Charlie looked at the dog dispassionately and kept his thumb on the bell.

The young man who trotted down the drive was wearing a smart grey track-suit and fancy Adidas pumps. He jogged with his elbows tucked into his sides, as though on a training run, and indeed he had all the appearance of a budding heavyweight. His His curling black hair was cropped short and his features had been rudely rearranged. His nose had been spread and broken, and reset slightly askew, giving his face a twisted look. Cut scars showed white in his brows and an overhang of thickened tissue bore witness to repeated hard blows. As he neared the gate, he called to the dog.

'Awright, Fritz! That'll do!' Then, to Charlie, 'Whaddya want?'

'Mr Kirby at home?'

'Who wants to know?'

'Tell him we're friends of the kraut.'

'Kraut? Who's Kraut?'

'The German bloke, sonny.'

'What German?'

'Look,' Charlie said, 'just run along and give him the message.'

'Wait here,' the bruiser said.

Where did he think we were going to wait? He caught a hold on the dog's studded collar and hauled it away up the drive, disappearing around a bend. Several minutes dragged by and then young Track-Suit came jogging back to open up the gates.

'Drive round the back, there'll be someb'dy waitin'.'

Charlie got back into the car and the Rover's tyres crunched on the gravel as I tooled up the curving drive. The house was a long sprawling ranch-type affair and an open porch along the front looked out over a steep-terraced garden. The garden, very well kept, sloped down to a crescent-shaped area on

120

which a maroon Rolls Royce was parked beside a little Japanese runabout. The Rolls, a magnificent Corniche, made the Datsun look look like a kiddie's plaything. The drive swept on around the side of the house to a roomy courtyard out back which was bounded on one side by a four-car garage with a service flat built on top. I parked in front of the garage and as we stepped out of the car we were met by a second young track-suited giant who had to be the other one's twin. They resembled each other almost exactly and before their faces got bent, they were probably identical. He beckoned us towards him with an impatient gesture.

'Come on, this way,' he said.

He led us in through an enormous kitchen which must have had everything ever featured in Ideal Home. Equipment and gadgets galore. After the kitchen a long wide hallway and at the far end of this, an oak door. From somewhere distant in the house came the unmistakable sounds of a child being taught to play the piano. A faltering stumble of notes repeated over and over again, each time with a different mistake. The bruiser held up a malt-shovel hand to halt up just short of the door and his diffident tap on the panels elicited a summons from within.

The bruiser turned the handle and pushed the door open wide and stood back to let us precede him. The big square room, part lounge and part office, could not have been called a study because there wasn't a book in sight. A modern glass-topped executive desk and a bank of four grey steel filing-cabinets clashed incongruously with a flowery fitted carpet and the big soft sofa and chairs in deep-buttoned peacock-blue Dralon. One corner had a built-in bar, the bottles reflected by mirror-backed shelves.

The man behind the glass desk was dressed in a thin black roll-neck sweater which looked as though

it might be cashmere, and smooth tailored slacks of dove-grey flannel. The gold Rolex on his thin wrist was as big as your average pocket-watch and the pinkies of both hands were adorned with large slab-cut diamonds. On the heavy gold chain around his neck, worn over the cashmere sweater, hung a twenty-dollar gold piece. Kirby was a man who liked his gewgaws.

And I hadn't expected him to be so young. Middle thirties, I guessed. He wasn't a big man, either. He would weigh not much more than ten stone. But there was an aura about him of fierce-burning energies. His deep-set pale blue eyes placed close together over a bird-beak of nose, had a wild and unstable look and I could well imagine why he was called Mad Geordie.

'State your business,' he said.

Not hello and how d'ye do, or sit down, or have a drink. It was stay on your feet and spit it out. But Charlie, perverse as always, sat himself on the arm of a chair, while the bruiser and I flanked the portal like a pair of temple dogs. It was a scene straight out of a Bogart movie. For a few seconds nobody spoke, then Charlie said:

'You're a wicked man, Kirby.'

'Can you hear him, Vic?' Kirby said.

The question was rhetorical and Vic did not reply. He just shot me a sideways glance and folded his arms on his chest, and adjusted his stance. I pulled out my pipe.

'Anybody mind if I smoke?'

Nobody answered. I struck a match and set the tobacco alight. What remained in the bowl was mostly dottle. It was bitter, and hot on the tongue, and the reek I made smelled like burning tyres.

'Yes indeed, Kirby,' Charlie said. 'Wicked. You've overstepped the mark.'

'What mark?' Kirby said. 'You two goons got a warrant, have you?'

122

'A warrant? Why no,' Charlie said. 'We're just here to give you a piece of advice.'

'What sort of advice?' Kirby said, 'I'm in the scrap-metal business, hinnie. Scrap, an' fruit machines, an' second-hand motors, an' —'

'Espionage.'

'What the hell's that?' Kirby said. 'Do you know what this bloke's on about, Vic?'

Again Vic voiced no reply.

'Espionage,' said Charlie, 'is an offence against the realm. This time, Kirby, you're out of your depth.'

'Stop talkin' a load of manure! Where have you come from, anyway?'

'That German,' Charlie said, 'the one you had a date with on Friday night, the one who never turned up —'

'I never knew no German.'

'Don't interrupt,' Charlie said.

'Vic —'

'I wouldn't, Vic,' said Charlie. 'My friend here's a terrible man — aren't you, Mr Farrow?'

'Oh, I wouldn't go so far as that, Charles.'

'He's modest,' Charlie said. 'He's been known to break a whole packet of breadsticks, and I've seen him —'

'All right,' Kirby said. 'You've got two minutes to say your piece.'

'This German, then,' Charlie said, 'when did he first get in touch with you?'

'I've told you,' Kirby said, 'I don't know any Germans.'

'All right, this foreigner, then.'

'I don't know any foreigners, either.'

'If you're going to tell fibs,' Charlie said, 'we're never going to get anywhere, are we?'

'*You* are,' Kirby said. 'You've already had one of your minutes.'

'Oh, we're in no rush,' Charlie said. 'We can stay here all day, if necessary.'

The little man's stare switched from Charlie to me, then back to Charlie again. He might have been mad, but he couldn't have been stupid, or he'd never have got where he was. Young Vic shifted restlessly, waiting for the nod, and I thought I heard a shuffling out in the hallway. I put away my foul-tasting pipe, hoping it wouldn't burn a hole in my pocket in the event of a violent affray. Charlie sighed, and conjured up a nailfile and touched up a cuticle which didn't need touching up at all. Kirby's eyes narrowed to slits, masking any reflection of the thoughts whirling round in his head. Suddenly he leaned back in his chair and stabbed with a forefinger, pointing his stabs at Charlie.

'You're askin' for it!' he said. 'You come here, into my private home, with my wife and kid in the place, and start to throw your weight around. Now, I don't give a shit — '

'But you *should* give a shit. Shouldn't he, Farrow?'

'Definitely,' I said.

'All right. Let's see some identification.'

'Sorry, can't oblige,' Charlie said.

'No reason why I shouldn't throw you out, then?'

'Oh yes there is,' Charlie said. 'In the first place, you haven't got half enough muscle. And in the second place, even if you had it would do you no good, Geordie. No good at all.'

Kirby placed a hand on his telephone and, 'In that case, mister,' he said, 'I think I'll get my solicitor here.'

'Please yourself,' Charlie said, 'but once you do that, it's official. It's no longer a quiet chat. It's you for the slammer, Geordie-boy.'

'Give over!' Kirby said, 'I'm a legitimate business-man.'

'You're a bloody crook,' Charlie said, 'who's managed so far to stay out of jail. But this time it's different, you see. This time, it's treason — and for your information, that's still a capital offence. Know

124

what a capital offence is Kirby? It's one they top you for. So let's be hearing about the German. Tell us in your own words.'

Kirby hesitated, one hand still on the phone, and his pale gaze fixed on Charlie's calm features.

'Get me a drink, Vic,' he said.

Vic pushed himself up off the door-jamb and crossed the room to the bar and leaned across it to reach down a bottle. Glenlivet, twelve years old. He sloshed a good tot into a wide crystal tumbler, clunked in a fistful of ice and put the drink into Kirby's hand.

'Nothing for me, thanks,' I said.

Vic came back to take up position. Kirby sipped at the malt and Charlie pocketed his nailfile.

'Good health, Geordie,' he said.

Kirby nodded. He had made up his mind. 'All right, listen,' he said, 'I got a call from this joker — '

'The German?'

'Who knows?' Kirby said. 'He could of been a bloody Hungarian.'

'Okay, so when did he phone?'

'Friday mornin', a quarter to twelve.'

When he'd been to the library, then.

'Was that the first time you heard from him?'

'I'm tellin' you,' Kirby said.

'What was his proposition?'

'It was a business deal,' Kirby said. 'That's what he said — a business deal.'

'Fifty thousand quid?'

'He did say something about that, yes.'

'Did he want to buy fruit machines?'

'Listen — !'

'All right, forget it. What else did he have to say?'

'He wanted a meetin' at North Road Station.'

'I take it you agreed?'

'I said we'd meet him there at eleven.'

'Yes, I see,' Charlie said. 'But he never turned up?'

'You askin', or tellin'?'

125

'Don't get smart,' Charlie said. 'My partner doesn't like it.'

'That's very true, Charles,' I said.

For an instant, I thought that Kirby would snap. But he took a swallow of Scotch and, with it, he managed to swallow his gall. Which couldn't have been easy for him and served to accentuate the difference between people with instinct and insight — or even the base low cunning of a man like Kirby — and those others who, like Billy Dickens, think that Brute Force Rules OK. Kirby, ruthless and mad as he might be, still had the sagacity to see that he was up against a deeply terrifying person.

'Okay, you're right,' he said. 'He never turned up.'

'Did he phone you again?'

'How could he?' Kirby said, 'He copped it on the way up there.'

'How'd you know that?' Charlie said.

'I sometimes read the papers.'

'Anyone else phone you?'

'No.'

'You'd better be very damned sure about that.'

'I am very sure,' Kirby said.

'And if anybody — *ever, at any time* — offers you any such deal again, you'd better by Jesus turn it down flat. If you don't, we'll be back to see you, and next time, we won't be so kind. Don't muck around with things you don't know about, Kirby. Stick to your usual filth.'

The madness made lasers of Kirby's eyes and as he fought for control his knotted fists shook on the glass desk top. Charlie rose to his feet and, having delivered his Parthian shot, he moved towards the door. Lacking a signal from Kirby, the bruiser stood his ground.

'Come on, son,' I said, 'shift the carcase.'

But Vic had still not grasped all this. Vic was rarin' to go, like an overgrown lamb to the slaughter. Instead of stepping aside, he lifted his fists and barred our way.

'I don't take that from nobody!'

'Let it go, Vic,' Kirby said.

'No!'

Vic took a roundhouse swing at me and as I ducked under the blow I felt a rush of wind at my side. Charlie moved so fast that I don't think any of us really saw it. But young Vic dropped like a stone and crashed against the bottom of the door, clutching at his gut. His pop-eyed face was literally livid. He was incapable of drawing breath, the muscles of his diaphragm paralysed by massive shock. Charlie put his hands back into his pockets, and:

'Shift him *now*, Farrow.' he said.

As we pulled away from Kirby's house, I looked across the car.

'I think you made an enemy there, Chas.'

'Christ, I should cocoa!' he said.

'Do you think he would have done a deal with Peltz?'

'I haven't the slightest doubt. Kirby's kind will do anything for money. It's just a case of how much is enough, and the fifty grand was only a sweetener. The job would have paid much more than that.'

'I wonder how the IRA got onto Peltz?'

'Maybe they didn't,' Charlie said.

'Come on, it was Bridie who set the yobs onto him!'

'Yes. But who put Bridie onto Peltz?'

'Maybe we'll find out, Chas.'

'No "maybe" about,' he said.

'Thing is, if Bridie knew that Peltz was carrying all that lovely money, why didn't the boyos do him themselves?'

'I don't think she did know,' he said. 'She just wanted him stopped from doing the deal with Kirby . . and in any case,' he went on, 'her buddies hadn't arrived then, had they? She could hardly mug Peltz on her own.'

127

'Yes, you're right. I'd forgotten about that.'

Slow down a bit,' he said, 'I want to talk to Royston before we get back into town.'

I eased up on the accelerator as Charlie unhooked the mike, hoping that Royston had not gone to lunch. He hadn't, but it took some little time to fetch him from wherever he was, possibly upstairs in the cafeteria, or perhaps he was in the loo. The control room had already established our call signs so that when he did come on, he came on without preamble.

'Royston.'

'About time,' Charlie said. 'Listen, this is important: I want Ruth Levinson picked up, and I want her held for at least an hour.'

'What reason do we give?'

'I don't give a damn what reason you give. Make one up,' Charlie said. 'Get her to help you with your enquiries.'

'Is it that you want her out of the way?'

'Never you mind the whys and wherefores. I want her picked up right now. Any difficulty about doing it yourself?'

'I'll have to talk to the Chief.'

'Talk to him, then, but get off your mark. And Royston — '

'Yes?'

'Don't let us down.'

After that, it was a case of consulting the street plan to pick out the easiest route to reach the upper end of Barnes Road. We did a three-mile right-angle to come out on Edgecombe Drive and I parked the Rover about a hundred yards up from Green's house. As I set the handbrake I looked at the dashboard clock. It has taken us seven minutes to get there. Too soon to expect Royston just yet.

But only about five minutes later, his grey Cortina drew up at the house and we watched him go inside. After another few minutes he came back

out again, accompanied by Ruth Levinson. The pair of them climbed in the car and we watched it perform a three-point turn and trundle away down the hill.

'Right,' said Charlie, 'let's set down there.'

Charlie did the front door lock and he didn't care who saw him. When we stepped into the hall, the first thing I noticed was a smell of cooking. Ruth must have been having her lunch, or maybe just preparing it. After I'd shut the door, Charlie turned to the telephone shelf and got down onto his knees and fished out his little steel nail-file. The small plastic lead-in box was fastened to the skirting board. He took the cover off and carefully used his nail-file to remove a flat black disc about the size and shape of a jacket button. He replaced the button with one from his pocket, then screwed the box cover back on.

'That looks like a brand-new type, Chas.'

'The receiver-disc's useless,' he said. 'Any damn fool can spot it.'

'What are we hoping to hear?'

'Maybe nothing. Better take a look round.'

I started with the upstairs, but it seemed that we had the house to ourselves. In the kitchen, I checked the oven. The heat had been switched off, but the dish of moussaka was done to a turn. *Moussaka*. That was strange. But strange or not it smelled delicious enough to make me salivate and turn my fancy to thoughts of lunch. I looked in the garage then, but it was empty save for the usual junk. I went through to the sitting-room. Charlie was perched on the coffee-table with a tape recorder held on his knee. It was roughly the size of a cigarette packet. The amazing micro-chip. He looked up as I entered the room.

'Nothing, Charlie,' I said.

'Oh yes, there is. Just listen to this.'

The tiny box made a whirring noise as he touched

129

the rewind tit, then a series of clicks as he made some adjustments. When the fine wire "tape" began to run there came first of all the ratchet sound of dialling, then the ringing-out, and then a *ping* as the receiver was lifted. I had settled myself in a chair, but the first voice I heard made me lean sharply forward.

'*Hello, Ruth. It's me . . .*' A brogue as thick as Kerry butter.

Then, very fast, '*Oh, hello! It's awfully nice of you to ring up.*'

'*Somebody with you?*'

'*That's right. I'm hoping it won't be for very long, though.*'

'*Jaysus! We haven't got trouble?*'

'*Well, yes, we have, in a way. But it's nothing for you to worry about.*'

'*Wait now, I'm not so sure about that. There's a feller here been askin' about me.*'

'*Where are you?*'

'*At the Goat's Head.*'

'*Oh, I see. So what do you think, then?*'

'*He's a big wan, I think he's a pig. Six-foot-some-thin', tough-lookin' bastat.*'

'*All alone, is he?*'

'*Yes. But listen, Ruth, I don't like it.*'

'*Oh, you mustn't get upset.*'

'*You don't think there's anybody onto us, then?*'

'*I don't thinks that's possible, dear — unless your young friends. .*'

'*No, they wouldn't talk. They'd know what they could expect — inside or outside the bliddy nick.*'

'*That's fine, then.*'

'*But what about you? Is it anything likely from your end?*'

'*Oh no, there's no real problem here.*'

'*Are you sure, now?*'

'*Quite sure, thank you.*'

'*What about this feller, then?*'

'*I've a feeling you'll know how to handle things.*'

'You mean we should take him off our backs?'
'I'll leave that to you, but do take care.'
'Will I call you afterwards?'
'I think perhaps not.'
'Well .. some time tomorrow?'
'That might be better, yes. But later, rather than sooner.'
'Ah yes, you're right there. Goo'bye.'
'Goodbye, dear, and thank you for calling.'

There was a *clunk* as the phone was put down, and I remember having to close my mouth.

'God Almighty!' I said. 'I can't believe it, Charlie!'
'You better believe it,' he said.
'But Ruth and Bridie — it's just too incredible!'
'It's nothing of the kind. Besides, you haven't heard the rest.'

He pressed the play tit once more, and after the familiar preliminary noises, the voices began again.

'Darlington double seven five three?'
'Is that you, Ruth?'
'It is.'
'Thank the Holy Jaysus! Can ye talk, now?'
'Yes, it's okay.'
'Listen — Behan an' Mooney are taken!'
'Taken?'
'Yes! They're in jail!'
'How did it happen?'
'That feller last night — he beat the both of 'em.'
'Are you sure they were taken by the police?'
'Sufferin' Christ, sure I'm sure! Didn't I see it happen with me own two eyes!'
'Just a moment, let me think . . .'

There was a long half-minute of silence, then:

'Bridie?'
'Yes, I'm still here.'
'What precisely do Behan and Mooney know?'
'Nothin', Ruth, not a thing. They just come over to do the job. They don't know what it was, nor where it was, nor nothin'.'

131

'However, they do know you.'

'Well, that much, o' course.'

'But they weren't told about us?'

'No, there's on'y me knows, I swear to God!'

'Good. So where are you now?'

'I'm stayin' with folks in Stockton — but listen, they're all in a sweat. They're not active, y'see, they're just sympathisers. They don't want any heat, an' they want me out of the house tonight. I'll have to get away, but the bastats will be watchin' the transports an' I haven't got a car.'

'These people you're with — would they give you a lift? Is so, you'd better come here.'

'Mother o' God! Wouldn't that be too dangerous?'

'Not if you do as I say. Do you know the Carmel Convent, here in Nunnery Lane?'

'Yes, I do, I know it well.'

'Get them to drop you there. You can walk the last half-mile to the house.

'But I might be seen!'

'No, you won't. Not if they drop you at midnight — no, make it a quarter to. That way, you'll be here just on twelve.'

'Are ye sure ye can get me away?'

'Don't worry, I'll get you away all right. Just do exactly what I've said. And Bridie — '

'Yes?'

'Don't come early. Don't come early, but don't be late.'

'No no, I won't, I'll be right on time.'

'That's good. Now, there's just one more thing. Talk to nobody — and I do mean nobody!'

'Christ, no, Ruth! I do understand!'

'All right, then. Don't panic, and I'll see you at midnight.'

'God bless ye, Ruthie. Goo'bye.'

That was it. The recording ran out. Charlie rewound the tape as I sat there stunned by the revelation. I could hardly believe my ears. The whole

132

shebang had been turned upside down and shaken up. It was weird. Now, *nothing* made sense.

Yet Charlie seemed quite happy. He was exhibiting the special signs. He was silently grinding his teeth and humming. A tuneless, nasal sound heard only at times of contentment and therefore very rare. It meant he thought he had all the answers or, at least, that he was well on the way to telling me how many beans made five. Which made of this job an all-time record, because we had worked on it less than three days. Two and a half, to be exact.

'All right,' I said, 'I give in. Let's have it.'

'Let you have what?' he said.

'Don't give me that, you've got it worked out.'

'Not yet, not quite,' he said. 'Top left-hand drawer of the writing-desk.'

'What about it?' I said.

'Packet of photographs. Let's have a decko.'

I fetched the photographs and stood at his shoulder as he riffled through them. Most appeared to have been taken at Whitby or down at Robin Hood's Bay. Charlie picked out one of Ruth sitting on the harbour wall and smiling into the camera. It had probably been taken by Green and, as snapshots go, it was pretty good.

'This one'll do,' Charlie said. 'Put the rest back where you found them and bring me an envelope.'

He sealed the photo inside the envelope and wrote something on the front before tucking it into his inside pocket. Something in the house had been bothering me and, suddenly, I knew what it was.

'What do you know about moussaka, Charlie?'

'Very little,' he said, 'except that they play it in supermarkets.'

'Not muzak, moussaka,' I said. 'It's a Greek dish, you eat it.'

'You might eat it, but I'm bloody sure I don't,' he said.

'No,' I said, 'and neither do Jews. Not orthodox

133

Jews, that is. Not when it's got a white sauce on the meat.'

'You interest me, Farrow,' he said.

'There's a dish of it out there in the oven.'

'Fancy some, do you?' he said.

'Look you want to hear this, or not?'

'Of course I do. Proceed.'

'Well, when we were here on Saturday, Ruth was cooking a meal, and I noticed she used separate sets of dishes. One for dairy stuff, and one for meat and such like. Now *that* is the orthodox way.'

'So?'

'So now she's very *un*orthodox.'

'Remarkable,' Charlie said. 'Not her — you.'

'How the hell d'you make that out?'

'She's just spent nine years in an Arab prison. Do you think they were orthodox there? Do you think they fed her a kosher diet?'

'Ah .. so she must have been doing it for Green.'

'Have you had any other brilliant thoughts?'

'Just a few,' I said, 'but I'm getting to be like you, boy. I'm keeping 'em up the sleeve.'

'Give me a for-instance.'

'What do you want the photograph for?'

'I want it for a keepsake,' he said. 'Something to remember her by, when we put her where she belongs.'

Well, I might have known he wouldn't tell me. But he didn't have to, I knew. He made a couple of telephone calls and then we left the house. First stop, Bank Top railway station where I sat out in the car while Charlie went in about his lawful occasions. Then we dropped down the hill to Park Place, where we found Royston waiting in his cubicle. The time was twenty past one and my stomach was rumbling like a train in a tunnel.

'Had your lunch yet?' Royston said.

'No, he hasn't,' said Charlie, 'and where's the woman?'

'She's having a cup of tea.'

'Being nice to her, are you?'

'Well, you don't think we — '

'Heaven forfend! I know you're not into Police Brutality.'

'She's asked if she can have Green's car.'

'Sounds reasonable. Let her take it.'

'She wants the body, as well. Something to do with Jewish burial rites.'

'Why not?' Charlie said. 'Let us observe the humanities.'

'You feeling all right, Chas?' I said.

'Do you want us to let her go now?'

'Where is she?' Charlie said.

'She's in the inspector's office. Devine's away for the day.'

'Lead on then, Macduff.'

'You want to see her?'

'Only to say goodbye.'

'What's all this? Are you leaving us?'

'Ask not the day, nor the hour.'

Charlie's expression never changed, but the way he was carrying on augured well for a speedy wrapping-up and a return to my ain fireside. As I tailed them along the lino-laid corridor I felt my step become light and I didn't even care if I went without lunch. Ruth had finished her tea and the woman constable keeping her company was clearing their cups away. Royston gave her the wink and she picked up the tray.

'Thank you, sergeant, that's all.'

Royston shot me a glance at this, but he followed the WPC and I closed the door behind them.

'Now then,' Charlie went on, 'how are you feeling, Miss Levinson?'

Ruth was suitably dressed in a black two-piece suit and a plain white blouse and black patent shoes with low heels. She was sitting in a wooden armchair with her knees pressed together and her head held high, handbag clasped on her lap. Her eyes were

135

red-rimmed, as if she'd been crying. She could have been rubbing them, though. She spoke with none of her old bravado.

'Are you in charge here?' she said.

'No, no. As a matter of fact, we're just leaving.'

'Why was I brought down here?'

'Didn't they tell you?'

'They've told me nothing.'

'It's the inquest, I'm afraid,' Charlie said. 'They want to make sure you'll be here for the inquest.'

'But I don't even know when it is!'

'It'll be held on the eighth, that's on Wednesday.'

'Well of course I'll be here!' Ruth said. 'But in the meantime, I've got things to see to, and they won't let me have Tony's car.'

'Have forensic finished with it, Farrow?'

'Yes, I think so,' I said.

'So there's no reason why Miss Levinson shouldn't take it?'

'None that I can see.'

Charlie turned to the woman. 'I'll have it released right away — but you won't be poling off in it, will you?'

'Of course not!'

'Good, then it's all okay.'

'It's not all okay. There's a question of burial.'

'Ah, now that,' Charlie said, 'is something we can't do much about. It's up to the coroner, you see. He won't release the body until his jury gives a verdict.'

'But — '

'Sorry,' Charlie said, 'it's no good arguing, Miss Levinson, because that's the way things are. I know it's only a formality — a clear case of suicide — but the law is the law.'

Ruth bit her lip. 'May I go now, then?' she said.

'Just a minute, I'll have your car brought round. Farrow . .'

'Right,' I said.

'There goes one helluva cool cookie, Chas.'

136

'She's a real professional,' he said.

'A professional?'

'Aren't you hungry yet, Farrow?'

'You kidding? I'm starving!' I said. 'But why this uncommon care and solicitude?'

'You know what Napoleon said: An army marches on its stomach.'

'It wasn't Napoleon,' I said. 'I've told you before, it was Julius Caesar.'

'Bullshit. Take the car, and go and indulge your favourite vice.'

'Why d'you want me out of the way?'

'Listen, if you're going to argue . . .'

'Jesus, no!' I said. 'This is a rare and momentous occasion!'

'Take advantage, then,' he said.

When I left him alone in Royston's office it was getting on for two o'clock and, knowing Darlington's restaurants now, I suspected that most would be closed. Or, if not closed, depleted of grub. Everything good on the menu now "off", and they'd be wanting to pile the chairs on the tables. I thought about the King's Head but then I thought, the hell with it. This looked like being the last day, so might as well be adventurous. Try somewhere else, for a change. Somewhere like the Europa, perhaps? Yes, I rather fancied that.

I opened out the Rover's huge engine and shot along Grange Road and was there in about three minutes. Actually, it was quicker and easier than nipping up to the Old King's Head, because there was no need for the time-wasting business of trying to find a place for the car. There was plenty of space in the carpark out front, not a dozen yards from the door and in very beautiful surroundings. With the golf-course all around, it might have been way out in open country. I was going to enjoy this lunch.

Incidentally, and to avoid confusion, do not seek the Europa now. It has reverted to its previous name,

the Blackwell Grange Hotel.

The lovely old 17th-century manor-house was equally attractive inside, in spite of its having been tarted up in psuedo-regency style. The chairs and sofas were all upholstered in a rich dark olive-green which went well with the gold and ivory decor. They were very comfortable, too. The big bar off to the left of the entrance was empty and seemed remote, so I patronised the one by the dining-room. The girl behind the bar, a pleasant lass with long blond hair, poured me a large Glenmorangie and assured me that lunch would be served until three o'clock, and maybe beyond. I relaxed and filled a pipe.

Half an hour later I was good and ready to get stuck into some scoff. The vast and airy dining-room had a splendid atmosphere and plenty of people still tucking in. It made me feel civilised and far removed from murder and muggings and unseemly brawling in parks.

In deference to the somewhat muggy day I started my meal with cold soup, a smooth and creamy vichyssoise. Then a big fat sole, tenderly grilled and left on the bone, with buttered asparagus tips and flageolets cooked with a whiff of garlic. I forbore from ordering spuds, because I'd seen the cheese-board as I came in and the Brie looked in excellent form. Perfect for finishing off the Niersteiner — just a half-bottle, of course — and after that, a Turkish coffee. The bill came to thirteen quid, but I paid up without a murmur. Witherspoon would faint with shock, but Witherspoon could go and stuff himself.

Driving back to Park Place, I felt replete and at peace with the world. Let there come what may, I was good and ready for it. I was certainly ready for any acid comment on my having been away so long, but my state of preparedness went by the board because when I got back to Park Place, my lord and master wasn't there. He was up at Durham jail meeting Commander Bill Hucklesby, head of the Yard's

138

terrorist squad. But I didn't learn this until later. All that Harry Royston knew was that Charlie had made a number of phone calls, borrowed one of their cars and had left the Station around three o'clock, forty minutes ago.

'. . . and he didn't say where he was going, Harry?'

'Does he ever?' Royston said.

'No. That was a stupid question. Well, when the cat's away. . .'

But I spoke too soon, because just at that moment Royston's telephone rang. He picked up the receiver and listened, then covered the mouthpiece with his hand as he passed it over to me.

'Look like you got back just in time.'

'Farrow here.'

'So you're back.'

'I've been back ages, Charlie.'

'Yeah, I'll bet,' he said. 'Anyway, here's a job for you. Find out when Bridie Keegan came to Darlington. I want to know the exact date, and I want to know where she came from.'

'Where are you now?' I said.

'Never mind where I am, just get on with it.'

'What time are you going to be back, then?'

'Never mind that either,' he said. 'Just you be there.'

'Oh, charming.'

'But I was speaking to the dialling tone. I stowed away the pipe I'd been filling and reached for my Burberry. Royston looked up, grinning.

'Going out already?'

'Yes. No rest for the wicked, Harry.'

'Is it something I can help you with?'

'No, not really,' I said. 'It's just an errand, but thanks all the same.'

'How long do you think it'll take?'

'Why? What's up?'

'Well . . thing is, Mark, I'd like to get away not much later than half past five. It's the annual school

139

concert tonight, and one of my kids — '

'Rest assured,' I said. I knew I was sticking my neck out, but such was my happy mood, I couldn't have cared less. 'I'm bound to be done before then, and when I get back you nip away smartly.'

'What about your boss?'

'Don't let that worry you. I'll handle Charlie.'

'Better you than me. Anyway, thanks, I'll phone the wife now and let her know it's okay.'

'Do that. See you later, Harry.'

'Mind how you go,' he said.

A brave sun was trying to break through the haze, so in spite of a spatter of rain I opted to leave the car and walk. It wasn't very far, but I had to get across the ring-road and by the time I reached the town hall my hair was feeling decidedly damp. However, my spirits remained unimpaired and the staff up there at the Housing Department helped to keep them that way. I had expected the usual bureaucratic runaround. What I got instead was an efficient bespectacled middle-aged lady who put herself about to get me the information I sought. It took a little time, but I was back at Park Place within the hour.

'That was quick,' Royston said.

'Any further messages, Harry?'

'Not a cheep,' he said. 'I think you mate's deserted you.'

'Don't take bets on that. You got anything else on your plate?'

'I wish I had,' he said. 'Frankly, it's getting a bit boring.'

'You might as well pack up, then,' I said.

He looked at his watch. 'It's only ten past. I'm not officially off — '

'Go on, catch the wife with the window-cleaner.'

He laughed. 'No chance of that. She's a one-man woman.'

'Lucky you.'

'Well . . . if you're sure, I'll be off. See you to-

140

morrow.'

'Enjoy your concert.'

I didn't say goodbye, although the chances of seeing him again were remote. If all went well that night, Charlie would not hang around. He'd be up and away before the smoke cleared, and I would be with him. Well, that was the nature of the business. It didn't pay to make friends or to establish lasting relationships.

That would be storing up grief.

Bridie Keegan and her dreadful old crone of a mother had hit the Darlington scene a little over ten months ago, on the 22nd of July, to stay with Bridie's sister and her builders'-labourer brother-in-law. It was thought they had travelled north from London, but how long they'd been living there seemed very much open to question. The sister and her husband had gone back to Ireland in the December of last year, ostensibly for the Christmas festivities. In fact, they had never returned.

Which left Bridie and the *materfamilias* ensconced in a council house which had someone else's name on the rent book. The council had thought about that and decided just to leave them there. It was easier and cheaper that way than to find them alternative accommodation, something they'd have to do if they turned them out of Inkerman Road. A situation far from uncommon.

'Isn't it marvellous,' Charlie said. 'We must be the biggest shower of idiots the world has ever known. We let these animals come and go exactly as they please, no checks, no passports, no nothing. Christ, we even give 'em the vote! They put their own kind into *our* bloody parliament!'

'Yes, I know all that, Charlie,' I said, 'We've been over it once or twice in the past.'

'Makes you want to vomit!' he said.

'What makes the date so significant?'

141

'Good God! You're as bad as them! Don't tell me you've forgotten what happened on the 21st of July!'

'No,' I said, 'I haven't forgotten. What I'm asking is, do we know of any connection?'

'The *date's* the connection,' he said. 'The date, and the fact that Bridie's description fits that of the woman in the case. The woman who was never found — remember?'

I remembered only too well. The papers had headlined it DAY OF BUTCHERY and, in more ways than one, it was.

A blue Morris saloon, registration number LMD 657 P, left among the cars parked on Hyde Park's South Carriage Walk, had been a lot less innocent than it looked. It contained a bomb made up of twenty pounds of ultra-high explosive and then thousand six-inch nails. The park was thronged with sightseers and tourists, men and women and kids, all waiting to see the Household Cavalry ride by. The "long guard" that morning comprised a troop of the Blues and Royals, sixteen mounted men. When, at precisely 10:44 a.m., the troop drew abreast of the Morris saloon, the bomb was radio-detonated by some brave soul skulking in the safety of a screen of trees a hundred yards away.

A huge explosion shattered the tranquil morning. Witnesses said the sky rained blood. The carnage was beyond belief. Men and horses flung into the air, their bodies ripped to tatters by a storm of hurtling nails, and hard upon the thunderous boom the terrible whinnying screams of animals in their death-throes. Bodies everywhere. Here an old lady with her foot blown off, there a mutilated child. Upwards of fifty soldiers and civilians injured, or dying, or dead. And that was only bomb number one.

The second explosion came two hours later, this time in Regent's Park, where the band of the Royal

Green Jackets was entertaining the crowds. The place, and the timing, were diabolical. Workers from nearby offices eating their sandwich lunch, others enjoying summer holidays. Six bandsmen were killed instantaneously, more died in hospital. Over half a hundred civilians were injured, many of them seriously.

Oh yes, I remembered, all right. I did forget at times, when like most other normal people I had other things on my mind. But not Charles McGowan. He *never* forgot. Not for one moment, waking or sleeping. He took it to bed with him and he woke with it in the morning. He ate it with his food and he drank it with his cup of tea and his occasional bitter lemon, no ice. He smelled it in the everyday smells and he breathed it with the air. And it wasn't only on account of his nephew. He had been exactly the same throughout all the years I had known him, and I knew him very well.

But the odd thing was, I knew nothing *about* him. I saw him only on jobs and never at any time in-between. He appeared unannounced out of no-where and I had no idea whence he came or where he went after he left me. I didn't know where he lived or what he did when we weren't together. I knew he was a bachelor, like me, because that was an inviolable rule of the Section. Should any of us disappear, there had to be no-one really to care. No mothers, no wives, no close friends. Our sort of life is no life at all. It is sterile, and lonely, and sad. James Bond and his women are the purest of fiction. It just isn't like that at all.

Thinking back on the parks explosions, 'It could be coincidence,' I said.

Charlie leaned forward with his forearms flat on Royston's desk. 'If you believe in that sort of thing.'

'And you don't, do you?'

'No. She's a co-ordinator, isn't she? She's a bloody setter-up. She set up the London operation, and she

143

was on the spot to set up things here. Now *that* might have been a coincidence.'

'Okay, so it's cards-on-the-table time, Charlie. How does Ruth Levinson fit in?'

'She doesn't, and she never did. If she's lucky, she's still in jail. My guess is, they've blown her away.'

'So that's why you put the photograph on the train. I thought as much,' I said. 'Has London identified this other one?'

'Oh, yes, no bother at all. They can't wait to be having a chat with her.'

'Can't they? Who is she, then?'

'Real name Yasmin Dawud, a.k.a. Jean Price, Dorothy Sharman, and now Ruth Levinson . . .'

Charlie went on to recite the woman's history just as though he were reading it from a printed dossier. Which, in an interesting way, he actually was. He was one of the very few people – and certainly the only one I ever knew – with a true eiditic memory. He could look at a document for several seconds and remember it word for word not only for days or for weeks, but for years. It was a wonderful facility and had he chosen to pursue a business career it would have helped him make the top of the tree.

Yasmin Dawud, daughter of a wealthy Sandhurst-educated Jordanian who later became a sinecure diplomat based permanently in London, spent most of the first seventeen years of her life in England. She was a spoilt child, wayward and rebellious, and in a belated attempt to instil into her some sense of responsibility, her despairing father sent her to a convent school. It was a very serious mistake, because this exposure to discipline came far too late. Yasmin hated it and her hatred was a festering thing. So the efforts of the nuns were counter-productive. Yasmin escaped as soon as she could, intent upon returning to Jordan.

Where she met and fell in with a group of insur-

gents headed by one George Habash.

George Habash, still alive and well and last heard of somewhere in Syria, was and is the Marxist-Leninist founder of the terrorist PFLP. Yasmin's natural virulence had found an outlet. She embraced the Palestinian cause and became one of George's most fervent disciples. She also became the lover of George's first lieutenant, a bloodthirsty fanatic by the name of Nayif Hawatmeh.

In 1973, at the time of the second Arab-Israeli war, Nayif lost patience with George's policy of restraint and broke away to form his own splinter group, the Popular Democratic Front. Exhilarated by the prospect of bigger and better acts of violence, Yasmin went along with him. She was put through an intensive course of training at one of the terrorist camps in Syria and it was there that she met, among her co-trainees, a contigent from the IRA. It was the start of an unholy alliance.

It was a foregone conclusion of course that Yasmin, first under one alias and then another, be sent to work in England. She was ruthless and clever, but an inherent recklessness led her to make mistakes and she came eventually under the eye of the Special Branch. She was promptly withdrawn for a spell, but she turned up a couple of years later, by which time she had learned to lie low.

In 1982, when Yasmin was thirty years old, two things happened: Israel signed a contract with Britain to buy the new Challenger tank and an Israeli army invaded the Lebanon.

The foregoing was fact; the rest speculation.

Nayif, only too well aware of the Israeli army's devastating expertise in the field of tank warfare, determined to prevent Israel from taking delivery of the new model by sabotaging production here in Britain. When his intelligence sources reported an item concerning the imminent release of Ruth Levinson, and when he learned further that she intended

to join an English family one of whose members actually worked for a firm of engineers supplying a vital component of the Challenger, he must have seen it as a heaven-sent opportunity. Yasmin was recalled once again and given a crash course in Jewish *mores*, and the substitute was duly made.

Charlie constructed this theoretical scenario and Charlie was usually right.

'Do you think Nayif knew that young Green was with MOSSAD?'

'I doubt it,' Charlie said. 'That was just another blessing from Allah.'

'What about the deaths of Green's folks?'

'Had to happen, didn't it? They were the only people alive who might just possibly remember enough about the real Ruth Levinson to spot, or suspect, that a switch had been made.'

'So the car crash wasn't an accident.'

'Was it hell as like. We are dealing here with people who do not mess about.'

'Jesus, two perfectly innocent old codgers — the entire family destroyed.'

'Yes, Yasmin murdered young Tony, all right.'

'Looks very much like it,' I said, 'and it also looks as though Green never told her he was working for MOSSAD.'

'That's right. He probably didn't want to involve her. But when *we* started nosing around, she thought up a way of taking the heat off. The bloodthirsty bitch put him down.'

'So we're partly responsible, Charlie.'

'Don't talk like a pillock,' he said.

'I must say she took one hell of a risk.'

'You're at it again,' he said. 'What was risky about it? She knew we thought that she too was with MOSSAD. Why should she kill one of her own?'

'So she slipped him some sleepers, stuck him in the car, took some sleepers herself and waited for somebody to find him.'

146

'You work that out all by yourself?'

'No need for sarcasm, Charlie — and there's still one other thing: how did she know about Josef Peltz?'

'She was watching Green, wasn't she?' he said. 'She could have found out in any number of ways. We're talking about a pro, we're talking about a lady with nous.'

'I suppose so. What now, then?' I said.

'We wait for the proverbial witching hour.'

'Let's go get some grub, then,' I said.

It was raining.

Charlie had insisted that we take up position soon after darkness fell, over an hour before midnight. We were parked on the corner of Mowden Hill View, at its junction with Barnes Road, about fifty yards above Green's house. There were two tall street lamps within that distance, one on either side of the road, and a number of cars squatting dark at the kerbsides. We were inconspicuous enough so that unless the Rover was known — and it wasn't — no-one would notice us as being in any way suspicious.

If Bridie took the obvious route from the convent in Nunnery Lane, she would approach us along Claxton Avenue, on the other side of Barnes Road, turn right down the hill and pass under a lamp-post. If she came the other way, up the hill from Lunedale Road, we would still be able to spot her although not quite so easily, because the street lamp she would have to pass then would be over on the opposite side.

I wound my window down and up to clear away the spots of rain, and resigned myself to the vigil. Green's front window shed dim curtained light.

'She might not be in there,' I said.

'She's in there, all right.'

'How can we be sure, Chas?'

'How do you think?' he said. 'Hucklesby's boys

147

have been keeping tabs.'

'Oh, we've got some help, have we?' I said.

'Don't start relaxing on that account, this is *our* party,' he said. 'All they're here for is back-up.'

'Well, in that case,' I said, 'I hope they're doing it at the back of the house.'

'Listen, Farrow,' he said, 'you just take care of your end.'

'You better tell me the drill, then,' I said. 'Do we grab the fair Bridie as soon as she shows?'

'No, we sodding well don't. We nab 'em well and truly together.'

'What for? We've got the tape.'

'The dame on the tape could be Old Mother Reilly.'

'Balls. Ruth called her twice by her name.'

'Your memory's improving, Farrow.'

'You're up to something,' I said.

'I'm up to taking them hand in hand.'

'Balls again,' I said. 'I know you, Charlie.'

'What you know would go on the back of a stamp.'

'Yeah — "Charles McGowan is a devious bastard".'

'Trouble with you is —'

'I know. Don't bother to tell me all over again.'

'Better check it,' he said.

'I checked it this morning.'

'Check it again.'

'Have a heart,' I said, 'I'm going to wear out the action.'

'I'll get you a replacement,' he said.

'I don't want a bloody replacement.'

'What you want,' he said, 'and what you get, are two different things. Now, check it.'

'What bullshit,' I said.

But I hauled out the Smith & Wesson and went through the old routine. He went through the self-same motions.

'Are you satisfied now?'

'Yes I am. Just don't hesitate to use it.'

148

'I don't shoot women,' I said.

'Knackers. You shot that lady in Burgos.'

'Lady! Jesus Christ! She was a millisecond away from blowing my head off! And in any case,' I went on, 'I didn't shoot her, it was Angie who shot her.'

'Ah, yes, so it was,' he said, 'your big fat American girlfriend.'

'She was big, but she wasn't fat.'

'Well, you ought to know.'

'As a matter of fact —'

'Watch the road,' he said.

'I'm watching it. As a matter of fact — '

'She was CIA, as well. You nearly slipped up that time, Farrow.'

'Slipped up, nothing!' I said. 'I got the job done, didn't I?'

'Yes, but only just.

And so we whiled away the waiting-time, sitting there in the car with the rain coming down and the cold building up. There were sporadic ripples of activity, unusual for a rainy Monday night, with dinner-guests leaving and residents returning from wherever it was they had been. I longed for a pipe and I could have done with a pee. Charlie reamed out his nose. A doddery old geezer walking his dog stooped to peer into the car and Charlie was very rude to him. The old chap shied away, dragging at his pooch to hurry back indoors.

'You've done it now, boy,' I said. 'He's probably gone to phone for the coppers.'

'Let him,' Charlie said. 'He'll get no joy out of Park Place tonight. They've been told to keep well away.'

'You think of everything, don't you, old buddy?'

'Yes and don't you forget it,' he said.

As the minute hand of the dashboard clock began its snail's crawl up towards midnight, Barnes Road quietened down. Fewer and fewer cars came and went and pedestrian traffic ceased. Ground floor

lights were extinguished to be replaced by lights upstairs and soon most of those had disappeared. Green's house had been shrouded in darkness for twenty minutes or so and I visualised Ruth — or Yasmin — sitting there in the gloom, waiting for her clandestine visitor. At five to twelve, I said:

'Do you think she's going to turn up, Chas?'

'No doubt about it,' he said. He switched on the windscreen-wipers. let them make a couple of sweeps, then switched them off once the screen was clear. 'Can you see all right?'

'Hang on — '

I rolled down my window and left it open. The cloud-bank was moving on, trailing a skein of ragged tatters across a watery quarter-moon. I kept snatching glanced at the green-glowing clock. Four minutes, three minutes, two.

'Yasmin must have warned her off, Chas.'

'Belt up and listen!' he hissed.

I held my breath, but I couldn't hear a thing except the tiny snicking of the clock. I had opened my mouth to say as much, when I *did* hear it. Very soft. The whisper of flat-heeled shoes on wet pavement. Almost instantly, she appeared. A small dark figure rounding the corner out of Claxton Avenue. She turned down the hill and increased her pace to trot through the circle of light shed by the street lamp she could not avoid. As she hurried in and out of its glow, I caught a good look at her hard, set face. Then she was just a dim shape moving quickly downhill to turn in abruptly at Green's ready-open front gate.

'By God, that's her! She came, Chas!'

'What did I tell you?' he said.

Tuesday

'Come on, Charlie, how much longer?'

'Just hold your horses,' he said. 'Give 'em time to get cosy.'

'Cosy? They're probably in bed!'

'Lovely. All the better.'

'All the better for what?' I said. 'I don't see the point in this hanging about.'

'Stop your bloody whining,' he said. 'I say we wait, and that's what we're doing.'

'But it's twenty to one!'

'I know. In an hour, it's going to be twenty to two.'

I hunched down low on the squab and laid my head back and closed my eyes. 'All right then, please yourself. You can give me a nudge when you're ready to move.'

'Stay alert, you idle sod!'

I took no notice. I knew I wouldn't sleep. I slumped there listening to the clock and the even sound of Charlie's deep breathing. He did it at times like these, to keep his blood-stream well charged with oxygen. I should have been doing it, too, as per the Sutherland training. My bad leg had started to ache and I shifted around for an easier position. It didn't stay easy for long and my shoulder came out in sympathy. With the onset of fatigue, all the old hurts reasserted themselves. I sat up and stretched and yawned.

Charlie was twisted round on the seat with his back against the door, looking past me through the open window, down towards Green's house.

'Can you see what I see, Farrow?'

'Such as what?' I said.

'Light from under Green's garage door.'

I stuck my head out of the window. 'Well . . . maybe . . I can't really tell. It could be a reflection

151

from the street lamp.'

'Just nip out and make sure.'

He reached up to deactivate the courtesy light before I opened the door, and I stepped out onto the murk. I crossed the narrow street and walked a few yards down the hill on the opposite side to Green's house, and crouched in the shadow of a hedge in a driveway. Charlie was right. It was there. A thin strip of white fluorescent gleam along the bottom of the garage door. I turned around and went back to the car.

'There's somebody in there,' I said. 'Unless she forgot to turn off the light.'

'She didn't forget,' Charlie said, 'it's been on less than a couple of minutes.'

He turned the ignition key and the powerful modified engine fired in fits and starts, temperamental as ever.

'*Come on, you bastard!*' he said.

'Give her a good burst of throttle, Charlie.'

'What — and wake the whole neighbourhood?'

The trouble with that big souped-up job was that it took some time to warm up, and Charlie had no time to spare.

'Give us a push,' he said.

'You *what*?'

'Get out, and give us a push! I'll coast her down the hill.'

I sighed and climbed out of the car again. The Rover weighed almost a ton, but I managed to start it rolling. Charlie steered sharp left and the big car began to freewheel down Barnes Road. It did not stop for me so I set off, trotting, after it. Charlie was showing no lights and now there were no coughs and spits from the engine. He must have switched it off.

As I angled across to the opposite pavement, several things happened at once. I heard the twang of springs and hinges as Green's garage door was

thrown up, and twin beams of light from dipped headlamps streamed across the road. The Rover's engine hiccuped then as Charlie tired to get power, and the big car bucked like a drunken mule. But now it was gathering speed, trundling down the hill under gravity.

Then I heard the fierce roar of another engine and a car shot out of the open garage and up the steep little drive, with the Rover on a collision course. I was running down the hill towards them, dragging the pistol clear. The car on the driveway didn't quite make it. It hit the side of the Rover with an enormous rending crash, just as Charlie was thrusting his door open. A loud yell of pain and rage and I feared the smash must have trapped his leg. I was still thirty yards away, closing as fast as my bad leg would let me. I saw the door of the small car swing open. A lithe dark figure sprang out and was off and away like Sebastian Coe, tearing down the hill.

The cars were locked together in the shape of a top-heavy "T". Charlie's door was jammed tight and, with it, the hem of his Burberry. He was trying to struggle out of the coat, all the time yelling at me.

'Use it! Use it, you bloody fool!'

I had no intention of gunning down what I thought was an unarmed girl. But as I swerved around the cars I felt my sick leg give way. I lurched against the Rover's nearside and just as well that I did, because I saw the red blast of a muzzle-flash and heard the booming report and could have sworn I felt the wind of a bullet. Yasmin fired again, and this time the slug caromed off the the bumper with a screaming banshee wail.

I flung myself down across the bonnet with the pistol gripped in both hands and the butt resting firm on the radiator top. A third shot from down the road shattered the Rover's windscreen, missing me by a foot. Where had she got the gun — from

Bridie? Where the hell were Hucklesby's boys? I swung up the barrel and sighted on her as she twisted to fire again. She was caught in the light from the lower street lamp and I had her dead to rights.

But I couldn't pull the trigger. A slug from a ·357 magnum placed anywhere in the trunk will collapse and destroy the nervous system and kill without a doubt. Hit a limb, an the man goes down and there's no way he's going to get up. I lowered the sights and squeezed one off. The recoil slammed at my palms and the huge blast thundered around the houses. Yasmin whirled like a top, then bounced off the sidewalk into the gutter.

Charlie was free of his coat and lunging across the inside of the Rover to get out of the nearside door. I hobbled down the hill towards the crumpled form, not knowing whether my aim had been true. I heard Charlie running hard on my heels and I knew that he wouldn't care. To him, she would be just another dead baddie. One less to worry about. As I stooped down over the still, shapeless form, he reached us and pushed me aside.

'Never mind this one — go find Bridie!'

'Christ, I'd forgotten about her!'

I started running back up the hill with the Smith & Wesson still in my fist. As I neared the crashed cars, there was a rush of movement at the side of the house and I swung the pistol up fast. But the figure which blundered into my sights was all of six foot tall. I kept my thumb on the hammer and yelled.

'Anybody leave by the rear?'

'No, we just heard the shooting!'

'All right, get back there, then. We're missing one.'

'Roger.'

The door of the smaller car was wide open. I stuck my head inside and saw that it was quite empty. She had to be still in the house. I ran through the garage and into the kitchen and started to search

the place, switching lights on wherever I went. Soon the whole house was ablaze and unless little Bridie was stuck up a chimney, she definitely was not there.

I opened the front door from the inside. Charlie was walking up the road, as though he had all the time in the world. I met him at the garden gate.

'You won't believe this,' I said, 'but our little Bridie's done the vanishing trick.'

'Is that fact?' he said.

'How is Yasmin?'

'You missed.'

'Did I hell as like miss!'

'Yes, you did,' he said, 'you got her just below the left buttock.'

'That's what I aimed for — a leg. I suppose you wanted her taken out?'

'That was the thinking,' he said, 'but you might at least have shot her kneecap off. That would have slowed her down. It would have slowed her down for the rest of her days.'

'You don't seem too worried,' I said.

'No, no, I'm not worried. We can always swap her. She's worth a good one of ours.'

'I don't mean her, I mean Bridie. The one that got away.'

'Got away? Don't be bloody naive.'

'All right, where is she, then?'

'Look in the boot.'

'Look in what boot?'

'The boot of the car, you daft sod.'

Of course. I leaned in to take the ignition keys and limped to the back of the Ford and opened the boot lid. And there she was. She appeared to be asleep, curled up in the foetal position. I put my hand on her neck, feeling for the carotid pulse. The skin was cold to my touch, like the skin of a partially thawed frozen chicken. Charlie was watching me, with the light from the windows glinting

on his glasses.

'So that's why we waited.' I said.

I lay on my back in the bed at the guest-house, too exhausted to sleep. There was a rush and gurgle in the water-pipes. Charlie, taking his bath. I saw him in my mind's eye, soaking himself and happily grinding his teeth and making his tuneless humming noise. He would wash, and brush, his hair, drink his nightly glass of lukewarm water and go fulfilled to his bed in his clean Marks & Spencer's pygamas. He would sleep like an innocent child.

I couldn't stop thinking about the women. Bridie seemed to have been poisoned, at first. We could find no marks of violence, no sign of any blood. Then one of the Special Branch men had loosened the neck of her blouse and we'd seen the tiny blue-ringed puncture in her shoulder, close to the neck. At that, Charlie made us search for a weapon, sharp-pointed and very slim, something like an ice-pick. What we found, in a kitchen drawer, was a pair of foot-long meat-skewers. One was very clean, as though it were recently washed and polished.

Charlie explained to us, then, the old Malayan method of legal execution. The condemned man sat on a stool and his executioner stood behind him with the ceremonial kris. The needle point was located in the hollow of the left collar-bone, then one swift thrust straight down into the heart. There was said to be no pain.

He had left the stricken Yasmin lying in the gutter. Best place for her, he said. When the shock wore off, and the agony came, she had started hideously to scream and she didn't let up until the ambulance arrived. Then somebody gave her a fix. By this time, the neighbours were out in force. There were lights in every house and people in slippers and dressing-gowns stood around in shivering groups and asked each other what the hell was going on.

One old chap came to quiz Charlie and was told to bugger off.

That Charlie had reckoned on Yasmin killing Bridie was sticking out a mile. She would never cop now for the London parks job. Too much time had passed. The clue lay in that last telephone tape. Yasmin had been at pains to make sure that only Bridie knew who she really was, and she'd told the Irish woman to speak to nobody. So with Bridie dead there was no-one left who could possibly give her away. Or at least, so she thought.

But Charlie had known that we had the goods on them both. He just hated the thought of a long-drawn-out trial costing half a million pounds, and so-called life-sentences reduced to ten years and protest marchers and such and idiot do-gooders lobbying for mercy. He said it caused a pain in the arse and made a mockery of the job.

Well, perhaps he was right.

Tuesday

'Is there a bus from Darlington to your place, Farrow?'

'Hey, listen, forget it!' I said. 'You picked me up, you can drop me off.'

'Look, I've got things to do.'

'I don't give an elephant's left testicle! You are effing well taking me home!'

'You're a bloody nuisance, you know that?'

'Maybe, but I've got the keys and, just to make sure, I'm driving.'

'Well, you'd better not linger, then. We've wasted enough damn time already.'

What he meant by that was I'd flatly refused to gobble my breakfast. I slung my bag in the back, and slid in under the Rover's wheel. The door did not close properly, but it closed well enough so it wouldn't fly open. There was a bullet hole smack in the middle of the windscreen, but the starring wasn't too widespread and apart from the draught, it would pose no great problem. We might draw some curious stares, but that was the least of my worries.

We said farewell to Darlington soon after nine o'clock and a good deal less than an hour later I was turning off the A1 with the signpost pointing the way to Masham. (Masham is *not* where I live. Yorkshire is a very big county.) After that, the lanes slowed me down and it took another twenty minutes of driving before I was home sweet home.

'Coming in for a cup of tea, Chas?'

'Shift yourself,' he said. 'I told you, I've got things to do.'

As he was changing seats, I leaned in the back to get out my bag.

'One thing before you go . . .'

He slipped the handbrake and held on the clutch.

'Oh? What's that?' he said.

'Just remember that *you* were driving when this lot happened to the car. I don't want any hassle about who was doing what, and whose fault it was, and all that bullshit.'

'Put it in your report.'

'That's the whole point. I'm not doing a report. That's your department, chum.'

'Oh yes, I forgot. You can't write, can you?'

He wasn't being acid, though. He didn't actually grin of course, but I could tell it was all in fun by his tone of voice and the way he nodded. Before I could reply, he let out the clutch and trod on the throttle and the big car roared away, leaving me standing there in the lane. As I turned in at the drive, Mrs Tidy came round from the back of the house with both of the dogs on their leads. When they saw me they threw themselves forward and she had to let them go or be jerked off her feet and dragged along behind them. They rushed at me and jumped up, and I put down my bag to fondle them.

'Well, 'ello!' Mrs Tidy called. 'You're early back, Mr Farrer, I wasn't expectin' you! Did you 'ave a nice little 'oliday?'

'Yes, thanks, it was lovely,' I said.

Minor Heresies, Major Departures

By John Espey

Reminiscences
Minor Heresies
Tales out of School
The Other City
Strong Drink, Strong Language
Two Schools of Thought (with Carolyn See)

Criticism
Ezra Pound's "Mauberley": A Study in Composition
Oscar Wilde: Two Approaches (with Richard Ellmann)

Bibliography
Margaret Armstrong and American Trade Bindings
(with Charles Gullans)

Fiction
The Anniversaries
An Observer
Winter Return

Fable
The Nine Lives of Algernon

Verse
The Empty Box Haiku

Minor Heresies, Major Departures

A China Mission Boyhood

JOHN ESPEY

UNIVERSITY OF CALIFORNIA PRESS

Berkeley · Los Angeles · London

This collection consists of all the chapters I wish to preserve from *Minor Heresies, Tales out of School,* and *The Other City.*

In somewhat different form, "Coals of Fire" and "She Bringeth Her Bread from Afar" originally appeared in *Harper's Magazine.* "People of a Deep Speech," "Every Man unto His Own Family," "To Keep It Holy," "Two Masters," "Making a Man Out of Him," "War Game," "The Cave-in," "Le Scouting en Chine," "Blasphemer," "Madame Polia-kov," "I Wait upon the Gissimo," "We May Not Climb the Heavenly Steeps," "Undine," "Ramon and the North American Attitudes," "Just the Way They Do It in the States," and "The Three Worlds" originally appeared in whole or in part in *The New Yorker.*

University of California Press
Berkeley and Los Angeles, California

University of California Press, Ltd.
London, England

Copyright 1944, 1945 by Alfred A. Knopf, Inc., 1946, 1947, 1948, 1949, 1973, 1975 by John J. Espey. New and revised material Copyright 1994 by The Regents of the University of California.

Library of Congress Cataloging-in-Publication Data

Espey, John Jenkins, 1913–
    Minor heresies, major departures : a China mission boyhood / John
Espey.
        p.   cm.
    "This collection consists of all the chapters I wish to preserve
from Minor heresies, Tales out of school, and The other city"–
–Colophon.
    ISBN 0-520-08250-8 (alk. paper)
      1. Espey, John Jenkins, 1913–   . 2. Missions, American—China—
–Shanghai. I. Espey, John Jenkins, 1913–   Minor heresies.
Selections. 1994. II. Espey, John Jenkins, 1913–   Tales out of
school. Selections. 1994. III. Espey, John Jenkins, 1913–   Other
city. Selections. 1994. IV. Title.
BV3427.E8A3 1994
951.04'1'092—dc20
    [B]   93-24516
                                                    CIP

Printed in the United States of America
9 8 7 6 5 4 3 2 1

The paper used in this publication meets the minimum requirements of American National Standard for Information Sciences—Permanence of Paper for Printed Library Materials, ANSI Z39.48-1984. ♾

A

Philip E. Lilienthal

B O O K

The Philip E. Lilienthal imprint honors
special books in commemoration of a
man whose work at the University of
California Press from 1954 to 1979 was
marked by dedication to young authors
and to high standards in the field of
Asian Studies. Friends, family, authors,
and foundations have together endowed
the Lilienthal Fund, which enables the
Press to publish under this imprint
selected books in a way that reflects the
taste and judgment of a great and
beloved editor.

For Carolyn See
who always believed it would happen

CONTENTS

INTRODUCTION

Shortly after I joined the faculty of Occidental College in Los Angeles in 1938 with the rank of Instructor in English, I found that
two other new members were, like me, the sons of Presbyterian
missionaries to what we then called, in our political innocence, "the
Orient." Together with our wives, we formed our own informal
social group. Living on modest salaries, we relied on California
sherry and our own wits for much of our entertainment. Those of
us who had grown up in the Anglo-American atmosphere of port-
city life enjoyed creating charades, riddles that rhymed, and other
word games.

"I've thought of a good one," someone said one evening. "If you
had to sit down right now and write your autobiography, what
would your title be?"

I hear my voice responding instantly: "*Minor Heresies.*"

The others booed and hissed. "You've ruined the game, John,"
the inventor said. "You could at least have held back long enough
to give the rest of us a crack at it."

"I'm sorry," I said. "It just popped out. I'm surprised myself."

"Well, you win, of course—that's a terrific title—but since you've
wrecked the game for the rest of us, you'll have to pay a penalty."

"That's fine with me," I said, assuming that I would have to

come up with a new game or provide the drink the next time we got together. "What's it going to be?"

"You've got to write the book!"

This provoked general laughter and we turned to some new contest. But for me it wasn't entirely a laughing matter. Though I knew no one expected me to pay up, I realized, as our evening fun continued, that I had possibly found my subject and my own voice after several years of blundering about in the literary world with no success. In my files I had the typescripts of a sonnet sequence, a painfully allegorical Jamesian novella, an Oxford B.Litt. thesis on British criticism of American literature from 1800 to 1850, an academic murder mystery, and a false/naive children's story written as a fable. Each had been returned to me more than once by a variety of publishers, sometimes with a letter expressing genuine regret and showing a thorough reading, more often with a perfunctory rejection slip.

Occidental, which was my own undergraduate college, prided itself on being a first-class "teaching" institution. I carried a full schedule, with weekly papers and reports to read, write comments upon, and grade. I rarely found time for my own writing until close to midnight, when I would put in an hour or two before going to bed. As the most junior member of the Department of English, I began my teaching day at eight o'clock in the morning five days a week.

Once started on this new project, I found myself writing with confidence and pleasure and was sometimes tempted to forego sleep altogether before going to the campus. As I got further and further into the book, I became aware of at least one tricky problem. After leaving Shanghai under gunfire in 1937, my parents had retired to Pasadena, following a year spent in the Philippines. Though I was

a son of the manse, I was a skeptical son, a disappointment to my father. If I was going to write about what my sister, three years my elder, and I had come to feel about the mission movement without disturbing our parents or their friends, I would have to skate on very thin ice. The Chinese part of me required filial respect; the American, truth to my own convictions.

I had grown up with an inherited knowledge of the Protestant mission movement that began in the middle of the nineteenth century and, with respect to China, was to carry through to the establishment of the People's Republic. For at least two generations, many of the most talented and idealistic youth in America and Britain—my father among them—had responded to the Student Volunteer Movement or the YWCA and YMCA and had answered the call to spread the Gospel abroad.

During my own boyhood, a conflict within most Protestant denominations persisted between Fundamentalists, who held to a literal reading of the Scriptures, and Liberals, who promoted a more free, symbolic interpretation of the Bible. As part of this division, the mission movement came in for examination and criticism. A committee of American Protestants, thanks to Rockefeller supporting funds, undertook an elaborate survey. Though its report, *Rethinking Missions*, came out in 1932, after I had left China, the entire discussion had been in the air for years.

For the United States, Kenneth Scott Latourette has written most exhaustively on this subject, and in his autobiography, *Beyond the Ranges*, he touches on the underlying force that sent many young men and women overseas when he quotes from Robert E. Speer's *What Constitutes a Missionary Call?*: "If you are a Christian, the burden of proof rests upon you to show why you should not become a foreign missionary." Latourette expands on this tenet: "The chal-

lenge was stated clearly: in the United States all have the opportunity to hear the Gospel; in Asia, Africa, and many other areas, millions have not so much as heard the name of Christ; therefore, if you are a Christian, unless some clear obligation stands in the way, you should become a foreign missionary."

What I suppose must be called the "logic" of this claim can be accepted only by those who believe that the exclusive road to the salvation of one's immortal soul depends on a belief in Christianity. Even here, some flaws might be exposed, but for anyone born and raised in part in another culture, such as China, the claim stretches the limits of absurdity.

My sister and I were born in Shanghai and spent the greater part of our lives there until graduating from the Shanghai American School. Though we felt quite at our ease in both the International Settlement and the French Concession, the Presbyterian mission compound outside the Little South Gate of the old Native City was our true home. As the only foreign children in the South Gate Mission compound, we grew up depending on each other, or at least I depended on my sister. In later years we came to feel that we had saved each other, not in any mission sense, but simply as individuals. Even though we lived a transplanted middle-class American life when it came to food and clothing, we lived another part of our lives in harmony with our Chinese servants. Neither our cook nor his wife, our amah, was a Christian. We found ourselves in a trying position, knowing not only that we should honor our parents but that we should do nothing to disgrace the household or risk anything that would make our parents lose face in the eyes of the Chinese. Sometimes the roles overlapped; sometimes they seemed irreconcilable.

A problem that had faced the earliest missionaries in China typi-

fied our own feelings. We had been told more than once that when it came to a Christian burial in the earliest days of the mission movement, the presiding foreign missionary had been shocked to find a Buddhist and a Taoist priest, as well as a representative from the local Confucian center, in attendance, generously offering their assistance in what they probably thought was a barbaric rite.

The missionary had had to make clear to them that they were not welcome, that they could take no part in the service. When we heard of this from the missionaries, the incident was treated condescendingly, used as an example of the ignorance of the pagans. But when we heard of it from our servants, we learned that it was a serious breach of manners, that these men were there out of courtesy, that though their individual creeds might be in conflict among themselves, and certainly with a foreigner's, they respected the right of foreigners to their own outlandish beliefs.

Those days were long gone by the time my sister and I learned of them, but when we talked this over in private, we found ourselves in complete sympathy with the Chinese view. After all, wasn't it better to take no chances? Quite apart from the question of manners, one of the other creeds might just possibly contain the truth.

As I grew older, this difference of viewpoints came to represent for me a typical American attitude that led self-righteously into policies supporting reactionary governments abroad and an unquestioning assumption of superior knowledge in all things. The so-called China Lobby in support of the weakening hold of Chiang Kai-shek's failing regime was the prime example of this when I began to write, and little in subsequent American foreign policy has led me to change my mind.

With my typescript completed, I began the familiar round of submissions, still an innocent in the world of publishing and igno-

rant of the chances of an unsolicited book being accepted for publication by a major house. Alfred A. Knopf was high on my list, and I was pleased to get an enthusiastic letter from one of his readers, Arthur Wang—could he be Chinese?—who thought my book somewhat thin, not in content, but in bulk. Knopf was definitely interested but wondered if I couldn't make it into a more substantial collection.

Could I recite the Twenty-third Psalm? I did my conscientious best to keep up with my classes and wrote into the early morning hours. Everyone seemed pleased with the new chapters. Finally a beautifully printed contract arrived, with an advance of five hundred dollars, a substantial sum in those days, approximately a quarter of the annual salary I earned as a recently promoted assistant professor.

I had written as lightheartedly as I could about issues that concerned me seriously. For myself, I had called into question the whole intent of foreign missions. The Chinese part of me had always resented this intrusion that frequently brought "not peace but a sword" as it challenged traditional Chinese values and broke up families. I did not doubt the sincerity of the missionaries, understanding that for persons like my father the salvation of an immortal soul made all disputes over policy pointless.

Still, I remained, as far as I could honestly be, a dutiful son of the house, and before I signed the contract I took a copy of my typescript to Pasadena when my wife and I went to our weekly Wednesday evening dinner with my parents.

After dinner the following week my father and I had some moments alone in the living room, my typescript beside him. His first question took me by surprise. "Are you putting any of your own money into this, John?"

"No, I'm not," I said.

"I'm glad to hear that," he responded.

"Actually, Father," I said, "Knopf is one of the most respected American publishing houses, known not only for its list of authors but also for its care in bringing out attractively designed books."

"That's interesting," he said.

I waited. When he said nothing more I asked, "Is there anything in the manuscript that disturbs you?" and braced myself for what I thought must be the inevitable attack.

"Yes, as a matter of fact, there is. You've used two things I don't like to read about, though I'm astonished that you know anything about them." He mentioned a South Gate scandal involving two sisters and an English acquaintance's abuse of his wife.

"Why, we heard all about things like that from the servants, Father," I said and stopped. I had been on the point of saying that we probably knew more of the details than he did. "You don't deny that what I've written is true?"

"No," he said, "but I just don't like to read about such things in connection with the mission."

"If that's the way you feel," I said, "I'll be glad to take them out. After all, they're not really central to the book as a whole."

"I would appreciate that," he said. "It's generous of you to do it."

"Not at all," I said and again waited for a frontal attack. When it failed to come I asked, "Are those the only things that bother you?"

"What else would there be?"

"Oh," I said, "I thought you might be troubled by my having made one incident out of two or my occasional juggling with times and places."

He looked puzzled. "What makes you think that sort of trifle

would upset me? After all, I've spent a good part of my life attempting to harmonize the Gospels."

This witty response and its deadpan delivery staggered me. Then I realized that my father hadn't intended this to be anything more than a simple statement of fact, and I managed to say, "I'm glad you feel that way about it."

Before *Minor Heresies* came out, Knopf sold two of its chapters to *Harper's* and four to *The New Yorker*. The reviews were largely favorable, and I wondered what Father would make of Adrienne Koch's remark in the *New York Times Sunday Book Review:* "The author's minor heresies manage a minor miracle: an artful decapitation of American missionary zeal."

He probably never saw it, but if he did, a letter he received from one of his Princeton seminary classmates more than made up for whatever doubts he may have had. This good man had recognized my name in *The New Yorker* and after buying a copy of *Minor Heresies* he had read it aloud chapter by chapter to this wife. He wrote: "I finished reading the last chapter aloud to Ruth last night. Then I closed the book and, slapping my thigh, I said, 'That boy's just a chip off the old block!'"

Once again, I was taken aback. If I was a chip off either of my parents' blocks, I had always supposed it was my mother's and not my father's. The effect of this letter was for me a major miracle. Father took over the book as his own, sending copies to his friends. When one of them would write a somewhat qualified letter of thanks, suggesting that his son's book might not be the best way to advance The Work—as missionaries called their commitment—Father would throw his head back and say (what I had often said of him), "You know, some people have absolutely no sense of humor!"

COALS OF FIRE

M R. LOGAN PEARSALL SMITH has given us in *Unforgotten Years* a lively account of his passage through the state of Justification and his attainment of Sanctification at the age of seven, a conquest of Satan and a gain of Grace that changed the lives of many "Red Indians, who were converted . . . in their thousands." Had I, during my childhood in the Presbyterian mission outside the old South Gate of the Native City of Shanghai, been the first cause of any similar movement, no matter how modest in comparison with Mr. Smith's, I should certainly exploit it to the limit of my talents. Humbly I confess that I was not so blessed, and I must content myself with a record of my failure. Yet even earnest failure brings its joy and its holy reward. Though Mr. Smith will doubtless shine in the courts of heaven under his ruby diadem, I am equally certain that I shall not be far distant from him, more modestly crowned, but crowned nevertheless, by a central yellow topaz set in a floral wreath of golden immortelles; and above this chaste design a single fiery opal will burn. For I have known what it is to heap coals of fire upon the heads of mine enemies, and I have felt the same coals scorch my own scalp in return.

The differences in degree and quality of Mr. Smith's success and my own are probably due to a multiplicity of causes, the most funda-

mental of which is the distinction between a Quaker child and a Presbyterian child. Mr. Smith had to be converted. As far as I know, this is a quite superfluous act of vainglory for any Presbyterian infant born in the faith. Although the Presbyterian Church has tacitly relinquished its right to election, and although it was never openly stated that election was hereditary, there still exists a gentlemen's agreement between the Lord and Presbyterians that they and their children keep the inner track to salvation and have a reserved section on the right hand of God. And I strongly suspect, anyway, that Western Red Indians are far easier to convert than the very simplest Eastern Chinese, all of whom are so well guarded against distracting influences that they even enjoy an endemic resistance to smallpox. They may bear the scars: they do not succumb.

And yet I cannot conceal my envy of Mr. Smith. Oh, how I should have liked, when I myself was seven, to whip into submission before the Lord those alley brats who lived opposite the mission compound in a crowded little street called Mulberry Lane! Instead, like Paul, I was halted on the road to Damascus. Paul was, I realize, converted; but then, Paul had not been a Presbyterian before his setback, though I think a strong case could be made out for his being a thorough one—and a missionary to boot—after it.

The alley brats were a constant thorn in the flesh of my sister, three years my elder, and me. A gang of twenty-odd arabs, they tore through the district on errands of malice, pitched rocks across the canal and bamboo fence circling our Presbyterian compound, harried the mongrel dogs on the streets, or, failing any of these amusements, fought fiercely with each other just to keep fit.

These alley brats were led by a savage young amazon known to us as the Lady Bandit. Only once was her leadership challenged. Another wild creature, an albino girl, invaded the district for six

days. We saw her leading the gang down the road across the canal, her pink hair bristling, her pale eyes squinting as she searched for prey. The Lady Bandit was missing. On the sixth night my sister and I woke to a wild scream across the canal. The next morning the Lady Bandit was back at the head of the gang. That is all I know, but we never saw the albino again. This should be enough to explain why none of the boys in the gang ever tried to lead it.

A variety of persecutions had been devised by the alley brats for the two foreign children. When we rode unescorted in a ricksha they leapt up and pulled off my sister's hair ribbons. If the ricksha man dropped the bars and gave chase, the rest of the gang surrounded us and taunted us with Chinese words I am sorry to say we understood perfectly. Or they would grab an end of my Windsor tie on gala days and pull out the bow and knot as the heavy silk scorched out through my Eton collar. Our amah grew worried over my diminishing stock of cravats, so one day she tied a square knot in a new Windsor before she made the bow. I bore the scar of that encounter for months. We were occasionally spat upon, and more than one stone sailed over the bamboo fence.

The sorest part for us was that we were under strict orders never to retaliate. We were living witnesses of a peaceful order come to help these people, and how would it look if we raised a hand in anger against them? I do not pretend that we could have taken on the feeblest alley brat and come out on top, but there were times when we would gladly have gone down fighting, spilling our life-blood for the pagan joy of gouging out a single eye. But no. If one had been spat upon in the face, one sat bolt upright in the ricksha, taut flesh quivering and tears held back, a living witness, until one reached privacy and a washbowl.

The climax of this feud was reached one spring when our gate-

keeper went on a particularly urgent opium binge. To inconvenience no one, he left the gate unlocked whenever he lay down for another pipe. Our garden was coming into early bloom and the alley brats saw their chance. Led by the Lady Bandit, they would dash across the bridge over the canal, sweep through the gate, and start ripping off the heads of the flowers. As soon as the servants or our parents saw them and shouted, they retreated with their booty. But one afternoon neither servants nor parents were at home. The gang swarmed into the yard and ran wild through the flowers. This was too much. My sister and I dashed out the front door screaming threats, and I picked up a brickbat from the border of the walk. Taken aback by this unusual display of courage, they all retreated to the bridge—all but one.

The Lady Bandit stood a good twenty feet inside the gate, feet planted wide. She sneered at me. Only by purifying her Chinese can I translate her words into: "Well, throw it if you dare, you dirty little bastard!"

"I will if you don't get out, you rotten turtle egg!" I retorted with equal delicacy.

"You wouldn't dare, you stinking little white ape's abortion!" she yelled.

"Throw it, John, throw it!" my sister urged.

"Should I?" I whispered, terrified.

"Go ahead," my sister incited me. "We've got to do something."

"Defiler of dead strumpets!" the Lady Bandit bawled.

"Putrid bitch of a running bitch's granddaughter!" I howled back.

"Good work, John, but throw it," my sister egged me on.

"Incestuous spawn of camel's dung!" the Lady Bandit screamed.

"Bloody mother of your own brother!" I shrieked and let fly.

Swift and true as the stone from David's sling, jagged edges twirl-

ing orange in the sun, my brickbat arched out and caught her squarely on the forehead.

She staggered and clapped a hand to her head. Reeling back, she tasted blood. Then, shouting the Chinese equivalent of Murder, Rape, Arson, and Slaughter as the gang dissolved before her, she fled across the bridge into the mouth of Mulberry Lane.

My life has not been without its simple joys, but I have never dared hope to feel again the surge of primitive triumph that swept me at that instant, the savage glee that raised the hackles on my neck and spread wide my nostrils.

It did not last. Both my sister and I knew we had sinned: we would have to pay. But before our depression set in completely, we discussed the miraculous flight of the brickbat. I had never before hit anything at that range. Was it—could it have been—the hand of the Lord that had guided me? Or was it—and we shuddered—the hand of Satan? We went back into the house, the clouds of Presbyterianism closing in upon us.

Late that afternoon, when parents and servants had returned, a wrathful delegation from Mulberry Lane swept into the compound and was fittingly received in the backyard. The Lady Bandit, still gory, was with them. Her parents addressed my father with a demand for compensation, since the marriage value of their daughter had been lowered. Father, sending for medicines and bandages, set himself cleansing the wound. He suggested mildly that their comely daughter had had no right to be in our garden. The Lady Bandit's parents sidestepped this detail and demanded money. Father, tangled in a bandage, assured them that he would charge them nothing for the medicines he was using on their daughter. He admitted that his son, who, he pointed out, was much smaller than their daughter, had acted in haste and with an angry heart, but he repeated that

their daughter had had no right to be in our garden. The medicine was still free.

The Lady Bandit's parents wavered. Listening from the kitchen window, trying vainly to control my reflexes, I wondered what sort of marriage value, if any, their daughter had ever had. In later years, I should add, the Lady Bandit was betrothed to a meek-shouldered artisan and went off to live with his family for a year before the wedding. Every six weeks or so she would run away and come back to Mulberry Lane, where she made the air blue describing her prospective mother-in-law. This worthy woman would wait a few days, probably in relief, before coming to collect the girl with the fine beauty mark on her forehead. Foolishly, she never asked my advice on how to handle her. But the Lady Bandit and I were quite good friends by that time. Our family was invited to her wedding, and some years ago I looked approvingly on her small son. This, though, lay far in the future.

While Father patiently held his ground, the Lady Bandit's neighbors, acting as seconds, cornered the cook and the amah, his wife, beneath the kitchen window, out of Father's earshot. The cook led off quickly when he saw what he was in for. What right, he demanded, did they think that snotty-nosed girl had to be in our garden wrecking the flowers? He did not doubt that his master would take the whole affair to court, and if he didn't get complete satisfaction there, he would order a fleet of twenty American gunboats up the Whangpoo and blow the living hell out of Mulberry Lane.

The seconds were thrown off balance and could only counter that the girl had been hurt.

Of course she had been hurt, and rightly, the cook snapped. She had probably reviled the boy.

That might be so, the seconds admitted, but at the same time, the girl said the little white devil was himself an artist in insult. The cook smiled broadly. And why not? he wished to know. They might as well realize at once that the superior son of this house was the only son of an only son, first cousin to the President of the United States and a nephew of the King of England; and though he was not, perhaps, physically impressive, he was endowed with a happy turn for felicitous phrases and the tongue of a five-clawed dragon. He would like to add as well, the cook went on, that the family he worked for was one of amazing refinement and wealth, so rich that they could spare two piculs of polished rice over a period of ten weeks and never miss it.

That, the seconds said, was a very interesting statement.

If they thought it was, the cook replied, they had better think it over, and that in a hurry, unless they wanted the twenty gunboats. As for himself and his wife, they had no more time to waste on alley trash, for they must retire and soothe the young master's wounded feelings.

The seconds drew away and got the ear of the Lady Bandit's mother. The cook and the amah came into the kitchen, where he winked at me and she hurried out to find me some clean underwear. We watched the council break up. The Lady Bandit's head was beautifully swathed. Her parents and her parents' neighbors bowed to Father and thanked him for the liberal gift of his rare medicines. Father returned to us, haggard but at peace, and we all relaxed. Mother had a little trouble balancing the household accounts for a while, but every seventh night for the next ten weeks the cook disappeared into Mulberry Lane carrying twenty catties of polished rice.

At this point my mother took an active part. Mother had married

Presbyterianism. She was born a Baptist, and from her childhood immersion she had retained a faith in the essential goodness of the human heart that years of contact with Presbyterians had as yet failed to eradicate.

Mother decided that the alley brats would make excellent subjects for her children's Christian zeal. She pointed out to us that the alley children were not really bad children at all. They lived hard, meager lives, barren of beauty. They did not mean to ruin our flowers out of spite. Every soul had a love for beauty deep within itself that craved satisfaction, and the alley children got this satisfaction by picking—picking, not stealing—our flowers. Now, if we didn't want the alley children to pick our flowers, what could be done about it?

The innocent light of purity struck our eyes. Almost in chorus we said, "They should have flowers of their own."

Mother smiled approvingly at this budding charity. Good, but how were they to have flowers of their own?

We hesitated and then rushed on. "We will give them flowers," we said.

Mother beamed. Gradually the plan was imposed upon us. First we gathered together thirty-odd tin cans and flowerpots. Then we slipped or potted the best plants we could find, and day after day that spring we watered and cultivated them tenderly as we watched for signs of growth.

Early in the summer we had about twenty sturdy little plants: geraniums, dwarf roses, daisies, pansies, a few bulbs. Most of them were in flower. And as the plants had grown, our plans too had waxed great. This was to be only a beginning. Slowly we would lead the alley children to God. We would cultivate their souls carefully; we would have Sunday school for them and teach them the meaning of brotherly love. Eventually the alley children, clean in heart and

body, would no longer whoop through the neighborhood, but, led by my sister and me, they would march up and down Mulberry Lane singing *Onward, Christian Soldiers* in Chinese, and we would win a myriad of souls for God.

Meanwhile the gang had stopped persecuting us. We went out alone in perfect safety, and the cook assured me that he had done nothing to lessen my reputation as a hurler of brickbats and epithets. So we had no trouble when we went out into the highways and byways to invite the alley children to the compound the following afternoon at three for a surprise we had made ready. We were just wise enough to tell them that there would probably be something to eat.

The next day found everything in order. On the edge of the veranda our plants glistened in beauty and love. On one table were set out pots of tea and Chinese teacups; on another table were arranged large platters of cookies and cakes.

The gang, led by the Lady Bandit, arrived in reasonable order, and we shepherded them to the tables, where they promptly gorged themselves. Then, after a tour of the garden and a few free-for-alls among five or six of the junior lieutenants, my sister addressed the bewildered group. She told them we knew they were not evil, that they wanted beauty in their lives and we wanted them to have beauty in their lives. So we had prepared a gift of love for them that we hoped would flower into a lasting friendship between them and ourselves.

After these elaborate flourishes I gave a few halting instructions on watering the plants and putting them in the sunlight. My sister then concluded by saying that we hoped to see them again, and that we would come to their homes and see how their flowers grew.

We then gave each one a potted plant, after presenting the two

best to the Lady Bandit as a mark of special favor. This ceremony over, we all moved towards the gate, the Lady Bandit leading the way, a flowerpot in each hand. At the gate the Lady Bandit turned and smiled at us, then bowed, and the rest did what they could to imitate her. Majestically, the Lady Bandit led the procession on to the bridge while we stood watching in the gateway, our hearts filled with love for all mankind.

When she reached the precise center of the bridge, the Lady Bandit, without a flicker of hesitation, poised the flowerpots and shot out both her arms. We gasped. A dwarf rose soared over the left railing, a white geranium cleared the right, and both plants splashed into the yellow water of the canal. As each alley brat reached the same spot another plant sailed out over the water. And the entire procession, not a one of them turning, went silently into the mouth of Mulberry Lane. Not until the last rigid back had disappeared round the corner did a ribald chorus of shouts and hoots rip the air and strike upon our horrified ears.

This was bitter bread that had come back to us. We looked up at Mother. Her eyes were filling with tears, her lips were trembling. Gently, my sister took her right hand and I her left. We turned her around and, burning foreheads held high, we walked with pride and Presbyterian hearts back to the house. If there had ever been a spark of Baptist fire in us, it was eternally quenched in those moments.

THROUGH THE SCENT OF WATER
IT WILL BUD

W̵E NEVER SPOKE of the canal as the most important thing in our lives. We never said, "It is the canal that has made this possible, that we live two lives," or "If it weren't for the canal, we wouldn't see it both ways at once, the way we do." We did say, instead, "The canal certainly went up in a hurry on that tide," or, and this was our usual tenor, "The canal smells pretty fierce in weather like this." When we said this we really meant that the canal stank, but on what was presumably our side of the canal nothing ever stank; even during the seasons of most penetrating decay nothing went beyond smelling pretty fierce.

It is this distinction between the real influence of the canal and our distorted expression of that influence that brings out the canal's genuine importance to us. When I say "to us," I mean to my sister and me. What the others thought, I cannot say. One of our gravest topics of conversation was whether or not the others thought at all.

Our canal was not a majestic waterway, a cool stream running clear beneath overhanging willow boughs. No roads arched bravely across it on camelback bridges. No luxurious houseboats moved over its waters to the mingled music of porcelain winecups and native violins. Ours was a less than ordinary Chinese canal, and its bridges were horizontally utilitarian. Its relation with the Grand Canal, if

any, was that between a dignified elder statesman and his disreputable remittance nephew. Yet, like the nephew, our canal had a rowdy liveliness about it that more than made up for its lack of caste. Our canal put on no false airs. It was a canal of great sociability, a canal given to indiscreet revelations that the elder statesman would surely have thought distressingly intimate.

It was a curve of this canal that cradled us in a bend near the Little South Gate of the old Native City of Shanghai. We lived on the south bank, cut off from the old Native City proper by the canal and a network of alleys. The most accessible of these alleys went under the name of Mulberry Lane, but that and its crookedness were its only carryovers from a dimly rural past.

The new foreign city of Shanghai lay to the north of the old Native City. It was a distant thing, a tree of exotic bloom and forbidden fruit. By daylight it could be visited safely, but its nightly flowering was a remote glow to the north, foreign indeed to anyone sheltering south of the canal. Whether or not its nocturnal fragrance could pass through the barrier of the canal's ranker smells is not a question to worry us here. It could and it did, but the canal was more than enough for any preadolescent nose.

We were not alone in our compound behind the canal. In a way, we and the other inhabitants of our refuge were mildly notorious. Throughout the mission the South Gate station was known as a group of eccentrics, to put the case in its best light. In its worst light the matter showed the South Gaters as a cluster of persons who might not get on well elsewhere. The sturdy nonconformists of the mission inevitably landed at, on, and in South Gate, where the Lord's work was manifold, offering something to each one's peculiar talent. Although this was common gossip, it never disturbed the South Gaters. Each one knew in his heart that he—the gender

is largely grammatical—was the one normal person placed there to give a point of focus and a core of sweet reasonableness to the others' gyrating oddities. Consequently, we had about a dozen focal points and cores of sweet reasonableness cutting across each other's orbits in kaleidoscopic variety and abruptness.

The inhabitants of our house—a large two-story red brick pile with two attics above the second floor, and handsomely arched verandas both upstairs and down—were disturbed least of all. Our case was just and true, founded on something more than a personal intuition. It was a fact, a thing that could be demonstrated. For though the Lord's work in South Gate was manifold, His blessings were naturally limited. Our parents were the only married couple of an age to have children about them. That my sister, born in 1909, and I, in 1913, were a point of focus and a core of sweet reasonableness the succeeding pages will prove beyond any shadow, any suspicion of a doubt.

My sister and I were familiar from early youth with the ugly rumor of South Gate's eccentricity. It filtered through closed doors at mission meetings. It was implicit in the way some people said "from South Gate." I will not go so far as to say that it was demonstrated before our eyes. That would be unfair, for when we were older and had ventured into other mission stations, we usually felt that theirs was the true eccentricity. This may, however, have been the result of our being in a small way South Gaters ourselves, so that we always saw others as trees walking. But granting that there was some foundation for the rumor, it is obvious that when I turn back to those days I have no difficulty in finding characters. There is no need to puff up any of the Courtesy Aunts and Courtesy Uncles to make them strongly individual personalities. Indeed, the problem is to soften them, to reshape them a little, so that they will

seem to the eyes of others as truly human as they were, and not as persons made fey by the touch of the Lord.

The Courtesy Uncles were few and were usually just Uncle John or Uncle Sidney, Uncle Jim or Uncle Enos, though we did have, from his Chinese name, an Uncle Mang. But the Courtesy Aunts were many and were curiously divided. Some of them were regular Aunt Emma, Aunt Julia, or Aunt Bess, but others were aunted with their last names and became Aunties. Thus there were Auntie Silsby, Auntie Cogdal, and, most curious of all, Auntie Moh, whose English surname was Morton. The general distinction was one of age, the older ladies being the Aunties, the younger the Aunts, though they were really an ageless group. Our own classification was made on the grounds of our reception: one sect welcomed our calls with cookies and weak tea, the other with a glass of milk and a Bible verse.

These were the South Gaters. With them were their servants, who had their own foibles. One of the Courtesy Aunts had an excellent old man who went on glowing drunks every other month. The Courtesy Aunt kept him on because he was such a good cook. My sister and I always wondered if she realized the blissful union of the two qualities and knew that most of her meat had been well seasoned with wine before it was borne to the table in unsteady hands. This cook was converted at regular intervals and thus was a source of constant rejoicing.

Another cook on the compound suffered from what his mistress called "an unfortunate hereditary malady." The gatekeeper was a slightly senile opium addict, but no one was greatly disturbed by that. This was quite sensible, for the worse he became, the more glorious would be his day of redemption. Our own cook had run away from home in his youth to join the army—what army I don't

know—and he varied his accounts of military adventure according to the size, age, sex, and degree of salvation of his audience. On the infrequent occasions when my friends applaud a story I have told, I secretly thank God that our cook taught me so early a decent respect for the truth.

Around all of us the canal curved, describing an accurate quarter circle. At least that would be the cook's way of describing it. Holding firmly to a higher truth, I am forced to admit that there was another compound across the canal on part of that arc. This housed the Boys' School, a place we rarely visited alone. It had its interests, chief among them a monastery adjoining its northern limit. If we listened closely by the monastery wall, we could hear the monks whiling away their holy hours at what I am sure were harmless games of cards and dice, aided by cups of what I am sure was tea. And the higher truth would insist that the canal did not describe an accurate quarter circle, but bent around us rather in the shape of a sickle.

Yet all this, as the cook would point out, is mere confusion. The Boys' School faced only a small part of the canal, and our own compound was the center of everything important. Our family's part of it was shielded from the canal by a bamboo fence. In front of the red brick house was a circle of grass that, by the higher truth, was really an oval. Near us was a double house of gray brick that usually housed two or more Courtesy Aunts. This little segment was cut off from the Women's Bible School on the north by a bamboo fence. On the south we were separated from the graveyard by a mud and plaster wall, and to the west were fenced off from the Girls' School. One bridge joined the Girls' School to the road across the canal, another did the same for the Women's Bible School, while the third bridge was our own. Gates led from one section of

the compound to another, and though they were supposed to be locked, they were usually left open. When I reached the age of thirteen, the regular locking of the gate between our backyard and the Girls' School, done at the insistence of one of my more worldly Courtesy Aunts, was a most premature tribute to my virility.

Until my manhood was thus rudely forced upon me, the whole compound was our playground. We could climb trees, try to roller-skate on the cement walks of the Girls' School, bang tennis balls against the graveyard wall, or romp over the mounded graves. We often consorted with the dead, especially those whose coffins had a startling way of exposing themselves after a heavy rain. Still, in spite of all these attractions, the canal and the road along the farther bank remained our greatest diversions.

A little below us, towards the Whangpoo River, the road and the canal passed a Buddhist temple whose priests prospered in getting the damned out of the many Buddhist hells. This they did, eye for eye and tooth for tooth, by ringing a specially dedicated bell at a high price. I once wandered into the bell tower alone and let go the swinging beam against the side of the bronze monster. I got in three strokes before the scandalized priests reached me and put an end to my design for free salvation. I have always been happy in the thought that somewhere a small part of a poor and anonymous sinner has been saved from eternal torment by this unselfish act.

Half a mile up the canal from us was a Catholic mission that we visited from time to time. Safe against the follies of popery in our triple brass of Presbyterianism, we were tolerant to the point of eating the pastries that the kindly Belgian Mother Superior gave us. Much as we enjoyed these and the company of the younger nuns, who were not above a bit of a game in the garden, the most attractive thing about the Catholic mission was its possession of an insane

asylum. This was vastly impressive to us, and no visit to the Catholics was a complete success if we had not been able to get at least a peek through one of the windows. One peek was good for a month's clairvoyant elaboration.

A pleasantly civilized exchange took place between these Catholics and ourselves. Whenever an unstable member of our flock found the strain of intellectualism too great and declined into a quiet madness, we would send him or her over to the Catholics, not having any separate Presbyterian insane asylum. The Catholics would cherish, comfort, and finally restore the stray to us. As far as I know, these wanderers always returned, so long as the bills had been paid, with faith intact; surely a most seemly and Christian arrangement in all its parts.

Beyond the Catholics and at the West Gate of the old city lived a group of Seventh-Day Baptists. They were very reasonable on the subject of Sabbath observance, by no means as rampant as Seventh-Day Adventists. One gentleman of this mission even told me quite publicly that he didn't think I would go to hell just for observing the wrong day. I like to think that that "just" was a slip of the tongue, for they were a gentle breed, these Baptists, and our very good friends.

These were the chief ports of piety along our canal. The canal may not have been the cause of their mutual tolerance, but it did it no harm. We heard wild stories from other parts of China, stories of battles between the lesser breeds for the souls of a few wretched sinners. This sort of thing was unthinkable along our canal. There were far too many souls about anyway, and if one person saw fit to become a Catholic, another to turn Seventh-Day Baptist, a third to remain a Buddhist, while a possible fourth elected himself to Presbyterianism, there was certainly no outcry of protest along our

canal. Even if there had been, the canal would have swallowed it up in its own noise.

It was a part of the canal's nature either to close us in or to lead us away from ourselves. There was always the road to watch, the road on the far bank with its daily traffic of small merchants and coolies. Droves of sweating pigs grunted past daily to the slaughter and were often allowed to wallow in the mud of the bank. A red-letter day brought a funeral or a wedding procession. It made little difference which; banners and brassy music went with each, banners and brassy music and richly gaudy garments over the dirty rags of the hireling marchers.

Two or three knotty and almost leafless willows kept their old stations in defeat, leftovers from the days when Mulberry Lane had been more than a fragrant name. Now they were degraded, these willows; their caricature limbs served as posts for the springes and limes of professional birdcatchers, while on cool evenings the branches were hung with the caged birds of lesser gentlemen who came out to air their best songsters. Though they worked hard, the birdcatchers rarely got anything more exalted than a myopic sparrow.

Carts and wheelbarrows screeched along the road, bumping over the cobblestones, and a few rickshas swayed past. But there were mostly coolies trotting along with carrier loads and pedestrians busy with their ordinary errands of everyday commerce. And yet the canal was ever there, both separating us from and linking us with the road.

The canal had its own life, beginning early in the morning with the boats on their way to market. As the first tide came in, the waters were crowded with jostling boats, and the echoes of Babel came with the gray dawn through our nursery windows. We were

still drowsy and warm as we lay in bed, so the rich oaths reached us faintly; yet they formed the foundation of what little mastery I retain over the Chinese language: a frank foundation, broad, deep, and earthy, utterly unsuited to the niceties of polished intercourse. The boats jockeyed for position, the bellows swelled like the roars of the bulls of Bashan, and traffic was hopelessly jammed until someone yielded under profane protest. Then the boats went on, only to snarl again in a few minutes.

Later in the day things were not much milder. The canal had a permanent population who lived out their cramped lives under our eyes in boats beached high in the mud. Here the business of life, the hatings and the lovings, the begettings and the dyings, went on regularly, if a little violently.

These canal folk were old-fashioned and clung stubbornly to the ways of their ancestors. Almost our only contact with them came from foot-binding. The shrill screams at night of a little girl whose feet were being pinched and bandaged for the first time would rouse at least one of the none too gentle Courtesy Aunts. She would sally forth from the gate, armed at all points with tracts and pamphlets, a Chinese Bible, the zeal of a suffragette, and, I hasten to say, a pure and compassionate heart. After two or three hours of contest with the ancient gods she would return in grim triumph. Sadly, from the skeptical detachment of my youth and the elevation of the second-story veranda, I often saw the next day that the boat had moved on, presumably to an anchorage where the little girl could be made beautifully and perpetually unstable on her lotus feet without creating an international incident.

To my sister and me foot-binding was a most vivid horror, far more terrible than the tales of the old neighborhood baby tower, where unwanted infants, mostly girls, were left to die or be picked

up and raised as slaves. It was already a thing of the past and seemed a pleasantly romantic rather than a frightfully real device. After one of these canal encounters we would whisper back and forth between our twin beds in the nursery, enduring unutterable agonies of the imagination as each encouraged the other to evoke still more dreadful sensations of pedal pain. Later this immature masochism turned into a keen curiosity, which was satisfied only when a temporary amah from the country reluctantly obeyed the young barbarians and exposed her naked feet to them. This is the one act of my youth that I still consider a sin, but after it we forgot the whole thing; our minds were satisfied.

The canal was at first our only water supply. A long row of earthenware crocks on the far side of the cemetery wall was our reservoir. The water was treated with alum here, then boiled in the kitchen, and finally filtered through absorbent cotton in the pantry before it came to the table: a spirited water, sparkling and tangy. Even after the mystery of running water arrived, we still had our steaming baths carried in wooden buckets from the hot-water shop in Mulberry Lane. This water had been boiled, according to the proprietor of the hot-water shop, so that whatever turned up in the bottom of the tub was sanitary if not altogether delicate.

For the surrounding district the canal was a place for washing the daily rice and a convenient laundry as well. But it had additional functions. Life in China—life anywhere, for that matter—produces refuse and excrement, and what gave the canal its real flavor was its service as an open sewer. Bits of rotten vegetables wavered tentatively on the tides down to the river. The bloated carcass of a dog or cat was no rarity. Although our most advanced Courtesy Aunt had a gurgling device in her home that required exquisite tact and persuasion in the pulling of its long chain, our own arrangements were

carried out with large quantities of Jeyes' Fluid, one of the ichors of my childhood, and the help of a creature euphemistically dubbed the Fairy Queen. At midday the flotilla of "honey boats"—the grossest euphemism I have ever known—went past us down to the river.

And all this was the canal: the women washing under the stunted willows; the boys and young men bathing naked on hot summer evenings; the lives in miniature of the canal folk; the swearing boatmen; the stink, heavy and sickening, that crept over us relentlessly on warm days. As I have said, we never spoke of the canal as the most important thing in our lives. But it was always there, a canal of the living and of the dead, an encircling moat holding off the noisy life swirling about us, but linking us to that life and to itself; so that we saw it all both ways at once, and we lived, at the very least, two lives.

PEOPLE OF A DEEP SPEECH

MY LIMITED TRIUMPH over the Lady Bandit ran its course while I was seven, but it was not my first direct contact with Chinese contemporaries. It seems only fair, then, to recount a slightly more dignified, if less active, exchange of courtesies that took place a year and a half earlier, for I am reluctant to leave the impression that we lived in a state of perpetual siege, constantly warring with all those whom we should have been clasping to our breasts in Christian charity. There is, I must say, very little clasping to the breast in what follows, but it should at least serve to show that we did not altogether lack delicacy of feeling in that area—a strange sort of delicacy to come from the canal, though I think, nonetheless, that the canal was its true source.

My sister, until she was prepared to enter the second half of the third grade in the Shanghai American School, was educated at home by means of an ingenious scheme that combined what my parents considered the salient elements of the Calvert System, Rousseau's *Émile,* John Calvin, John Dewey, Madame Montessori, Professor O'Shea of the University of Wisconsin, under whom my mother had studied, and phonetic spelling. I myself gained much from this eclectic mélange, since I nibbled from a distance at its educational feast, picking up whatever crumbs my sister let fall. This lively curric-

ulum was suspended for a few months one fall in order that my sister and I might attend the Chinese kindergarten connected with the mission at South Gate. My sister has always asserted that she was sent along only because I was too timid to go alone. This view I repudiate utterly, choosing to think that our parents thought it would be good for both of us to mingle with other children and improve our Chinese.

What happened was no doubt educational enough, and in a way it could, I suppose, be called a mingling. My sister, a full three years older than the rest of us in the kindergarten, naturally felt quite superior and had a tendency to sit bolt upright in her kindergarten chair, sniffing at the antics we performed. I, on the other hand, immediately fell in love with the teacher, a Miss Zung.

Miss Zung stood something under five feet, and she was blessed with a cheerful spirit and a bubbling laugh. She threw herself enthusiastically into all our activities and enjoyed everything quite as much as we did. I recall being soberly informed once by a scholar that it was said of Sidney Lanier that he could get more out of a flute than any other man of his time. This is not faint praise even for a Southern poet, but I can do Miss Zung yet greater honor: Miss Zung could get more out of a baby organ than any traveling evangelist living or dead. Her small feet pumping furiously under the skirts of her blue serge gown, she would attack the stops, swells, and keys to bring forth rare and bewildering melodies that were always severely bound together by the repeated sounding of a major chord in the bass.

We did, I suppose, what everyone does in kindergarten. We drew pictures, counted up to twenty in Chinese, constructed elaborate edifices with blocks, and sang the Chinese versions of "Good Morning to You" and "Happy Birthday to You" at appropriate intervals.

When our interest in any of these activities flagged, Miss Zung would sit at the baby organ and we would march around the room or form a circle holding hands, skipping first to the right five times and then to the left five times. Though I was by no means the most finished performer in the room, I could hold my own. With an adoring face directed towards Miss Zung, I proceeded to do so.

Yet not everything went quite as our parents had planned. It was not that my fifteen or twenty Chinese schoolmates resented my being in love with Miss Zung. I am sure we were all too young to hold any serious views on miscegenation, and anyway all the rest of them were in love with Miss Zung too. In fact, the whole point of that kindergarten was to be in love with Miss Zung, and it has always seemed to me a very good point for any kindergarten. Even my sister on her superior level was not left untouched. No, it was not this. Nor was it the fact that I was not Chinese. After their first inevitable reticence at the presence of two strangers, our schoolfellows, boys and girls alike, were quite ready to accept us as equals despite our clothes, which must have looked bizarre to them in contrast with their own small and severely cut gowns. No, the real difficulty lay in my doubtful mastery of Chinese.

My sister was quite capable of carrying on long windy discourses in perfect order and correctness. Indeed, she did just that from time to time, discussing with Miss Zung over the heads of the rest of us some of the finer points of her education to date. But aside from these occasional demonstrations my sister withdrew into herself to picture the sophisticated pleasures of going to the second half of the third grade in the Shanghai American School the following spring.

This left me in a most embarrassing spot. I was more than eager to communicate with my potential Chinese friends. I was perfectly capable of understanding everything they said. Yet when on the

third or fourth day of going to kindergarten I ventured to take part in the give-and-take of conversation, I found that there was something wrong with my spoken vocabulary. In later years I never attained more than a halting lack of fluency in conventional Chinese conversation, and I have always believed that it was my early experiences in kindergarten that so inhibited me.

My small Chinese neighbor said something quite innocuous to no one in particular, and I replied in a spirit of good fellowship, using a phrase of jocular unbelief that I had often heard from the canal. The canal let me down badly. The whole class shivered. My sister rapped out a grim "John!" and Miss Zung looked at me with astonished and reproachful eyes. I confess I haven't the courage to translate my remark into unvarnished colloquial English, other than to say that I had told my little neighbor to commit on a member of his own family an act that neither he nor I was capable of performing at that unripe age. I had only a very vague idea of what my phrase meant; I doubt if anyone but Miss Zung really understood it, and she, I trust, in only an abstract sense; it was simply a phrase that cultivated persons did not employ in public. And yet it was a trifling commonplace on the canal, a joshing sign of good feeling between generous friends.

Miss Zung's eyes made it clear that this was the last thing she had expected to hear from the only son of my father. My sister continued to glare at me, and the class went on timidly with its projects. On the verge of tears, I bit my lips and turned back to my building blocks.

In a few minutes all was forgotten. My neighbor smiled shyly at me, and Miss Zung seemed willing to continue accepting my mute adoration. The rest of the day progressed as usual, and I kept my mouth shut. This was to be the final pattern. As long as I kept my

mouth shut except for saying "Good Morning," "Thank you," or "May I leave the room?"—formulas not difficult of mastery—everything went well, but the instant I opened my mouth to make a general observation on life, something went wrong. My idioms were all too highly flavored. The alley brats would have loved them; the well-bred members of the kindergarten were not amused. After two or three further attempts that first week I subsided into wounded silence under Miss Zung's eyes and the puzzlement of my schoolmates.

Once I had learned this lesson, kindergarten went on smoothly. My Chinese playmates accepted me as a silent partner. No one hesitated to take my hand when we marched or skipped in a circle; no one shrank from me when I sat down at the work table. I smiled at them and they smiled at me. They said nothing and I said nothing. Miss Zung's eyes were constantly merry again and we all continued to adore her.

As autumn deepened into winter our kindergarten projects began to take shape and direction in preparation for the Christmas program. I showed such an avid desire to work on the red and green paper chains for the tree that I was placed at a table in a corner of the room with two other little boys and two little girls. My task had been chosen not because I had a special gift for sticking together bits of paper, but because I had always had a discriminating palate for paste.

My first day on the paper chain was a disappointment; the kindergarten supplied only insipid flour gruel. The next day I lifted a jar of Carter's Library Paste—still my favorite brand—from Father's desk and presented it to my fellows. Whenever Miss Zung was busy elsewhere, drilling a quartet or inventing a new dance, I thrust my index finger into the firm spicy substance and then offered it to a coworker. Soon all five of us were devotees of Carter's Library Paste. I am pleased to say that I showed no favoritism. As opportunity offered, I went

round the circle of the table with strict impartiality, and I dare say few persons in the world today can boast an index finger as well and internationally sucked as that of my pale right hand.

After Miss Zung had tentatively organized her program, a happy thought came to her. This Christmas, she announced, should be an especially happy one for the kindergarten because we had two little foreign children with us, the son and daughter of those who had brought the story of Christ across the sea to the Chinese. Wouldn't it be a very fitting thing if these two would sing a special duet on the program? The room agreed that it would. Frankly, I doubt if they thought of us any longer as foreign children. I believe they accepted my sister as a superior elder being and me as a smiling deaf mute who provided lively refreshment with a free hand. But everyone always agreed with Miss Zung, and my sister and I agreed more vociferously than the rest, though I confined myself to shouting "Good!" in Chinese instead of the more natural Chinese equivalent of "You're damn tooting!" which had almost escaped me.

The following day Miss Zung set to work with the two of us at the baby organ while I kept an alert eye on my paste pot at the paper-chain table to be sure that my deputy was giving each friend his just share. The tune Miss Zung had chosen was a cheerful one, but we found trouble with the words. In one of the pauses my sister whispered to me in awe: "It's in Mandarin!" This made the effort doubly worthwhile. No one at home spoke Mandarin, that exalted dialect of the north. I now hold the view that the Shanghai dialect—one of the Wu dialects, which are, I have been told, immeasurably older than other Chinese dialects—is a far more sensitive and suave instrument than Mandarin, which even then we thought could be well imitated by pretending that we had hot rice in our mouths as we spoke. This view may be simply a reflection of the fact that

the Shanghai dialect was the only dialect I ever came near to mastering, but the prejudice appeals to me as an intelligent one.

There was no denying, however, the social prestige of Mandarin; so that afternoon we announced to Mother with keen relish that we had been chosen to sing a Mandarin song on the program. The song was called "Gau Lei Tzu" as far as we could tell, since those syllables formed its first phrase. (My romanization is probably shamefully inaccurate, for that is another field of scholarship I never conquered; yet my method is certainly no more confusing than the ordinarily accepted systems.) Mother confessed she didn't know the song, but suggested that when we learned all the words we should practice it at home with her help.

What with paste-sucking and practicing dancing in a circle, as well as drilling for all the choruses and special features, it was not until the day before the program that Miss Zung finished teaching us the two stanzas of "Gau Lei Tzu" that we were to sing. That afternoon we announced to Mother at tea that we were ready to give her a dress rehearsal.

Mother put down her cup. We stood in the middle of the sitting room. After my sister had given the pitch, we struck gleefully into the rollicking song.

Ordinarily Mother gave a fairly good imitation of being a Presbyterian, but we had scarcely completed the first line, which ran *Gau lei tzu mei li jen loo mung,* before her baser and more loosely disciplined Baptist nature began to come to the surface. By the time we had shrilled through the first stanza she was hooting and shouting with joy in most lamentable abandon.

We were hurt and a little scandalized by this display, which seemed excessive even for a Baptist and made one think of the Holy Rollers.

When she had subsided at last, Mother choked out at us: "My dears, that's English! You're singing an English Christmas carol!"

"It's Mandarin, Mother," my sister said stubbornly. "You don't know any Mandarin."

"Maybe I don't," Mother whooped back at us, "but I do know English!"

"So do we," I shouted, thoroughly miffed. "So there!"

Mother calmed herself by degrees and in the end persuaded us of the truth. We had spent two earnest weeks memorizing Miss Zung's version of "God Rest You Merry, Gentlemen," carefully imitating each nuance of her accent.

It took a tactful quarter-hour for Mother to make us see the exquisite irony of the situation, though once we had sensed it we yielded to a few reserved Presbyterian chuckles. Then we fell to, and Mother taught us the correct English words in no time. It was only at the end of this drill that a sense of uneasiness began to come over us. No matter how untutored Miss Zung's ear might be, it was too much to think that she would fail to recognize the difference between *Gau lei tzu mei li jen loo mung* and "God rest you merry, gentlemen."

At the program the next day Mother sat smiling with the other mothers as they all exchanged graceful compliments on their accomplished offspring. The kindergarten went through its performance, and at the appointed time the two foreign children took their places beside the baby organ. Miss Zung gave the pitch. Then with happy eyes the two foreign children, the son and daughter of those who had brought the Christmas story across the sea, gravely burst into the strains of their favorite Mandarin carol, "Gau Lei Tzu," while their mother modestly nodded her head in restrained and quiet approval.

EVERY MAN UNTO HIS OWN FAMILY

O UR SPECIAL PROVINCE in the house was the nursery. This was a large well-lit room on the second floor, its woodwork painted white and the calcimined walls tinted a light blue or pink. The color was presumably left up to our choice: one year my sister had her say—these were the pink years—and the next I was supposed to have mine—these were the blue. I say "supposed" because I never really chose blue. Purple was my favorite color, and every other year, when Mother said, "It's your year now, John, so I suppose it will be blue again," I would answer, "No, I think it should be purple. I want purple. I've never wanted blue."

Mother would hedge in typically Baptist compromise. "Well, at least it could be lavender, couldn't it?" I would ask. But Mother would look dubious, and after a few minutes of silent deadlock she would say, "Really, I think blue is a very nice color." "I want purple," I would reply. And every other year the nursery was blue.

In winter the nursery was heated by a tin drum, provided it was working as the excellent Chinese who made it for us assured us it would. A large cylindrical creation with a maze of passages inside, the drum was supposed to heat, or at least temper, the nursery. But the soot from the soft coal clogged the passages after a few days'

use, and though wisps of gas and some flecks of smut came from the joints, the heat often lost itself in the inner mysteries.

The pipe to the drum led through a register in the nursery floor, directly above the elaborate cast-iron Montgomery Ward stove in the living room. When the stove was taken away for the warm weather, we could remove the cover of the register and shout into the lower floor, though this was the least effective of its uses. During large tea parties, when my sister and I were sent upstairs to drink our cambric in isolation, we used to open the register and sprinkle down cake crumbs on the innocent head of any guest standing below. When we were brought downstairs to say goodbye to everyone, I often heard some good-natured advice being given Father on just how whitewash should be applied to prevent flaking. Once we tried to land a lump of sugar flush in the center of an inviting cup of tea being held within our range. Our aim was not perfect. The cube nicked the victim's shoulder, glanced off the edge of Mother's best white and gold Haviland, and shot out of sight, but from the approving buzz that followed we knew the attempt had been well received. On one memorable occasion, I am happy to admit, we drooled a little spit onto the head of a boisterous and unpolished boor from the YMCA.

Mother's social affairs were always well attended and deservedly popular; I like to think that these small divertissements arranged by my sister and me had a little to do with her success. The most exciting use we ever made of the register came during a dinner party. This dinner party was so formidable and correct that we were already in bed, our prayers said, when the guests arrived. We lay in bed, wondering what we could do to signal our interest. The dining room and the living room were separated by sliding doors that made so much noise whenever they were moved that they were always left

open. Our final scheme was effectively dramatic. Getting out of bed, we crossed to the register and lifted off the cover. Pulling up one leg of my pajama pants, I slowly lowered my naked foot and leg down through the ceiling. My leg hung there for a few moments, and then I began waving it to and fro, slowly and gently, the toes wriggling. We were rewarded by a wild feminine scream, the clatter of silver on china, and the crash of a dining chair going over. Then, and I hesitate to say it of my parents' home, all hell broke loose.

"That's Father," said my sister as a second chair hit the floor. I withdrew my leg, not hurriedly, but with dignity and a final flourish, because we had learned just how long it took Father to get to the nursery. When he arrived we were both in bed, dazed by our success. Father had not been able to identify the leg, so despite my confession we were both well thrashed, on the general theory that if one of one's children is an imp, the other too is probably a limb of Satan.

Only my devotion to the higher truth keeps me from combining this incident with a fascinating story my parents brought home from someone else's dinner party. According to this tale, the hostess, halfway through her fish and chatting cleverly with the gentleman on her right, suddenly clapped a hand on the general region of her stomach, said "Goodness! Please excuse me," went upstairs, and had a baby. Just that. When the dinner was over, the guests ascended and admired the child. This, at any rate, was the story brought home, and I have always liked it. Why my own performance was not equally rewarded I do not know. But, on reflection, this was not the disorderly sort of thing to be met with in our house.

Our own introduction to the formal social life of South Gate was occasioned largely through the game of Rook, known familiarly as "missionary bridge." The whole question of card playing was a delicate one at South Gate. We never used playing cards, as distin-

guished from Rook cards, because the Chinese gambled with them. I think that the minds of our Chinese servants and friends were credited with a supra-Chinese subtlety in our hoping that they would understand the difference. One of my Courtesy Aunts, I learned from the cook, was considered just a trifle madder than the rest of us because her servants reported that she found pleasure in gambling with herself for hours on end in the evening.

We continued, however, to make the fine distinction between Rook cards and playing cards, though my mother, I am sorry to say, did keep a deck of miniature playing cards locked in her bureau drawer. When she was sure the servants were not going to interrupt her, she locked the bedroom doors, pulled down the shades, and, giving way completely to her Baptist emotions, played a fast wicked game of Canfield in the gloom. When I returned from boarding school one vacation during my teens, I overlooked a deck of cards in one of my suitcases. Fortunately for our family reputation, Mother unpacked for me and my big deck joined her little one. I was of course examined on why I had cards with me, and at last the horrendous truth came out that I had learned to play poker at school.

"Poker!" Mother exclaimed.

"Yes, Mother," I said guiltily.

"Well, let's see how good you are," Mother answered, enthusiastically riffling the deck. "Just sit there on the other side of the bed."

I sat down, and when I got up I had acquired a number of pointers that added to my pocket money once I was back at school.

Rook is not so severely logical a game as either whist or bridge, and for that reason it was probably a better relaxation for missionaries than either of the latter. We were introduced to the public playing of the game by slow steps. At first the family played alone, and at these sessions we were instructed in the theory and practice of Rook.

Then we watched others play, often giving helpful hints that were not fully appreciated. Eventually Mother and Father decided to risk us in public by letting the two of us play one hand in cooperation. Each of us was endowed with a certain degree of card sense, and if we wriggled in our chairs it was only in order to peek into our opponents' hands in search of intelligent leads.

It was in this atmosphere of quiet pleasure and intrigue that we lived; but a reader basing his or her visual image of me on contemporary American youth is in sad error. As for me, I may as well admit that since the age of eighteen months, when I ate too many fresh figs in California and later vomited over my mother's new green silk going-ashore dress in Honolulu Harbor, I have been chronically underweight, racked by frequent attacks of asthma, subject to insomnia, and possessed of legs like those of Chaucer's Reeve: *Ful longe were his legges and ful lene,/Ylyk a staf, ther was no calf ysene.* The only nickname ever given me that hurt was Toothpicks, and I sprang into long pants at the first opportunity, rarely to be seen out of them since. This first pair was not the complete success it should have been, since the Chinese tailor, accustomed to cutting his cloth on liberal outpost-of-Empire lines, left ample room in the seat for the buttocks of Solomon, whereas I had been sternly reduced by frequent punishment. I personally supervised the tailoring of my next pair, and my new nickname, which had been in whispered circulation behind my back, died out before it confronted me face to face. I still quiver at the fluttering ghost of those words: Droopy Drawers.

If the reader can clothe this young family skeleton in long ribbed black cotton stockings reaching above the knee, a pair of blue serge shorts, and a blouse, he will begin to see me as I was in those days. The socks, which turned a dark metallic green after much washing,

hitched to garters hung from a foundation garment of light canvas called a waist. This waist was striped with tape and circled by three tiers of buttons. One tier anchored the garters, the next held up the shorts, and the third held down the blouse, which was gathered together by a drawstring whose bow kept popping out from its hiding place. In winter my ankles bulged with folds of long woolen underwear; in summer the whole effect was topped by a large heavy pith helmet or a sailor straw lined in Turkey red, under my chin a broad elastic dangling limp and sticky from repeated chewings. Beneath all were the shoes. Our parents, wisely frugal, bought sturdy button shoes, which my sister never wore out and passed down to me when she had outgrown them. We both suffered, for our parents were always quite neutral in their choice, and until my sister was thirteen the two of us wore shoes so strictly sexless that even the mates of a pair were identical.

The cook and the amah were naturally members of the household as essential to its unity as ourselves, but at the same time they were a source of recurrent embarrassment to our parents. This arose from their extreme sincerity. Although most of the other servants on the compound had welcomed salvation as they would an extra bowl of rice, this was not true of our servants. Naturally it was a rather sore point in the family that the servants who were in daily contact with us should not see the light a little more quickly than they did. Every six months or so this affair would come to a head, and a graceful ritual followed.

This ritual never varied. Mother, who was in closer contact with the servants than Father, would approach the amah—as woman to woman—and suggest that perhaps the time had come. The amah was all agreement. To her it seemed a good thing. If it were only herself, yes. But—and there was always this suspense-filled

"but"—her husband, the cook, was not yet sure. He still had a few minor scruples. And until they were overcome, was it not a good thing for husband and wife to live together in harmony? She was quite ready, certainly, but would it not be presumptuous to make up her husband's mind? My mother would invariably agree—as woman to woman.

Now it was Father's turn to tackle the cook. The cook, it always appeared, was about a half step closer than he had ever been before. And yet, and yet, there were indeed certain things of which he was not quite sure. As my father would readily understand, this was a serious thing, a thing to be thought on deeply. Now, certain persons were much too willing to do this thing. There were even, the cook would suggest, certain Chinese very near to us who did it simply as a matter of convenience. And yet this was a thing to make a great difference in one's life. If one did this thing, certain established customs, customs such as the ten percent squeeze on the comprador's monthly bill, would have to be given up—even though this was a very old and very honorable custom in China. Now, as my father could see, it would be very easy just to give lip service and go on taking the squeeze, as indeed certain not too distant persons were well known to do. But with him it was different. He knew my father was a good man, a sincere man, who would wish to be dealt with well and sincerely. And until he could be certain of these things, the very honesty that, he might say, my father was forcing upon him made it necessary that he hesitate. If one did this thing in a real way, it must be done wholly and with an open heart.

There was, of course, no answer, and we would settle down to another six months of patient brooding, fortified by a vast admiration for our cook's honesty, so superior to the attitude of many not too distant persons.

My sister, upset by the cook's perennial doubts, suspicious of his delays, once set about trapping him into salvation through an Oriental scheme of her own. After a series of preliminary negotiations including the proper number of red herrings, she led him, indirectly and cleverly as we both thought, into a contract that practically guaranteed his conquest for Christ. According to the terms of this contract, and she saw to it that the amah and I were present as witnesses, the cook would be converted the moment my sister was able to say the Lord's Prayer in Chinese faster than he could.

The battle was all but won. My sister spent a few days practicing. She could be heard ripping through the Chinese cadences of the Lord's Prayer at all hours, picking up speed and polish until she could do the whole thing in a breath and a half. It began to look like an easy victory, and we were both jubilant at the thought of telling our parents that the cook was converted at last.

At the first trial my sister sat on the kitchen table and the cook stood beside her. The amah and I acted as starters and judges. On our count of three my sister's piercing treble and the cook's light baritone burst into a duet of sibilants and explosive vowels. At *Thy kingdom come* my sister had a lead of two syllables, which she held until the cook pulled even on *our daily bread,* and they coursed together until *Thine is the Kingdom,* when the cook spurted, and just as my sister was screeching *for ever and ever* the cook shouted his *Amen.*

The amah and I applauded. We agreed it had been the best Lord's Prayer we had ever heard. Nor was my sister overly dismayed at first; a little more practice, and the cook's soul would be safe in the Everlasting Arms.

For two weeks we had almost daily contests. Time after time the cook's soul was on the verge of being snatched from everlasting

torment: *Amen* after *Amen* he shot ahead and was lost to God. My sister developed really furious speed. She got down to one breath, and there was no question that the cook was hard pressed. When the contests reached this point the cook was not saved only because my sister failed to be Oriental enough. I noticed that the amah sometimes looked a little embarrassed. Sensing foul play, I listened very carefully the next time and was quite sure the cook had skipped *the power and the glory.* I suggested haltingly to my sister in private that she herself might well do a little squeezing in such a good cause, but she was made of sterner stuff than I and would have none of such double-dealing.

We had reached an impasse. There was no use accusing the cook; he was still a heathen. If he had already been a Christian, we could have brought him to account. As it was, what did we know about the honor of the heathens? Perhaps it was honest from his point of view. Perhaps my sister had better abandon the project. Reluctantly, after a few nearly breathless attempts, she did. The cook gave us especially choice handouts for some days, until the slight look of guilt faded from his face and we all went back to normal.

PRAYING AT ALL SEASONS

WE SHOULD HAVE BEEN unspirited indeed if praying had meant nothing to us at South Gate. Our regular day was marked by a trinity of prayings. What Sunday brought us to I shall make no effort to detail; it would be a sin of intellectual pride to describe our bilingual devotions on the Sabbath, and it is unlikely that anyone would credit the catalog. Even this everyday account may seem lurid to a lay reader's eye. South Gate's unwritten motto was *Vita brevis, prex longa.*

Our praying began immediately after breakfast, excluding, of course, grace before that meal. The blessing was important, but we took it so in our stride that it seemed a little trivial in comparison with the three other prayings, and we got down to serious business right after breakfast with Chinese Prayers. These were primarily for the servants and the exercise of our Chinese. The servants came into the sitting room and ranged themselves stiffly on the chairs. The first step was the serial reading of a chapter from the Bible. Verse by verse we took it around the room. My turn was always a slight relief for everyone else. I knew no character, I still know no character, but daily I read my verses. One of the servants coached me in stage whispers, and I solemnly repeated syllable for syllable, suffering and intense. I suffered because I was stupid enough to think that no one

knew I couldn't read Chinese, and I didn't want to give myself away. It was not until I was at least eleven that I realized everyone knew I couldn't read, and that my stuttering agony had been payment for the sin of hypocrisy.

Each time my verse was finished, things moved on smoothly—my sister was better at character than I was—and after a few expository remarks from Father at the end of the chapter we got down to serious work. This was no namby-pamby rite. We whirled and went down on our knees, buried our faces in the chair seats, shut our eyes firmly, and held on. Father and Mother did most of the praying, but we swung into a stirring chant of the Lord's Prayer in Chinese as the finale.

Very early I sensed that there was no reason for my taking Chinese Prayers too seriously. Obviously the Deity would have the courtesy to address me in English, if He saw fit to address me at all. I also disliked having my eyes shut, so I hit upon the idea of setting myself up as a watcher, a sort of guardian angel over the others as they knelt there, so awkward, so very vulnerable. I kept a sharp lookout over them, my innocently unconscious flock, and peered about the room, even looking through the windows to make sure that nothing could take us by surprise. If, by chance, anyone else opened his or her eyes, I glared severely. Was I not there to watch over him, to make his praying a prayer of undivided attention? Was I not risking my own salvation to make hers certain?

Thus my reasoning grew upon me, and except for the discomfort of kneeling—how easy it must be to be pious and fat!—I found Chinese Prayers quite pleasant. I couldn't follow everything, but I always got in on the end of the Lord's Prayer and was good for a hearty, clearly articulated *Amen.*

I must have taken my position a little too seriously, for when I

was six I was humiliated by the Lord in a most subtle way. One morning as I watched while the others prayed I was enchanted to discover a little gnome across the room. He was standing under the leaves of a large potted plant in one of the windows. A charming, winsome sprite, dressed in green, he stood there smiling at me. I estimated his height as six inches. My heart dilated as I thought of catching the tiny fellow and having him for my pet. He might have come straight from the fairy stories I had had read to me, his green cap tilted slyly over a berry-red face. It was good to know that my parents had been reading me the truth instead of a series of childishly adult lies as I had thought. I wondered if he would be able to help me with my German.

Although it seemed a sensible thing to be up and across the room instanter and nab the tiny man, I restrained myself. After all, prayers were being said and it would be most impolite to stir, as well as a bad example to the servants. At last the Lord's Prayer came on, and with my *Amen* I leapt up and darted across the room. Ah, what a cruel punishment for my presumption! What a stinging reprimand for my overweening pride as a watcher! When I reached the window my precious gnome fell apart into a cluster of hanging leaves and a small bunch of berries.

I understood immediately and swallowed the bitterness of the truth. The Lord had shown me. He had sent this false image of my mind to reveal unto me that I too was a small green imp in my self-appointed role. I choked up and wandered off to be alone, trying to solace myself by noting that I had been right about little green gnomes all along. From that day on I tried during Chinese Prayers to combine at least a minute of prayer with what I hoped was very humble watching. I think I satisfied the Lord; at least I never saw another forbidden gnome grinning out from the druid leaves.

Round two was scheduled for noon, just before lunch. Lunch, though, was not lunch in Shanghai; lunch was tiffin—an odd Briticism for South Gaters to affect, coming as it does from "tiffing": drinking. This particular bout was known as Station Prayers. Everyone on the two compounds assembled at one of the houses for mutual encouragement, and though the place was changed each week, the ceremony was always familiar.

We left little to chance; in my mind, chance and the Devil were very early identified. I suppose that it was quite reasonable for the station as a whole to pray for other stations, since the purpose of this contact was the strengthening of all in their work, or The Work as it was called. The leader first read the list for the day from the *Foreign Book of Prayer* and followed this up with the day's list from the *China Prayer Book*. These lists were, of course, confined to missionaries under the Presbyterian Board of Foreign Missions. I often wondered if, on their particular day, the Presbyterians working, say, at Bangkok felt themselves stronger than any Episcopalians, Catholics, or anyone else rash enough to hang around. No doubt they did.

This reading was by no means the dull affair it may appear at first blush. All missionaries traveled and met other missionaries. Almost every name that was read meant something to at least one person present, and it was only fair that we should learn a little intimate detail of our subjects for the day.

And so: "Yes, I remember him well. Came out together after my second furlough. *Golden State*—terrible ship—butter went bad halfway across. Oh yes, a most remarkable man, done good work there in the school. Had a wart on his chin, left side—no, maybe it was the right. Fine fellow—stood up to the Boxers."

Or: "A lovely woman, a real lady. We were together two summers ago at Peitaiho. She was so ill—thin and peaked, but then they

never get anything but wheat and millet in the northern interior. No, almost no rice. But a really lovely woman—a real lady." And on through the list.

Then again it was down on one's knees, face in chair seat. The leader prayed first for the chosen of the day, and my mind would wander off, picturing a man standing up to box, a wart shifting from side to side on his chin as he sparred for position; or a real lady, so thin and peaked because she had no rice. These visions did not long endure. It is still a mystery to me why my knees never became truly hardened, but they would begin to ache and I to fidget. Finally, unable to keep still, I would start on my grand tour. Never leaving my knees, I scuffed from one kneeling form to the next, nudging each gently, and smiling graciously with what must have been a nauseous coyness whenever noticed. Occasionally a restraining arm would be put around me, but not for long. I would draw away, and no voice was raised to stop my pilgrimage. Naturally I omitted visiting either Mother or Father.

It was not as if there had been only one prayer to weather. After the leader's prayer, anyone moved to do so prayed on any topic he was moved to pray on, and many indeed were they who were moved.

When our own station turned up annually in the lists, a pretty variation occurred. We all became extremely modest and self-effacing. The leader rushed through the names perfunctorily as if apologizing for this unnecessary bother, and the prayers that followed were noticeably grand and general and astonishingly brief. To my Occidental eye this was clearly a performance full of humility, but when the cook's influence was in the ascendant my Oriental eye saw it as an assurance to the Lord that He needn't worry particularly about improving us. After all, were we not the salt of the earth, the South Gaters? And surely the salt had not lost its savor.

The *prex precum,* the Prayer of Prayers, at these sessions was rarely realized, but it was worth a year's waiting. It usually followed an especially vivacious mission or station meeting at which some topic of mission diplomacy or station policy had been disputed. A dispute in which each of the contenders knows that the Lord is acting personally as his second and the Devil is leering over the shoulder of his opponent is likely to assume Miltonic force, and the reverberations often lasted for weeks. Station Prayers gained an intensity far beyond our normal zeal as one member prayed in veiled fashion for the salvation of all obstructionists and the triumph of truth, only to be answered by another prayer of equal eloquence expressing the hope that we would not be deluded by wolves in sheep's clothing.

There was a Chinese charm about this that pleased me. God became an interested middleman, celestial in all senses, passing messages back and forth, bargaining a little, deprecating this suggestion and approving that in a not altogether orthodox or charitable manner. And through it all I, the little Levite, shuttled back and forth on my knees, a visible emissary, carefully avoiding my mother's eyes if she were so impious as to open them.

The veil was torn in my presence only once. My most senior Courtesy Uncle, his white spade beard following up his periods, prayed that one of my more junior Courtesy Uncles might have his neck humbled, his proud and willful spirit broken. From the rigid backs and the quivering heads, any heathen could have seen that something walked among us. When the prayer ended, the junior uncle came back hitting hard and brilliantly, though even I thought the reference to whited sepulchers a bit below the belt. There was at least one rebuttal from each side. So powerful were the currents in the atmosphere that I found myself stranded in the middle of the carpet, unable to move, as the contest raged and the winged

spirits clashed about my head. When the South Gaters rose at last from their knees, their faces flushed, I knew that I had felt a presence and had heard the gift of tongues.

Noteworthy as these two prayings of the day were, for me they were little more than daily initiations, times spent largely in observation and the acquisition of material for my own private use. It was in Family Prayers at night that I had my chance to inform the Lord of many things I thought should be brought to His attention.

Family Prayers came off just before my sister and I got into bed. They were at their best in spring and summer, but if the tin drum in the nursery was working well, even winter was acceptable. Either Mother or Father began, once we were all on our knees between the twin beds. Then my sister and I had our turns, alternating successive nights, and whichever parent was left provided the final bracket. There may have been a time when my sister and I were timid about praying, but we soon got into the spirit of the thing, and, modeling our entreaties and confessions on the prayers we heard during the day, we prayed with might and fervor, within, of course, the strict bounds of Presbyterian decorum. Not for us any gasping or tremors of the voice, any whining requests, but a clear intellectual control over passion and a dignified restraint as we offered our thanks and delivered our suggestions: Presbyterian to Presbyterian. Better, Northern Presbyterian to Northern Presbyterian, for the Southern branch, though laudable, was inclined to secede from the mathematical joys of logic and indulge itself in an arbitrarily personal bias.

Soon we began to vie for the favor of the Lord. Night by night our prayers increased with the seasons. A tacit understanding existed between us that on cold nights when the drum was ineffective, a snug bed and a hot-water bottle were more precious than salvation.

But as winter gave way to spring and the nights grew temperate, we renewed our rivalry. The American slant of our minds was revealed in that we strove for quantity rather than quality. One of my earlier and more simple devices to this end was a foolish repetition of what I had already said. Mother and Father stopped this by pointing out that God was not forgetful and could be trusted with one telling. Perhaps they were right, but it seemed to me that if they were, the world, our world at least, did a vast amount of unnecessary praying from day to day, year to year.

There was a point in this rivalry at which the law of diminishing returns began to function. Usually my sister reached it first, and then we called off the whole thing for a few weeks. My sister won because she could control her rate of speech far better than I could mine, and she was more ingenious than I in remembering almost endless catalogs of relatives on whom to call down blessings, catalogs that put to shame any genealogical table in the Old Testament.

As for me, I became so eager to help the Lord that I grew excited and rattled things off too quickly, so I had to depend in large part on my sins and then throw in whatever relatives I could remember all in a heap at the end. Each day my sins were numerous and varied. I had been nasty to the cook's daughter; I had stolen my sister's crayons and frightened her canary; I had asked a Courtesy Uncle what "eunuch" meant when I already knew; I had sworn at one of the alley brats; I had only pretended to brush my teeth in the morning; I had poured a Courtesy Aunt's offering of milk into a potted plant and left without thanking her; I had imitated a Chinese Christian speaking English; I had even told the amah I was really a Eurasian orphan plucked from the filth of the gutter at the age of six months. Best of all, I often had to ask forgiveness at the end for confessing to sins I had not committed.

My parents would solemnly approve my frank confessions, and as Mother tucked me in she would say, "Now, you won't do any of those things again, will you?" "No, I won't ever," I would answer instantly, happy in the knowledge that I already had the first item for the next night's confessional. Sinning was not only pleasant, it was plainly virtuous.

As I have said, my sister ordinarily beat me in our competitions. I had only one clear-cut victory, unless my review of the Ten Commandments might count as a cumulative score. I had been memorizing them when it occurred to me that the Lord might enjoy a little discussion. The first night I assured Him that I had had no other gods before Him, generally and at great length approving the whole plan of things, and the second night I got in a few sly comments on the Buddhists and Catholics. By the fifth night I was in my stride and I assured the Lord that my parents were noble souls, that I would always honor them, and that He had certainly had a fine idea when he thought up that one. The sixth commandment gave me a chance to review everything I could remember having killed, and I pleaded extenuating circumstances for the slaughter of a number of mosquitoes, houseflies, toads, lizards, angleworms, grasshoppers, and snails. If anyone is expecting an indiscretion on the seventh night, he will be disappointed. I told the Lord that, as far as I knew, I had never committed adultery, but that if I ever did I would probably be sorry and I should be glad to tell Him about it. When I reached the tenth night, I could say with a clear conscience that I was without fault. Our neighbor, a Courtesy Aunt, had a house smaller than ours, no wife, a dipsomaniac cook, a cross-eyed amah; and she raised no cattle.

The family endured this patiently enough, perhaps even enjoying my elementary exegesis, but the night of my one undisputed

triumph, which occurred when I was eight, may have been rather more trying. My sister prayed first. From her deliberate tones and her completely tedious catalog of all relatives, I knew she was making her bid to end the current series. After the *Amen* I kept a firm grip on myself and started calmly. I thanked God for every hour, nay, for every half- and quarter-hour of the day, for the sun's rising, each passing cloud during the morning, the breeze that sprang up at noon, my afternoon nap, my tea, and on through without a gap. This was a slight innovation—I could feel my sister's admiration and jealousy. Next, still under control, I commented on the behavior of everyone I had met during the last twenty-four hours. The cook had given me some cake, for which I thought he should be commended, even though he was not a Christian; the amah had not sewn the button on my blouse—black mark; Father had forgotten to find a book he had promised me, but I hoped he would be forgiven for this oversight since he was a very busy man. Similar minutiae followed, including the demand for a Courtesy Aunt's punishment for having raised her voice rudely in wrath against me as I climbed a tree in her garden. A rather conventional list of sins followed. The rest of the family stirred in anticipation of the end. But I had two surprises for them. I had mastered all the relatives at last, and I called down blessings on grandparents living and dead, grand-aunts and great-uncles, uncles and aunts, cousins, half-cousins, second cousins, cousins of various removes, and in-laws on both sides. Still not satisfied, I included an extensive selection of friends and acquaintances, good and evil, with appropriate footnotes. Then I asked for the salvation of China and as many other countries as I could recall from the atlas.

At this point I knew that I had at least equaled my sister, so I flung in my last section to clinch the title. Starting with the

west attic, going on to the east, then to the second and first floors of the house, I named every article I could remember, including my parents' academic diplomas in a trunk, and asked that each be dedicated anew to the Lord's use. Progressing grandly through the dining and living rooms, I swept on through the pantry to the kitchen and asked blessings for every single pot and pan we owned, elaborately describing each so the Lord would have no trouble identifying it. Closing with the iron spider the cook used for killing centipedes, I ended my prayer secure in victory. Father just managed to stagger through the Lord's Prayer, and his joints cracked as he rose from kneeling. Mother's eyes were glazed. Only her admiration and envy of my revolutionary novelties had kept my sister awake.

That prayer remains the most inclusive of my public prayings, nor did it go unanswered. For at least a month every dish from our kitchen was a chef d'oeuvre, and we all relished piously the sanctified succulence of our daily bread.

Thus far I have described only praying that, no matter how personal its qualities, was essentially public. But we were always given to understand that any time in the day was appropriate for a bit of Private Prayer. This was one of the rewards of being a Presbyterian. The Lord might have special hours and forms for receiving the prayers of other sects; He might admit the blanket prayers that covered the sins of Episcopalians and Catholics, but His ear was open to us at all times. Consequently, whenever we got into a tight place we knew a little prayer would do no harm.

Missionary parents can be divided into two groups on this point. There are those who recommend prayer, and I am thankful my own parents were among them; and then there are the foolish ones who advise stopping and saying to yourself: "Now, what would Jesus do?"

Aside from verging on blasphemy, this second formula is definitely dangerous. The children of this group seemed to us to live in constant peril and to behave on occasion with a complete lack of realism. One summer I pulled from the swimming pool a half-drowned little girl of the What-Would-Jesus-Do? school who had asked the question before trying to get to the other side.

What, I often wonder, would have happened to me on Market Street in San Francisco at the end of our second furlough had I been raised a What-Would-Jesus-Doer? We were in the city for a few days before our ship sailed for China. Father was out having our Model T Ford, which had brought us across the continent, crated for shipment to Shanghai. Mother was raiding the local five-and-tens, building up a seven-year supply of hooks and eyes, snaps, elastic in all widths, paper clips, buttons, dishrags, potholders, hair curlers, and Ping-Pong balls. I had been told I could take a walk if I cared to, and since my sister was pretending to write a letter, I set out alone. At some point I must have crossed Market Street half consciously, for on my way back to the hotel I found myself stranded in the middle of that ugly thoroughfare. That San Franciscans needed four sets of car tracks on one street was, I suppose, their own business. I found myself in the center of Market Street, two clanging streetcars bearing down on me from one direction, two equally noisy cars surging forward from the other. I judged the distances, saw I was caught, and froze in the space between the two pairs of track. With luck, I thought, I might get through with only an odd hand or foot missing. Now, had I been raised in the What-Would-Jesus Do? school, there is no telling what folly I might have committed. I might simply have commanded them to stop and then walked on, or I might have tried to elevate myself and glide over the cars. In any event I should obviously have gotten into a worse

spot than I was in already. Instead, I let out all my breath, closed my eyes, and prayed furiously.

My prayers were answered. I heard a gruff voice saying, "Hurry up, you little son of a bitch." I said my *Amen* quickly and opened my eyes. There before me, his arms spread wide, was a policeman. The cars had stopped. I will swear on the Bible that there had been no policeman within sight when I began to pray. This blue-clad creature, whose very language set him apart, was an angel of the Lord. Pulling myself together and breathing deeply, I bowed briskly in polite Chinese fashion and said, "Thank you, sir. Thank you very much." As I scuttled on across, I heard the angel give further witness of his origin. "Well, I'll be God-damned!" the seraphic voice rumbled. I turned when I reached the sidewalk. The four cars were passing one another. When the space cleared, it was as empty of policemen as when I had started my prayer. To my knowledge, this is the only demonstrable instance in the entire history of the United States of a link between Church and State.

I was never again thus fortunate: the remainder of my Private Prayers went unanswered. But then, I never again got stuck in the middle of Market Street. This lack of response was, I was given to understand by various Courtesy Uncles, a result of the inscrutable nature of the Lord's mind. It was always difficult to reconcile this with the need for a certain type of praying, and though I have had this reconciliation demonstrated to me, I have no space here for the required theological apparatus.

Eventually in my Private Prayers I set out on a series of experiments. My sister, I have learned since, was doing the same thing, though she was far rasher than I. She wondered if there would be any visible difference in her life if she dedicated her Private Prayers to Satan. Somewhere she had heard that anyone doing this would

be smitten by the Lord and struck dead. The idea interested her, and for a week she prayed privately to the Devil. Nothing happened and she grew bored. To this day she is tolerably well, but it is not for me to say that she will never receive her just reward.

I started simply. I might have forgotten, soon after puzzling over it for the first time, the fatal passage on faith's moving mountains had it not been for my sister's praying aloud one night, a month before Christmas, for a pink silk parasol. Moved by her request, I began to pray for a baby brother, surely an unselfish demand. I prayed secretly at first, since my sister's display struck me as unduly ostentatious. Perhaps this was my error. Each night she pointed out how much she would appreciate a pink silk parasol, and each night, once I was in bed, I prayed silently for a baby brother.

Radiant in my faith, I went downstairs Christmas morning. My sister got a pink silk parasol. I got a clockwork train.

I could find no excuse for the Lord. A few feebler public attempts, ranging from a baby brother to a baby sister—a sad decline for a Chinese—to a flush toilet, and I knew that there were a number of things on which I and the Lord did not see eye to eye.

At last I let the whole effort drop, but I would not have been part Oriental if I had not got some good out of Private Prayers. When I was about ten my sister and I moved from the nursery into separate rooms. Mine had a large closet with space enough for a small desk. On top of my stamp collection and the latest additions to my herbarium lay my Bible, a green silk marker falling elegantly from its pages. Here at odd moments of the day I would retire. When I heard a pair of leather-soled shoes coming upstairs—the servants wore cloth, and the servants would never have been taken in—I flipped open the Bible, cast myself on my knees, and prayed loudly to the Lord to make me a better Presbyterian, to keep me

from the sins of pride and hypocrisy. One favorite request ran, "O Lord, keep me from being irritated or irritating." The shoes would pause for a few moments outside the door. My voice rose and fell in disciplined cadences until the shoes went back downstairs. Then I would turn back to my stamps or my herbarium, leaving the inscrutable mind of the Lord free to sinners who needed Him more than I.

THE FIG TREE

MY SISTER MUST HAVE BEEN about eleven when the oval of grass between our house and the front gate became a testing ground on which four South Gate wills struggled for supremacy. The contest opened sluggishly years before it reached its climax, but when my sister saw the necessity of our entering it—for she and I made up the fourth will—its tempo picked up and we cut through the opposition to a satisfying close. Our own part in this clash was the result of our crossbred nature. Our Western directness was augmented by our Chinese practicality and the choice of means, while our knowledge that we were the only real family at South Gate deepened in us our Oriental sense of family pride and the need for saving the honor of the house. This combination produced in our minds a stronger feeling than the casual family loyalties of the West, a feeling of intense urgency that required satisfaction. As Chinese we knew we must not lose face; as Americans we knew we must act efficiently; as South Gaters we knew we must be right.

The oval was just large enough for a tennis court, and Father wanted very much to have it made into one, so that he and I could practice at home instead of going across the canal and road to the Boys' School compound. True, there would be almost no space behind the baselines. The bamboo fence was a low barrier along

one side, so during each set a brace of balls would probably go into the canal. The cemetery wall, too, was a little inadequate for a backstop, but our house and windows, and the double house and windows of the Courtesy Aunts, would take care of the other two sides perfectly. This was Father's point of view.

The Courtesy Aunts in the double house, though they rarely agreed on anything, did feel that a tennis court was less than desirable. One in particular had a notion that the lawn should be dotted with flowering shrubs in a strictly mathematical design. This was the second, the most dangerous point of view.

Mother was not particularly enthusiastic about tennis. She had no racket, anyway, after giving me the cork-handled, flat-topped one her brother had used in 1902 when he won his college championship and approached the state championship of Iowa. Mother favored a stretch of open lawn, just as the oval was. If it had to be a tennis court, she would not object greatly, but whatever it was, it was not to be mathematically dotted with shrubs. This was Mother's point of view.

Whenever the subject came up in public and I was present, one of my dimmer Courtesy Uncles always looked archly at me and asked, "John, do you know where tennis was played in the Bible?" Since this was the only daring joke the Courtesy Uncle had ever understood and mastered, I always said politely that I didn't know. Waggling his head in pride of his wit, the Courtesy Uncle would then crow, "When Joseph served in Pharoah's court."

Though at first we thought Father would win, we later decided that Mother, already supported by the inertia of the status quo, might succeed through her passively conservative tactics. I was inclined to be on Father's side, while my sister, who never gained any great dexterity in tennis and disliked fagging balls, supported

Mother. Neither of us was markedly impressed by the Courtesy Aunt's ridiculous proposal.

The affair dragged on so long, and everyone was so accustomed to its moves and variations, that the Courtesy Aunt's swift stroke one spring was as electrifying as an unexpected backhand volley. My sister and I were having our tea one afternoon when we heard Mother and a Courtesy Aunt from the Girls' School compound exclaiming excitedly in the next room. On our way to see what was happening we passed a window. Glancing out, we halted in amazement. In the very center of the oval stood a large shrub. The earth was packed down neatly around it, and this parvenu stood there insolently, just as if it were a permanent part of the scheme of things.

We listened carefully by the closed door to the conversation in the next room. The Courtesy Aunt from the Girls' School compound was saying decisively, "No, it doesn't do. It ruins, simply ruins the vista." This particular Courtesy Aunt had suffered from vistas ever since subscribing to *House and Garden*. Everything had to be or have a vista. The first time I heard the word she was reprimanding me for standing in front of her window by saying, "My dear boy, step aside, step aside. Can't you see you're getting in the way of the vista?" Since only the two of us were in the room, I ran home as soon as I politely could and announced that this poor Courtesy Aunt was the victim of hallucinations.

To return to our eavesdropping. Mother said, "Well, I don't think it was ever much of a vista."

"It's ruined, anyway, simply ruined," the Courtesy Aunt answered dolefully.

"I don't like it, but I suppose we'll get used to it," Mother replied. "Perhaps it will die. Maybe it would help if we put a curse on it."

The Courtesy Aunt laughed. "All right, let's," she said.

My sister and I looked strangely at each other. We heard more laughter in the other room.

Then through the door we heard the voice of the Courtesy Aunt ring out as she declaimed, "Bush! I put a curse on you that you may die!"

My sister and I stood dismayed. Next we heard Mother's voice, deeper than usual, fill the air as she rumbled, "Bush! I put a curse on you that your leaves may shrivel, your branches wither, and your roots rot until you are dead!"

We could imagine the gesture, hand outstretched and finger pointing, as these two witches uttered their blasts. Most shocking of all was the gale of laughter that followed. Then the ordinary chitchat of the tea table was renewed, and my sister and I crept back from the door to consult with each other.

"Is that all they're going to do about it?" my sister asked in disgust.

"Do you think it can possibly work?"

"Don't be silly," she said tartly. "Who ever heard of a curse working except in a fairy story?"

"There's the fig tree in the Bible," I offered meekly.

"That's different." My sister's voice grew stern as she went on: "In fact, it's blasphemous of you to mention it. It's probably only an interpolation anyway."

"Isn't it in both Matthew and Mark?"

"Now, stop blaspheming and be sensible. The cook curses hundreds of things every day and you know nothing happens to them."

"He isn't a Christian," I said doggedly.

"You don't need to be a Christian to curse," she answered. "When

you curse you call down the Devil. Anyone can call down the Devil, but it doesn't work."

"Then the fig tree in the Bible was really killed by—?"

She interrupted me sharply. "Don't start blaspheming again, John!"

"Maybe Father will do something," I suggested.

"We'll wait and see," she said gloomily. "But if he doesn't, we'll really have to. That's all there is to it."

Father was a wretched disappointment. He shrugged his shoulders when he came home and gave up his tennis court as if it were nothing. The next morning he actually took off his hat to the guilty Courtesy Aunt just as usual.

My sister and I were completely upset and enraged. Was this the way a family took an open insult? What would become of a house that lost face in such an absentminded manner? If our elders were weak and blind, we must be strong. Now that the bush had lasted the night, I was converted to my sister's views on cursing and I blasphemed no more.

We waited until the day of an evening station meeting. That morning we went out to the cook and asked him if we could have ice cream for tiffin. He thought we might. We told him to use plenty of salt on the ice and to save the water in the freezer for some Western scientific experiments we planned to conduct. (My sister, though not too sound on miracles, had a good nose for practical passages.) We then bore off a couple of heavy cleavers, which we assured the amah we needed in our work. I thought of offering to help crank the freezer; on reflection, I decided to conserve my strength.

Although Mother couldn't remember ordering it, the ice cream was very good. My sister said so, at least. I have never liked ice

cream and I ate it only as a fraternal duty. The cook assured Mother sympathetically that she had definitely ordered ice cream, reminding her that she had told him to use plenty of salt to get it well frozen. We both backed him up so enthusiastically that he had to frown at us to keep us from overdoing it.

After tiffin we put the salt water and the cleavers in the coal shed and waited impatiently for evening. The cook, a wise man, asked no questions. After supper was over, Mother and Father cautioned us not to stay up beyond our usual bedtime as they left for the station meeting.

Dusk was falling. We told the cook and amah that we were going to conduct our experiments on the front lawn, but it was important that no one see us. The amah said she was too lazy to move and frankly wasn't interested in Western scientific experiments. The cook thought he might go over to the double house and have a chat with the servants there. A few minutes later we carried our bucket of brine and the cleavers out to the front lawn. From the servants' quarters of the double house the cook's voice could be heard starting on the unexpurgated version of his most gripping military reminiscence.

We began by playing a short jumping game. First one and then the other tried to clear the bush. Our work well started, we took the cleavers and hacked deep into the soft ground near the base of the central stalk. After feeling the edges bite something more than earth we poured the salt water into the gashes we had made and carefully patted down the dirt. Then we ran round the oval a couple of times shouting loudly so that the cook could edit his story if it was tiring him. In the backyard again, I assured the amah that science was what made America superior to the rest of the world. She looked at our legs and remarked that science was rather violent,

though if it was the only way to get to the root of a matter she supposed it was a good thing.

Over a period of five weeks, the shrub died a beautiful, lingering death. Slowly one branch after another drooped. When the leaves of a branch were yellowed and dry the Courtesy Aunt would come out to inspect it and then snip it off. We enjoyed the sight of the creator destroying her own unsightly abomination. Apparently we had not caught all the roots: for a few days in the fourth week it looked as if the remainder of the shrub might pull through, and we ate a great deal of ice cream. At last, when the bush was clearly beyond all hope of life, the Courtesy Aunt's outside coolie dug it up and carted it away.

Mother laughed lightly at supper that night. "You know," she said to Father, "I put a curse on that bush."

"Dear me," Father answered, "I never thought of doing that."

After a mutual glance of disgust my sister and I looked down at our plates.

"Perhaps we can have a tennis court now," Father suggested, but without much conviction in his voice.

"Oh, I like it just as it is," Mother said quietly. "Just a nice green stretch of lawn again after the grass covers that spot."

The grass took more than one season to conquer the barren soil. Mother worried us time and again by joking with Father and the Courtesy Aunt from the Girls' School compound about how the place seemed permanently accursed. After one such remark my sister asked, "Do you really think, Mother, that your curse killed the bush?"

"Why, of course not, dear," Mother answered. "It was just a joke."

"Then why did it die?" I demanded.

"Oh, I suppose it—well, I guess it just died. Lots of plants die, you know. It was just a coincidence."

This was a great relief. We were pleased that Mother cherished no foolish notions on curses.

"Of course, there was the fig tree in the Bible," I persisted, provoking an indignant glance from my sister.

"That's a little different, John," Mother said.

"Yes, I know," I sighed, feeling at last that I surely did.

THE PROMISED LAND

I KNEW A STRANGE WORLD beyond the normal childhood worlds of fantasy, a world that was quite real in my mind, and a world that I knew existed in the ordinary sense. It was an earthly paradise, this place, a land flowing with milk and honey, filled with creatures who, though human, were as demigods to other humans. It was a world where no sorrow endured for long, where all men lived as brothers, where the sun shone with an especial brilliance and brought to fruit a country of great richness, watered by rolling rivers and sheltered by giant forests. In this country no one starved; the rulers of the land served justice with a devotion and a fervor elsewhere unknown; the highways of the land were smoother than slate; the people of the land were the greatest of all the peoples on whom God had set His mark.

Nor was all this casual hearsay. The spies had gone down into the land and had found it good. There was no conflict in their reports. The fruits they brought back were rare and strange. And this land was known among men as the United States of America.

None of this information was, as I remember, given to me direct. It was absorbed as normally as are prejudices of race, caste, or party. I was amazed later to find that even in the prophylactic atmosphere of South Gate I had in some way acquired a prejudice against Jews

and a feeling that all Democrats were socially unacceptable. These later biases have been altered by tiresome steps of education; the picture of America was dealt with more boldly and immediately.

The map of the United States was a familiar sight, yet the intimate geography of the land was my own creation. My first misconception came from a failure to grasp the location of the District of Columbia. I knew all about the French and Indian Wars, the Declaration of Independence, the crossing of the Potomac, the Battle of Yorktown, and the Continental Congresses. To this point my history was as sound as anything learned from a textbook can be. But when it came to choosing a site for the national capital, the founding fathers had, it seemed to me, gone astray.

I read the accounts carefully and they all said the same thing: Washington was placed centrally, without regional favoritism, in order to best serve the thirteen states. Then I would look at the map again, just to make certain, and there were Washington and the Columbia River up in the northwest corner, cut off from the thirteen states by leagues of prairie, wilderness, desert, and mountains. This did make it easy to understand why it took so long for things like elections to be settled. I could see the members of the Electoral College, guided by Daniel Boone, Lewis, and Clark, set out across the continent, all of them tight-lipped and secretive until they reached Washington. Here they cast their ballots, and the next day they started back on their grueling trail to tell the people what had happened. I felt that this was really going too far in the interests of disinterestedness. Though I hope few will believe me, I retained this impression until I was twelve, had already spent two conscious years in America, and had gone back to China. Meanwhile I continued to get A's in American history.

Washington did not trouble me too much, because I knew it was

no longer a very important part of American society. Washington had early been displaced as the center of all American life by 156 Fifth Avenue, New York City, New York, U.S.A. This address was, as everyone should know, the home of the Board of Foreign Missions of the Presbyterian Church in the United States of America. It was a perfectly respectable building, rather gloomy and drafty, where the menservants and the handmaidens of the Lord successfully disguised themselves to look like everyone else in New York. But in my youth 156 Fifth Avenue was the earthly representation of heaven, the temple of the Lord in the New Jerusalem. Its corridors sparkled with golden pavement; its lamps were glowing carbuncles; the rooms and halls were lined in chalcedony, marble, alabaster, and beryl; the fragrant furniture was made from the cedars of Lebanon; and within the central courts, each on a jewel-studded throne of Ophir, sat the High Priests who always saw to it that the humblest workman at South Gate was worthily paid for his hire.

Ah well, that vision is faded, but I once, at the age of seventeen, felt a certain degree of the old warmth return when I wandered into 156 from Europe and, unbeknownst to my parents, drew out part of Father's next check.

There was only one other spot in the city of New York of the slightest importance. This was Grant's Tomb, where Mother had wheeled me when I was twelve months old. With me beside her, she had posed for a photograph in a smartly tailored suit, a peacock plume rising from her newest hat.

Quite close to New York was another city of heavenly importance. This was Pittsburgh, Pennsylvania, and it was a more spiritual place than New York. Whereas 156 Fifth Avenue was slightly tainted by business, its annex, the First Presbyterian Church of Pittsburgh, was a House of God so detached from the world that, although it sup-

ported us, it preferred to send the money to 156, which was more accustomed to handling these things. In this Holy of Holies a majestic gentleman, who resembled William Howard Taft, served the Lord with pomp and glory as Senior Elder. That he was my grandfather was only right and just.

The temporal powers, then, huddled in the Northwest. In the East, where the sun rose, stood the Cities of God. Between the two, in the precise center of the continent, was raised a massive structure, the home of commerce, where all the best of America's material wealth was gathered up and placed on shelves stretching out of eye reach. Once a year this great mart, this all-providing emporium that made other centers of trade appear as nothing, sent us a large crate crammed with everything we needed from America. The cook prized off the cover, and then we leapt as leap the young lambs in spring while one treasure after another was lifted from its bed of excelsior. But here I must interrupt myself for a few paragraphs.

When I began going to day school in Shanghai, I arranged to be picked up on the corner of the Bund and Avenue Edward VII by Robert Dollar II, a classmate, in his private limousine. This enabled me to save part of my carfare for candy. My sister (whose character shows throughout, I hope, in a better light than my own) decided this was not particularly honest, though she didn't mind sampling the candy later, and she continued by streetcar. So Robert Dollar II and I would roll in gentlemanly grandeur to the gate of the First and Second Grades Building, where we were gravely handed out by the chauffeur. One day, as soon as I had settled myself into the cushions, Robert drew from his pocket a thin, flattened, and altogether anemic-looking gold watch.

"My father," he said, "sent to America to get me this."

"Oh?" I asked politely.

"Yes," he said. "It comes from Tiffany's."

Fumbling in my jacket, I finally drew out my own watch on the end of a shoelace. Its nickel case was plump and well filled. Its movement was audible even in the limousine.

Dangling it casually and with an air of quiet superiority, I said to Robert Dollar II in the tone of one who knows the best from the merely good: "My watch comes from Montgomery Ward's."

One of the most sapid prospects of my America was the variety of food eaten there. It was always perfectly cooked and served up in abundance. I knew this because South Gaters repeatedly said, "At home you get really good beef" and "At home the vegetables have a fuller flavor." Home was America, even for me. We used the word in two senses. If we said, "When we go home tonight," we meant our house at South Gate; but if we said only "When we go home," we meant America.

Nothing was more revealing to me about this real home than knowing that one could eat fried chicken there nearly every other day. Our chickens were scrawny stew-things, though they put on a lively spectacle in the backyard after the cook had slit their throats with a razor and pitched them into the court to die. In America chickens sprang from their shells almost as large as capons, and when they were fried they tasted like nothing else on earth. For years fried chicken was rated higher than caviar on my mental palate.

Though food may have been my primary interest, I was also socially conscious, happy to know that in America impartial justice controlled society. Did I not hear time and again, "Now, can't you just imagine what would happen to anyone at home who tried to get away with that?" This usually followed an exposure of local graft. The common response would come: "Why, no one would ever dream of trying that at home."

I couldn't quite grasp what sort of work Americans did. I knew they worked a little, but working could hardly be a great part of their lives, since the land was so rich. America was full of refined, charming persons with leisure to cultivate their minds. Everyone I met on the mission field—except my own family—seemed to be related to someone of great wealth and power. I often heard, "Though I don't like to advertise the fact out here, my father was. . . ." or "Of course, if I felt it was right, I could just write home to my sister to buy one for me, and, mind you, she would do it without. . . ."

Not only was everyone rich and powerful, everyone—except my own family—was extraordinarily talented as well. We received only the overflow in China. We knew a bishop—only a Methodist Episcopal one, at that—who spoke annually on how he could have been one of the world's greatest violinists, but had preferred sacrificing this life of the fleshpots to the greater glory of saving the Chinese. The number of prima donnas who had dedicated their voices to the Lord instead of the Metropolitan was large enough to presage a decay in New York opera. Others had turned their backs on careers as big businessmen, politicians, diplomats, authors, playboys, and millionaires. The nobility of these virtuosi in surrendering themselves to the mission field impressed me. If they had come to China, think of the geniuses left in America who had not heard The Call.

Best of all was to learn that almost everyone in America was a Christian. In that green and happy land there was no need for missionaries, except to the Indians and Mormons. The greater part of the population, I gathered, were Presbyterians, and all Presbyterians, with a few exceptions in the South, were decent Republicans. No wonder I tingled in anticipation of the day when I would be going home.

I was almost nine when I first saw America, excluding the time I spent there between the ages of six and eighteen months that allowed me to say glibly, "Of course I've been to America," and then frown down any further questions. I had only one warning that America might not be all clear sweetness and Christian light. On hot days I grew accustomed to hearing Father say, "Oh, what I'd give for a chocolate ice-cream soda this afternoon!" Mother would answer, "Don't talk about it—you make me want to take the next boat home just to taste one." That rare creation, a chocolate ice-cream soda, foamed and frothed at the very pinnacle of sybaritic dissipation.

One late spring afternoon Father came back from the International Settlement with the nearly revolutionary news that the Chocolate Shop on Nanking Road had begun to serve ice-cream sodas. Immediately we planned a family expedition for the coming Saturday.

Dressed in our best, the four of us marched into the Chocolate Shop and sat down in a booth. Father delivered our order with an air. My sister and I sat in an agony of expectation. When the gassy concoctions were put before us at last, we seized our straws in trembling fingers, put the straws to our lips, and sucked. After the first swallow we looked at each other squeamishly. A wrenching belch shook me, and my nose seemed to catch fire for an instant. Eyes watering, I turned to Mother and Father, who were guzzling greedily.

"Is this a real ice-cream soda?" I asked.

"Of course, dear," Mother assured me between gulps. "Isn't it wonderful?"

Another gas pocket came free and interrupted my reply. Doggedly I stuck it out. I had not yet learned that all semicivilized pleasures

are refinements and adaptations of discomfort and pain, that only in civilizations of antiquity are pleasures genuinely simple.

"Perhaps," I said voicelessly to myself, "I am not a real American at all." Awful thought! I beat it down as each fresh convulsion shook me.

On the way back to South Gate I clamped my jaws in a fixed smile and prayed for control. In the nursery bathroom and alone at last, I vomited luxuriously. The first taste of America had not been good.

When Mother, my sister, and I boarded the *Empress of Asia* a year later, I had foolishly forgotten about the crude Roman pleasures of the ice-cream soda. At last we were going home, a year early. Father would come later, and when he arrived the Mayo Clinic would have made me into a little Atlas and an orthodontist would have pulled my sister's and my jaws into shape. No longer could my sister say tartly, "No, John, you do not remember a thing about America," or, as I looked at the *Maid of the Mist* in the family photograph album, "You can't possibly remember Niagara Falls, John. We left you in Chautauqua when we went there." I would make no more blunders as to the language Americans spoke or the dress Americans wore, mistakes that were instantly caught by my sister and corrected emphatically. I would know.

Robert Dollar II—who insists on cropping up—was on board the *Empress of Asia* with his mother and sister. I played with him in the drawing room of their suite when exhausted by the vulgar pleasures of the deck. At the children's dinner sitting my sister and I sat with Robert, his sister, and their governess. Here Robert and his sister were held to a strictly limited diet. I think they were envious of the way my sister and I galloped up and down the long menu unsupervised.

As the *Empress of Asia* slid into her berth in Vancouver Harbor I glanced over the wharves. Then I pulled Mother's sleeve. "Are those white men doing that coolie work Americans?" I asked, pointing to some stevedores.

"Why, yes," she answered.

Utopia threatened to collapse. "Real Americans like us?"

"Well, they're Canadians, of course," Mother said.

"Canada isn't part of the United States, is it?"

"No, Canada is part of the British Empire."

"Oh, well," I murmured happily.

Our car from the Canadian Pacific Railway entered the United States at Portal. We went through customs at midnight. In my upper berth I was almost breathless with fear that we might be refused entry for some reason. As the train started up I gasped in relief.

Portal is in North Dakota. I have nothing against North Dakota as North Dakota; but North Dakota early in the morning as the realization of my dreamworld was disaster. Not lasting disaster; I was too resilient, too Chinese, for that. I stared at the hot landscape and my sweating fellow passengers. During the next hours I absorbed the truth: Americans were just duller versions of South Gaters. In one day I gained an international vision.

As the train clacked on, I assimilated my discovery. I thought I had made a good job of it until I overheard my sister saying quietly to Mother, "When Father comes, he can look after John, and you and I can go home where we belong, can't we?"

"But we are home, dear," Mother answered.

"I mean," and my sister's voice came close to breaking, "I mean our *real* home—in China."

I secretly felt the same way. Yet my ancestors could have rotted

in their graves and their dust been blown from the face of the earth before I would have admitted it. American was still a proud name. Even if it killed me, I was going to be one. From that day to this my sister has been slightly more Chinese than American, and I have been slightly more American than Chinese, still half expecting at least a few of my early visions to spring into real life.

TO KEEP IT HOLY

THE FAIRY TALE about Rapunzel so irked me on first reading that I became furious with my sister for liking it.

"It's impossible to climb up anyone's hair," I insisted.

"It isn't," my sister replied coldly. "You've never tried."

That night in the nursery while the amah was brushing out my sister's waist-length hair, I seized my chance and showed her. The hairbrush and all that followed failed to shake my critical views.

Stories in which animals carried on long colloquies or fantasies like *A Connecticut Yankee* were, on the other hand, quite acceptable. The whole point, it seemed to me, was to keep one's worlds properly defined. If the thing pretended to be fact, it ought to be fact; if it shrugged its shoulders and said, "This is just a good story, and no one would ever think to believe it," that was fine; but to dash back and forth was simply a sign of weak-mindedness and bad taste. I yawned in particular over one ill-conceived tale of a man who whipped around the North Pole at such a rate that he went centuries backwards and forwards, and, I suppose, came out more or less where he went in, probably with a bad cold. Even the fall of Jericho and Joshua's halting of the sun were saved from my censure only because they were in the Bible, and then they were such whoppers that it was almost worthwhile to believe in them out of daring.

Though I still bring much of this feeling with me to any fictional event, I am no longer as critical as I used to be. Ever since I crossed the Pacific in 1923 on the *President Pierce* I have known that miracles, or at least half miracles, are not beyond ordinary human experience.

Shortly after boarding the *President Pierce* in San Francisco, I saw it wasn't a patch on the *Empress of Asia*. As an American ship, it affected to be one-class. This did not mean one-price. It meant that some cabins were cheaper than others, and whoever gave the biggest bribe got the best service. The cabin that Father and I shared was, we soon decided, marked down because it got the full blast of all galley smells. When the wind sat in a certain quarter, the porthole scoop caught bits of sour bread and decomposed fish. After two years in America I knew that this was very democratic in its own way, so I shut the porthole and went up on deck.

1923 was one of the flapper years; consequently there was always plenty to see. From the opening of the unofficial bar to the last waltz in the ballroom, ship's life was an eye-opener. There were even women on board who smoked brazenly in public, to the horror of the missionary contingent. The line between the sheep and the goats was distinct, and we of the Chosen People looked in sad wonderment at our doomed fellow passengers. I was myself saved from perdition only by the strict action of my parents when they caught me in a benefit performance of the shimmy for the other missionary offspring.

We spent mornings wandering about the deck, or we wrote long letters on ship's stationery. After lunch we played shuffleboard, pitched quoits, or disported ourselves in the swimming tank, a large canvas bag that sloshed its water back and forth to the roll of the ship. In the evenings we watched the dancing and kept an eye on the unofficial bar until we were sent off to bed.

It was during this crossing that I had the only uncontested athletic triumphs of my life. On the afternoon of the inescapable races my parents firmly shoved me forward when my age group was called. I hated these days on trips because I never won a prize and I always felt unnecessarily humiliated. But this too was a part of democracy, so I dragged myself glumly to the judges' stand and waited for the others. Everyone waited. Then it became apparent that I was the only person of my age on board. After brief consultation the judges handed me all the prizes for ten year olds, and I retired in the face of prolonged applause. Democracy, I felt at that moment, wasn't so bad as long as you didn't have to be democratic with anyone.

In fact, the only thing that seriously marred that crossing was the weariness of getting through Sundays. If the missionaries had had their say, the ship would have been hove to every Sabbath, and we would have wallowed piously in the waves. Luckily, the missionaries had nothing to say about the ship, but we did more or less heave to on Sundays as we drifted through the day's doldrums. Mornings were spent at devotions. These were tedious, ecumenical services. The Catholics took over the ladies' lounge and performed their abominations after their own manner, sensibly and without interference. The Protestants, however, tried to be tolerant and democratic. They took over the main lounge as one group. This was an error. We should have got on much better if the Episcopalians had been put into one room, the Methodists shut off in another, the Baptists left to the swimming tank, and the YMCA sent out on deck, while the Presbyterians nipped through their Calvinistic simplicities in any convenient corner. Instead we had a community service, which spun out endlessly because we had so many gods to satisfy. We shouted through a Baptist hymn, and then flopped to our knees for a string of Episcopal prayers. These always seemed to be ending,

but started up again after each *Amen* in the most absurd fashion and left a good Presbyterian in midair between his seat and his knees. A Presbyterian hymn might follow, and then a Methodist sermon, topped off with the Lord's Prayer, during which everyone got in a mess between *debts* and *trespasses.* Then we groped for the Prayer Book and rattled through some responses, followed by a long YMCA prayer that obtusely criticized the sermon at length and came to an athletic conclusion as it demanded funds for work with the U.S. Navy.

Meanwhile, the unregenerate spent the morning muttering in the passageways and grumbling on deck as they waited for the unofficial bar to open. Generally the missionaries and the damned got on tolerably well, but on Sundays we lived through an armed truce. Most agonizing were Sunday afternoons. These wretched people and their children splashed in the tank and had the shuffleboard, quoits, and deck tennis to themselves, while we made a pale pretense of devoting our minds to mastering another section of the Shorter Catechism. The Shorter Catechism is a splendid piece of work, but there are times when its limitations are almost unbearable.

It may be that the captain played *deus ex machina* just for fun; it may be that things really fell as he announced. In any event, a fantastic rumor began circulating exultantly among the missionary children one Saturday afternoon a few days out from Honolulu. When my sister and I picked up the tale we ran to the bulletin board. It was true. We decided to hold our fire until evening.

After supper that night our family strolled the deck. At last my sister spoke. "You know," she said, "I can hardly wait until tomorrow afternoon to go in swimming again."

"Me too," I echoed obediently.

Mother looked at us. "But, children, tomorrow is Sunday," she

pointed out patiently. "We don't go swimming on Sunday, you know."

"I beg your pardon," I said politely, "but tomorrow is Monday, and we do go swimming on Monday."

"Don't be silly, John," Father broke in. "Today is Saturday, and of course tomorrow is Sunday."

"I beg your pardon, Father," my sister said calmly. "Tomorrow is Monday."

"Stop being absurd, children," Mother put in mildly.

"We aren't being absurd," I said, unable to hold it back any longer. "Today is Saturday and tomorrow is Monday. Tonight we cross the International Date Line!"

"That's the truth," my sister said with authority.

Presbyterian logic was, for once, powerless. The captain wisely kept himself to the bridge. No services were posted for the next morning. During the rest of the evening my sister and I held fast and refused to be shaken by any tricks of seminary sophistry. By the time we went to bed, we knew that for the Catholics, the Baptists, the Methodists, the Episcopalians, and the YMCA the next day was Monday. But Father stubbornly withheld a Presbyterian ruling. We knew, we had always known, that Presbyterians were creatures apart, yet for this once we had no wish to make our superiority conspicuous. When we got into bed we still did not know what the next day was to be.

At midnight I wakened to the ship's bell and sensed the fleeting influence of the Lord's Day brush over me and slide into the past as I turned over into the new day.

Breakfast next morning was a silent, tense meal. Not until it was over and we were ready to leave the table did we speak to Father.

"Well?" my sister said at last.

"Well?" I echoed.

Father took a sip of water and then delivered his judgment, a judgment that set us apart as Presbyterians, a judgment that, in my eyes, made Solomon little more than infantile beside Father.

"Children," said Father with scarcely the trace of a smile—"Children, today is Sunday until twelve o'clock; after twelve o'clock today is Monday."

TWO MASTERS

W HEN I WAS ABOUT TEN and my sister thirteen, we came
to realize that one thing was lacking to complete the comfort
of whatever guests we entertained at South Gate. We ourselves by
this age whisked about all over Greater Shanghai unaccompanied
and were often guests in the homes of our more worldly friends.
Many times we thought the brand of hospitality we received quite
inferior to what we offered at South Gate; yet there was, we had to
admit at last, one thing in which South Gate was lacking.

In these other homes all the servants spoke English. If you wanted
another fork, you simply said, "I'd like another fork," and the table
boy would produce one. In fact, if you took the trouble to say it
in Chinese, the table boy would look down his nose at you and
probably bring you a dirty spoon just to let you know that he understood English. At our house if you said in English to the table boy
or the cook, "I'd like another fork," he would stare at you blankly
and wait for a member of the family to translate. Not, of course,
that we ever failed to have the correct number of forks on the table,
but any sort of request addressed in English to our servants got
nothing but a blank stare in return.

This lack worried us because we looked on guests at South Gate
with a special feeling. The courageous few who fought their way

out to South Gate were, we felt, deserving of the nicest attention. We ignored all their inane dicta on the character of the Chinese and their language. We clucked soothingly over them as they raved on about the stench of Fish Market Street or the degrading spectacle of the men's open-air public urinal on the road between the Big South Gate and the canal. After they had returned to a state of approximate calm we led them down pathways of cultivated conversation and fed them a good meal. The cook could produce finely flavored and abundant food; every member of our family considered himself a polished conversationalist; and after a genteel period in our house one guest in three was usually willing to risk the trip again after a three months' period in a quiet rest home.

The cook really understood a great deal of English, but he never admitted this. When my sister and I offered to give him English lessons, he informed us that Chinese was an ancient mode of expression that had been found adequate by his people since the beginning of time. Was there anything anyone wanted to say that couldn't be said in Chinese, and at that probably a lot more effectively than it could be said in English? We granted there wasn't anything we knew of. We could never get the cook to see why he should learn English.

It was because of this that we looked at Oo-zong with great interest when he came to work for us as outside coolie. Dr. Lin Yutang in *With Love and Irony* proves conclusively that there is no such creature as a coolie in China. I understand his feeling and sympathize with it. I try to use the word sparingly, but there are times when it cannot be avoided. After all, Oo-zong really was our outside coolie.

Oo-zong was the cook's nephew, a large raw-boned fellow who was about twenty when he came from the home village to work for us. His gown was narrow at the shoulders and ended at his calves.

His teeth were always in evidence, because he went about his duties with an idiotic grin spread over his face. His hair was cut very short, exposing all the bumps of his skull. Furthermore, Oo-zong, with his enormous hands and feet, was about the clumsiest individual we had ever encountered. Whenever he ventured into the house, something was certain to be smashed to bits and Oo-zong would be found sprawling on the floor in the midst of the wreckage.

My sister and I agreed that he didn't look promising, but having been raised in the Presbyterian atmosphere of South Gate, we knew the value of attempting the impossible. We decided to give Oo-zong a chance. After he had become accustomed to our yard work he was gradually introduced by Mother and the cook into the subtleties of being a table boy. This meant that he was going to stay on at South Gate, so my sister and I cornered him in the servants' quarters one afternoon and broached our scheme. By devious routes we told him of the qualities of the English language. The Chinese tongue, we admitted readily, was a beautiful thing, but English had its own advantages. Wouldn't Oo-zong like to have us teach him English so that he could understand what our guests wanted when they spoke to him? No, "Goddam" was not the only phrase aside from "Damfole" that was useful in speaking English. We could teach him many more phrases, like and unlike, if he wanted to learn them.

Once he had understood our plan, Oo-zong was most enthusiastic. After lesson one, which consisted of teaching him that my sister must always be addressed as Miss Espey and I as Master John, we dragged out our old primers and started in with "This is a dog. This is a cat. The dog is chasing the cat." No one, I am sure, had ever paid much attention to Oo-zong's mind, yet it took us only a few hours to make him grasp this basic concept of Western civilization, and, once started, there was almost no holding him back.

After a few weeks we used the direct method. Oo-zong would come into the room with a freshly laundered tablecloth in his hands. "What are you carrying, Oo-zong?" I would ask.

"I do not know the English name, Master John," Oo-zong would reply in slow syllables.

"That article is called a tablecloth, Oo-zong," I would say.

"Then I am carrying a tabrucroth, Master John."

"No, you are not carrying a tabrucroth, Oo-zong. You must learn the difference between l and r. It's a tablecloth. Now say it again."

"Yes, Master John. Tabblecloth."

"That's better. Now listen. Not tabblecloth, but tablecloth."

"Yes, Master John, thank you very much. Tablecloth."

"That's very good, Oo-zong. Say it again."

"Thank you, Master John. Tablecloth, tabru—no, tablecloth, tablecloth, tablecloth."

"Good work, Oo-zong."

"Thank you, Master John. Can I repeat?"

"Not can, Oo-zong—may. 'May I repeat?' Yes, you may repeat, Oo-zong."

"Thank you, Master John." Oo-zong would say, and return to the pantry only to emerge the next instant.

"What are you carrying, Oo-zong?" I would ask.

"I am carrying a tablecloth, Master John," he would reply.

"Very good, Oo-zong."

"Thank you very much, Master John."

Meanwhile Mother was guiding him through the intricacies of serving from the left and removing from the right and methods of distinguishing the rank and importance of male and female guests. Oo-zong was puzzled by the serving of ladies first. To Oo-zong it was obvious that Miss Espey and Master John were the most important

mouths to be filled. We agreed with him in private, but told him he had better do as Mother instructed.

The cook, too, was taking a part in Oo-zong's education, teaching him to decorate the pats of butter with delicate flower designs and how to arrange things on a tray, as well as how to keep his thumb out of the soup, or in any event not to lick it until he was back in the pantry.

Oo-zong's progress was not a constant, unmixed triumph. At first he was so awkward that he kept breaking dishes right and left. The grin would immediately leave his face and he would fall screaming to his knees to beg forgiveness. My sister and I took him aside after this had happened two or three times. It was not good taste, we informed him, to bawl in this way. Everyone knew that the Chinese were emotionally very reserved, so he would please in the future just pick up the pieces and walk with dignity to the pantry.

As we got to thinking about it, there were many things in Oo-zong's nature that weren't a bit Chinese, so we began to remold him into a member of his own race. There was his grin, for example. We had to explain to Oo-zong that the Chinese are an inscrutable people who rarely show joy or sorrow in public. He was to make his face, we told him, blankly intelligent. The effect, we added, would be heightened if he were to droop his eyelids a little. Then when he was addressed he was to tighten the corners of his mouth ever so slightly, which was as far, he should know, as any Chinese ever went in showing amiability. The cook and the amah whinnied in endless entertainment at the frozen mask of detachment we finally got Oo-zong to assume. It took hours of patient work in front of a mirror, but the result was the most Orientally bland face in all China.

Once we had given Oo-zong a truly Chinese face and had forbid-

den him to go to a barber until he had our permission, we set to work on his clothes. He was still stumbling about in the short, narrow, rusty black gown that the village tailor had probably fobbed off on him as the latest Shanghai style. We contributed some money of our own and gave Oo-zong careful instructions. The sleeves were to cover his wrists, and the shoulders were to be cut broad and square. The gown should come all the way to his ankles so that his feet could be better hidden, and we recommended a pair of soft Chinese cloth shoes with old-fashioned corded seams instead of the leather-heeled yellow monstrosities he sported for house wear. We didn't presume to dictate everything, we said, but we did suggest either a soft silky gray or a pale dusty blue as the best color for the gown.

When he had been outfitted thus—he chose the blue—we got to work on his posture and walk, for Oo-zong still loped into a room, head stretching forward, as if he were in pursuit of a water buffalo. We made him stand up straight. This at first produced an appalling result; he thrust his Adam's apple out in front, his rump out and up in the rear, the skirts of his gown riding high on its rounded eminence. After great effort we taught him to pull in his chin and tilt his pelvis forward, so that his truly elegant gown fell in an unbroken line from the back of his shoulders to the floor, while in front it left his broad chest in another beautiful straight line. This, we were happy to tell him, was what made Chinese clothes so pleasing to the eye and so superior to the chaotic and contradictory lines of Western dress. Though Oo-zong had never before realized this, he was happy to agree with Miss Espey and Master John.

Once Oo-zong had been taught to stand correctly, we had to teach him to walk. His normal step was about four feet long, making

his gown fly in all directions and exposing his trousers well up the leg if he was turning a corner. Patiently we taught him to flex his knees slightly and take smaller, more deliberate steps. After some weeks we were delighted by the sight of Oo-zong, swimming as it were over the floor, the light forward motion carrying his gown quivering along with him, always on the point of breaking its lovely lines but never quite doing so, its sharp cut modified in movement by spontaneous modulations. At last, we congratulated ourselves, we had taught Oo-zong the Oriental glide for which Chinese servants have ever been justly world-famous.

The more I think of it, the more I realize how essentially responsible my sister and I were for making Oo-zong conscious of the habits of his own race, for making him, indeed, really Chinese. Without us he would probably never have known the true qualities of his own nationality.

While Oo-zong's movements were being chastened and curtailed, his English was leaping ahead. He soon exhausted our primers and we took him on to more advanced reading. In this intermediate stage it was not uncommon for him in the middle of an adult tea party to call out from the other end of the room in an elegantly worked query. His clear articulation silenced all conversation as he said, "Is this not then a beautiful afternoon, Master John?" Master John, cringing in a corner, would reply, "Indeed it is, Oo-zong. Please get some more hot water now." Then Master John would follow Oo-zong to the pantry and explain to him that this type of familiar badinage was acceptable only in the bosom of the household; on public occasions Oo-zong would please be good enough to speak only when spoken to, and then only in his quietest tones. "Yes, Master John," he would whisper, the lips of his characteristically Oriental face scarcely moving.

The complete process took us about a year. At the end of that time Oo-zong was an unparalleled table boy and, in the Western phrase, a true son of Han. Although his literary bent broke out from time to time in such overwrought sentences as "Indeed, Miss Espey, it is but a pleasure for me so to do," or "What say, Master John, to the consumption of an omelet this morning?" his English was so much better than that of the average International Settlement servant that my sister and I felt we had done everything we could for him. We leaned back and enjoyed the astonishment of a visitor when Oo-zong in clipped accents greeted him with "Just give me your coat, sir. This way to the downstairs bathroom, please." What more, we questioned ourselves, could our long-suffering guests ask of us?

For almost two months we lived in this fool's paradise. Oo-zong conducted himself magnificently. My sister and I congratulated him daily and ourselves hourly on his success. No longer did we need to look embarrassed when anyone addressed our table boy in English. He was ready, often more than ready, with an adequate and cheerful response. Our hospitality was perfect now, and in our childish way we thought that all we had to do was sit back and enjoy it. Mother let fall a few ironic remarks from time to time on the excellence of our product, but we assumed that, inconsistent as it was with her character, she must be just a touch jealous because she hadn't thought long ago of doing the same thing.

At the end of our two perfect months we noticed that Oo-zong during his free hours was leaving the compound for the outer world instead of staying at home and reading another chapter of Dickens's *Child's History of England.* When we asked him where he went, he usually told us he had been paying some calls in the International Settlement. We romantically assumed that he was conducting a

high-class love affair and were totally unprepared for the shock of his coming announcement, for when Oo-zong at last revealed his plans to us we were crushed. Oo-zong announced that he had been investigating openings for English-speaking table boys in the International Settlement and now planned to leave us. Dazed, we asked him why he wanted to go. With just a hint of the pre-Chinese Oo-zong in his face, he said, "But, my two dear friends, surely you know that an English-speaking table boy is paid at least three times as much as a Chinese-speaking one?"

We had not known, but now that we did, we saw readily there was nothing else for Oo-zong to do. We were Chinese enough for that. We also knew that our parents were certainly not going to triple Oo-zong's pay. But that our hand-turned product should go to a home in the International Settlement, possibly to the home of some of our own acquaintances, was almost too much to bear. Did we, we asked, know the people Oo-zong was going to work for? Indeed we did, replied Oo-zong, for they had been guests at South Gate more than once. In fact, they had approached him, and not he them, on the subject. The only satisfaction we ever got out of this was learning later that on his first morning's service Oo-zong had nonplussed his new employer by greeting him with a gay "Hello, fellow."

So Oo-zong left us, though he did not fail each year to send appropriate gifts to Miss Espey and Master John, the founders of his career. As he rose in the English-speaking hierarchy of Shanghai servants, we took a certain pride in his advance, for after all we were his unwitting sponsors. Whenever we were guests at the homes in which he worked, we smiled approval at his perfect Oriental glide, his air of true Chinese detachment in performing his duties.

After Oo-zong left, Mother continued to drop ironic remarks,

and at the end of a week the cook imported a fresh raw-boned nephew from the home village. For a day our hopes revived. The new nephew certainly looked unpromising, we told each other, but then, so at first had the unmatchable Oo-zong. The new nephew, we also noticed, acted almost as if he were waiting for us to propose teaching him English.

We mentioned this hopefully to Mother. "Don't you think once is enough, children?" she asked.

We were forced to face the facts. A vision came to us of an endless stream of raw-boned nephews coming up from the home village one by one, year after year. Year after year we would begin with "This is a dog. This is a cat. The dog is chasing the cat." Year after year we would be giving advice on the cut of a Chinese gown. Year after year we would teach the Oriental glide, correct the tilt of the pelvis. And year after year our hand-finished products would go off to the International Settlement or the French Concession at triple pay.

It was an impossible future. Happy as we were to teach the Chinese their true nature, we were not going to make it a life work. Nor could we feel that our highest contribution to society was the providing of our guests with servants better trained and of a sweeter disposition than any they could hire elsewhere. Oo-zong we could be proud of in our own fashion; the second nephew could surely find sufficient expression in Chinese for any thoughts he might have. Yes, we agreed, once was definitely enough.

In later years, when our harried guests said, as if it were the last straw of being entertained at South Gate, "Dear me, don't your servants speak anything but Chinese?" we had our answer. Lowering our eyelids slightly and looking down our noses, we let our faces freeze into the well-known passive mask of the Oriental as we said

haughtily, "But of course not. After all, this is China, you know. Our servants are Chinese, you know. And, if you would only take the trouble to learn the language, you would find that there is really no good idea in the world that cannot be expressed clearly, adequately, altogether wittily, and with nice distinction in the Chinese tongue."

SHE BRINGETH HER BREAD
FROM AFAR

MISS MARY ELIZABETH COGDAL had been in the mission for some years when I was born, so I have no clear recollection of our first meeting. She, on the other hand, might have been able to bring up a striking scene in her own memory of the only son's only son who was to cause her some trouble and, I hope, a little joy. Legend has it that she bent over my crib, pursed her lips, and said, "Well, they always come that way."

Miss Cogdal was born on a farm in Illinois and later moved to Kansas. She knew the earth and was familiar with horses; no better preparation has yet been devised for a missionary. Somewhere in her past lay a romance. We never heard much about it, but it hovered there in the background, the young lover dead, the girl turning all her passion to teaching. I always gathered that it was the unreliable conduct of this young fellow that made Miss Cogdal into a militant feminist who began to teach in a country school at the age of sixteen. From that day to her death she declared herself a man-hater, and like all of that breed she could be got around by any fairly subtle male.

All her life Miss Cogdal was a little slow in paying attention to anyone, and the Lord was unable to get through to her with His Call until she was in her middle twenties. After making herself ac-

ceptable to 156 Fifth Avenue, Miss Cogdal, still paying no attention to anyone, started putting her affairs in order. Knowing in her own mind that life in China would hold no luxuries and that she was on the point of renouncing the world, she gave away all her possessions. When she buckled the strap on her one suitcase, it contained two changes of nunlike garments, her Bible, one knife, one fork, and one spoon. The last three items were to see her through her apprenticeship with chopsticks, and then they too were to be cast aside. Her clear voice always broke in notes of bassoonlike laughter when she told of the South Gate ladies eagerly waiting to see the latest nineties fashions, only to be dismayed by Miss Cogdal severely attired in a rustling black creation of her own design. Miss Cogdal's establishment never quite lost its original nakedness. "Why should people worry about their houses," she would ask, "when half the children in China haven't clothes to their backs?" And she would sweep out and clap a garment on the next child she met.

Miss Cogdal came to grips with South Gate immediately. Starting with a private teacher, she soon acquired a hold on Chinese that remained a curious delight to all who heard her speak. Then she turned to the Girls' School. The principal of the Girls' School at that time was an Englishwoman who did not like cucumbers. Miss Cogdal doted on cucumbers. She and the Englishwoman ate their meals together. Whenever cucumbers appeared on the table the Englishwoman snatched up the dish, rushed it out to the kitchen, and hurled the cucumbers into the garbage pail. At the end of six months Miss Cogdal became principal of the school and the Englishwoman left South Gate for a place more to her tastes.

The Englishwoman disposed of, Miss Cogdal turned to the girls. She was offended by them. They were apathetic, thin, flabby, delicate, finicky—in short, they had not grown up on a Kansas farm.

Miss Cogdal went about getting what she could to take its place. She drew up a stiff regimen of physical training for all the girls. The girls shuddered—the girls' parents shuddered. One did not go in for flinging the body about wildly in China. Miss Cogdal stood firm for flinging the body about. Then the Orientals outsmarted themselves. Smiling up their sleeves, they said that everything would be fine if—and they thought it was an insuperable *if*—the foreign teacher did the same exercises. Miss Cogdal was shocked. "Of course I'm going to do them," she replied. "How do you think they'll learn if I don't teach them?" The Chinese had been had, though Miss Cogdal went on blithely flinging the body about without realizing that she had had them. Not only did Miss Cogdal do her calisthenics; she started her own vegetable garden to get more exercise by spading, hoeing, and weeding. When the girls saw this they knew that the world had come to an end. And, indeed, that world had come to an end.

In her own way, Miss Cogdal set a good pace for the emancipation of Chinese womn. Her pupils soon adored her to the point of imitation. She had large feet, so the Chinese girls began to frown on bound feet. She was vigorous and athletic, so the Chinese girls tried to be vigorous and athletic. Her most daring advance was made late in the twenties. The short-hair question was agitating the councils of the church in those years. If it had been anyone but St. Paul who had laid down those absurd injunctions, Miss Cogdal might have conformed. But she got to thinking about Paul, who was after all a mere man, and she decided that he hadn't known his own mind. While everyone else was debating whether or not a woman with short hair could get into heaven, Miss Cogdal took a streetcar into Shanghai. She went to no beauty parlor, for this was not a move of vanity. She went to an ordinary barbershop and demanded that

her hair be cut exactly like a man's. She thought of this, I am sure, as the most humiliating method she could follow. On her return the station gulped collectively. Miss Cogdal was very calm. "It feels better," she said. "It's more convenient and it saves time."

The station hastily decided that Miss Cogdal would not go to hell, and the next day the braids in the Girls' School began to fall. Ironically, this haircut was the most beautifying thing Miss Cogdal could have done to herself. Big-boned, with great hands and feet, she had sensibly never gone in for frilly clothes or flower patterns, but the hair drawn back into a knob at the back of her head had always looked a little silly. Now, in her sixties, the close-cropped graying hair went well with her bold nose and strong chin. In her austerely cut suits and dresses she could have stalked into any of Shanghai's more sophisticated spots and been accepted as a distinguished woman of the world. This, in fact, was just what she was.

Yet underneath it all there seethed a great unrest. At the risk of appearing old-fashioned in my psychology, I think she wanted children. She may have wanted a man, but I doubt it, unless it could have been for the pleasure of hitting him over the head and plucking out his hair. She used to come and look at my sister and me when we were still small. Gingerly she held us in her arms. But at the first squawk, the first dampness of the diaper she jumped up, thrust the infant back, and declaimed: "Let them as wants babies have 'em. I don't!" She came back to the nursery time and again.

Eventually she experimented with vicarious motherhood and took under her guardianship an ugly duckling at the school. She fed her and clothed her, paid for her education, and even stooped to finding her a husband. This experiment was not a great success, since the

husband turned out to be an opium addict and the girl not altogether grateful. Her second daughter was more satisfactory. Miss Cogdal spotted her in Mulberry Lane, a dirty little girl of three living with her newly widowed father and five or six other ricksha coolies. Miss Cogdal offered to take the girl and rear her. The father was glad to be rid of his daughter, so Miss Cogdal bundled her over to our house, where she and Mother filled a bathtub and stripped the child of her rags. They scrubbed the skin off her, using tub after tub of water and ignoring the girl's screams. Satisfied at last, Miss Cogdal thrust her into some clean clothes and took her to the school dormitory. Next morning she was gone. Miss Cogdal strode to the hovel in Mulberry Lane, turned down the filthy bedding on the one bed, and found the girl asleep, her face tearstained. Without hesitation Miss Cogdal snatched her up and, her own eyes brim-full of tears as the girl fought and wept, bore her back to cleanliness. After that she stayed. As she grew up, a completely undemonstrative tie was formed between the two self-willed and determined women, a tie that was closer than Miss Cogdal normally came to sentiment.

Her unrest had some sportive manifestations. It was a fine scene of a moonlit night to see Miss Cogdal, long-sleeved nightgown whipping about her, stride back and forth on the upstairs veranda of her house as she walked in a nightmare, waving her arms about as she shouted, "Help! Murder! O Lord, O Lord!" until someone led her back to bed. For no known reason this convinced her she was a light sleeper, and she refused to lock her house until a thief got in one night and rifled her bedroom successfully.

There were other nights when Miss Cogdal did no sleeping at all. If she found a book she liked, and she was an omnivorous reader, she sat up with it until half an hour before breakfast. Then she would fill her bath with cold water, leap into it, come out refreshed,

dress, go down to breakfast, and appear at school to lecture the girls on the necessity of regular habits.

I wish I knew more about her reading. I know that it followed no plan, that she had spells when she read magazines, novels, biographies, and murder stories, anything she could lay hands on. It would, I am certain, make an interesting list. When I came back from boarding school one vacation, Miss Cogdal asked me what we were studying. After I had said something about European history of the seventeenth century she remarked, "I know a book you would like, and it would do you a lot more good than any history text. It's called *The Letters of Madame de Sevigné.*" There is a spell to conjure with, but I cannot complete the charm, though I remember her recommending to me *Tom Jones* and *Barry Lyndon.*

When somnambulism and reading failed to release her, she required physical expression. Once, on learning of a tragedy that had overtaken one of her girls, and that seemed to her unjust, she dragged a big log from her woodpile. Taking the outside coolie's ax, she savagely smashed the log into tiny chips before going in to eat her supper. Another time she reacted with an even finer sense of violence. What we referred to as the Q Trial provoked her. The Q's were two sisters who made so much trouble in the mission that their dismissal was considered. The investigating commission was presided over by a man, not a South Gater: two bad mistakes from Miss Cogdal's point of view. Not only was the creature a man, he was a small man, about half Miss Cogdal's height. The insolence of this male midget's sitting in judgment on not just one woman but two women automatically brought forth Miss Cogdal's feminism to do battle against him. She won, as South Gate knew she would. But when the trial was over—and it dragged on for days—Miss Cogdal was still not satisfied. That night as she combed her hair

before going to bed, her pent up fury swept over her. Stubbornly setting her jaw, she grasped the heavy comb and, slowly and relentlessly, one by one she broke out all its teeth.

The upshot of the Q Trial was that Miss Cogdal had to go safe-conduct for one of the sisters and live with her. Her defense of this woman had not been made because she liked her. In fact, she didn't especially, but she took up the cross good-humoredly and laughed when the Chinese pastor said the two of them were just like man and wife: they fought for and with each other.

Late in 1918 Miss Cogdal was practically incapacitated by sprue, and I was not doing too well either. A dictionary will observe airily that sprue is a tropical disease with ulcerated mucous membrane of the mouth and chronic enteritis. In the same lexical tone the dictionary will note that asthma is a disease of respiration, characterized by difficult breathing, cough, and so on. Neither definition is even suggestive of these two tortures.

Everyone at South Gate got the idea about the same time. Miss Cogdal, going on fifty-five, was ill and should go to the mountains for a rest. I, going on six, was ill and should go to the mountains for a rest. Ergo, Miss Cogdal and I went to the mountains for a rest early in 1919. This was a Presbyterian syllogism. My sister was trundled off with us, and a green amah and Miss Cogdal's cook completed our party.

The trip up the Yangtze to Kiukiang by boat and then into Kuling Valley by sedan chair did not improve anybody's health. My sister was acutely homesick, but she had been told not to make me unhappy, so she mooned around, lips clamped, looking like Niobe suddenly gone dry. Miss Cogdal suffered from sprue, the cook went on a bender in the bowels of the boat, the amah was riversick. I viewed it all impartially. At the age of four and a half, during an

attack of amoebic dysentery, I had overheard the doctor saying to Mother that he didn't think I was going to live. This is a mistake doctors often make with our family, but I didn't know this at the time, and I was so invigorated at the thought of beating the rest to heaven that I got well in a few weeks. But whenever things got very hectic I assumed the doctor had been right, and I leaned back, waiting for death to remove me. I leaned back most of the journey to Kuling, wondering if the rites of burial at sea were effective on a river.

Once we had arrived safely in Kuling, Miss Cogdal got down to curing her sprue and knocking us into shape. We spent our mornings at a small American school. In the afternoons Miss Cogdal took over. One of our daily tasks was writing home, an alarming process. First we drafted the letter in pencil. Miss Cogdal edited. We made a second copy in ink just to limber our fingers. Miss Cogdal read proof. At last we got a fair sheet of paper and transcribed our final copies. It took me a month or so to adapt myself to Miss Cogdal's epistolary style. Frequently during that period my first draft contained some such statement as "Auntie Cogdal beat me this afternoon until I cried." On coming to this in her editorial capacity, Miss Cogdal would look up and fix me with a not unhumorous eye. Rapping my fingers with her pencil, she would say, "Boy, tell the whole truth." My revision would come out on a piece of scratch paper: "The cook called me a bad name so I threw a mud pye at him and Auntie Cogdal gave me five wacks when I cried to make her stop." Miss Cogdal's eye would brighten at this as she corrected *pye* and *wacks*. "Is that all?" she would ask. I would twist a bit, take back the scratch paper, and emend to "After I called the cook a bad name this afternoon he called me one so I threw a mud pie at him and Auntie Cogdal gave me five whacks when I cried to make her

stop. It didnt hurt." Miss Cogdal would insert the apostrophe, smile at me and say, "All right, and while you're copying that, I'll just step out to the kitchen for a few minutes." By the end of four weeks I developed a satisfactory method and was even guilty of things like "I was a bad boy this afternoon but Auntie Cogdal was very nice and just gave me five whacks."

Miss Cogdal also left her marks on my speech. Not a very advanced conversationalist at that age, I nevertheless enjoyed talking. When I got hold of something to tell I tried to say it all at once and interrupted my own sentences, backtracked, leapt ahead, and generally made a hash of the story. After a few weeks of listening to me, Miss Cogdal pulled me up short one day in the midst of a long backwards harangue and said: "Form your sentences in your mind, boy. Speak them clearly. Then close your mouth." Not bad precepts, though for some time my conversation was rather halting as I formed a sentence in my mind, spoke it clearly, then closed my mouth and began forming another sentence in my mind, only to discover when I was ready to speak it clearly that I had lost the floor to Auntie Cogdal.

What with her belief in exercise, Miss Cogdal took us for long walks. It is not too strenuous to take a long walk with a victim of chronic enteritis; even so, we thought some of the hikes a bit too much, and one day we took Miss Cogdal for a walk. Pretending that a mountain gully was a path, we started up. Miss Cogdal was not a graceful rock climber, and by keeping about fifty yards ahead of her we brought her panting to the top of the mountain. She played the game well, congratulating us on the trip, and never after insisted that we go any further than we wished.

The sprue inspired a thoroughly perverse game we invented. Only a child raised by the canal can appreciate it, and all delicate readers are

advised to skip this paragraph, for it reveals only the bad effects of living in a country that does not consider comment on bodily functions very bad taste. Miss Cogdal's bedroom and the dining room had originally been one large room. The wooden partition, thrown up in casual Chinese fashion, ended in the middle of a window and was a foot short to let one get at the latch. When Miss Cogdal was audibly in the throes of her suffering we liked to thrust our heads around the end of the partition and shout "Boo!" Miss Cogdal, enthroned, would look at us calmly and say, "All right, children, pull your heads back in. There's no need to be vulgar about it." And as we drew back, her great laugh came crashing against the partition. I admit there is a very canalish touch to this, but the real point is that Miss Cogdal thought it was just as funny as we did.

The series of events that convinced me that Miss Cogdal was one of the superior women of her day reached its climax slowly. My first grade teacher was reasonably competent, but she was a trifle frail in a Victorian way. One hot spring morning she was standing by the blackboard demonstrating $2 + 2 = 4$. As we concentrated on this problem she suddenly wheeled towards the door, said, "Oh, my God!" and collapsed on the sill. A few of us ran up to her, and then I, putting two and two together in my own Presbyterian arithmetic, went into the other classroom, where my sister's class worked. The teacher looked up as I entered, and I said to her firmly, "Our teacher has just said a bad word and God has struck her dead." The effect was very satisfactory, and the first and second grades spent the rest of the morning in the playground.

The next day we had a substitute, a missionary mother whose ideas on education were decidedly embryonic. Her first question was "Can anyone here count up to one hundred without making a mistake?" I put up my hand and volunteered. "Go ahead," she

ordered. Wondering at this elementary task, I set out towards one hundred, galloping through the twenties, thirties, and forties, droning on into the fifties, sixties, and seventies, and then rattling off the rest at breakneck speed. "Very good," the substitute said. "You are a well-educated boy." I thanked her, and she started around the class, asking each member to count to one hundred. As it happened, no one else was able to; so for the next week the first grade was taught to count to one hundred. This was done by the chorus method. Obviously, there wasn't much for me to do. I could join the chorus automatically. Therefore, I sat twirling my glasses in my hand and pondered the meaning of life. On Friday of that week I twirled my glasses once too often: a temple snapped, and the chorus was hushed.

The substitute came over to my desk. "What have you done?" she asked.

"I've just broken my glasses," I said.

"Can you read without them?" she demanded.

"No," I said, although this was not strictly true.

"Then there's no use your staying the rest of the morning," she told me.

This I couldn't understand, since reciting to one hundred did not demand very keen eyesight. But I kept my mouth shut and got up to go.

"You are," the substitute said, "a wicked, bad boy to break your glasses. When you get home you must get on your knees and ask God to forgive you."

Until this moment I had not realized that I had sinned. The thought depressed me as I walked reluctantly back to the house, for if the substitute thought I had sinned, probably Miss Cogdal would think so too.

Unwillingly I went through the door. Miss Cogdal looked up from the book she was reading at her desk. "Why are you back so early?" She asked. "Is anything the matter?"

"Yes," I said bravely. "I was twirling my glasses in school while we counted to one hundred and I broke a temple. The teacher sent me home and said I must pray to God on my knees to be forgiven for this sin."

Miss Cogdal's head jerked back. Her deep brown eyes flashed. "Are you telling the truth?"

"Yes," I said.

She took a deep breath, looked in my eyes, and saw that for once the truth was in me. Then she jumped up, book in hand, raised her arm, and with a wild shout of "Sin!" hurled the book to the floor. She picked it up instantly, and down she flung it again to another magnificently bellowed "Sin!"

Thoroughly frightened, I asked, "Should I get down and pray right away?"

Miss Cogdal relaxed. Her eyes filled with tears, and for the only time I can remember she put her arm around me. "My dear boy," she said, "if we pray for anything we will pray for that idiot woman's soul." She grinned, and I felt much better. "She's not a Presbyterian," Miss Cogdal chuckled, and then grew stern again as she added "but that's no excuse." Turning her eyes full on me, she continued, "It is the silliest thing in the world to pray to God over nothing. You haven't sinned. No one your age really can sin. And remember this: when you break a thing, when you make a mistake, never, never get down on your knees and whine about it. Just get it fixed if you can." Again her anger seized her, and she let go of me to smack her fist down on the desk. Her eyes lit up. "The Bible says, John, that you're in danger of hell fire if you call your brother a

fool." She hesitated. "Well, I won't call that woman a fool. No, I won't—she isn't worth it."

I had gathered by this time that Miss Cogdal was on my side. She smiled at me and said, "Now you may play for the rest of the morning, and when your sister gets back and we've had tiffin, we'll all go down to the Gap and have your glasses mended."

The Gap was the name given the village in the pass at the head of Kuling Valley. The three of us set out on this unusual expedition in high spirits. Miss Cogdal was quite as excited over this irregularity as we were, and that may have been the cause of her accident.

As a feminist, Miss Cogdal was always somewhat unconventional about her clothes. Instead of wearing the regulation two petticoats and an underskirt, she was in the habit of breezing about with just a pair of voluminous black bloomers under her walking skirt. We got the glasses fixed and set out to see the sights on the Gap's one street. Somewhere on this journey the elastic of Miss Cogdal's bloomers gave way. My sister and I, afraid to say anything, saw what was coming. Down, down, came the bloomers below the hem of Miss Cogdal's walking skirt. We looked at them, hypnotized. Miss Cogdal finally noticed that we were staring at her. "What's the matter, children?" she demanded. My sister pointed feebly and quavered, "Auntie Cogdal, your bloomers." Miss Cogdal looked down. With a snort that brought everyone's eyes on her, she bent over, grasped one leg of the garment and stepped out of it, then balanced and pulled off the other leg. Rocking with laughter, she held the things up and shook them out before folding them carefully and stuffing them into her reticule. She smiled at the Chinese audience that had gathered. "There," she said, "we can go on now." After a few paces she hitched up her skirt and commented, "I wonder why that never happened before. You know, it's a lot more comfortable

this way." My sister and I looked at each other, eyes wide in admiration of such aplomb. Was this not a wonderful woman? we asked ourselves; and we agreed that she was.

In the years following our stay at Kuling Miss Cogdal returned to her teaching at South Gate. I know little of this part of her life save that she won the unfailing tribute of a great teacher: the personal affection and respect of her best students. If her methods were similar to those she had used on me, I have no difficulty in understanding her pupils' devotion.

One thing that surely characterized everything she did in and out of the classroom was her enthusiastic curiosity over whatever lay at hand. On one occasion a pupil told her that angleworms made noises—"talked," as she said. "Tommyrot," Miss Cogdal replied, or at least its Chinese equivalent, "I'll eat the first one I hear talking." After the next rain the girl called Miss Cogdal out to listen to the worms. Miss Cogdal put her ear to the ground. She heard something. Getting a trowel, she dug in and brought up some angleworms. According to my story she ate them. Others say this was the only time in her life that she broke her word. If I could get hold of our cook and amah and talk for a few minutes with them and with my sister, I should have three incorruptible witnesses on my side. I am satisfied to rest my case there.

My own contacts with Miss Cogdal during this period came from ours being the one really normal household in South Gate and from her delight in the game of Rook. She was fond of normality and incurably addicted to Rook, though I imagine that she learned to play the game only after coming to South Gate. Certainly her original suitcase had not held a deck of cards.

Rook leads you temptingly on to a high bid with no real indication of your partner's strength. The winner of the bid has the privi-

lege of picking up a four-card kitty and then discarding four cards from his hand before naming the trump. It was this kitty that was Miss Cogdal's undoing in a Rook game. To have four accessible cards face down on the table so aroused her curiosity that she often had to be reminded that the bid could not go above the maximum number of points that could be won in a single hand. Her desire to hold the unknown led her time and again into overreaching herself, whereupon she would go set in a dazzling collapse, revealing as the cards were played that from the very beginning she had not held a single quick trick. Possibly this accounted for the reluctance of some of the more conventional South Gaters to have her for a partner.

For my sister and me, when we played a hand in cooperation, she was ideal. She usually took the bidding away from us, but when it came to playing out the hand—there is no dummy in Rook—my sister and I went into long huddles of whispering. If we failed to reach an agreement, I would peek into the hand on our right and my sister would do the same for the one on our left. Auntie Cogdal gazed over our heads and launched into an interesting tale for the benefit of our opponents. The three of us made an almost unbeatable combination when Miss Cogdal curbed her curiosity over the kitty. At times she trumped our tricks, but no one cared, least of all the two of us. And I think she enjoyed playing with us as much as we enjoyed her, for when she was paired off with one of South Gate's Mrs. Battles she realized too late always that she had put her partner into a bad hole and felt compelled to say loudly, "I'm a goose, a perfect goose, I know. But those four cards face down there are just too tantalizing." Her partner would look acidly in Miss Cogdal's direction, but Miss Cogdal often failed to recognize acid and was probably already well into some recent event that had delighted her.

On the whole, I think that I prefer Miss Cogdal's type of game to Mrs. Battle's, for I share with Auntie Cogdal the unusual view that games are meant for entertainment. Though Mrs. Battle may have been the soul of whist, Miss Cogdal was the very heart of Rook.

After I went off to boarding school I saw Miss Cogdal only during vacations. One Christmas I came down with asthma, and Miss Cogdal, knowing that I would be upset by missing our annual Christmas Eve dinner at the home of some friends, brought all her gifts up to my bedroom and spent the evening with me. Her gifts were characteristic. A woman who spent almost nothing on herself, Miss Cogdal gave the best of everything to her friends, and what she would have considered mildly sinful to own herself she happily thrust into the hands of another.

That evening as I gasped and coughed between my jerky sentences—with plenty of time to form them in my mind—she sat wrapping her presents, and we talked over old times in Kuling: mud pies, my glasses, her bloomers. She shook her cropped head and laughed until she was in almost as bad shape as I was. But then she asked me with a tremor in her voice, "Do you think I did a good job? Was I all right for a mother?"

I was fourteen at the time, an age that does not lend itself to easy expression of sentiment; but I was able to catch my breath firmly for an instant and, with no need to form my sentences, I assured her that she had been all right, that she was marvelous, and that my sister and I adored her. I wonder if she had ever been praised to her face before. Her brown eyes grew luminous and her features softened.

The next breath I went into a coughing fit. "Good heavens, boy!" she exclaimed. "There's no need to choke yourself to death flattering an old woman."

"Who—said—old?" I strangled out.

Then for the only time in my life I heard Miss Cogdal giggle. It was not a silly giggle; it was a flight of full-throated meadowlarks rising at sundown.

When she left that evening, Miss Cogdal turned at the door. "I've always thought it was a pity you had to be a boy," she said. "But now I'm not so sure."

I scarcely know what more I can say of her. She herself would think that I had already said too much, that if I really had to write a book about South Gate I ought to concentrate on the interesting people, the Chinese, though Miss Cogdal never found the Chinese very puzzling, for she met them all on a basis of complete equality. She had no unctuous condescension in her, none of the superior laughter that shrills through many an Old China Hand's remarks on the quaintness, the oddity, the weirdness (all meaning the inferiority) of the Chinese. I believe the only thing that ever angered her from them was their query in the country districts as to whether she was a man or a woman. To Miss Cogdal nothing was weird, odd, or quaint simply because it was not Kansas. She never confused difference in manner with difference in quality. She was that rarest of foreigners in China, one who accepted unconsciously the right of the Chinese to think, to act, to be human beings. She accepted everything until Kansas common sense told her something was wrong, and once she was convinced a thing was wrong she flew to remedy it, not with superior cluckings and shakes of the head, but with a clean heart and an impassioned spirit.

There was no studied policy in this acceptance. Miss Cogdal was incapable of either forming or following a policy. She had no systematic knowledge of Chinese art, but she did not sniff with supercilious amusement at paintings that lacked Western perspec-

tive. She knew little of Chinese literature, but she never sneered at things she did not understand. Perhaps the best way to describe her attitude—which was not really an attitude—is to say that the Chinese were not the Chinese to Miss Cogdal; the Chinese were honest-to-God people.

When the Girls' School was turned over to a new principal, Miss Cogdal had the good sense to leave the compound. She was not going to get in anyone's way. With a friend she made a home in the International Settlement, where she created a job for herself by keeping in touch with her former pupils, who were to her her own children, devoting her waning strength to helping them in every way she could. Not entirely satisfied with this, she, who had shaped a great school, did some teaching in a small struggling school in the city.

In 1932 the Japanese swept over that part of the city. Some of her girls were killed in the streets, some were subjected to indignities, others were able to flee. This barbarism threw Miss Cogdal into a frenzy. Back at South Gate, where she herself had had to seek refuge, she could not sleep for thinking of the outrages being committed. At last, wangling military passes for herself, she swept down on the Japanese. Exposing herself to scorn and insult, she did all she could to get the Chinese and their possessions out of the rioting district. The Japanese soldiers were, after all, men—and small ones.

When the temporary peace was restored she went back to her home in the city. Only then did she learn that she had developed Hodgkin's disease. After reading all the literature she could find on it and learning that her condition was incurable, she refused to leave China. Instead she went to a hospital for a few weeks, but finally returned to her own bed.

Hodgkin's disease is a proliferation of the lymphatics. In its latter

stages the victim may suffer a complete agony of the body. Miss Cogdal was no pale and resigned martyr. Exhausted and gaunt, weeping over a wounded China, she was uninterested in dying a nobly restrained death. If she was to die, she was to die, and the quicker the better. As the pain racked her in her last days she cried out time and again, "How long, O Lord, how long?" After five hours of unconsciousness this great-hearted pioneer woman died.

At one time or another, a hot controversy on the value of foreign missions has burned. At times I have found myself in sympathy with the more severe critics, but always at some point I would stop. The case for foreign missions was entirely Mary Elizabeth Cogdal's case.

THE SERVANT IS FREE
FROM HIS MASTER

MANY GAPS, most of which will not be filled, remain in this casual record. There is one, however, that is so apparent that I must say something about it even though I am unable to stop it adequately. An outline of what it should be is plain enough; it is so familiar that I think I could fake it without the slightest risk of being found out by anyone outside of my own family. This should be the story of my firm friendship with a Chinese boy of my own age. The chubby, fair American lad, advancing in a frank and friendly manner, takes the shy hand of his Chinese companion and leads him into the ways of Western thought, receiving in return a sense of the deep intuitional feeling of Chinese life, a knowledge of its complex mysteries. Together, hand in hand, the two small friends supplement each other: The American gains a shrewd understanding of China's wisdom; the Chinese comes to recognize American direct-ness as open-faced generosity. The happy interchange ends in the cementing of the bonds of international love and law, plus a few cutting remarks on Kipling's famous statement about the East and the West.

Somehow for Kwei-ling and me it didn't work that way. I make no pretense of penetrating very far into his mind, but I did get far enough to understand most of his difficulties, and I know perfectly

well what my own were. The picture was wrong from the start, even visually. I was not fair, but just about as dark as Kwei-ling, and though my hair was a deep brown instead of black, it was just as straight as his. And Kwei-ling, not I, was the chubby one, though he was solid rather than chubby. As for holding hands, neither one of us, I think, ever considered such an undignified mode of behavior either in public or in private. And the mental and intuitional part was confused too. I was the shy, impractical, inactive one, and something of a dub when it came to Western science and the direct approach, while Kwei-ling, although he was shy with me, was otherwise perfectly self-sufficient, literal-minded, and practical, always a little bored by anything that smacked of the imagination.

Yet before I go any farther in this thwarted account, I should make it clear that I am perfectly willing to accept anyone else's tale of an East-West friendship, knowing from my own American contemporaries in China that they are nothing out of the ordinary. Kwei-ling and I might even have managed one of our own if it hadn't been for South Gate, his parents, my parents, and too much sensitivity on the part of us both.

Kwei-ling was the cook's son by his first marriage. We were almost the same age, and since we were members of the same household all of South Gate certainly expected the usual pattern to follow. I had no other boys to play with, which was another point in our favor, since everyone knows that sisters, though good companions, cannot share all a boy's interests. What these unsharable interests of mine were my sister has never explained to me, but everyone knows they exist. So Kwei-ling and I were shoved at each other and were expected to solve all the problems of Chinese-American relations. I dare say we could have solved them unaided with little hesitation, but we had so much assistance that we never got down to it.

I was about seven when a misguided relative gave me a soccer ball. I had begun to kick it around halfheartedly on the front lawn one afternoon when a Courtesy Aunt passed by and announced that it was foolish to kick it around by myself—why didn't Kwei-ling, who had come up from the home village a few weeks earlier, kick it with me?

Until this time Kwei-ling and I had looked at each other around corners, and though I think neither of us had reached any definite conclusion on the other's character, we were perfectly prepared to say hello when we happened to collide. Probably we would have gone on in this fashion for some months, and though we were not, I suspect, designed to be close friends, we could have had a quite normal relationship.

But while I was kicking my soccer ball around, Kwei-ling was produced by the cook and the amah, his stepmother, and as they looked on and my parents looked on, Kwei-ling and I silently kicked the soccer ball back and forth, back and forth across the lawn. He was much stronger than I, but he never kicked out of my range, a tactful consideration for which I felt grateful. Kwei-ling, however, did kick the ball in a peculiar way off the side of his foot, so that near the end of this Chinese-American interplay I tried to tell him that he was doing it all wrong, not realizing that to kick a soccer ball in orthodox manner was unwise when wearing a soft Chinese shoe. Kwei-ling sensibly announced that I didn't know what I was talking about, and we went back to kicking the ball silently back and forth, back and forth across the lawn. Finally my parents gathered me into the house, and Kwei-ling's parents gathered him into the servants' quarters. I can't remember what happened to the soccer ball.

Once in the bosoms of our respective families, we found that we had got off to a bad start, something that neither of us had noticed.

My parents informed me that just because Kwei-ling was the cook's son was no reason for me to begin giving him orders. He was as free an agent as I was, and I needn't be so cocky about knowing how to kick a soccer ball. At the same time Kwei-ling was being given a lecture by his parents on the duties of a servant to his master. He was to understand that the little American boy was the only son of the house, and when the only son said a thing it was right, as far as Kwei-ling was concerned, even if it meant that he had to break a toe proving it.

Instantly Kwei-ling and I ceased to be a couple of small boys and became self-conscious miniature adults trying to keep their proper places. What was worse, each of us came to realize the instructions that had been given the other, and our young brains were so occupied in dealing delicately with each other that there was simply no time or energy left for us to worry about becoming friends.

The approved method for two males to become friends is, I believe, for one to knock down the other. I have never used this method myself, possibly because I have never been physically capable of knocking down anyone I cared to have as a friend, in addition to a feeling that I am not interested in being the friend of anyone who would care to knock me down. But the theory is good: you should at least have the free option of knocking down your friends, and although if one of my friends ever knocks me down I shall get up and walk off to find another and better one, wondering at my original lack of judgment, I think I could see out of my unblackened eye that friendship should be an open exchange, not too closely hedged about by conventions. With Kwei-ling and me this atmosphere was immediately removed. Neither of us, I am sure, would have thought of knocking down the other, but we ought at least to have been given the chance.

Instead, we got into a tangle about our names. I was usually called Little Brother in Chinese, but Kwei-ling felt he couldn't call me that. I didn't think he should either, for that matter, but I didn't see why he couldn't call me by my Chinese given name, the equivalent of John. As from servant to master, this too was impossibly familiar in Kwei-ling's way of thinking. On the other hand Little Master was something I obviously couldn't tolerate, for we were equals. Therefore I was unable to call him Kwei-ling since he couldn't call me John. The upshot was that he called me nothing and I called him nothing. As far as possible we made our rare remarks strictly impersonal, and when it was necessary to go beyond this we said "you." And we went on saying "you" during the difficult intervals in which we cultivated our ideal international friendship.

These intervals were infrequent, for we both managed to keep fairly busy. Our parents, meanwhile, thinking that they had given us a good start and the right cues, left us to work out the rest by ourselves. We worked it out by considerately avoiding each other as much as possible.

A year or so after our soccer game we came to high-jumping. At this time I was being reminded constantly of the sterling example of Theodore Roosevelt, who conquered his childhood asthma by bullying it out of himself, roughly riding over his physical shortcomings to make himself into a good God-fearing American who persuaded some Colombians they wanted to be Panamanians and let us cut a canal through their property. I was already a God-fearing American, and I already had a hero in the person of David Livingstone. I was not especially impressed by Dr. Livingstone as a missionary; what I did enjoy was his being the first white man in a strange land. I had my own mind set on Tibet, and one of the many reasons why I am trying to explain about Kwei-ling and me, instead of

being smuggled into the palace of the Dalai Lama with a Tibetan translation of the Bible hidden in the seat of my pants, is that a lot of other fellows got to Tibet before me. Be that as it may, the toothy face of T. R. was put up as a false god before me, and a pair of jumping standards came into my life.

I discovered after a few days that I enjoyed high-jumping, after all, so I spent a number of hours leaping over the crossbar. Then, of course, someone had to think of Kwei-ling. Here again was a splendid chance for two boys to play together in amicable fashion and learn to know each other better. Kwei-ling was produced, and we set about high-jumping. Although his style was extremely bad, I was careful to make no comments, but after a few jumps, I realized that Kwei-ling always followed me when we moved up a peg. On the next peg I tried to communicate, without giving an order, that he should go first. The communication itself was strained enough, but Kwei-ling at last understood and failed to make the jump. I assured him that I was certain he could do it. He tried again and failed. Then he proposed that I attempt it. I successfully hurled myself over, to his applause. Kwei-ling then thought he would try that height just once more. He dashed at the standards and cleared the bar by at least four inches, just as I had suspected he would. From there on, our high-jumping was essentially ludicrous, but it was full of distress for both of us. Whenever anyone passing by paused to watch us we were the victims of an intense inner drama. Kwei-ling would be told that he ought to be able to jump much higher than he was jumping. I would then make wild efforts to clear a height that would give him an opportunity to show what he could do. I always failed in this and then suffered in thinking of Kwei-ling's sufferings at not being able to clear his reputation as a high-jumper.

Once again we avoided each other. Since we were both going to school we found this fairly simple, and though persons were known to remark that Kwei-ling and I were certainly a queer pair of boys, Kwei-ling and I knew that we were perfectly all right and were merely taking no more chances. Whenever anyone suggested that I go play with Kwei-ling I would be very tired or buried in a book. Kwei-ling had, I am sure, no impulses to come and play with me, but even if he had had an impulse he would have been compelled to wait until he was requested to appear.

We reached another sad climax the Christmas of 1922, just before I was ten. Mother had taken my sister and me shopping at Wing On's, one of Shanghai's large department stores, where I decided that I wanted to buy a huge red balloon about three feet long and half as wide. When I got it home I blew it up and began batting it lightly around the living room. Soon the cook came in and admired it so much that he went to get the amah. Then, of course, someone asked where Kwei-ling was, and there we were again. Why didn't we bat the balloon back and forth? We began, and everyone laughed happily except Kwei-ling and me. After all, balloons break after a certain amount of batting. I wouldn't have worried over my balloon's bursting except that I knew it was worrying Kwei-ling. This was the young master's balloon, and it was up to Kwei-ling not to break it if he weren't to get a lecture or worse from his parents. I soon saw that it was up to me to break it if we were to do anything else for the rest of our lives besides batting a red balloon. I began to strike harder and harder, using the tips of my fingers in the hope that my nails would pop the wretched thing. Kwei-ling returned the balloon gently each time for the kill, hoping, I am sure, that I would finish it off on the next stroke. I kept on hitting with full force, but I couldn't burst the balloon. With a furious wallop at last

I struck the balloon such a blow that Kwei-ling, in trying to return it, could do no more than let it glance off his hand. The huge red balloon careened out of reach into a hanging lamp and burst loudly.

Luckily, I was prepared for this. As the last echoes of the explosion died, I jumped up and down in frantic glee, shouting, "Hurrah for Kwei-ling! He broke the balloon! Isn't that splendid? Wonderful work for Kwei-ling!" Kwei-ling looked relieved, and his parents, who were on the point of scolding him, broke into smiles. My parents were, I think, a little surprised by my sudden enthusiasm at having my balloon burst, but Kwei-ling and I knew what it was all about, and each of us retired hoping that the great theme of Chinese-American friendship would be dropped forever.

All three of these major encounters were slightly athletic, a fact that may seem unusual. Yet this was the natural result of a further difficulty. Kwei-ling knew very well that he couldn't sit down in my presence. His father never sat down with my father, and he therefore couldn't sit down with me. I, on the other hand, knew that to sit down and keep Kwei-ling standing was unspeakably rude and a thing that my parents would lecture me on or worse for allowing.

Once Kwei-ling did sit in my presence, but I think he brought himself to do it only because he was told to and because I was stretched out in bed with an attack of asthma. Kwei-ling had started a stamp collection. I too was a collector and often gave him foreign stamps by giving them to the cook so that Kwei-ling and I needn't go through another farcical interlude. On this occasion I was almost thirteen. Boarding school had in the meantime made life much easier as far as the great Chinese-American friendship was concerned, but one vacation I was laid up at home, and immediately it was proposed that Kwei-ling come up to my bedroom, where we could work together on our collections as we reviewed our happy boyhood

memories. Once in the room, Kwei-ling was forced to perch on a chair, which he did with as small a part of his body as he could and still maintain his balance. Whooping and wheezing, I offered Kwei-ling one of my duplicates. He insisted that it was too rare for me to give him. I assured him that it wasn't rare at all, that I should like to give him a rare one, but I didn't have any. Then I went into a coughing fit and blew all the loose stamps off the bed. Kwei-ling hopped up to recover them. I tried to apologize and another coughing fit started. Kwei-ling probably thought I was going to die, but he stuck manfully by his master as for an hour we struggled along, interrupted by visitors who peeped in at the door to admire the Chinese lad comforting the American lad in his sickness.

That was our last effort. After it each of us had so perfected his technique of avoiding the other that we led our separate lives peacefully and with a full understanding of why they had not grown into a beautiful international friendship. Kwei-ling soon began to push far ahead of me. After finishing school he learned a trade and moved away from South Gate to become a citizen of the greater world. While I was still a gangling high-school senior Kwei-ling married and within a year became a father.

I doubt very much if Kwei-ling ever again thought about me and the difficulties we had had together. He had a family to raise, and I am sure he set about raising it very well. But I have thought of Kwei-ling from time to time, regretting our failure to set an example for all nations to follow. I think of him even as I might think of an old friend, with a certain amount of affection, for if Kwei-ling and I never had any hours of unalloyed joy together, we at least suffered in common, and that may be an equally good basis for friendship. Indeed, I suspect I think of Kwei-ling with far greater affection than I should think of him had he ever knocked me down.

CHANGES AND WARFARE

I F I HAVE GIVEN the impression that South Gate was something of a self-contained backwater, creating its own life and standards, nurturing its own peculiar strength of character, that impression has not been shaped entirely by accident. In most ways South Gate was definitely something of a backwater, a fact that only adds to its excellence in my eyes, a backwater being the best place I can think of for a child to be raised in. The greater, worldly Shanghai was nearby, ready for sampling once the smaller world of South Gate had been mastered. I sampled the greater Shanghai later on, yet I am not so rash as to claim that I ever mastered South Gate. South Gate was in its very nature unmasterable. And when I compare the greater Shanghai, glittering cheaply at night, nervous and hectic, a little shrill in its laughter, a little uncertain of itself always because it knew it was a rather tawdry imitation of a second-rate European capital—well, when I compare that Shanghai with South Gate for qualities of true greatness, South Gate wins in a walk. For that matter, South Gate wins without moving a muscle. In Shanghai people ran about and did things; in South Gate we stood pat and meant things.

Granted that it was a backwater by everyday standards, through a geographical accident South Gate more than once did find itself in the whirlpool of national and international affairs. To my knowl-

edge, no professional historian has ever mentioned South Gate's outwardly rather passive role in the history of China, so I shall go back to days before my own life began, in an effort to furnish the background for South Gate's attitude towards such events, an attitude that had become a tradition by the time I was myself personally involved in the Battle of South Gate, which was fought to a finish during a day and a night in January—or was it February?—of 1927. My individual failings as a historian are immediately evident, for I cannot give the exact date of that battle, nor can anyone else in my family, because in 1937 Japanese troops put the torch to our house and burnt up all of my mother's carefully kept five-year diaries. Anyone eager for state papers or precise days and hours may be disappointed in my cursive narrative of South Gate and the world at large. I have no documentary evidence to offer, but I can, I think, blow a little life into the stories that I heard as a child.

The mission at South Gate was founded about 1850, so it must have had a few years of external peace and quiet before the outbreak of the Taiping Rebellion. No one seems to be certain now whether the zealots who swept through the Native City of Shanghai—it must have been about 1858—were genuine members of the Taiping or only a good imitation, but they were at least impelled by the same mad spirit of Christianity and mysticism to cleanse their country by violent means. The missionary family then at South Gate stood pat until the last possible moment. The story is so conventional that they were just sitting down to a meal, the food already on the table, when word reached them that they must flee to the International Settlement. I hope no one misunderstands me when I say we stood pat at South Gate. Ordinarily we did stand pat in a physical sense, and always in a spiritual sense; but when there was clearly nothing more to be gained by sticking our necks out, we pulled them in

and, at the last possible moment, galloped into the International Settlement, carrying with us our sense of spiritual patness.

As it happened, this particular Taiping leader made a great point of the fact that his mission in the world was not a destructive one. His men were under strict orders to harm nothing, aside, I suppose, from the persons he thought could be killed with moral profit to the world. I have always nursed a secret sympathy for the Taiping Rebellion, and it may be that the conduct of this leader is responsible, for when our archetypal South Gate family returned ten days later, they found that the men had been as good as the word of their leader. The table, a little dusty perhaps, was in perfect order, the food still in the serving dishes waiting to be eaten. Though it is not a necessary part of the tale, I am certain that this first of South Gate families promptly sat down to their dinner just where they had left off and cleaned up the meal with dispatch. If there was any hesitation, it could only have been a short pause to debate the point of whether or not they had already said a blessing over the food before going to the International Settlement.

The reason for the Taiping leader's having to disturb South Gate was at the root of most of our experiences in warfare. As the land lay, South Gate stood in a direct line between the Arsenal and the most strategic point on the Whangpoo River for bombarding the Arsenal. Consequently, if anyone wanted to capture the Arsenal he came through South Gate. Or if anyone on the other side of the Whangpoo wanted to annoy the holders of the Arsenal he had his artillery brought up to the bend in the river, casually adjusted the sights, and fired at random, letting a few shells fall into or near South Gate while he gradually found his range.

It was not a totally uncommon experience to dig up an old rusty cannonball in the garden at our house. We added it to the collection

of four or five that we already had and never knew quite what to do with. Some of these cannonballs must have been fired during Boxer days. By this time—1900 was the Boxer year—the gentleman who was to become my most senior Courtesy Uncle was at South Gate. He was a member of a local volunteer group, and though he too eventually took his family into the Settlement, he did so only after patrolling South Gate with a gun, quite prepared to shoot any malicious Boxer who failed to be persuaded of the folly of attacking South Gate. This was in the end unnecessary, for a complicated bit of political management involving the alteration of a government telegram by the Chinese authorities in Shanghai came between and the Boxer menace passed, leaving South Gate still in a direct line between the bend in the Whangpoo and the Arsenal.

For an interval between the Boxer Rebellion and the revolution of 1911 South Gate was again at peace with everyone but itself. Like most revolutions, the 1911 uprising was not over with in a day, and this caused difficulties for the residents of the Native City, since the district changed hands a number of times. For a few months it would be a loyal part of the tottering Empire, only to find itself the next day in the very van of the republican supporters. These shifts had their embarrassments, because a loyal Chinese became a son of the revolution by cutting off his queue as a sign of emancipation. He was often not even given an option in the matter, since the revolutionists posted emergency barbers at the gates of the city and the queues fell where they might. To return to the Empire was not the work of a moment. At least it wasn't until the Chinese learned the expediency of keeping at home a spare queue that could be pinned into the skullcap every Chinese gentleman wore in public. After this discovery no man in Shanghai worried too much over his politics.

The first time the Republic reached South Gate in 1911 my father

and my most senior Courtesy Uncle, the Nimrod who stood off the Boxers, were disturbed one morning by a loud clatter of gunfire and shouting. After making sure that our own South Gate was intact they ventured into Mulberry Lane and walked up to the Little South Gate, where they found an animated crowd admiring the sight of the local yamen being burnt to the ground. It developed that everyone had known for days that this was to be the signal for Shanghai to release her revolutionary fervor, and the citizens of Shanghai were doing so by enjoying the fire. In addition, a few shots were being lofted over South Gate from the river towards the general vicinity of the Arsenal. The yamen officials, it developed further, had been quite as aware of the plan as everyone else and may even have thrown a few imperial documents into remote corners of the building to make it burn more brightly. The next morning every house sported a white flag, the sign of the revolution. Some of the flags looked more like soiled bed linen and towels than standards of progress, but the new powers saw no reason to complain.

The revolution continued to disturb South Gate off and on for a couple of years, achieving its most dramatic outburst in 1913 when a sporadic postrevolutionary revolt was directed against the Arsenal. Whether this group was to the right or the left of the main revolution no one recalls. Shells flew overhead as the troops on the Whangpoo and the troops in the Arsenal decided which way to jump. One night a dud landed on the roof of a Courtesy Aunt's house. After investigating, the Courtesy Aunt decided that there was still plenty of time for standing pat and went back to bed. The following morning the servants went up into the attic, worked the unexploded shell loose, and carried it off to the canal, while the Courtesy Aunt, annoyed by the interruption, went on with the more important work of saving souls.

Ordinarily when the cook, naturally our chief military authority, heard gunfire he was quite unconcerned. "Nothing to worry about," he would say. "They're going to sell out after firing five rounds." And he would be right; five rounds, and the winning general had bought over the losing general's army. On one occasion, however, a gunboat was unexpectedly boarded and seized on the Whangpoo. It was anchored, I need hardly point out, in the most favorable position for firing on the Arsenal. The crew remained loyal—to what I am not certain—and when the insurgent officers ordered them to fire on the Arsenal the crew obliged at pistol point by screwing up their guns to a maximum elevation and turning them on anything that wasn't the Arsenal. A few shells were lobbed clear to the north of the International Settlement, but a number of shrapnel bursts scourged the compound at South Gate. In the middle of all this, as Father stood in the yard trying to get a clear picture in his mind of what was going on, the cook came running out to him, not to drag him to cover, but to shout in an aggrieved voice, "This cannot be. There is a mistake!" Father asked him what he meant. As the story goes, the cook, while shrapnel whistled through the air about him, looked at Father in astonishment and said, "There has been no announcement!"

To this point my part in these flurries has been inconspicuous, not merely, I think, because I failed to be present at most of them, but also because of my nature. Had I been a Chinese living during the revolution, I feel quite certain that I would never have left my home without a spare queue coiled discreetly in my pocket. Nor would I have failed to hang out a large clean sheet each time the revolution triumphed. By 1926, on the other hand, things had changed. The sense of an important movement was in the air, something that was possibly really worth worrying about. Yet I am not

one to sneer or laugh too boisterously at the internal warfare of an unsettled and groping China. I have never understood the point of view that insists that the shooting of men in a largely pointless struggle is a subject for great hilarity. The opera bouffe preliminaries, yes; but if a man happened to be killed in the Taiping or Boxer Rebellion, or was caught in one of the dozen revolutions or counter-revolutions, I cannot see why he or anyone else should find the event especially stimulating to his sense of humor simply because it was all rather meaningless.

In 1926, though, we began to feel that there might be a meaning to the revived Kuomintang Party when its National Army began to push up from the south. I make no claim that South Gate really understood the internal politics of China, but we did get at least an inkling of change. The National Army, it became apparent, was actually willing to fight a battle if necessary, and the National Army was also known to be notoriously antiforeign.

In early December I came down the Yangtze from boarding school in Kuling, above the river port of Kiukiang. Kuling had already fallen to the National Army. The British ship on which I sailed was sandbagged on the upper decks to protect us from any potshots that might be fired at us from the bank. Although the captain informed me one morning at breakfast that we had been fired upon during the night, I think he did so only to satisfy the bloodthirsty spirit he thought a boy just turning fourteen should have. Aside from this very dubious attack the journey downriver was peaceful.

Shanghai, however, where the Northern forces were still in possession, was aquiver with excitement. In the International Settlement barriers had been erected and barricades thrown up at all points of entry. Out in South Gate we lived under rather lax martial law and

had to carry large official passes to walk through the streets at certain hours. This tension increased as the year ran out and we learned that the National Army was approaching. By the middle of January we could hear the heavy artillery of the advancing army far to the southwest. More passes had to be issued, and the American Consulate General of Shanghai renewed its timeworn struggle with South Gate. This consisted in an exchange of messages, opened by the Consulate's "advising" us tactfully to leave Chinese territory. We would reply that we thought there was still plenty of time. A day later another message would come in, this time just "advising" us to leave. We still stood pat. Finally a message would come through shorn of all semblance of tact, stating that if we were killed the Consulate General really could not accept responsibility, further implying that the Consulate General not only would refuse to send any flowers to the funeral but would consider the event good riddance.

It was during moments such as these that the members of the American Consulate General were reputed to turn a deep envious green at the mention of the British Consulate General. By some virtue of parliamentary law, the officials of the British Consulate General had the right to "command" His Britannic Majesty's subjects to get out of dangerous territory, whereas the weakened powers of the American Consulate General could do no more than "advise strongly" that we retreat. We continued at South Gate, hoping the National Army would give us enough time to complete another segment in the education of the students at the schools—whose vacation would not begin until the Chinese New Year—and the chance to save a further brace or so of souls.

The artillery fire drew nearer. At night we could see the distant flash of heavy guns and hear the rumble of explosions. A battle

developed slowly on the southwest outskirts of Greater Shanghai, but the Northern troops still held the Native City. Then one night the National Army thrust a prong in from the southeast. We could hear machine-gun fire in the streets close by, and in the morning we looked out to find a group of about ten soldiers manning a machine gun in the mouth of Mulberry Lane. This was the van of the National Army. At least, that is what I shall call it, though at the time it was really part of the force of a local warlord who was willing to see the merit of the National Army's point of view.

We shouldn't have minded having the van of the National Army mount a machine gun in Mulberry Lane had it not been for the fact that we soon spotted another group of soldiers, the last element of the Northern rear guard, installed in the tea shop at the corner of the road leading from the canal to the Big South Gate. It was impossible to see this tea shop from the mouth of Mulberry Lane because of the curve in the road, but the National Army showed its progressive spirit by aiming its machine gun directly at the Northern group. That this meant they would be shooting straight into the windows of the Women's Bible School apparently was the least of their worries. The National Army pulled some food out of their pockets and sat down to refresh themselves before advancing. This ended the first phase of the Battle of South Gate.

The second phase, as far as this narrative is affected, is in the nature of a diversion. With South Gate turned into no-man's-land, it became painfully obvious that it would be a good thing to get as many as possible of the students to their homes, particularly since we began to remember that the National movement was antiforeign. The gates into the French Concession and the International Settlement were, we decided, probably all locked by this time. All the members of the Consulate General were no doubt purple with rage,

wondering how they were going to explain our imminent massacre, a thought that so heartened us that we instantly set about organizing the evacuation of the students.

Father cast about for some impressive mark of authority, since he had been unable to obtain any military passes. He found it at last in the declaration, signed and garishly sealed by the American Consulate General, that all the property and buildings at South Gate were, by virtue of their American ownership, under the protection of the government of the United States of America and were subject to the privileges and considerations of international law and extraterritorial rights. This impressive statement Father put in a large frame and proposed to present, in lieu of anything better, to soldiers of antiforeign sentiment who were not only opposed to extraterritorial rights but were also, fortunately, quite unable to read English. That the most strict martial law was in force, permitting none but the military to circulate in the streets, troubled Father no more than the fact that their machine gun was pointed directly at the Women's Bible School troubled the van of the National Army.

His most impressive calling cards ready for instant distribution, Father, together with the other teachers, led the crocodile of students, marching two by two, out of the compound, holding up before his chest in typical South Gate humility and Christian meekness a sworn statement that all our buildings were American property. Thus armed, South Gate's first army was hurled against the barricades. Mother, meanwhile, an impressive figure in her brown silk fleece-lined Chinese gown, went off with a close non-Christian Chinese friend of the family who wished to move part of his own family closer to the International Settlement.

Left to myself at home, I wandered through the house, wondering what I could do for the cause. That I was left alone had horrified

Father's Chinese friend, who couldn't decide whether this was a total lack of responsibility on my parents' part or a sign of Christian superiority. After the battle he confessed that this singular devotion of Mother's was the only thing that would ever make him consider becoming a Christian.

Tiring at last of inactivity, I opened the third phase of the battle with reconnaissance duty. I went to the upstairs veranda and observed the group around the machine gun. Comfortably sprawled on their bedding rolls, they made a picturesque cluster as they smoked their cigarettes and gossiped. After a moment's thought I waved to them. They waved back and giggled a little. I went downstairs and slipped out the front gate. These notoriously antiforeign warriors smiled as I approached, though that may have been the result of my appearance. I was in my last stage before going into long trousers. During this period I affected droopy plus-fours that reached almost to my ankle bones in a gracefully draped effect that I hoped would disguise my deficient legs. To go with these I wore a sloppy sweater and tried to draw attention to the upper portions of my body by haltering my neck in a loud and heavily knotted tie.

The National Army recognized me instantly as a child of peace. Using an international dialect of gesture and exclamation, I presented myself to them. They were quite interested, and in the end we were able to establish a sort of subhuman communication through gesticulation and isolated Chinese phrases. They showed me how their machine gun worked. I pointed out that it was not really aimed at anything but American property. They laughed at this and gave me to understand that they were not going to riddle the Women's Bible School. By wild contortions that brought my plus-fours almost to the ground, I illustrated an attack on the Northern men. They grinned and shook their heads. Apparently they had no intention

of forcing the issue. I looked at them questioningly, and they shrugged their shoulders. After what I think were suitable compliments on both sides I returned to the compound.

Walking through the Girls' School grounds, I got to the gate across the road from the teahouse where the Northern men were stationed. I opened the gate, waved to them, and stepped out. They too smiled slightly at my approach, but seemed quite happy to receive me. In the same language I had used a few minutes before, though with suitable alterations for climatic change, I presented myself. These men had no machine gun, but they were armed with antiquated rifles. They let me know that they understood all about the National Army just round the bend. I looked at them with my most expressive questioning face, and they smiled and shrugged their shoulders. Again compliments were changed and I went home. The third phase was closed.

Late in the afternoon Mother and Father returned with handfuls of students whose parents they had been unable to find. About the same time my sister wandered in unconcernedly from her supposed safety at the Shanghai American School, where she was a boarding pupil. She reported that stray bullets from the main battle had been finding their way to the school grounds, leading her to think that South Gate would be a better place to spend a quiet weekend. She seemed to think nothing of her feat in getting back to South Gate. Father had been threatened more than once by armed guards. He and the other teachers had waved calling cards until their wrists were weak. But when everything else had failed, the Consul General's signature and seal had carried the crocodile through to victory.

Now that most of the students were cared for, South Gate began to draw up orders for itself against a surprise in the night. One of the Courtesy Aunts soon produced a plan that for tactical efficiency

has probably never been equaled, though to me it remains as incomprehensible today as it was then. This Courtesy Aunt proposed that after supper Mother and my sister go to her house and sleep in an improvised bed. Father and I were to go to the Boys' School compound and sleep on the third floor of an old residence there. The only glimmer of reason behind this that I can find is the possibility of the Courtesy Aunt's thinking that someone of American nationality should be in each part of the mission. Perhaps there was an added motive behind this separation of the sexes. I don't know.

Nevertheless, the Courtesy Aunt carried the day, and shortly before bedtime Father and I crossed to the other compound, where we tried to sleep on an old bed that had newspapers spread between the mattress and the springs. We could hear an occasional rattle of machine-gun fire, but all we had to do to drown it out was roll over.

The night was uncomfortable and tense. About two in the morning a rifle-shot banged out almost under our windows. Father leapt to a window, but could see nothing. We heard a shout. Then dead quiet again. We did not know it, but the Battle of South Gate had just concluded its fourth and final phase.

We were up early and dressed ourselves quickly. On our way back home for breakfast we passed the tea shop, which was still filled with soldiers—but this time they were the soldiers of the National Army whom I had last seen in the mouth of Mulberry Lane. After breakfast, with the interpretative aid of half the servants on the compound, we learned the details.

Well after midnight the men of the National Army had put down their guns. Leaving one man to guard these and the precious machine gun, still trained on the windows of the Women's Bible School, they sauntered round the curve of the road and signaled to

the Northern soldiers. In a brief parley they informed the Northern men that they had no guns with them, that they wanted to declare a truce in order to drink some tea and smoke a few cigarettes with the Northern men. They were told to advance slowly. Certain at last that they were unarmed, the Northern men welcomed their enemies to the tea shop and out of elementary courtesy stacked their arms as a sign of good faith. The two outposts fraternized for half an hour over their tea. Finally the leader of the National group shattered his teacup against the floor, and at this signal his men jumped up and grabbed the guns of the Northern men, who were then told to run for their lives. The Northern men yelped in terror and streaked away. The Battle of South Gate was over.

In March South Gate gave up standing pat and moved into the International Settlement. The National Army, now victorious throughout southern and central China, pressed against the small outpost of Europe and America. The times were not pleasant, and out near South Gate a foreigner was likely to be more picturesquely reviled than was customary. When his back was turned he might get a stone in it.

The Battle of South Gate and our evacuation to the Settlement took place during the period so vividly dealt with by André Malraux in *La Condition humaine*. I am afraid that there are few things in common between Monsieur Malraux's narrative and my own. I don't think that South Gate even knew there was a purge of Communists going on in the Kuomintang Party or that we were seeing the beginning of the long trek inland described by Edgar Snow in *Red Star Over China*. Instead of concerning ourselves with these matters we waited in the Settlement until we were able to go back to South Gate, where we felt really comfortable. At least that was the way it looked to one South Gater.

MAKING A MAN OUT OF HIM

B ECAUSE I AM the son of a missionary, the muddy flat on which Shanghai stands is all that I can lay claim to as my native soil. I had a happy childhood in the compound of the Presbyterian mission at South Gate, outside the old Chinese city, but I never really throve there. After I had suffered a number of setbacks during the autumn of 1923, my parents decided that the best thing they could do for me was to take me out of the Shanghai American School and put me into the American School at Kuling, a resort in the mountains above the river port of Kiukiang, on the Yangtze, about three and a half days by boat from Shanghai. When the other members of the mission at South Gate heard that my parents were planning to send their only son to boarding school, the general opinion among them was that this would go a long way toward making a man out of me. The news went around shortly before my eleventh birthday, and if this impresses anyone as a rather early age for the putting on of one's manhood, I can only say that the wish was quite characteristic of most of the South Gaters, who had a tendency to force themselves and others whenever possible. My parents' real hope was to preserve me alive for such maturity as might come with the years, but since to point this out to their neighbors might have appeared a little impolite, they let the matter ride and went on with their plans.

I myself did not at first look upon the move with any great favor, not so much because going from the Shanghai American School to the Kuling American School was rather like having to leave Harvard for the hinterland as because I was afraid the school at Kuling might not have a Boy Scout troop. There was an active one in Shanghai, and for years I had been looking forward to becoming a Scout when I reached the age of twelve. Now it seemed as if I might be cheated of this rare privilege. Whereas my mother and father looked through the school prospectus sent us from Kuling with an eye to the choice of textbooks and the academic degrees held by the teachers, I looked for information on Scouting. Only when I discovered in a list of the faculty that one of the men at the school acted as Scoutmaster did I reconcile myself to the move, and even then I was not carried away by enthusiasm, for I had already changed schools five times and the process had never been a painless one.

My coolness was not lessened by the way in which my Courtesy Aunts and Uncles insisted on telling me what a wonderful thing it was to go to boarding school, what a lucky boy I was to be going, and what fun I would have once I was there. There was a certain professional cheer and enthusiasm in all this that was both familiar and suspect, so, though I accepted the change as inevitable, I spent very little time clapping my hands at the prospect. But I was at least partially won over to the idea by the most junior member of the mission station, who was a recent graduate of Princeton and so young that I called him by his first name. This man, unlike the other members of the mission, had himself attended a boarding school, though not, he had to admit, a coeducational one, as the Kuling American School was, and when he said that it was really a splendid experience I felt that I had to believe him.

During the Christmas holidays my mother and our amah spent

many hours sewing name tags on my clothes and checking the list giving the exact number of towels (face) and towels (bath) as well as all the other items without which one could not hope to enter the Kuling American School as a boarding pupil. The amah was also supposed to give me a course in bed-making and elementary cleaning. But the idea of my actually having to make my own bed or use a dustcloth and broom impressed her as being so absurd that she was satisfied with merely having me watch her make my bed one morning. As she pointed out, there was little sense in worrying about sweeping and dusting, since I had often seen her perform these duties. I agreed with her and we let it go at that.

I had entertained a few wild dreams of being allowed to make the journey alone, but I was not surprised when a Courtesy Aunt who owned a summer cottage in Kuling decided that, in spite of the cold weather she would find in the mountains, January would be a good month to take a short vacation, during which she could inspect her property there. She said that she would be happy to act as my escort.

As a concession to my doubts about going to boarding school, my parents allowed me to stay in Shanghai until I had passed my eleventh birthday—a delay that meant I would reach Kuling a fortnight after the reopening of school for the winter term. The postponement must have been quite trying to the missionaries at South Gate, all of whom were forced each year, by the custom of the community, to give birthday presents to my sister in the middle of December, Christmas presents to the two of us a few days later, and birthday presents to me in the middle of January. Now, to have to give me not only a birthday present but, immediately afterward, a going-away present as well must have seemed excessive, but I made it clear to everyone that this was the only decent thing to do.

Just which one of the Jardine, Matheson steamers took us up the Yangtze I have forgotten, but it was probably either the *Tuk Wo* or the *Kut Wo* that my Courtesy Aunt and I boarded in the Whangpoo late one January evening. Most of the members of the mission came down to see us off, and my cabin was piled high with gifts. Any number of last-minute bits of advice were given me, and my sister and I managed an awkward exchange of kisses to satisfy the proprieties. After prayers had been said, the party broke up and my Courtesy Aunt and I went to our cabins. There was a touch of anticlimax in this part of leaving for Kuling, since the boats usually did not sail until midnight or later and one's friends simply walked down the gangplank and went home instead of standing on the wharf waving their handkerchiefs at a disappearing ship. I locked my cabin door and set to work opening all my going-away presents. Satisfied that everyone had come through handsomely, I undressed and went to bed.

I have only two clear memories of the trip to Kiukiang aside from recalling that my Courtesy Aunt was devoted to dragging me on brisk turns around the deck and that we were able to get excellent hot curries at almost every meal. One of these memories has to do with breakfast on the second morning of the voyage. Since my Courtesy Aunt and I were the only first-class passengers on board, we ate with the captain, and when I announced that morning in low tones to my Courtesy Aunt that the boiled egg I had just opened was bad, she must have been flustered by the captain's presence, for she answered, "Now, you're just being fussy, John."

"I am not," I said, and passed the egg to the captain, who was sitting on the other side of her at the head of the table. "Isn't this egg rotten, sir?" I asked loudly.

The captain took one sniff and said, "My God! Here, Boy, take it away," and he handed it to a waiter.

I was under the impression that I had proved my point until I received, after breakfast, a lecture on duty and obedience from my Courtesy Aunt. "You embarrassed me very much by what you did," she said in conclusion.

"But just think of what would have happened if I'd tried to eat the egg," I protested.

"That's not the point," she replied. "You could have handed it quietly to one of the table boys."

"If I had, you would have noticed and called it back," I retorted.

"Remember your manners, John," she answered sternly.

"Yes, Auntie," I said.

My other memory has to do with Chaucer. The Princeton graduate's going-away present to me was a small book of selections from *The Canterbury Tales* done into simple English prose for young persons. Since I had almost nothing else to do, I spent part of each day wrapped up in a steamer rug in a deck chair reading. The weather was chilly, so I wore gloves, and after I had carefully polished my glasses on them I would read a few more pages of Chaucer. The result is that even today when I hear the names of Palamon and Arcite, Constance or Chanticleer—for of course it was only this type of tale that was included—instead of picturing the color and detail of the medieval world I see the yellow waters of the Yangtze, beyond them a small Chinese fishing village, and between this scene and my eyes the pattern of the ship's rail.

What with Chaucer and brisk turns around the deck, we finally reached Kiukiang in the middle of a Monday morning, and after eating a very early lunch and saying good-bye to the captain, we left the boat. I had been to Kuling for the summer holidays several times and remembered how, during the summer months, the trip from Kiukiang to Kuling was made exciting by a constant traffic of

vacationers. At that season the baggage carriers tended to squeeze a little on the established rates and the chair bearers were likely to insist that a passenger hire an extra pair of men because of his weight. In the winter, however, few made the trip and we found what little bargaining was necessary at the transportation office in Kiukiang was quite perfunctory. We crossed the plain between Kiukiang and the foothills in a rickety bus, sharing it with a number of Chinese. There were patches of snow on the ground, but the red dirt surface of the road was clear and we made the trip in good time.

Once out of the bus, and after our baggage had been started up the trail, we got ready for the chair ride up the mountain. I was wearing a brown corduroy suit, over it a green and red plaid mackinaw. I put on my heaviest gloves and a piece of knitted headgear modeled after a balaclava helmet. My Courtesy Aunt and I carried rubber hot-water bottles, which we had filled at a tea shop, and we got into our sedan chairs, put the bottles next to our feet, and wrapped our steamer rugs around our legs. We had had almost no argument at the transportation office over the number of bearers each of us would require, and my Courtesy Aunt, who in summer would certainly have had to hire eight men, now was obliged to take only six, and no one even suggested that I, who weighed less than a hundred pounds, should have more than four, the minimum. After a short delay for testing the chair poles and the balance of each load, we left the foothill village, my Courtesy Aunt's chair, at her insistence, in the lead, to the annoyance of me and my bearers, because we knew she would hold us down to a sober pace.

When we had left the village behind us, we began a gradual climb, going past terraced paddy fields at first and then through groves of bamboo. There had been a ice storm in the lower foothills, and the bamboos were still weighted down with ice and snow, each tree

arched in a gleaming curve, its leaves flashing as their glassy coating caught the afternoon sun. I had never before seen anything like it, and as we went up through the crystal groves, I felt that I was being borne through a magic world. Whenever a bit of snow or ice fell from a branch, the entire shining arc of the tree would shudder and I was surprised to find that I could hear a tinkling sound as the leaves brushed against one another.

My mood of wonderment was broken when the two coolies in front of me jerked the chair poles to attract my attention and I saw that my Courtesy Aunt had turned partway around in her chair and was calling to me.

"What do the bamboos make you thing of, John?" she shouted.

"Why, I don't know!" I called back, puzzled.

"Oh, you must make a comparison for them!" she shouted back impatiently.

"A comparison?" I yelled.

"Yes!" she cried, her voice shrill from the effort to make herself heard. "You must think of what they look like. There's really just one thing. I'll ask you later." She waved her hand and turned around.

I stared at the bamboos again. To me they looked like bamboos bent over by the weight of the ice on them, gleaming in the afternoon sunlight. This, I knew, was not a comparison; it was what they were. I felt troubled, as if I were missing something. For a time I thought the bamboos might be compared with the jade trees the Chinese made for ornaments. I had seen some whose leaves were all of white jade. But I rejected this comparison, since I had never seen a jade tree made to look like a bamboo.

The coolies were getting warmed up by this time and began to shed their wadded jackets. The two men in front tossed theirs over my feet, in the footrest, and the two behind hung theirs over the

back of my chair. I could smell the body odor from the coats as it reached me faintly through the cold air, and this distracted me from my worry about the bamboos. We had already gone beyond the groves, anyway, and my Courtesy Aunt's question had shattered some of their wonder for me, so they seemed not quite so strange and fine as I had first thought them.

Now we mounted rapidly, as one flight of stone steps followed another. The cover of snow on the mountain slopes around us was broken here and there by a jagged rock or a tall tree. The chair men had to step carefully in their straw sandals for fear of slipping on the icy stones. The white walls of the mountain looked familiar to me as the sunlight glinted off them and I thought this strange, for I had not been to Kuling for some years and I had never before gone up the mountain when it was covered with snow.

The chair ride to Kuling is usually interrupted twice, each time at a small mountain village where the coolies can get tea and a little food while they rest for a quarter of an hour or so. When we reached the first of these villages, I noticed that the coolies carrying my Courtesy Aunt let go of her chair while it was still two or three inches above the ground, a sure sign that she had done something to annoy them. Probably, I thought, it was because she had kept turning around to make certain that I was following close behind, thus upsetting the balance of the chair. My own coolies set me down gently, and this pleased me so much that I flipped them a silver twenty-cent piece and, since I could not speak their dialect, I pointed to the teahouse and made a gesture of drinking.

What pleasure I got from this attempt to act grown-up was short-lived, for as soon as we handed in our hot-water bottles for refilling at the teahouse, my Courtesy Aunt turned to me and asked, "Have you thought of what the bamboos look like?"

"Well, no, not exactly," I said, "unless it's a grove of white jade trees."

She laughed. "That's not very good. I'm afraid you haven't much imagination. There is really just one perfect comparison for those bamboos."

"Is there?" I asked stupidly, feeling that I was going to be a dreadful flop at boarding school.

"Yes, and I guess I'll have to tell you what it is." She paused. "The perfect comparison for those bamboos is a white ostrich-plume pen on a lady's desk. Isn't that beautiful?"

"A pen on a desk?" I asked, puzzled.

"Yes—you know, an ostrich-plume pen."

"But the bamboos were cold and shiny. They were—well, they were different," I said in confusion. "Anyway, I use a fountain pen. Almost everyone uses a fountain pen."

"That isn't the point," my Courtesy Aunt said testily. It was unnecessary for me to answer this because she quickly turned to another subject. "I noticed when your chair was set down your coolies had hung their jackets on the back and the footrest."

"Yes," I replied glumly, suspecting what was coming.

"You mustn't let them do that. The coats are very smelly, and besides you might get a disease from them."

"What disease?" I demanded, knowing that I was being difficult.

"Oh, smallpox or something like that," she answered.

"I've been vaccinated every few years," I said, "and just last summer I had typhoid and paratyphoid shots."

"Now, John," my Courtesy Aunt began, but I said, "I'm sorry," before she could remind me that it was unnecessary to be rude.

We got back into our chairs and wrapped up in the steamer rugs. Again my Courtesy Aunt took the lead and after a few minutes her

coolies shed their jackets. The coolies carrying me took off their coats and, as before, they put them on the footrest and the back of the chair. But my Courtesy Aunt turned in her chair and shouted, "Make them put them on the poles!"

"I don't know the dialect," I called back. "I can't make them understand."

At this she ordered her coolies to stop, but since they couldn't understand her Shanghai dialect, it was some time before she was able to make them hold up. My chair, of course, had to stop behind hers, and then, with a wealth of gesture, she demonstrated to my coolies that their jackets were to be hung on the poles, just as her coolies' were. I sat silent throughout this, but once we started again and my coolies were grumbling a little, because a jacket often slips off a chair pole, I tried out a small Shanghai expression in what I hoped was a Kiukiang accent. What I said was, I knew perfectly well, a libel on my Courtesy Aunt's ancestry and behavior. One or two syllables must have meant something to my men, for they shouted with laughter and bounced me high in the air. I laughed, too. One coolie after another took up my remark and worked what I was sure were very ingenious variations on its theme, but I was unable to follow them with any certainty.

I could see my Courtesy Aunt turning around, to the obvious annoyance of her coolies. "What are you laughing at?" she called out.

"Nothing!" I shouted back. "I guess they can't understand my Chinese."

She looked unconvinced.

This exchange somehow made me feel better and I looked happily at the white slopes rising around me. As I stared at them I slowly came to a realization of why they looked so familiar. They looked exactly

like the paintings of snow-covered mountains I had seen on Chinese scrolls, and for the first time in my life I sensed that Chinese art was not a matter of quiet and inaccurate whimsy. The discovery pleased me so much that in my imagination I improvised a scroll of my own with an abruptly rising white mountain slope, a trail, going up its side in long flights of stone steps, and on one of the flights a chair borne by four men, their breath smoking out into the cold air.

Soon we settled down to hard climbing. The men began to sweat and puff as the flights of steps grew longer and steeper. Once one of my men slipped, but the others were able to steady the chair until he recovered himself. After an hour or so, we reached the second village. Again my Courtesy Aunt and I had our hot-water bottles refilled, but we found little to say to each other as we walked up and down, stamping our feet to warm them. I went back to the chairs before she did, and as I settled into my steamer rug, I noticed that my four bearers were almost finished with their tea. I motioned to them and, raising my eyebrows and grinning, pointed up the trail with my chin. Before anyone else realized what was happening, they had run out of the shop, lifted my chair, and, uttering high, falsetto screams, started running up the trail. My Courtesy Aunt called out, and just to show her that my heart was in the right place, I yelled "Stop!" four or five times, feeling certain that the coolies couldn't understand a word of English and that even if they could they wouldn't dream of stopping. Our escape exhilarated the men so much that they dashed up the first few flights of steps at great speed and there was never any question of our being overtaken. Soon I had two wadded jackets over my feet and two more hung over the back of the chair. In the interest of truth, I must record that they did smell quite strong, but they represented something that seemed much more important to me than my own comfort.

The winter afternoon was waning. When the trail went along the western side of a valley or followed a streambed, we could feel the chill of the evening air. By the time we reached the upper slopes of the mountains the sky was already losing much of its light, but the tops of the mountains were lit up by the rose-yellow afterglow of sunset. Near the end of the ride the trail leveled off for about a mile before it reached the Gap, the Chinese village at the head of Kuling Valley, and we covered that last mile, as the light died out around us, in a burst of speed and laughter and profanity, finishing at a dead run.

In the transportation office at the Gap we waited at least twenty minutes for my Courtesy Aunt's chair to catch up with us. She was quite indignant when she finally arrived and gave everyone a sound, though not very colorful, scolding in the Shanghai dialect. No one was greatly impressed, but my men did their best to look contrite. My Courtesy Aunt settled our account at the office, and after lanterns had been lit for our chairs, we started on the mile-long trip down the valley to the school, my Courtesy Aunt's chair again in the lead. Around us we could just make out the shapes of the summer cottages, boarded up and lightless. The road ran beside the stream that flowed down the valley, and the lanterns on our chairs cast circles of orange light over the snowy boulders and onto the streambed. Because the road went downhill and was smooth, and because the coolies were hungry, we were taken along at a rapid dogtrot that shook us up violently.

As I was tossed from side to side, I felt myself seized by a wish to say something to my Courtesy Aunt that would startle and perhaps shock her, something with just a touch of vulgarity in it, to show that I was unimpressed by her system of comparisons. An expression that I had once heard came into my mind. The phrase

was an odd one, "It's like to shake my liver pin loose!" That, I thought, would really show her. How startling it would be to have that called out through the darkness as we jounced along in our sedan chairs! Once or twice I was on the point of calling out, even though the motion of the chair might, I knew, make my voice unsteady. Just when I thought I really was going to shout it at her, we turned off the main road up into a steep side path. As we topped the rise, I realized that we had arrived and I forgot about everything else. A feeling of uncertainty came over me as, for the first time, I became fully aware that I had left South Gate behind me and that it would be almost six months before I should see my family again.

Our chairs were set down and we stepped out of them. When my Courtesy Aunt asked me how I felt, I smiled at her and said "Fine!" wondering how I could have felt such an aversion to her so recently. I pulled off my balaclava helmet as we went up the steps of the school into the entrance hall, on the main floor. Here I saw my baggage piled up, and a group of boys and girls gathered around it, looking at the labels and tags. As they turned to look at me, the warm air of the building made my glasses fog over so that I couldn't see my new schoolmates.

After a few moments the headmaster came out and greeted my Courtesy Aunt. She went off with him to his office. When my glasses cleared and I could see, I stared, expressionless, at the boys and girls around my trunk and suitcases. There was a smell of school in the corridor, and a spasm of nausea came over me. I swallowed violently in an effort to control it. Then one of the boys, obviously the clown of the group, came over to me and said, "Do you know what we're going to call you? We're going to call you Jibby Jones because you have a big nose and skinny legs and wear glasses."

Jibby Jones, I knew, was a character in a series of comic stories

then running in a boys' magazine. I also knew that I must say something, that I must strike the right note or be lost forever. The boy stood looking at me, a taunting smile on his lips. I looked back at him and said, "You must forgive me if I don't die laughing." The girls behind him giggled and I knew I was safe for a little while.

Just then the headmaster and my Courtesy Aunt came back and an electric bell rang in the hall. "Time for study hall," the headmaster said to the students, and they left without saying anything more to me. I was taken to my room on the floor above by the matron, who showed me where I could wash up for supper.

My Courtesy Aunt and I ate with the headmaster, his wife, and their two small children. The main course was a fairly dull curry, the regular Monday-night supper, I was to learn—nothing to equal the curries on the boat or the cook's best efforts at home, and there was no chutney to go with it. I picked at my food in silence while the headmaster and his wife carried on a conversation with my Courtesy Aunt about Shanghai and our trip up the river. She related that the chair coolies had run away with me, but even the memory of that incident failed to cheer me.

After supper the matron took me back to my room and helped me unpack my trunk. She told me I shared the room with two other boys and slept with them on an adjoining sleeping porch and showed me my locker and chest of drawers and my section of the wardrobe. When everything but my bedding was put away, the matron said, "Well, I'll leave you now and you can make your bed. Your room-mates will be in from study hall in about half an hour, and half an hour after that it's time for lights out in this room." She went away and I was left alone.

The amah and I had made a bad mistake. I went out to the sleeping porch next to the room. I knew that one slept between

sheets, but I couldn't remember what the pad was for and I started to put it under the mattress. Then I thought of going over to one of the other beds and folding back the covers. Working with this model, I made my own bed more or less. After I had put the counterpane on, I stretched it tight and my bed didn't look too bad.

Back in the room, I sat down and waited for my roommates. My Courtesy Aunt had disappeared forever, it seemed, and I was surprised to find that I remembered her with great affection. When my roommates came in, I was glad to see that neither of them was the clown of the lower hall. I told them my name and they told me theirs. We looked at each other for a while, and then one of them said, "What grade are you in?"

"I'm in the second half of the sixth grade," I answered. "What grade are you in?"

"We're in the second half of the fifth," he said, "but we're only eleven."

"I turned eleven just a few days ago," I said.

They got a washbasin for me and showed me where I could keep it in the bathroom at the end of the hall. We found very little to say to each other when we had returned to our room and were undressing around the wood-burning stove. After we were in our pajamas, the matron came in. She glanced through the glass doors to the sleeping porch and said, "I see you know how to make a bed well, John."

"Thank you, ma'am," I answered.

"Is everything all right?" she asked. "You boys are going to all be good friends, you know."

We said nothing and she said good night. We said good night and she left us.

A bell rang. "That's our lights-out bell," one of my roommates said.

We turned off the light, went out to the sleeping porch, and climbed into our beds. Mine was not very comfortable, but I pulled the eiderdown up around my shoulders and snuggled into it. I felt completely deserted and still a little sick from my journey by chair and wondered if I was going to lose what curry I had eaten.

Then one of my roommates whispered, "Say, did you have a good trip?"

"Yes, I did," I answered. "I had a swell one, especially up the mountain in the snow." I felt a little confidence returning and I went on: "But from the Gap on down to here, the men ran so fast I got all bounced around. As a matter of fact, for a while I thought it was like to shake my liver pin loose."

"What?" came from the other two beds.

I smiled in the dark. "I said it was like to shake my liver pin loose," I repeated.

One of them snickered. "That sounds funny, doesn't it?" he said, and the other agreed, "Yes, that's good."

"We often say that in Shanghai," I said.

Then as a sixth-grader speaking to two fifth-graders I whispered good night, and my roommates said good night to me. I wondered if I could keep from crying until they were both asleep. As I waited, I knew that I had weeks of loneliness ahead, that I would feel nausea and uncertainty for days. Yet lying there in the dark and reviewing the events of the journey from Shanghai, it seemed to me that, as far as the South Gaters were concerned, the chief purpose of my going away to school had already been pretty thoroughly achieved.

WAR GAME

ONE OF THE MOST popular sports at the Kuling American School was war game. Although the school was a coeducational one, war game was played only by the boys during the years I was there. There had been a time, I was told, when the girls too had joined in, but they had proved themselves too savage for the gentlemanly recreation of war, and after they had been offered a couple of chances to redeem themselves and had failed, they were permanently barred from playing. That was the official account, at least, but perhaps I should add that there was an unofficial explanation, to the effect that some of the older boys and girls had shown a tendency to forget the real purpose of the game and instead had indulged on the side in a few friendly skirmishes of their own.

In spite of the great popularity of war game, we played it only two or three Saturdays a term because it took an entire day and required a certain amount of organization. First, two generals were appointed by the teacher in charge, and then the two armies—usually designated as Red and Blue—were chosen by the generals. After this, a fort was decided upon; it might be the porch of a summer cottage or one of the passes in the mountains. Then one army was appointed to defend the fort for the first half of the game while the other army attacked. The roles were reversed for the second half,

the dead of both armies having been brought back to life between halves, when we ate lunch. Whichever army, when it was on the attack, got more men alive into the fort won the war.

Each soldier had a "life," which was a piece of yarn (of red or blue, depending on which army he belonged to), tied around the upper left arm if he was right-handed, the upper right arm if he was left-handed. A soldier was killed when one member of the opposing army succeeded in breaking his "life." Most of the fighting, therefore, was a matter of dodging or, if two soldiers were attacking a single man, of having one of them hold the victim's arms while the other man broke his "life." In the case of simultaneous deaths, the teacher in charge acted as umpire, but often the two casualties would decide, without consulting the umpire, that neither had been killed and would restore their own lives. It may possibly have been a feminine inability to grasp such technicalities that made the girls unsuitable for war game.

On the Saturdays that we played, the school put up lunches for us, so that we could spend the whole day out of doors. Even if killed early in the game, a boy could have a good time dawdling about over the hills, waiting to have his life restored in the afternoon, after everyone had eaten. At times a few of the braver spirits among us were suspected of taking their own lives in order to enjoy this liberty.

There were a number of interesting war-game campaigns while I was at Kuling, but in only one of them did I play anything like a prominent role, and this was the first one I participated in. It is true that later on I did distinguish myself once by wearing a bright red sweater that could be seen for miles, but I prefer to forget that incident. And I also prefer to forget the time the leaders of the army I belonged to decided that the only way to get anyone alive into

the fort, which was a high cottage porch, was to pick me up and hurl me in over the heads of the defenders.

My first war game was played on a Saturday early in March, a little less than two months after my arrival at the school. The winter had broken for a few days and we were enjoying a false spring. Because twilight came early at that season, the fort selected was little more than a mile from the school. It was the center of the foreign cemetery. The cemetery itself was a walled square of ground on the top of a mountain spur, and a square space had been marked out for the fort where the two main paths that crossed the enclosure met. After Saturday-morning inspection of our rooms, all the boys reported to the athletic field, on a terrace in front of the main building. Here the teacher in charge of us for the day appointed two of the older boys generals. He then told them to toss for first pick, after which they began to choose sides.

The process of choosing sides was one of the terrors of my childhood. It was not that I ever expected anyone to be so perceptive as to pick me straight off, far from it; but I constantly dreaded the humiliation of being the last boy chosen. Indeed, I would have served faithfully and with utter devotion anyone who would rescue me from being left in the dismal no-man's-land between the two sides until I stood there alone, the last boy to be picked. As the newest of the younger boys at Kuling, I knew on this occasion that there was very little chance of my not being left to the end, but for a time I kept up my hopes. One of the other younger boys had broken an arm a few weeks before, and though he was being allowed to play, his arm was still in a sling. I thought there was an almost even chance of my being preferred over him, and I waited, trying to look unconcerned as the generals picked us off one by one. The Kuling American School was a small school, and each army was

made up of twenty-five boys at the most, but the choosing seemed endless. When there were still five of us left, the boy with the broken arm was chosen and I knew that I was going to be the last. I had already begun to edge toward the army that would have to take me—it was the Red one—when my general finally said to me, "Well, come on, whatever your name is."

Since the Reds were to be the defending army for the morning, we had our "lives" tied on first, and after we had collected our lunches, we set off for the cemetery. I tagged along near the end of the line. Ahead of me the general and his particular friends discussed strategy, but without much animation, and one of the boys near me said that there wasn't much to figure out because the cemetery had been used a few times before and everyone knew what would happen.

Our general divided the greater part of the Red army into two groups and placed one of them at the only entrance to the cemetery, the gate in the middle of the east wall, and told the other to go to the south wall. Some of the faster runners were sent out as scouts to cover the main approach to the gate from the northeast and the smaller path coming up from the south. Then our general, to my great pleasure, singled me out and said, "You can stand guard over in the northwest corner." At last, I decided, my talents had been recognized. I went over to my post. The cemetery wall was about four and half feet high. I climbed on top of it and saw there were no paths on either the north or the west slope. They were both quite steep and covered with brush. Either slope looked to me almost ideal for a surprise attack, and I walked back and forth along the top of the wall, imagining how I would give the alarm and save the battle for the Reds. The more I thought about this, however, the more I saw that something was wrong with the disposal of our army.

If the main force of the Blue army attacked from the north or the west, the two groups of defenders were in the worst possible places to meet the attack. This worried me so much that, after mulling it over for some time, I jumped off the wall and went to the general, who was standing in the fort.

"What's the matter?" he said, grinning at me.

"Say," I began eagerly, "if they come through where I am, nothing can stop them."

"Listen, kid," he said, "we know how they'll come. One bunch will attack at the gate and another bunch will come over the south wall at the same time. No one ever climbs up on the other sides—they're too steep."

"Oh," I said, aware that I had been made a fool of.

"If you want to, you can go over with the others on the south wall," the general said.

"No, thanks," I answered and walked back to my appointed post.

When I got to the wall I climbed onto it and sat with my back to the cemetery. Perhaps, I thought to myself, this time they really would come up the north or the west slope. I would hold the enemy off single-handed until help could reach me. I would be Horatius at the bridge. I peered into the patches of brush, hoping to catch sight of one of the Blue's forward scouts. Nothing stirred.

Soon our own scouts began to report back. The Blue army was coming up in two groups, they said, one along the main path from the northeast, the other circling the spur to reach the path that came from the south. These reports didn't interest me greatly, for if anyone was coming from the north or the west, he would be quite invisible to our scouts.

Reports kept coming in. A couple of our scouts had tried to pick off a decoy ahead of the main Blue force and had been killed. To

the south, one of our scouts had been successful in ambushing a Blue, but there was a vigorous argument going on over the legality of the attack.

Shortly before noon the teacher who was acting as umpire came up the south path. He said it was true that one of our Red scouts had killed a Blue. Then he sat down near the gate. Our remaining scouts came running in, saying that both groups of Blues were very close and were leaving the paths to advance under the protection of such cover as they could find. By this time I had turned around and was greatly tempted to leave my post. Still, I thought, someone *might* be coming up the slope at my corner.

The bushes near the entrance began to shake, and suddenly a body of the enemy leapt out and tried to storm the gate. No sooner had they been engaged than the group at the south wall shouted that the other Blues were coming over. The battle raged. One of the Blues broke through the gate and made for the fort, but our general headed him off and killed him.

I took one last look down the slopes at my corner. The brush was motionless. Then I jumped off the wall into the cemetery and ran toward the gate. By the time I reached it, the battle was over. Not one Blue soldier had reached the fort. In fact, all of the Blues and about two thirds of the Reds had been killed. No one seemed to notice that I had done nothing at all, and I felt no need to mention the fact.

The Blues went off to pick up their lunches, which they had cached near the cemetery, and when they got back, both armies sat down outside the entrance and ate. From the conversation, I gathered that the last time the fort had been the cemetery neither army had won, and the Blues were now saying that they would easily kill off all the Reds in the afternoon game. The Reds said that they

wouldn't all be killed off, but there wasn't much conviction in their boasts.

After we had finished our lunches, the teacher restored the "lives" of the dead and everyone had a drink of water from a nearby spring. Then the armies separated, the Blues going into the cemetery, the Reds going down the main path to the northeast. In about twenty minutes we reached a point where another path, which circled around the spur, crossed ours. The army halted. Our general divided the older boys into two groups and said that each of the rest of us could choose to go with whichever group he preferred.

I had been at the school only a few weeks and had not yet made any close friends. Both my roommates were in the Blue army. I did get up enough courage, though, to suggest to two boys my own age that we might try to approach from the northwest. They were startled by my plan but finally fell in with it, and during the confusion of dividing the army we slipped off the path into the brush. After a walk of perhaps half an hour we reached the northwesterly base of the spur.

The climb did not prove to be so difficult as we had thought it might. We worked up slowly and were careful about taking cover. Yet when we were about halfway to the top, my companions began to have doubts. "Maybe we should go around to the south and meet the others," one of them said. The other agreed.

"But then we'll be killed just like the rest of them," I protested.

"That's the way we always attack the cemetery," the first boy insisted.

"Come on," I said, "or we'll get there too late," and I started to climb again. They didn't follow, so I added, "Well, you can go to the south if you want to. I'm going this way."

By all accepted formulas of behavior this should have brought

them to heel, but, instead, one of them said, "I guess we'll go to the south, then."

"Go ahead," I answered, and went on. They circled away to the south and I was left alone, knowing that part of their reason for leaving me was that I was a new boy and that they had been considering the social hazards of following me.

I kept on climbing, and when at last I could see the wall above me, I made my way to a point on the west side where I had noticed a bush overhanging the wall. I straightened up slowly and looked over the wall through the bare branches. As I had hoped, the Blues were arranged almost as the Reds had been in the morning. They did, however, have a man standing in the southwest area of the cemetery. He looked as if he could easily outrun me, so I hoped he would be drawn into the fight at the gate when the attack came.

I crouched down out of sight again and waited. I kept thinking what a hero I would be when I had won the war. Perhaps my army would lift me up on their shoulders and give me three cheers. Next time we had to choose sides I would not be left to the last. I lived in this dream until the Blue scouts came in to say that the Reds were almost there. I stood up cautiously and looked over the wall again. The boy in the southwest corner was still at his post, his back to me now.

The attack opened just as it had in the morning. The boy in the southwest corner started to trot toward the gate. The attack from the south developed, and I scrambled onto the wall.

My plan had been to sneak over to the path running from the entrance to the middle of the west wall and then to run down it to the fort as fast as I could. The Blue general had been standing in the fort, giving his orders, but I hoped he would be drawn into the

battle at the east entrance. As I jumped, I saw that he was already involved at the gate, and I started out for the path. Then I saw the boy who had been nearest me look back as he zigzagged through the graves. He stopped as if he couldn't believe his eyes and then he let out a yell. I was closer to the fort then he was, but I saw that I couldn't possibly reach the path without his cutting me off. I took the only way left and lit out in a straight line for the fort. I had no real hope of beating my opponent, but he didn't seem to be gaining on me and I kept on running.

"Stop that!" I heard him shouting, and I thought he was foolish to waste his breath.

When I was about fifteen yards from the fort the boys fighting at the gate saw me. They were too far away to cut me off now, but I still couldn't believe that I hadn't been caught. At last I was at the fort and inside the square marked out on the paths.

A few seconds later my pursuer came up. "You cheated," he panted at me.

"I did not," I said.

The Reds, all of whom were now dead but me, and the Blues came running up, the teacher behind them. This was my moment. I would be lifted to the shoulders of the Reds and given three cheers. My career at the Kuling American School was made. I smiled generously at them, only to realize that something had gone wrong. All the Reds and the Blues stopped at the edge of the fort, looking at the two of us in the center.

"He cheated," the Blue soldier announced.

"I did not," I repeated.

"You stepped on the graves," the Blue general said, horror in his voice.

"Of course I did," I answered. "It was the shortest way."

The Reds murmured among themselves. Surely, I thought, the Red general would back me up. But all of the Reds just stood there looking embarrassed.

"Isn't that cheating, sir?" the Blue general asked the teacher.

The teacher cleared his throat. "Well, of course this has never happened before," he said.

I gave a frantic look at the Reds and saw that I was no longer one of them; I was just a new boy who had done what had never been done before. Although I had been frightened at first, I felt myself growing angry.

"It's sacrilege to walk on a grave," the Blue general announced.

"It is not!" I almost shouted at him. "In Shanghai we have a cemetery right next to our house, and my sister and I often play in it and run up and down the mounds."

"Oh, well, those are just Chinese graves," a Blue put in.

I drew myself up. "All souls are equal before God," I pronounced. Confident of my theology, I turned to the teacher and asked, "Isn't that right, sir?"

His face was contorted, almost as if he was trying not to laugh, and he blushed and stuttered.

"Of course," the Blue general said, "it may be all right in Shanghai."

My fear was entirely forgotten. "Listen," I said, "my father is an ordained minister of the Northern Presbyterian Church, and if it weren't all right to walk on a grave he would have told me. You're just superstitious, that's all."

Again there was a murmur from the Reds and I looked hopefully at them, but the noise died down almost immediately. Everyone was silent, and I thought that if I could be the first to speak I might still win out. An idea came to me. "Isn't this a war game?" I asked.

"Sure," the Blue general answered. "What's that got to do with it?"

"Well," I said, "you must have heard the old saying that all's fair in love and war. Almost anybody would know that."

Everyone looked impressed. The Blue general gurgled, and I knew that I had scored a telling point. The teacher had got hold of himself by now and he said, "I think it would be just as well if we didn't run over the graves again, but since all *is* fair in love and war, I rule that the Red army wins by a score of one to nothing."

I looked over at the Reds. Now, surely, they would embrace me. But the Reds and the Blues were already turning away silently and beginning to drift out of the cemetery on their way back to the school.

My two roommates didn't exactly shun me as we went down the path. They merely walked ahead of me and talked rapidly to each other. The more I thought of the matter during that bleak return, the more it seemed to me that the girls probably understood war game a lot better than anyone else did, a view that received support from the interested glances sent my way by a number of girls at supper that night.

THE PINE TREE PATROL

WHEN I HAD SPENT A YEAR at the Kuling American School and was old enough to become a member of the local troop of the Boy Scouts of America, I faced the problem of choosing, or at least being chosen by, a patrol. There were three patrols in our troop, the Pine Tree Patrol and two others. The others must remain nameless not from any conscious snobbery on my part, but because their names have so completely slipped my mind that I know it is hopeless for me to try and remember them. They were perfectly decent patrols in their ordinary way, and each was named after a wild animal. Of that much I am certain, but of little more.

It is easy to be mistaken about even the most important details as one looks back over the years, and it may be that one or two members of the Pine Tree Patrol came from the less prosperous sects. However, I seem to remember that the membership was made up entirely of Presbyterians and Episcopalians. The Episcopalians looked down on the Presbyterians whenever they thought about the matter, and the Presbyterians smiled back and looked down on the Episcopalians. We Calvinists knew that though our fathers would never be bishops, they would always give us allowances substantially larger than those of our fellow patrol members,

and we were happy to let the matter rest on this sound economic basis. When it came to a pinch we knew that we had what it would take.

It is probably evident by this time that I became a member of the Pine Tree Patrol. Our average age was a little less than that of the members of the other two patrols, but we never felt ourselves inferior in any other way. It is true that many of us remained Tenderfeet, or at the most Second-Class Scouts, throughout our Scouting careers, but this was the result of our looking with a jaundiced eye on the more spectacular and exhibitionist phases of Scouting, like firemaking and knot-tying, and not of any lack of ability.

The exact details of my being admitted to the Pine Tree Patrol I have forgotten, but I do remember that I pulled a number of strings and spent my allowance liberally for some weeks. I cultivated the son of a bishop and the son of a probable bishop. It may be that the members of the other two patrols were under the impression that they were maneuvering me out of their patrols and into the Pine Tree Patrol. If they thought so, they were welcome to the illusion. When I took the oath, gave the three-finger salute for the first time officially, received the hand clasp from the Scoutmaster, and was welcomed into the Pine Tree Patrol, I felt that a period of my life had ended and a greater period had begun.

For the sake of those who have not received the benefits of Scouting, it is necessary that I explain briefly the nature of a patrol and the spirit that exists among its members. The patrol is a unit made up of a dozen or so Scouts who stand somewhat in the relation of blood brothers to each other. They are to heed the cries of help of any other member of the patrol and speed to his aid. All of this relationship is symbolized by the patrol's emblem, which is usually

a wild animal. A detailed, and probably quite meaningless, study of totemism in modern American life could no doubt be written on this subject, but here it is enough to point out only one thing: the members of a patrol are expected, when hard pressed, to call to each other by using the sound of the totem animal.

I do not know what the feelings of the average American-born Scout are when he has to resort to yelping like the coyote or slapping his tail like the beaver. I do know that to a boy born and raised in China, where man is still held to be a trifle superior to the other orders of being, there is something in these acts that appears ludicrous, if not downright degrading. Because of this, we who were members of the Pine Tree Patrol always snickered when the other patrols had to do any signaling. Not that this happened often, for anyone in really dire straits would have had sense enough to shout "Help!" or call for a servant in a loud voice; but as a good Scout and a loyal patrol member, one was supposed to keep in practice on the patrol calls.

We boys of the Pine Tree Patrol were never embarrassed when we had to give our call. Though we were occasionally told by dim-witted and envious rivals that we should sigh like the wind blowing through pine needles or shout like the rising sap, we smiled condescendingly on such suggestions and referred their authors to the official *Scout Handbook*. Here anyone who could read might see that the approved and official call for the Pine Tree Patrol was made by placing a pine cone in a tin can and rattling it. The sound was said to carry over great distances. Thus it was that a member of our Pine Tree Patrol, whether he was an Episcopalian or a Presbyterian, was always able, even under the most trying circumstances, to keep his dignity.

THE CAVE-IN

ATE IN THE SPRING of 1925 the headmaster of the Kuling
L American School decided that the courtyard behind the main
building of the school should be enlarged in order to give the servants
more space to work, and to improve the drainage of rainwater from
the upper grounds. The main building stood on the slope of a hill.
There was already a twelve-foot vertical cut in the slope at the rear
of the building and a level space perhaps twenty feet wide between
this cut and the building had been excavated to make a court. The
headmaster proposed to have the width of this court increased by
seven feet.

It was not long before a Chinese contractor was engaged and a
crew of twenty-odd coolies set to work digging into the reddish clay
of the hillside. Other coolies carried the earth away in large baskets
hung from poles, some loads going to level up parts of the school's
athletic field and others to fill in a terrace at another of the contractor's construction projects.

For a day or two everything went smoothly. During what free
time we had, groups of students, both boys and girls, would gather
behind the building to watch the men, not because this was an
especially unusual sight but because it gave us an excuse for loitering
outside. The headmaster was also keeping an eye on the progress

of the work, and soon he felt it necessary to express disapproval of the contractor's methods. The coolies had been put to work at the base of the existing cut and had been doing all their digging from head-level down. This, the headmaster pointed out, was dangerous. The conversation took place in the courtyard before an interested audience of us children. The headmaster said that the entire face of the cut was being undermined, and that if the men went in much further, there would almost certainly be a cave-in. This, the contractor replied, was precisely what he himself expected to happen. Indeed, he couldn't have offered to do the job at such a low price if he had planned to have the men dig down from the top. The headmaster was not visibly impressed by this answer and asked the contractor how he could be sure that none of the coolies would be injured when the crash came.

The contractor, who spent most of his time sitting around in a white linen gown drinking tea, smiled at the headmaster's naivete and told him that the Chinese had been doing this sort of excavation in just this manner for centuries, that he would know when the danger point had been reached, and that when this moment came, he would send all the coolies up to the top of the bank to jump up and down. The jumping and their weight would loosen the soil and the whole bank would crash down, saving no one knew how many days' work. He thought it would be a fine sight and he strongly recommended that everyone try to see it. Afterward, the coolies would carry off the earth. This was the way to do the job, he said, and he implied, in conclusion, that if the headmaster would just stick to what he was paid to do, he himself would be happy to do likewise.

Though the headmaster looked anything but convinced, he gave up for the day, and as soon as he had left, we children were treated

to quite a show by the contractor as he mimicked the headmaster's accent and gestures. Then, flipping open his large, gentleman's fan, he shouted at the men to get on with the work and stop standing around with their mouths hanging open.

This exchange between the headmaster and the contractor was repeated the next day. The coolies meanwhile had dug deeper into the bank and the situation did begin to look a little precarious. Failing again to get satisfaction, the headmaster announced at breakfast the following morning—the day was a Saturday—that no one was to venture into the courtyard or walk along the top of the bank. Late Saturday evening it began to drizzle and most of Sunday there was rain. We wondered whether enough water would fall to overweight the bank and bring it down. Some of us spent a good part of Sunday afternoon and evening on the sleeping porches at the rear of the building, just in case the headmaster knew what he was talking about. There were, naturally, one or two boys present who took pleasure in quoting the contractor's better thrusts.

By Monday morning the rain had stopped and the coolies were back at work. The contractor announced loudly that the moment had almost come, that some persons might think it even now time to stop digging, but that to one of his experience it was plain that still more dirt must be removed. He clicked his fan open and shut a number of times and stood a good distance from the bank.

Although it would be an exaggeration to say that we children went to our first classes that Monday morning with a sense of impending disaster, and though much of our anxiety was merely that we would not be there to see the coolies jump up and down on top of the bank till it collapsed, some of us hoped secretly that everything might not go as planned. It was in this mood that we gathered for chapel services, so when the matron came into the assembly hall,

which was on the second floor of the building, and spoke to the headmaster in the middle of the opening hymn, we stopped singing almost before the headmaster raised his hand, despite the fact that we had heard no sounds from outdoors.

"A bad accident has just occurred," the headmaster announced. "The nurse and the members of the Scout Troop will come with me. Everyone else will remain here for the rest of the service, after which classes will be held as usual."

Feeling very important, I stood up with the other Scouts, and we followed the headmaster and the nurse out of the hall. When we reached the stairs, we heard the noise mounting in the courtyard. As we went down, we could see through the windows on each landing that the earth had caved in along the entire length of the bank. The school servants were running about in great excitement when we reached the court itself. The contractor had lost his aplomb and was shrieking commands in a hysterical voice. Some of the workmen were digging out the men who had not been completely buried, and one man, whose left leg was caught under a great heap of fallen dirt, was shouting to the others to rescue him before any more of the bank fell. Near one end of the cave-in, five or six men were digging frantically and calling for others to come to their help.

The headmaster silenced the contractor by telling him to find out how many of his coolies were missing. The older Scouts were told to take up any shovels and picks they could find and help the men already at work. The school nurse commandeered one of the classrooms on the ground floor and sent me and another of the youngest boys, whose name was Walker, to the infirmary for her first-aid supplies. Some of the servants and the rest of the younger Scouts were ordered to bring basins of water to the classroom and to move out most of the chairs.

By the time Walker and I got back to the improvised first-aid station, some of the casualties had been brought in, among them the man whose leg had been pinned down. The nurse found that the leg was broken, and she had the man lie down on a folded blanket and told one of the younger Scouts to clean him up without moving the leg. Some of the men in the room had been badly bruised or cut, and the nurse set about patching them up. While she was doing this, two of the older Scouts carried in a man who was covered with clay from his waist up. "He's still breathing all right," one of them said, "but he seems to feel best sitting up. We don't know how badly he's hurt."

"All right," the nurse answered. "Prop him up in that chair." Then she spoke to Walker and me. "You two get a basin of warm water and some washrags and wash the dirt off him. Some of his ribs may be cracked, so go easy."

Walker and I got a big basin of warm water, and each of us took a washcloth from the supply of towels and cloths that one of the servants had brought in. The man was wearing nothing but straw sandals and a pair of faded blue trousers. His mouth hung open and he breathed through it heavily, moaning occasionally. Half afraid and half curious, I reached out and took an experimental dab at his forehead.

As I touched him he gave a grunt. "It's all right," I said, pulling my hand back. "We're going to help you."

"What's the matter with you?" Walker said scornfully. "He can't understand English and his ears are covered with mud anyway." This was true. The man's whole head was an irregular sphere of reddish clay, in which his mouth was the only opening.

"Let's work from his waist on up," Walker said, and I sensed that he shared my reluctance to touch the man's head.

Gently we began washing him, scraping the clay off with our fingers first and then using the cloths. As we uncovered his ribs, the man groaned a few times, but we went on washing him, sliding our arms behind him to get at his back.

While we were doing this, other men were brought in, but Walker and I scarcely noticed them. We emptied and refilled the basin five or six times before we had finished washing the man's chest and arms and back. At times he moaned but he made no attempt to resist.

When we had refilled our basin once again, I said to Walker, "Well, now we've got to start on his head."

"Yes," Walker said. "Where should we begin?"

"If we start on his ears," I suggested, "maybe you can talk to him and tell him what we're doing and ask him where the worst pain is." Walker's home was nearer to Kuling than mine, and there was more chance that the man would understand his Chinese. My own knowledge of the Shanghai dialect would, I knew, be useless.

"Well, let's begin," Walker said.

Working one on each side of the man's head, we scraped away the clay. "Perhaps we should have done this first," I remarked.

"It's too late now," Walker answered.

The clay had been forced into the man's ears, and we had to get swab sticks from the nurse's supplies before we could dislodge the plugs of dirt that had been formed. Walker bent down and spoke in Chinese.

"What are you saying to him?" I asked impatiently.

"Shut up," Walker said. "How can I talk to him if you keep yelling at me? I'm just telling him who we are and what's happened to him. I don't know if he understands."

But the clay-laden lower jaw moved a little and the man whispered

what even I knew were the two syllables for "thank you" in the local dialect.

"Why, he's thanking us!" I said in wonder. A feeling of great tenderness came over me.

Walker nodded. "Yes. Now I'll ask him if there's any special place that hurts." He leaned over the coolie and spoke to him, but the man only groaned and again whispered, "Thank you."

With great care we washed his lower jaw and upper lip, wiping away the slime around his mouth. We had to use the swab sticks again when we came to his nose. Slowly we worked at his forehead and from time to time were startled afresh to hear the man's whispered "thank you." It was only when we began to work on his eyes that he whimpered.

We kept on carefully as we could until I drew back suddenly. "Stop, Walker! Stop!" I exclaimed, and pointing I said, "Look, look there." I had washed enough of the clay off one eye to see that the man's eyelids were opened and that the clay was packed in over the eyeball itself.

Walker gasped. Then he washed a little more and said, "It's the same with this one."

We paused. I reached out at last and touched the clay covering one eyeball. The man trembled and his hands came up in protest. His breathing grew jerky and he sobbed a little.

"I'll tell him we can't do any more now, that somebody else will do the rest," Walker said. He spoke to the man, who smiled weakly and said something. "He wants a cigarette," Walker said. "Do you suppose we'd get into trouble if we got one for him?"

"Of course not," I answered with more certainty than I felt. I went to the door, thinking to get a cigarette from one of the servants, but I saw the contractor standing in the hallway. I made a motion

of lighting a cigarette and then held out my hand. He smiled and bowed, pulling out a pack of Ruby Queens and a small box of safety matches. I took a cigarette and the matches and nodded to him. He smiled and bowed again. Perhaps he thought that my father held an important official position.

"Say, we'll have to light it for him," Walker said when I returned.

"That's right, we will," I answered. Facing the wall, I struck a match and lit the cigarette. As I turned back I let out a puff of blue smoke.

"Do you know how to smoke?" Walker asked, in considerable awe, as I put the cigarette between the man's lips.

"Well, not really," I admitted with some reluctance. "I smoked once in America, the last time I was there."

The man inhaled deeply, raised one of his hands slowly and took the cigarette out of his mouth, and said, "Thank you, thank you." We were glad to see that he could move his arm at all.

Now that the man was as comfortable as we could make him, Walker and I began to look around the room. Five or six bandaged men were lying on blankets on the floor. The school doctor, an American, who had been called from his home, arrived, followed by Chinese officials from the Gap. These officials began to question the headmaster and the contractor. I was unable to follow much of what was being said, but the contractor looked as if he were worrying more about the size of the bribe he would have to pay than the sufferings of his coolies.

I felt Walker jerk my sleeve. "Over there," he said, pointing to the corner of the room farthest from the door. What he had seen were two sheets stretched out over what we knew must be the bodies of two dead coolies. We said nothing, staring at the motionless white crests and hollows. I turned to the man we had been washing, as if

in fear of finding him, too, dead. But he was still smoking his cigarette, reaching up to take it from his mouth between puffs, but sitting motionless otherwise. When he had finished it, Walker took the butt from his hand and threw it into the basin.

The doctor was now free for a moment and we told him about the clay on the man's eyeballs. "I'll attend to that later," he said.

As we stood there wondering what to do next, one of the older boys came in and joined us. He looked over at the corner where the dead had been laid and abruptly said, "It was awful."

"What was?" I asked.

He looked puzzled. "Didn't you hear? The second one."

"Second one?" Walker asked.

"Yes—over there," he said, looking at the sheets. "We dug him out almost as soon as we started to work. He was breathing and almost right away he asked for a drink of water. I got him one and held up his head to help him drink it. Well, he swallowed most of it, and then he—well—he sort of gurgled, and then he—he just died." The boy's eyes looked hurt. "Do you think it could have been the water that killed him?"

"You mean he died just like that?" Walker demanded.

"Yes, he drank the water and then he died."

"But that wouldn't have killed him," Walker said. "He must have been broken inside. You ought to be glad you did something for him."

"Of course," I put in. "Nobody would die of a cup of water." The boy looked a little relieved.

"Have they got everyone now?" Walker asked him.

"No, there's still one they haven't found. I guess maybe I'll go out again. They're still digging."

Walker and I stood by our man until the nurse and doctor got

to him. "Now you two may go," the nurse told us. "It's almost time for lunch and you must clean up."

"Couldn't we stay?" I asked. "Maybe we could help. I mean, we're interested, you know," I went on in confusion, unable as well as unwilling to say right out that Walker and I felt a bond with the man sitting there, his face masklike with its two patches of red clay over the eyeballs.

"No, you'd just be in the way," the nurse said. "Just run along now."

We backed out of the room and then went outside. In the courtyard the uninjured coolies and the older Scouts were still digging. One of the teachers watching from an upper window saw us and called for us to come in and get ready for lunch. The girls and the younger boys were all gathered at the windows above us, but from time to time their heads would be drawn in as a teacher came by and tried to get them away from the windows.

Walker and I went back into the building. The boys not yet old enough to be Scouts gathered around us, envious and questioning, but we had little to say to them. After lunch, of which I ate only a few mouthfuls, all of us were kept indoors until classes resumed. One of the teachers told us, in answer to our questions, that the body of the last man had still not been found, and it was not until the middle of the afternoon that word came in of its discovery.

When Walker and I were finally able to get away, after classes, we learned that all the injured men had been moved from the school. We asked the nurse about the man we had tried to help.

"Now just which one was that?" she inquired.

"His eyes were pressed in with dirt," I told her.

"Oh," she said, and I felt sure that she remembered him. "You know, there were so many hurt in one way or another that I can't

really recall them individually." I was certain that she was lying to us.

"Do you think if a person was hurt like that, he would have a chance to see again?" Walker persisted.

"Oh yes," the nurse said, much too cheerfully, and then betrayed herself by adding, "Of course, there are lots of things a blind person can do to earn a living, you know."

Feeling utterly lost, we left her.

"He seemed so nice," Walker faltered. "And the way he kept saying 'thank you.' "

"Yes," I said.

At supper I still had no appetite, and all during study hall I stared at the pages of my books without trying to read them. While I was getting ready for bed, one of my roommates came in, in great excitement, saying he had just learned that, because of some official red tape, the bodies of the three dead men hadn't been moved from the building yet.

"Let's sneak downstairs after lights-out and look in," he proposed.

"I don't want to," I said.

"Oh, come on," he urged, and told me that he and my other roommate and one other boy had decided to do it.

"All right," I agreed at last.

Shortly before midnight we sneaked down the hall in our bare feet. Using the servants' stairs, we reached the ground floor. Through the pane of glass in the door of the classroom, we could just make out three white forms in the far corner, for a light burning outside the building lit the room dimly.

"Do you suppose we can get in?" one of my roommates asked.

"The door's locked," I said in panic.

"How do you know?" He tried the knob and the door opened.

We stepped inside. The whiteness of the sheets seemed to draw us to them, and we found ourselves standing beside the covered bodies.

"Don't!" I whispered as one of the other boys reached out his hand, but he paid no attention to me and drew back the sheet from the head of the nearest body. The face, which we could see only faintly, looked crushed.

Then terror took hold of us. We ran to the door, closed it, and raced upstairs. When my roommates and I were in our beds again, we said little to each other. If it was not that night, it was only a few nights later that I dreamed for the first time of a man coming toward me, hands outstretched. It was a dream that came back night after night. He always came toward me in the same way, and only when he had murmured something in Chinese would I notice that he had patches of red clay over his eyes and be shaken by fear and tenderness.

Plates

The Espey house (left) and the double house for single ladies. Presbyterian Mission Compound, South Gate, Shanghai.

1906–07 (?). The faculty of Miss Jewell's School, Shanghai. Front row, third from left: Mary Lucretia Jenkins, the future bride of John Morton Espey and mother of the author. Extreme right: The author's great-aunt Janette Rosbrook; to the left of her (unhatted), Mary Macphail, later Courtesy Aunt Mary Myers; and to the left of her, the redoubtable Miss Jewell.

Summer 1907. The tennis courts at Mokanshan.

Summer 1913. Swaledale, Iowa. The author and his sister,
John Jenkins and Mary Frances Espey.

1915 (?). The author with his parents and sister.

Opposite: Summer 1914, Swaledale, Iowa. Left to right, back row: Frances and Florence Jenkins; their half-brother, Louis Jenkins; his sister, Mary, mother of the author (in her arms); the author's father; Alice Woodward Jenkins, wife of Louis. Center row: Margaret Hales; Bessy Carr Jenkins, second wife of John Thomas Jenkins, seated to her left; Meta Jenkins Hales, mother of Margaret, and the author's maternal aunt; Frank Hales, husband of Meta and father of Margaret. In front: The author's sister with cousins Burke and John Jenkins, sons of Alice and Louis Jenkins.

Summer 1916 (?), Mokanshan, China. From left: The author's mother; Courtesy Aunt Mary Myers; Courtesy Aunt Bess Hille of South Gate; Courtesy Aunt Mary Elizabeth Codgal (see "She Bringeth Her Bread from Afar").

1916 (?), South Gate. The author and his sister blowing bubbles.

Christmas 1918, Garden of Girls' School, South Gate. This picture was later trimmed and used for the first American passport, issued early in 1919, of the author and his sister.

1921, South Gate. The Espey family's first automobile, a Chevrolet Baby Grand Touring Car. From left: The blurred author; a Miss Eddy of Newark, New Jersey; Scott Crawford, the author's SAS classmate; the author's sister; the author's mother at the wheel.

The main building of the Kuling American School.

1927, South Gate. The author and his parents at home.

1930. Senior picture, Shanghai American School.

1935. Senior picture, Occidental College, Los Angeles.

Summer 1935, Peitaiho, North China coast. The author (right), with his parents (center), and his sister and brother-in-law, D. Theodore McAllister (left).

Late summer, 1935. The author and his sister, together with their guide, on the Great Wall. (Photo by D. T. McAllister.)

Summer 1936, Merton College, Oxford. Lo, the Rhodes Scholar! (Photo by Margaret Calhoun Hostetter.)

March 1938, Baguio, Philippine Islands. "All the expression has been taken out of our faces—too much retouching; but Dad imagines we look like this, so never mind even tho we don't."

LE SCOUTING EN CHINE

S INCE FRENCH was the only foreign language taught with any seriousness at the Kuling American School, the language naturally became a medium for many juvenile efforts at verbal humor. Nothing delighted us more than to be reported to the headmaster for the grave offense of "swearing in French" by teachers whose Gallic spirit was as weak as their French vocabulary. My one success in this line was to be reprimanded for exploding into *"Parapluie! Parapluie!"* when a classmate jostled me in the hall. When we learned that the French called a dinner jacket *un smoking,* my classmates and I could scarcely contain ourselves, and we immediately set out to Frenchify everything we could think of by adding *ing* to it and honking out the syllable with what we hoped was the true Parisian timbre. Soon I began to speak of the activities of the Kuling American School Troop of the Boy Scouts of America as *"le Scouting,"* and whereas few jokes seem deader to me now than most of these attempts to be funny, I have felt more and more strongly as I have grown older that *le Scouting* is the only term to describe the actions of our troop, and especially of the Pine Tree Patrol. For I have learned through occasional and unsought contacts with the male youth of America that what it calls Scouting is a far, far different thing from *le Scouting* as I knew it in Kuling.

Even as a boy, this difference was apparent to me to some extent. For example, only one member of the Kuling troop owned full Scouting regalia in all its correct glory, and when the three patrols gathered for meetings or hikes, their members were clothed in a great variety of outfits. To own an item of official equipment set one apart, especially if it was an item of some importance. There were perhaps five regulation shirts in the entire troop and about the same number of trousers. Four of the Kuling Scouts owned correct hats, and a few more sported official belts and knives, the latter usually hung from the waist for display. One lucky troop member owned a canteen whose canvas cover bore the Scout insigne. On long hikes he allowed his intimates to drink from it, an act that they performed reverently and with little regard for the principles of hygiene.

Shortly after I joined the troop I was made happy for a time by the prospect of owning an official Scout hat. I had written to my father in Shanghai, asking him if he couldn't get me one, and in a few days he wrote back that the parcel was on its way. His promptness made me suspicious, since American Scout hats were hard to come by in Shanghai stores, which naturally catered to the Boy Scouts of China rather than the Boy Scouts of America, and I wisely said nothing about the matter to anyone. When the package arrived, I waited until I was alone before I opened it. My chagrin and my relief at being alone were about equal as I pulled from the wrapping not an official American Scout hat but an official Chinese one, which was a few shades darker than the American model and had a leather strap instead of a ribbon around it. Though I enjoyed, and quietly cultivated, a small reputation for eccentricity at the school, I knew that even my closest friends would think I had gone too far if I were to appear with a Chinese Scout hat on my head, and I hid it instantly at the bottom of my steamer trunk.

This experience left me so shaken that I was not particularly surprised a few months later by the collapse of a deal I had made to buy a hat from the only Scout in the troop who owned two. This boy's father was, like mine, a Presbyterian missionary, but his intellectual training, unlike my father's, had been completed in a medical school instead of a theological seminary, and he was, therefore, given to making and maintaining dogmatic rather than logical statements. He stopped the sale of his son's hat as soon as he arrived in Kuling for the summer, not because he objected to the price we had agreed upon but because he insisted that the maiden aunt who had given my fellow Scout his second hat would have her feelings seriously hurt if she ever learned of its sale. Since this good woman lived some thousands of miles distant, in the eastern part of the United States, the probability of her learning anything at all about the hat was remote to say the least, and I pointed this out as tactfully as I could to the doctor and his son. The doctor, like so many of his kind, refused to budge from his original position, whereupon I offered to buy my friend's first hat. But this hat, I was told, had been given to him by an uncle, also living in the United States, and his feelings, too, might be hurt. I then pointed out that my friend had already worn both hats and couldn't any longer, as a matter of fact, tell the aunt's from the uncle's; so that I would, I said, be happy to buy either one. I couldn't, I went on, see how anyone's feelings would be hurt, since even the doctor himself would never know for sure which hat I had bought. As I have already said, my friend's father was beyond logic, and this altogether reasonable proposal, which would have delighted the mind of any well-educated theologian, shocked his medical sense of professional ethics. I finally let the matter drop, though not before I had given silent thanks for being a member of a family that recognized the attractions and uses of pure reason.

Thus it was that at the meetings of our troop I had to be satisfied with my tarnished Tenderfoot badge, pinned to an ordinary sports shirt, and a pair of rather faded, but nonetheless authentic, ribbed khaki socks on my scrawny legs as the only strictly correct items of my wardrobe. Scout socks were fairly common, and almost anyone could get hold of a pair by using a little ingenuity. There were often a few pairs on the market at school, so it would have been possible for me to buy them outright. This, however, struck me as being a reckless waste of capital, and I obtained mine in the best tradition of *le Scouting* by doing a series of arithmetic lessons for another, and less academically inclined, member of the Pine Tree Patrol.

The best example of *le Scouting* was the two-week camping trip taken annually by our troop during the summer vacation. The year I became a Scout I went on this trip despite my parents' fears that I was really too young and delicate for such a rough experience. As soon as they had arrived in Kuling to spend the summer, I had demanded permission to go camping, and though they finally yielded, it was with some concern that they and my sister watched me, one Monday morning, take the path that led down the mountainside at the north end of Kuling Valley. When I reached the last point from which I could see the veranda of the cottage our family was renting that summer, I turned around slowly and waved. My parents and my sister waved back. Then I squared my shoulders, turned forward again, and started down the path. I had to handle myself with deliberation because I was carrying on my back a large U.S. Army knapsack that my father had bought on his last furlough. This splendid piece of equipment would, I knew, be an object of envy, for it had "U.S." stenciled in large letters on one of its flaps, and it was controlled by an astonishing number of adjustable straps, spring clasps, and buckles. These were probably well adapted to a

fully developed male figure, but once I had them all hitched to my belt, the full knapsack played the devil with my khaki shorts and threatened to geld me. My load, moreover, was increased by a blanket roll slung over the top of the knapsack in the best *Scout Handbook* form. But, regardless of my physical discomfort, I felt that I was at last acting in the great tradition of Scouting as I had absorbed it from the pages of *Boy's Life* and from dozens of American books celebrating the joys of roughing it.

I had taken only a few steps when I was surprised to see our cook walk out into the path just a short distance ahead of me. With him was the local outside coolie who was hired for the summer to carry in our water and do other odd jobs.

"What are you doing here?" I asked the cook. "I thought you were still at the house."

"Well, you were mistaken, Little Brother," the cook said. He always called me Little Brother when he was about to give me either advice or orders, saving my purely formal title of Little Master for public occasions. "Since it is impossible even for your parents to keep you from rushing out over the mountains to live like a wild animal, I say nothing of the stupidity of what you are doing, but I can at least see that you don't disgrace yourself and everyone connected with you by walking through the valley loaded down like a donkey."

"But that's part of the idea," I protested. "This is the way everyone does in America when he goes camping." Knowing no Chinese word for "camping," I used the English one.

"You see, it isn't a civilized thing," the cook said. "If there isn't a Chinese word for it, you can be sure it's barbarous."

"I don't know about that," I answered, "but I do know I'll be late meeting the others if I stay here trading thoughts with you."

"All right, then," the cook said. "Just unload yourself and we'll go right along."

"Are you going to carry my things?" I asked.

"Am I a camel?" the cook demanded, letting his voice shoot up into a falsetto shriek. He pointed to the outside coolie. "This man is going to carry your things, of course."

"Now, look here," I said. "I know you think you'll be disgraced if the other servants see me carrying this stuff through the valley. But *I'll* be disgraced in their masters' eyes if I *don't* carry it."

"At least let this fellow carry the bundles down to the main road," the cook pleaded, and I realized that this short haul would get us past most of the homes where he was known. Since most of my own friends lived farther down the valley, it seemed best to yield.

"All right," I said, unbuckling the knapsack and slipping it off. The outside coolie slung it over his shoulder and, tucking the blanket roll under one arm, started down the path.

"Not so fast!" the cook said to him sternly. "Little Master and I will go first." He straightened his gown and stepped ahead of the outside coolie. "Will you go ahead of me, Little Master?" he asked.

"Oh, don't be so fussy, we'll walk together," I answered. And so the cook and I walked side by side down the path to Brook Road at the bottom of the valley. Whenever we passed a house where he was known, the cook spoke to his Little Master in a loud voice, thus gaining, as he hoped, quantities of face from the spectacle of his Little Master beside him and of the outside coolie meekly following along behind with my luggage.

The three of us halted when we reached Brook Road. "I've been thinking," the cook announced. "For a very small sum of money, you could hire this ox to go all the way with you and look after you at the camp. He could make your bed and take care of your

things, though I suppose he is really too stupid to do anything very well. But at least there would be some reason to hope that you would come back alive."

I was scandalized by this proposal. "That's impossible," I said. "That isn't what camping is like. You're supposed to do everything yourself."

"Why don't you let the coolie carry the things down to the meeting-place, anyway?" the cook countered.

"It's true, they're very heavy," I answered. "And I ought to save my strength for the rest of the trip. I'll tell you what—let him carry the big bundle and I'll carry the blankets. But make him walk a long way behind me, and maybe it will look as if I'd just forgotten the things and he was trying to catch up with me."

"You're very hopeful," the cook remarked, "though it isn't too bad a notion." He gave the coolie his orders and then said to me, "Well, I must leave you now. If you aren't brought back in a coffin I'll cook roast beef and Yorkshire pudding for your first dinner."

"What's the Chinese for Yorkshire pudding?" I asked.

The cook snorted. "It's amazing how often people who are ready with their tongues come to a bad end."

"Good-bye," I said, and started down Brook Road. When I glanced behind me I could see the outside coolie about fifty yards to the rear. As I passed various homes where I was known, people called to me from their verandas, and I bowed and said yes, I was going to the Scout camp at Incense Mills, and yes, it was good to have a fine, clear day, not too warm, for the six-mile hike, and no, I wouldn't get lost in the hills or cut off my foot with an ax, ha-ha!

Just before I reached the south end of the valley where the campers were to assemble at the American School, I had what seemed to me

a good idea and I waited for the outside coolie to come up to me. When he did, I took the knapsack from him and put it on my back. He then insisted on taking the blanket roll. In the end, I had to give in to him and I came staggering onto the school grounds under the weight of my knapsack, the outside coolie a few paces behind me with the blanket roll.

One of the older Scouts saw me and called out, "What in the world's the matter with you, Espey? Why don't you have your coolie carry the pack?"

"Oh, I just wanted to get the feel of it, you know," I said as the others gathered around me.

"You mean you've come all the way from your house up at the other end of the valley like that?" a member of the Pine Tree Patrol asked.

"Yes, I've come all the way from there," I said, feeling that this statement violated nothing in the Scout code of honor.

Luckily the members of the troop became interested in my knapsack and instead of asking me any more questions they began to investigate its fastenings with respectful interest. This inspection was stopped by an older Scout who came up to me and said, "You'd better hurry and turn your things over to the baggage coolies."

"The baggage coolies?" I asked, bewildered.

"Yes, they're over there, just about ready to start off," someone else said.

I looked where he pointed and saw seven or eight coolies making up carrying loads out of a collection of packs and blanket rolls. "Yes, of course," I said, and walked over to them. I slipped off my knapsack for the second time that morning and motioned to the outside coolie to put down the blanket roll. Then I waved him off home.

Two members of the Pine Tree Patrol joined me. "Say, you got

here just in time," one of them said. "The supply coolies left about twenty minutes ago."

"The supply coolies?" I bleated.

"Sure, you know, with all our food—the canned things and dry stuff. The tents, too, of course."

"Oh yes, of course," I said, quickly revising my notions of camping.

The baggage coolies heaved up their loads and were out of sight in a few minutes. After allowing them a fifteen-minute lead, the troop itself, unhampered by heavy luggage, started. In justice to the honor of my fellow Scouts, I must admit that some of the older members of the troop did not go entirely unburdened. One or two carried blanket rolls and the boy who owned the official canteen carried it and a small pack as well. The residents of the lower end of the valley waved us good-bye, and with many an *En avant, mes braves* and *Après vous* we got under way.

The day was, as had been pointed out to me several times, very fine, and with the other members of the Pine Tree Patrol I enjoyed the easy hike over the hill trails. Most of the way we went downhill, for our camping ground was located in a meadow in one of the lower valleys through which the main stream of Kuling flowed. We caught up with and passed the baggage coolies in an hour, and a few minutes before we reached Incense Mills we caught up with the last of the supply coolies. Once on the ground itself, the three other new members of the Pine Tree Patrol, who were to be my tentmates, and I staked out our claim to what we thought would be a good spot for our tent and then set about putting it up. This, I felt, was getting down to the realities of camping, and for about ten minutes I ran around untangling guy ropes and driving in stakes. After an interval of work the four of us had succeeded in getting the tent

partway up, its top sagging and the side flaps trailing on the ground. The ridgepole and the two end poles wobbled back and forth, and the whole structure looked menacing.

At last one of us, who happened to be a bishop's son and may have inherited a talent for assuming authority, said, "Really, we aren't getting very far this way."

"I know we aren't," I said, "but I hate to ask any of the others for help."

"I know what we'll do," the bishop's son said, and walked off towards the Scoutmaster, who was settling with the coolies, our baggage having just arrived.

For a moment I thought we were going to be disgraced by having the Scoutmaster himself find out what a mess we were in, but instead of going to him the bishop's son approached two of the coolies standing off to one side and came back in a few minutes with them both in tow.

"Now just what do you think needs doing?" he asked me.

"First, they ought to get the poles in a little more firmly," I said, "and then maybe while we hold one side of the tent they can get the other side stretched out tight and pegged down. By the way, what's this going to cost?"

"Oh, I just said we'd give them a little wine money," said the bishop's son. "Haven't you got your pocketbook with you?"

"Of course I have," I said, for though I had had no idea what use money would be out in the wilds, I had not been born a Presbyterian for nothing. "I just wondered if you'd settled on a price."

The coolies were greatly amused by the whole process of putting up the tent. After everything was made shipshape, they ran in and out of the tent, giggling, until I paid them off. Before we ate lunch, the Scoutmaster made a tour of inspection and complimented us

on the neatness of our work, which he thought was especially re-markable since we were all very young.

I had supposed that each Scout would cook at least a part of his own food, but I was pleased to discover that for this first meal, anyway, box lunches had been provided. We all sat in a circle around the site of what was to be the evening campfire. As we munched our sandwiches, I noticed a Chinese man coming out of the brush with some wood under his arm.

"I wonder if he lives near here," I said. "I didn't think anyone lived near here."

"Why, that's the wood coolie," an older Scout said. "He collects wood for the fire and keeps it going."

Another Chinese man followed the wood coolie across the clearing.

"That's another coolie to help," the older Scout said. "We don't have a real cook because the Scoutmaster likes to do most of the cooking—I don't know why—and everyone has to help him a little."

"Do we have any more servants?" I asked.

"Well, not exactly," my informant answered. "Of course, there are the coolies who bring in fresh supplies every day from Kul-ing—stuff like meat and eggs and milk."

By this time I had revised my idea of camping so often that I was almost afraid to ask any more questions, but I did risk another one. "Are we expected to pass very many tests while we're camping?" I inquired.

"Oh, no," the older Scout answered. "You can always pass tests during the year at school if you want to. I don't think anyone cares much about tests while he's camping, there's so much else to do."

"Yes, I suppose there is," I answered, but I really couldn't imagine what it would be.

Incense Mills got its name from a small group of water-powered mills, each little more than a stone hut housing a waterwheel geared to trip-hammers. When the mills were running, these hammers slowly pulverized pieces of sandalwood into incense dust. Most of the year the mills were out of use and after lunch my tentmates and I went inside the buildings to inspect them, and we poked around in the corners of the rooms hoping to find some pieces of wood that had been left behind. We soon got into an argument on just how the waterwheels worked and paid no attention to what anyone else was doing. We were therefore surprised when a group of Scouts came down from the camp to the path by the stream, wearing bathing suits. One of them called to us, "It's time to go to the pool now."

Afraid of being late for what we supposed was an official ceremony of the day, we rushed back to our tent, flung off our clothes and climbed into our bathing suits. Then we ran down the path, buttoning our shoulder straps on the way, to a point where the stream spread out into a large natural pool. Around its edge were large boulders, many of them flat enough for comfortable sunbathing.

"Are we too late?" I gasped to the first Scout I saw.

"Too late for what?" he asked. He was taking off his bathing suit and putting it on top of a rock, apparently planning to lie down on it.

"Somebody said it was time for us to come to the pool."

"Oh, he must have meant it was an hour after lunch," the Scout answered. "The Scoutmaster won't let us come down until an hour after meals. You'd better pick out a good rock for your sunbath. We have to wear our suits down here just in case we meet some hikers from Kuling on the trail, and it's a good thing to keep them in reach."

My tentmates and I chose a big flat rock on the other side of the pool. After we had swum over to it we took off our suits and stretched out to await developments. From time to time a Scout would dive into the water and swim around. Some of the Scouts timed one another to see how long they could stay under water. Every now and then someone would try to duck someone else. The sun was hot on our bare bodies and I drowsed through a good part of the afternoon. Only when the eastern slopes of the mountains were deep in shadow did we put on our bathing suits and stroll back to camp. The Scoutmaster and his coolies had cooked up a big stew for us, and all that the boys who were posted on the list to help with supper had to do was open some cans of peaches and pass them around. After supper we went down to the stream and everyone washed his own dishes with water and sand or dirt. Then the campfire was heaped with branches the wood coolie had brought in during the afternoon and we chattered around it for an hour or so before turning in.

The next day, an hour after we had finished breakfast, most of us went down to the pool and claimed our rocks after the ritual of putting on our suits at camp and taking them off again at the pool. Late in the morning a Scout who had been badly sunburned the day before came down the trail to tell us that the mail had just arrived. Everyone hurried back to the camp.

"I didn't know we could get mail in camp," I said to one of my tentmates. "I don't suppose there'll be anything for me."

But my parents had somehow learned that mail could be sent daily to Incense Mills by the coolies who carried in the perishable supplies, and I was cheered at receiving a letter. My mother hoped that I wasn't trying to do too much, and reminded me that I wasn't as strong as I might be. She also wrote that my father would come

down to visit me the following Monday and that if I had found things too rough going by then, I could return with him.

After lunch we lay on our cots waiting until an hour had passed and it was time to go to the pool. I found that two of my tentmates had brought a few books and magazines with them, so we read a little and talked a little to while away the interval. When it was time we put on our bathing suits and went to the pool.

As the days followed one another, the same pattern of languid activity was repeated with few variations. The only break for me came the night I had to stand watch. We were supposed to be on guard against a sham attack that had been arranged to keep us constantly on the alert. We knew that one night during the two weeks a group of three or four men from Kuling would sneak up on the camp and try to get in without attracting attention. The bishop's son and I thought of approaching one of the coolies when our turn came, but we decided it would be rather fun to keep the campfire going and sit up part of the night; so we took our turn and were disappointed when nothing happened.

On Monday of the second week my father strolled into camp about lunchtime. He looked very natty in white duck shorts, and carried with him a quantity of photographic apparatus. I thought his appearance did me credit, and I welcomed him cordially. After he had eaten lunch with us he asked me how I felt and I told him I was fine. He wanted to know if I had been doing a great deal, and I said no, I was being very careful. Satisfied with the condition of his son, he left the camp and climbed the rocky slope behind our pool in order to get some angle shots of the cliffs below and to explore generally for striking effects and possible pictures. When we campers reached the pool after our usual rest period, we could see him working his way around a group of rocks high above us.

When at last, in about an hour, Father started down toward the pool, taking shots along the way, one of the older Scouts splashed over to the rock I was on and said, "Say, will your father mind our not having any bathing suits on? You never can tell about people who weren't born in China. And, naturally, he's an ordained minister."

I wasn't at all certain, now that the question had been raised, what my father's reaction would be, but I decided to gamble everything and I said, in what I hoped was an unconcerned tone, "Oh, he won't mind. You know, my people live in Shanghai and they're used to a lot of things." Then I added, "And, of course, he's a Presbyterian," though I wasn't sure that this made sense.

I could feel my heart hammering as I lay there, hoping that Father wouldn't let me down. When he stepped out of the brush and came to the edge of the pool I got up to swim across to him, but he called out, "Just stay where you are." Then, while all the other members of the troop looked on in awe, and I looked on in pride that brought out gooseflesh on my arms and legs, Father first stacked his tripod, cameras, and plate-holders, next took off his clothes, and then made a neat racing dive into the water and swam across to our rock, using a brisk Australian crawl. He pulled himself up beside me and, grunting luxuriously, stretched out in the sun, apparently quite unconscious of the fact that he had just sent the stock of his family and his religion soaring clean out of sight.

The second week of our stay in camp was very like the first. We successfully repelled the "attack" the night before I was to stand watch again, so I was relieved of that chore. On our last day at Incense Mills we all scurried around early in the morning packing our things. We found that it was much easier to dismantle the tent than it had been to erect it, and by the time the baggage coolies arrived, everything was ready for them. After the coolies were loaded

and sent up the trail, we took a last swim and then started about forty minutes behind them. We overtook them only at the edge of the school grounds, and here we sorted our things. I was not especially surprised to see my family's cook and outside coolie standing with some other servants who had come down to meet their Little Masters. The effect on my character of two weeks of primitive living could be gauged by the way in which I pointed out my knapsack and blanket roll to the outside coolie and told him to pick them up.

After I had said good-bye to the Scoutmaster, I set off up Brook Road with the bishop's son, behind us the cook, behind him the outside coolie and the bishop's gardener. At the bishop's house I said good-bye to my friend, after making a tennis date for the next day. Then I told the cook to walk beside me, and we went up the valley, bowing to right and left, and I said yes, it was fine to go camping, but of course it was good to be back, and yes, I was very lucky to have had the experience, and no, we hadn't had any rain and wasn't that fortunate?

At dinner that night the cook served up a fine roast of beef and an excellent Yorkshire pudding with it, somewhat to my mother's surprise, since she couldn't remember ordering that particular meal. But then, she was getting used to having roast beef and Yorkshire pudding whenever I turned up after an absence of any length.

The next year at school when names were being taken for the camping trip, I thought the matter over and finally said to one of my friends in the Pine Tree Patrol, "*Ah, mon vieux,* I don't think I'll go this year. After all, I know how to look after myself in the wilds now. And then, there's something a bit strenuous about it—washing your own dishes, and in dirt, at that. One can, *vous savez,* have almost too much of *le Scouting.*"

SINS OF THE FLESH

I N THE SPRING of 1926 the headmaster of the Kuling American School took a vacation and left the school in the hands of a temporary headmistress. This woman, a Miss Blanchard, soon displayed what seemed to many of us somewhat primitive standards of conduct, and though there had been times when our headmaster, a Quaker, had been stern, his more or less impartial justice seemed in retrospect preferable to the regime that Miss Blanchard saw fit to impose upon us.

Most of the trouble began when Miss Blanchard undertook to search into the lives of the younger boys with more detail than any of us felt was the privilege of her sex. She was always bobbing up at odd times and observing our conduct with a suspicious eye. At first she found nothing really discreditable, though she thought it perfectly legitimate to inspect one's ears and fingernails at all hours of the day. This exercise satisfied her for some time because she found a good bit to correct. How much can be gathered from the fact that those of us known to clean our fingernails more than once a week were considered effete eccentrics by the other boys.

Possibly Miss Blanchard would have remained content with pointing out the wickedness of having dirty fingernails if she hadn't one night wandered into one of the boys' dressing rooms ten minutes

before lights were to be out. This particular room was the largest one on the second floor and was used by five boys. As it happened, all five of them, while undressing, had become involved in a pillow fight (an ordinary form of entertainment at the school, particularly among the sons of the less sophisticated sects of Protestantism) and the fact that none of the five had any clothes on was something everybody but Miss Blanchard felt should be overlooked.

Miss Blanchard, however, was scandalized. "Boys! boys!" she called out as they stopped their fighting and looked at her. "Have you no decency? Can you stand there uncovered without shame?"

Since it was Miss Blanchard who was intruding, none of the boys took her seriously for a moment, and as one of them observed to me later, it did seem a little absurd for a woman of her age to be upset by this display. But at last they realized she was quite serious, for as soon as they had all put on their pajamas she insisted that they go down on their knees with her and ask forgiveness of God.

The next afternoon we younger boys were called together in the study hall by Miss Blanchard and given an illuminating address on the sins of the flesh, with pronounced emphasis on nakedness. Since we had lived most of our lives in China, we were not inclined to be concerned over nakedness, and I think many of us became conscious that day for the first time of its existence. Miss Blanchard pleaded with us not to forsake the heritage of our fathers—something we couldn't understand at all—and wound up her speech with a peroration in which she declaimed, "Never, never, not even in your most private moments, should you be altogether naked. Keep some part always clothed that you may know the evil of the body."

This idea was completely novel. We looked at each other with wonder and a new sense of the wickedness of life. I, together with many of the others present, was bothered by one particular point,

and was about to ask Miss Blanchard a question when I saw Peter Martin, the clown of the eighth grade, raise his hand.

"Yes, Peter?" Miss Blanchard asked.

"Well, Miss Blanchard," Peter said with false innocence, "there's just one thing I don't quite understand. Miss Blanchard, how do you take a bath?"

Since this was the one question all of us had had in our minds, the room was filled with a gabble of "yes, yes" and "that's what I want to know, too," and in another instant we were roaring with ribald laughter. Miss Blanchard flushed and said, "Peter, I want you to stay after the others have gone." Then she dismissed us, and we left the hall trying to suppress our giggles. As we expected, Peter got a thrashing for his joke, but he probably felt the pain of it a small price to pay for the popularity he had gained.

Not long after this, Miss Blanchard instituted a schedule of early morning exercise for the purpose of taming the flesh of the boys in the school. Ten minutes before breakfast we lined up and answered roll. Miss Blanchard passed down the line, looking at our hands and ears. Then, when she was certain that everyone was clean for the day, she led us in front of the main building to the athletic field, where we had to run a half mile before breakfast.

The folly of this was apparent to everybody the first day. Running on an empty stomach was a decidedly poor notion, and though we did not doubt it was an excellent method of taming the flesh, we wondered if we really deserved this treatment. The running was made thoroughly ridiculous by a school rule that anyone who came into the dining hall a minute after the blessing had been said lost the sugar on his porridge. And anyone who came in three minutes late lost his porridge altogether. The curious result of this was that those who found it difficult to complete the half mile in time to

make the dining hall before the blessing—in short, the weakest of us—got the least food. As if this were not bad enough, we had to sit through breakfast feeling thoroughly sticky and uncomfortable, something that I, and probably my neighbors as well, found extremely distasteful.

Miss Blanchard was so clearly pleased by her system of subduing the natural Adam that we knew no direct appeal would do any good, so we tried to think of some other way to protest. Finally we hit upon the plan of having one of us faint as the blessing was being said. I thought this an excellent idea until my schoolmates elected me to do the fainting. As they pointed out, I was in the infirmary a good part of the time; everyone knew I wasn't very strong; and though they didn't want me to take them wrong—and they paid me the compliment of keeping out of range of my arms when they said this—I really was about the feeblest-looking boy in the school. There was no denying this, and I said that I would have to think about the matter.

Each morning the next week I ran as hard as I could to be sure of getting to the dining hall before the blessing was said and worked up an even worse sweat than I would have otherwise. And each morning as the blessing was being pronounced by Miss Blanchard, the other boys would look at me as I tried to screw up my nerve to pull a faint. My chief difficulty was that, though I couldn't deny I was the feeblest-looking one of the lot, I had never in my life fainted and I wasn't at all sure that I could give a convincing performance. And each morning after breakfast the boys would gather around me and ask me what the trouble had been. I would tell them that I was just waiting for the right moment and hoped secretly that I could manage it the next day. But the week went by and we still found ourselves puffing around the field every morning.

It was not until Wednesday of the third week that anything happened. The blessing was being said by Miss Blanchard when everyone started at the sound of a marvelous groan. This came from the table next to the one I was standing at, and as I turned I saw one of my roommates, Edward Lowry, who was quite an athlete and did not look at all feeble, swaying back and forth. He groaned again and then began to fall backwards. As he fell he reached out and grabbed the tablecloth. Almost as if in slow motion he went over, his back stiff, bringing with him the tablecloth and a cascade of tumblers, cream pitchers, and silver in a grand clatter. One of the girls at his table let out a screech as Ed hit the floor, giving the back of his head a hard bump, which filled me with admiration, for I had planned to faint crumpling forward.

That Ed should generously do this for me gave me the warmest sort of friendly feeling, and as I knelt down to loosen his collar I whispered, "That was swell, perfectly wonderful!" Ed, as everyone will have guessed by this time, continued to play his part perfectly, not even flinching when a slightly hysterical high-school girl threw a glass of water in his face; for, of course, he had really fainted.

After Ed had been carried out of the room by one of the high-school boys, we sat down to breakfast, though not until after another blessing had been said. Throughout the meal everyone made a point of saying how dangerous it was to have to run on an empty stomach and that we were all probably developing bad hearts and the next thing anyone knew somebody would die of a heart attack. The echo of all these words must have reached Miss Blanchard's ears, for after that we had to make the round of the athletic field just once, and only at a slow trot. Although even this seemed quite a little to demand, we were happy that Miss Blanchard had been partially thwarted and we felt that we

could get along under her rule by being careful. This was especially true since we learned that some of the teachers had been heard to comment on the narrowness of Miss Blanchard's attitude. Mme Poliakov, who taught French, had been overheard observing to Mrs. Ames, the English teacher, that she felt Miss Blanchard was "a little—how you call it?—puritanian." And Mrs. Ames had said that Mme Poliakov was probably right.

From time to time we still quoted to one another Miss Blanchard's remarks on nakedness, and we often let our imaginations run riot on the theme of the Blanchard ablutions. This was particularly true of the time when we ourselves were taking baths. Each boy at the school took two baths a week. We were divided into shifts and assigned to a Monday-and-Thursday, Tuesday-and-Friday, or Wednesday-and-Saturday night bath schedule. The bathrooms were at the ends of the hall on each floor of the main building. The school coolies carried the hot water up to the galvanized iron tubs in five-gallon Standard Oil cans. Though we had cubicles for bathing most of us found it more satisfactory to pull the tubs out into the central part of the room. In winter this meant that we would be closer to the sheet-iron wood-burning stove that heated the bathroom, and at all seasons it made for an easier exchange of conversation and soap.

Bath night was a social occasion, and during the months the stove was in use, the bathers were expected to provide refreshments for themselves and the other boys. We never had anything more elaborate than toast, which we prepared by putting bread on the top of the stove and letting it scorch. The product could be appetizing only to boys on bath night, but it had grown into a school tradition. And there was something very friendly about standing around the stove with the three or four others who had taken baths, drying in

the heat of the stove, and turning over the pieces of smoking bread. The room was usually so full of steam that we could hardly see from one end to the other, and its atmosphere was both intimate and strange. As the tradition grew, it became imperative for those whose bath night it was, not merely to provide the bread, but to steal it from the dining hall. This was a simple thing to do, and on bath day a boy always filled his pockets at both lunch and supper in order to have enough bread.

One cold night in the late spring my roommates and I had finished our baths and were standing around the stove, the steam swirling about at the other end of the room, as we toasted our bread and handed pieces of it to the boys coming in to wash before going to bed.

"What would you do if Miss Blanchard came in now?" Ed Lowry asked me as he turned over a piece of blackening bread.

"What would I do?" I said rhetorically, as I wound my bath towel around my head, getting ready to give an imitation of a Sikh policeman in Shanghai. "Why, I would say to her, 'My dear Miss Blanchard, you see me now as God made me.' " Everyone laughed approvingly, for it was unthinkable that Miss Blanchard or any other woman would come into the bathroom.

Just as I was going into my Sikh act, the door was thrown open and a woman burst in. We froze around the stove, the bread sending up streamers of smoke. For an instant I thought the intruder really was Miss Blanchard, but when she stepped forward and closed the door, I saw through the smoke and steam that it was Mme Poliakov.

She took another step into the room. "Boys, I thought I have smell a burning," she said. Her eyes lit on the bread. "What is that dirt?" she demanded.

I was the first to find his tongue. "That's our toast," I said. "We always make toast on bath night. It's a tradition."

"A tradition?" she asked sharply.

"Yes," Ed Lowry said. "We always make it. It's part of being at school."

Mme Poliakov peered at us all. We felt quite self-conscious and I wondered what Miss Blanchard would do when she heard of all this nakedness.

But for the moment Mme Poliakov was more interested in the bread. "Where does it come from?" she asked.

We hesitated. "It comes from the table," Ed said at last.

"You mean you steal?" Mme Poliakov asked in surprise.

"Oh no—at least, not exactly," I said. "You see, it's really been served to us and we just save it for later."

Mme Poliakov looked at me sternly for a moment. "Very clever. Very, very clever," she said finally. "Well, in Russia we have not this tradition—a very filthy one it seems to me—but, of course, you are Americans."

We waited, tense, for the punishment that was going to fall on us for our shame. Yet Mme Poliakov simply stood there, the steam swirling around her head. Then she said, "It would be easier to get from the servants."

Only after she had made this sensible remark did she seem to notice that my roommates and I were standing there without a stitch on. Her eyes lit up and I thought that now we were really in for it. She stepped closer to us. Then she smiled. "Really, it's picturesque," she said, "to see young boys stand like this. Very charming. In Russia the lower classes bathe thus in the Moskva." She continued to smile and stepped back as if to look at us in a better light. Then she laughed and said, "You need a little more flesh, Jean."

"Yes, Madame," I said. "I'm sorry you caught us like this."

Mme Poliakov laughed again. "But why be sorry? It is really picturesque, most picturesque." She opened the door, then paused and said, "The poor Miss Blanchard!" We heard her giggle as the door shut, and looked at each other without speaking. It was a few minutes before I could pull myself together and go on with my Sikh imitation.

BLASPHEMER

W HEN THE RUMOR that Max Silber had been blaspheming started to go around, I was not especially interested in it. Max and I were rivals in a sense. We were the only students at the school whose homes were in Shanghai. Whenever any question came up about Shanghai, or city life in general, one or the other of us was consulted. Sometimes we would both be consulted at the same time, and when this happened, Max and I almost never agreed. After a number of clashes I found that I could usually swing everyone over to my side by prefacing what I had to say with "My father is an ordained Presbyterian minister, and he told me. . . ." Whenever I fell back on this formula, Max usually gave up the argument. Had it ever occurred to him to say in reply, "My father is a Jewish businessman, and he told me . . ." he would probably have found that he was only contributing to the defeat of his cause, for, with the exception of a few Standard Oil children and one or two students whose fathers were with other business concerns, practically every-one at Kuling came from an American missionary family and looked at the minority with an almost Victorian contempt for their being "in trade."

Not until one of my friends went into detail about Max's blas-pheming did I become interested; indeed, what my friend had to

say was of such importance that it was impossible to remain indifferent. Max was reported to have declared that most of the missionaries in China were ignorant imposters exploiting the Chinese for their own ends, and that Christianity wasn't a real religion at all.

Though Max, like myself, could certainly not have been called a very popular member of the school community, he had always succeeded in getting along fairly well. His career had, in fact, met only one serious check. Whereas all the other boys automatically passed the preliminary Scout tests as soon as they turned twelve, and became members of the school troop, Max had repeatedly failed to pass. For many months I couldn't understand why Max never made the grade. A vast throng of American males can testify that no very high quality of intellect is necessary to master the odds and ends that prove one is qualified to be a Scout, and it was not until the fourth or fifth time Max took the test and the Scoutmaster told him, with apparently genuine regret, that he hadn't come up to par again, that I began to connect his failure with his father's religion. Even then I was not sure my suspicion was correct, for though I certainly did not expect him to become a member of the Pine Tree Patrol, I saw no reason why either of the other two patrols in our troop should not welcome him.

The circumstance that he was still trying to pass his Scout tests made me surprised that he should do anything so foolish as to blaspheme, and for a short time I refused to believe that he had. It seemed to me impossible that Max, who during our trips down the Yangtze to Shanghai at Christmas always made a point of letting me shoot his slug gun at the flocks of teal rising from the river, should start uttering anything as ridiculous as the charges he was said to have made against missionaries. Each winter we agreed to a truce on the boat and would admit frankly to each other that there

were parts of Shanghai neither of us knew much about, and that the parts we did know about didn't overlap in many areas. But by the time three or four classmates told me that Max had really said these dreadful things, I lost whatever fairness and critical judgment I had had and began to share the growing hysteria that was taking hold of the other missionary children.

The older boys, after a series of conferences, decided that something must be done to put an end to Max's remarks. To take the matter to the authorities would not be satisfactory for Max had attacked us in our persons, as it were, and it was up to us to bring him to account. We would punish him ourselves, but just what form the punishment would take we younger boys were not told ahead of time. I do not know how the Standard Oil and other business sons felt about Max's remarks against missionaries, but most of them were questioned with such keenness on their religious beliefs that they became ill at ease and were only too happy to fall in with any sort of plan.

From day to day the reports of Max's blasphemy grew. Just who heard him say the bad things that were daily attributed to him it was impossible to learn, for everything came to us at third or fourth hand. But soon our excitement and our desire for revenge had grown so large that it never occurred to us that, since no one was speaking to Max anymore, we must be making up the reports ourselves.

One Friday morning the word went around that Max was to be taken care of during the soccer game that afternoon. There was a soccer game every afternoon except Saturday and Sunday. Since everyone could not play at once, teams were selected by the headmaster, and the names of the players for the afternoon game were posted on the school bulletin board each morning. That particular Friday morning Max's name was on the list. Also posted on the board was

a notice that the teacher who usually supervised the game would be in a faculty meeting and that his place would be taken by a member of the senior class. So we decided that the playing field, which was on a terrace below the main building, would be a fine place to look after Max without running much risk of discovery. When a heavy mist blew into the valley shortly after one o'clock in the afternoon, we felt that things were really working out just right for us. There was no danger that the game would be called off, for we played soccer during the heaviest fogs, even when it was impossible to see from one end of the field to the other.

I was not on the list for that afternoon, so instead of going directly to the playing field when my last class was finished, I went to my room. I found my two roommates there, each busily preparing a stocking club. This peculiar weapon was made by stuffing a rolled-up pair of stockings in the foot of another stocking, the leg of which was then knotted. Next, the foot of the stocking was soaked in water to make it heavier and to add to the sting of the blow. The approved technique was to whirl the stocking club three or four times around your head and then lay a blow on your opponent's face, head, or neck. Although the weapon was by no means deadly, a well-placed blow could black an eye or bloody a nose.

Even though I had been as enthusiastic as anyone else about bringing Max to judgment, it had never occurred to me that we were going to beat him up. As I watched my roommates readying their stocking clubs and listened to them going into detail as to just how they were going to hit Max and where, I experienced a faint sense of distress. When one of them asked me why I wasn't making a club, I said I thought there would be enough clubs without my making one, and I sat down and waited for them to finish. I still believed that Max should be punished, and I was only moderately

concerned at the thought of his being beaten up, but I, too, had felt more than once during my career at Kuling that I was standing alone against the rest of the boys, and I knew the sickening feeling that used to come over me at such moments.

When word came up to those of us who were not on the teams that the soccer game had started and that Max was playing in the south goal, we left the building and made our way to the north end of the field. The fog had grown so dense that it was impossible to see more than thirty or forty feet, and by kicking the ball around and shouting, the boys at the north end were able to put on a good imitation of action at the north goal. After all the boys had gathered, we fanned out in a line across the field. When one of the older boys raised his arm as a signal, we began to trot forward, the wings running a little faster than the center, and we swept down through the fog to the south goal, yelling as we ran. The line closed in on the goal posts and we halted in a half circle, the two ends of the arc just outside the posts.

Max, who was wearing a heavy white turtleneck sweater, came running out of the goal, thinking at first that the opposing forwards had come through his fullbacks and were attacking the goal. But when he saw all of us, players and nonplayers, standing there, he stopped dead.

"Say, what's the idea?" he asked, his voice shooting up and cracking. We were standing only a few feet from him and through the mist we could see his head thrown back, his dark eyes wide, and a look of almost animal terror in his face.

One of the older boys stepped forward. "We've come to fix you, you dirty blasphemer," he said, and swung his stocking club at Max, landing a blow on the side of his head.

The other boys carrying clubs stepped forward, some of them

saying, "That's right." One boy yelled, "You aren't going to forget this, you little Jew!"

Another blow landed on Max's face, and his arms went up to his head. He stepped back and shouted, "Stop! stop! what have I done?"

We had not yet turned into a mob and one of the seniors said, "Didn't you say that missionaries were no good and that all Christians were fools?"

"That's right, that's what he said!" someone called out. Max shouted, "No! I never said that! I never said that at all!"

Three or four boys stepped in again, their clubs swinging, and Max took their blows without yielding any ground, though it was clear that they had hurt him. His eyes were filling with tears, but he kept his head and said, "Who heard me say that? Whoever heard me say that, let him say who he is and I'll fight him."

The club swingers hesitated, and Max followed up his advantage. "I may have said that my religion is as good as anyone else's. I may have said that, but I never said any more than that. If anyone says I did, I want to know who he is."

We stood there in the gray mist looking at Max, who still faced us, his lips trembling. The sport seemed to go out of the thing, but with most of the boys it seemed to be replaced by anger rather than by remorse. The boy who had taken the first swing at Max stepped in again and hit him with his club. "Well, see that you don't say anything more," he said.

Three or four others hit him with their clubs, but Max just stood there taking the blows, his eyes overflowing with hate.

On the outskirts of the group someone said, "Well, I guess that's taught him."

I myself felt sick. For an instant I thought I might go up to Max and speak to him, but I hadn't the courage. We began to drift back

into the fog, away from the goal and toward the dormitory, leaving Max standing there, breathing hard, his eyes full of hate, but also full of scorn.

Two boys walking through the mist ahead of me kept assuring each other that Max Silber was really fixed for good now, but their voices sounded troubled and hollow.

Of course, after what had happened, it never occurred to anyone to put in a good word for Max with the Scoutmaster. As far as I can remember, Max never tried again to get through the preliminary Scout tests.

MADAME POLIAKOV

S HORTLY AFTER Mme Poliakov came to the Kuling American School as our new French teacher, we realized she was going to be a welcome relief from the self-conscious American monotony of our everyday routine. With the exception of one of the men on the faculty, an Englishman, everyone in authority at the school was an American. This made Mme Poliakov's descent upon us more vivid and, we felt, more "Russian" than it might otherwise have appeared.

My own awareness of the difference Mme Poliakov might make in the life of the school came a few days after her arrival. I was walking down the second-floor hall of the main building when I heard an outburst of sharp yelps and screams from one end of the hall, and a few seconds later a Great Dane came around the corner at a dead run—right after him, her yellow hair flying out behind her head, her legs bare, a young woman whipping the animal with a leash. As she beat the dog, she shrieked a series of what I was sure were wonderful Russian oaths. I had halted at the main entrance to the building, where a flight of steps came up into the center of the second floor, and when the dog reached me he made the turn, paws skidding and scratching on the floor. The woman made the turn with him, and chased him, still swinging the leash, to the top of

the steps. Here she stopped and continued to curse the dog, which ran down the steps and off into the school grounds.

I was fascinated not only by the cursing—the fluency of which I could appreciate, even if I couldn't grasp its nice detail—but also by the fact that a European woman would lay into a dog in such an athletic fashion. Having been raised in the belief that to beat a dog in anger was only a little less dangerous to one's hope of salvation than neglecting to say one's evening prayers, I was both frightened and attracted by this exhibition.

The woman was still cursing when I heard an icy voice from the end of the hall calling, "Galina! Galina!" I turned and saw Mme Poliakov come sailing down the hall, the full sleeves of her dress trailing out behind her, making her look like a dignified and somewhat worldly angel as she bore down on us. Her gray hair was put up in small curls, and what I took to be diamond pendants sparkled in her ears. "Galina!" she said again, and the woman who had been chasing the dog faced about.

Mme Poliakov addressed her in rapid Russian, and the woman who had been called Galina answered. For a few moments they spoke to each other. Then Mme Poliakov noticed me and switched into English. "You see, you fright the children," she said. "What is your name?"

"John Espey," I said.

"Ah, Jean Espé, a French name," Mme Poliakov said. "It must be a French name. Beautiful! I apologize for my daughter."

"I don't know if it's French or not," I said. "My people are Presbyterians. And I really couldn't understand anything your daughter was saying, but it sounded wonderful."

Mme Poliakov looked startled. Then she smiled at me and laughed. "Oh, it was indeed, wonderful," she said. "Very wonder-

ful!" And since her daughter seemed to have difficulty in following English, Mme Poliakov said something to her in Russian. They both laughed. Galina reached out and patted me on the shoulder. I had some notion that I ought to kiss her hand, but instead I satisfied myself with a jerky bow. The two women, still laughing, turned and went down the hall toward Mme Poliakov's apartment. Later in the day I saw Galina collect her dog and leave the school, going in the direction of Russian Valley.

Soon Mme Poliakov was the principal topic of conversation at the school. Everyone became familiar with her girlhood on an enormous Russian estate; her education, which she had received in the company of the Czar's daughters; her flirtation in Paris with a young man of good family but no means; and her later marriage to M. Poliakov. Before long we all knew the details of how she and her husband had been living in an eastern Russian town, where he had held a government post, when the revolution broke out, and how they had made their way to Vladivostok, where they had lived until the Soviet regime took over Siberia. Mme Poliakov revealed most of these details either during meals or in her French classes. It was often possible to throw her off the lesson by introducing some bit of Russian lore dug out of the Britannica and asking her about it.

She began to make herself felt in the life of the school. For one thing, she was certain that for a boy to walk with his hands in his pockets was about the most wicked thing he could do, and to whistle in a building was almost as bad. Since the headmaster himself always walked around with his hands in his pockets and whistled from time to time when he was indoors, Mme Poliakov had difficulty in convincing us that she was right about these things, but she continued her crusade nevertheless. Just a little below these two offenses was sliding down banisters.

Whatever difficulties we had adjusting ourselves to Mme Poliakov's notions of propriety, they could have been as nothing compared with her trials in fitting herself into the life of an American
school in China. We heard that she had two children, Galina and
another daughter, that they had been successfully married off since
the family had fled Vladivostok, and that her husband, who suffered
from the incapacities of his rank and station, was living in a cottage
over in Russian Valley, unable to do much but let his wife support
him.

One thing Mme Poliakov soon told us in class was that when
one had been educated with the Czar's daughters, one never made
a mistake; when one learned a thing, it was learned forever. We
found this difficult to believe, particularly since, though she spoke
adequate, if at times stilted, English, Mme Poliakov made frequent
errors. The knowledge of her fallibility did us no good, however,
and as Madame tried to conduct us through the *New Complete
French Grammar* by MM. Fraser, Squair, and Coleman, we found we
were not getting very far. This was the result of Madame's insisting
whenever anyone made a mistake in recitation, composition, or
dictée that the entire class go back to the lesson in which that particular point was covered and start the book over again from there. The
rule brought great tension into our classes, for after working our
way heroically up to Lesson XIV ("Partitives"), someone would
make an error involving pronoun objects, which had been taken up
in Lesson IV, so back we would go to Lesson IV and start from there.
When we had struggled forward again to Lesson XII ("Feminine of
Adjectives, Irregularities, Position, Interrogative Adjective"), someone would probably make a mistake involving a section of Lesson
X ("Plural Forms, Contractions, Use of *il y a* [ilja]"), and back we
would go to Lesson X. This unending review had its value, but

when the headmaster discovered near the end of the year that we were stuck at Lesson XV ("Past Participles, Compound Tenses, the Past Indefinite, Word Order, Use of Past Indefinite, Idiomatic Present Indicative"), he had to step in and assure Madame that the members of the Kuling American School could not hope to approach the daughters of the Czar in perfection. Since Madame had suspected this all along, she settled down at last, doing no more than cluck despairingly at our errors and conduct weekly rapid reviews in which she bombarded us with tricky questions.

Before this the headmaster had had to interfere in another of Madame's activities. One of the things about her that enchanted us when she first came to the school was the variety of her wardrobe. Almost every day she wore a different dress, and when she appeared for the first Saturday-night games of the term in black velvet décolletage, with what I thought were diamonds in her ears and in her hair (though some said they were only rhinestones), and her back held with a peculiar rigidity acquired from her life with the Czar's daughters, she made all the other teachers look like oafs. We knew then that school would never be quite the same again, and many of us were rather thankful. Madame's wardrobe however, puzzled us. If she really had to work for a living—and none of us was so fatuous as to think that she was there for the love of teaching—we were unable to understand how she could afford so many clothes. Once or twice a week her Chinese tailor came to school carrying a bundle tied in a large square of cloth, and Madame continued to astonish us by the frequent change of her costumes.

The term was half through when I saw what amounted to a repetition of the scene with Galina and the Great Dane, but this time it was Mme Poliakov and her tailor. I was just coming in from a walk on open bounds Wednesday afternoon when the tailor dashed

by me, almost knocking me down, and behind him came Mme Poliakov, her voice not raised as high as her daughter's had been when she chased the Great Dane but with a more cutting quality to it. As the tailor reached the front steps and started to run down them, Madame let fly with a book. She halted, her eyes fiery, and shouted "*Canaille!*" an expression for which MM. Fraser, Squair, and Coleman had not prepared me. "*Canaille!*" repeated Mme Poliakov. Then she turned to me and went on, "That is the wrong with the world. Never let the *canaille* get you!"

"No, madame," I said. "I'll try not to."

"Good!" she said emphatically.

It was not long before we learned by the school grapevine that the headmaster had had to intervene and adjust matters with the tailor, because Mme Poliakov owed him a sum greater than her salary for the entire year. Just what the final settlement was we never heard, but thereafter Madame appeared in a limited wardrobe, wearing each dress more frequently than she had before. We discovered to our wonder that heretofore—even, we were given to understand, in Vladivostock—Madame had never worn a dress more than four times, and then only if it was a special favorite. The young American woman fresh from college who taught my Sunday-school class tried to point this up as a lesson in the foolish use of one's money, but she failed miserably as far as I was concerned, and I had an even greater respect than I had had before for Mme Poliakov.

Once Madame had pretty well broken us boys of putting our hands in our pockets and whistling in the building, she decided it was time to stop the slamming of the screen doors. All the dormitory rooms had screen doors equipped with stiff springs, and most of the pupils let them bang shut. This, Mme Poliakov insisted, reminded her of the bombarding of Vladivostok—which she had

been through and which had left her nerves very susceptible to loud noises—and was unmannerly anyway. Since I had been trained at home not to slam any sort of door, I thought little about the matter until one evening, as I was leaving my room for supper, I was stopped by Madame's voice coming down the hall.

"Who is that?" she called out. "Wait a minute, I must see. It's too dark." And Madame surged toward me.

I couldn't imagine what I had done. When Madame recognized me she said, "Ah, the little Espé! It's the little Espé. But how *gentil*! You do not bang the door."

"Oh, no," I said, relieved. "I'm always scolded at home if I do."

"Then you have been raised a gentleman," Mme Poliakov said, with obvious approval.

Though it had never occurred to me whether I had or hadn't been raised a gentleman, I said, "Thank you, madame," and from then on, Mme Poliakov took a personal interest in me that continued for many years. It was, I learned, her hope that she could do something for me, a benighted American child. Though she was happy to work in an American school, which paid better than anything else she could hope for, she never doubted that America was a peculiar land, a bit savage and uncultivated, and I am afraid the years she spent with us in Kuling did little to alter her view. I do not know how many times Mme Poliakov told me about her life in Russia, the country house with its conservatory housing a collection of exotic plants and birds. She talked almost as much about Paris—the Paris that was to her, now that Russia was no longer her country, more real than any other place in the world.

Mme Poliakov would, in fact, have been delighted to be mistaken for a Frenchwoman, as I discovered when we were required to write an original French composition about an animal, preferably a cat,

for Madame was very fond of cats. Thinking to pay an oblique compliment to her native land and its history, I wrote an extravagant tale about a kitten named Napoléon, who set out one winter's day to explore the grounds of the house next door. The grounds proved to be enormous, and little Napoléon found himself wandering through wastes of snow, almost frozen to death by the cold. In a most pathetic passage I described the sad spectacle of Napoléon's tiny paws, crusted with ice—*ses petits pieds complètement glacés*, as I thought it should go in French. Finally little Napoléon returned to his home, bedraggled and discouraged and half starved. The moral—we were reading some of La Fontaine at the time—read to the effect that little Napoléon would have done much better to stay at home.

I was thoroughly puzzled when this artless theme threw Madame into a fit of despair over me. She refused, in fact, to speak about it for some time, other than to say that I had attacked the true Gallic spirit, that I had derided one of the great men of Europe, that I was a hypocrite and probably had criminal tendencies, and that there was no hope of my salvation. Only after Madame, consulting with the headmaster and a number of the teachers, discovered that they thought my exercise harmless in the extreme, not to say a trifle dull, did she consent to forgive me.

From that time on, I did my best to be discreet, since I had a great affection for this woman with the energy and courage to turn to, after she had reached middle age, and earn her living. I made only one other error. Madame was on occasion depressed, as I can well understand now, and there were days, I think, when the school must have been almost too much for her to bear. At these times Madame was electric in her teaching, ready to snap up the slightest mistake and hound the poor student she had caught. During class

one such day I wrote in the margin of my French reader, "She is crazy again today," for the benefit of the boy sitting beside me. He refused to read it, keeping his eyes on his book, and I jogged his elbow. He blushed and looked straight ahead. When I glanced up, I saw Mme Poliakov standing beside me.

"What have you written?" she asked, and snatched the book from me. She read my scrawl, then handed me her own book and said, "I will keep this." I sat through the rest of the period as if I were waiting for a clap of thunder.

What Madame intended to do I had no idea, but after lunch I gathered up my courage and went to her apartment. When I heard her call out "*Entrez!*" in answer to my knock, I went in and found her lying on a couch.

"I am desolated!" she said when she saw who it was.

"I am very sorry, madame, for what I did," I apologized in French. "Really, it was I who was crazy, not you."

Mme Poliakov sat up abruptly. "That's very pretty," she said. "You have style. That is what I know from the beginning. If you work hard, do special work, you can polish your French. Shall I give you special lessons?"

This sudden turn was too much for me, and whatever style I had vanished for the moment. But it seemed such a delightful solution that I consented, and I never regretted my decision. Madame handed me my reader, I gave her hers, and we were fast friends from then on. That was the day she gave me the nickname of Jean le Terrible. As the result of her offer, I enjoyed a special "tutorial" each Wednesday afternoon, and even if I learned less French than she had hoped I would, she opened up for me a new world, albeit one already dead.

The tutorials had their moments of embarrassment. Shortly after we had started them, Madame, in an effort to make her apartment

more like the wonderful conservatory of her girlhood home, decided to keep two pairs of uncaged canaries in her sitting room. One had to rush through the door and close it quickly so that the birds should not escape, yet without making any noise, in order to save Madame's nerves. Unfortunately, this was only the beginning of the complications the birds brought with them. The first time I had a tutorial after she had acquired them, I was shocked by the state of the furniture.

Madame spread a newspaper over the couch for me to sit on. When she noticed the expression on my face, she said, "Don't speak of it, Jean. It would be vulgar to notice."

"Yes, Madame," I said, but I found the four birds, fluttering about the room, clinging to the curtains, and calling to each other, not the best accompaniment for mastering the uses of the conditional anterior.

Madame herself was eventually forced to recognize the impossibility of her arrangement and she gave the birds to her husband to keep in his cottage in Russian Valley. She was disconsolate for some days, until a scrawny black kitten wandered into the backyard of the main building. Madame snatched it up and thereafter cherished it, feeding it milk and taking it scraps of food from the table. She confined it to her apartment, making the servants, who thought the whole business a nuisance, bring in a box of fresh dirt for it every day.

Two weeks after Madame had adopted the kitten, I went to her apartment for my regular Wednesday-afternoon tutorial. The kitten was lying on the couch, and I sat down beside it. Shortly after the lesson began, I reached out to pet the kitten and was astonished when I found myself touching a cold, unresponsive body. I looked at Madame and was on the point of speaking when she held up her hand to stop me.

"*Non, non, Jean le Terrible!*" she said. "Don't say a word, not a word. The little cat is asleep. Some might think the little cat is dead, but *non*. I know, and you must believe, the little cat has been asleep now for one day. Isn't it a charming little cat?"

"Oh, yes, Madame," I said, trying to come up to what was expected of me. "Some cats, especially kittens, sleep all the time, for days and days." Stimulated by this invention, I went on and fabricated a tale of how a cat of mine in Shanghai had once slept for a week.

"Just pet it a little," Madame said, her eyes full of tears.

Trying to conceal my distaste, I put out my hand again and scratched the top of the dead kitten's head.

"Ah, that is charming," Mme Poliakov said. "Very charming. You have the right feeling, *un coeur aimable*. And now the irregular verbs in *-ir*. The principal parts of '*acquérir*,' please."

"Yes, Madame," I said, and from time to time during the following hour I reached out and touched the little black kitten curled up beside me.

I WAIT UPON THE GISSIMO

THE SUMMER OF 1926, which I spent in Kuling with my family, was perhaps not as refreshing to the resort's polyglot vacationers as we could have wished. We followed our usual round of pleasures, but as rumors from the south about a young Cantonese general with ambitions puffed into verified reports of a nationwide military campaign, an uneasy alertness spread through the American-European community. The general and his southern army were said to be trying to oust the northern Peking government in an effort to unify the country, and were also said to be somewhat antiforeign. Finally the colony felt compelled to organize. As a member of the Pine Tree Patrol, I was naturally called out on messenger duty.

On my first day of duty I reported at two in the afternoon to a "key post," which happened to be the cottage of a young American missionary. He was writing at a table on his veranda. He settled me in a chair nearby and gave me a copy of next week's Sunday-school lesson to read. At four o'clock his wife joined us for tea. I drank four cups of unsugared green tea, ate two sesame-seed cookies, and finished with a wedge of chocolate cake. At five I went off duty.

Though I thought my services competent, I did not consider them brilliant, no messages having come in or gone out. Even so, I was immediately promoted to the "central post," and on my next

turn of duty—we worked every third day—I reported to the Athletic Club, Kuling's most noticeable outpost of empire. Here my superior was a middle-aged Englishman, who looked very military in khaki shirt and shorts. I gave him the three-finger salute and he ordered the bartender to get me a bottle of ginger beer and some copies of *Punch.* I was then posted in a wicker gentleman's chair on the club veranda. My superior settled himself into another wicker gentleman's chair just inside the door. Staring coldly at the leader in an old London *Times,* he slowly put down a series of Scotch-and-sodas.

This pattern was repeated every third day into early September. I got a fresh bottle of ginger beer each hour; I learned as much about the English from *Punch* as I did from my superior; and I almost came to enjoy the bubbling of ginger beer as it fizzled through my nose and made my eyes water.

One day I thought there was really going to be a message. The Englishman clapped his hands several times, and when no servant came, he called out to me and said, "Would you mind going to the bar and getting me some more Gold Flakes?"

"My father doesn't smoke," I told him as I got up.

When I came back with the cigarettes, he said, "Thank you," and I said, "You're welcome, sir."

Though there were no messages, we knew all the time that the Cantonese general, whose name was now definitely known to be Chiang Kai-shek, was pushing northward. Nobody was made any more comfortable by the further knowledge that with Chiang as a personal adviser was one Michael Borodin, known to be a Soviet agent who was directly responsible to the Kremlin.

By the middle of September only the small year-round colony was left in Kuling. My English friend disappeared. My parents returned to Shanghai as soon as the Kuling American School took up

again, and I went back to the dormitory and to my algebra and Latin. But the blood of the Pine Tree Patrol was up, and when we heard that the local residents were continuing their alert, we volunteered for further duty. An elaborate plan of lookouts was drawn up, and two or three days a week I would leave school shortly after breakfast, with either the bishop's son or the probable bishop's son, to climb one of the rocky spurs that commanded a stretch of the Yangtze Valley. From these points, it was assumed, we could easily spot an approaching army and relay word by semaphore to the next lookout, who would pass the news on in the same way until it reached the school. Just what was to be done then, I have no idea; no doubt there was another elaborate plan for that.

So we boys would sit on our mountain and talk about life, our books, which the headmaster insisted that we take along, stacked neatly under a rock. Now and again we sent friendly inquiries to the next post. "WHAT HAV LNCH," we might ask, and the answer would come back, hesitantly, from the red and white flags: "CHS SANWCH BANAS."

The autumn days were mellow and fine; it was pleasant to sit on a mountaintop with a bishop's son and look through a pair of field glasses into the valley. I am not certain from what direction Chiang Kai-shek and his army approached Kuling; I do know that we never saw the dust cloud of a marching army rise from the valley floor and spread beneath us. This, we had been told, would be a sure sign.

One morning in late October the Chinese servant who lit the stove in our dormitory dressing room woke us with the news that Kuling had been captured and that the new flags were flying in the Gap. We were to keep in close bounds. As the day went on, the school servants brought in reports of how the few northern soldiers

in the Gap had left well in advance of the southern army's van. The servants also reported that Chiang Kai-shek himself and his entire personal suite planned to come up the mountain for a few days' rest.

The general's bodyguard reached Kuling within a week and roamed over the valley, bright orange-red tassels swinging from their holsters. It was said that the general had set up headquarters at the Fairy Glen Hotel, half a mile up the valley from the school, and that he had sent a delegation to assure the headmaster that we would all be quite safe. Close bounds were lifted. A few days later, on a path near the school, I met a man who, by his clothes, I knew must be a Russian. Removing my cap, I bowed with Calvinistic grace and said, "Mr. Borodin." Borodin stared at me, grinned, and walked on, leaving me wondering if I should have addressed him as "Comrade."

Clearly, the invaders were not dangerous, and we wondered if it would be possible for us to see the general. Some of us of the Pine Tree Patrol walked past the entrance of the Fairy Glen the next afternoon and came to no harm. We did not attempt to pass the sentries. We had heard that the general and his intimates took occasional strolls accompanied by a double file of his bodyguard, pistols drawn, but this must have been during school hours, for we saw no such sight that day.

The Pine Tree Patrol was not discouraged. We determined to get past the sentries and see Chiang himself. We knew the Fairy Glen Hotel very well; there was a half-hidden gate in the rear of the gardens that might do for a way to sneak in. We set out again the following day, taking along a Eurasian schoolmate who went by the unresented nickname of Chinky and claimed a hereditary knowledge of the Cantonese dialect.

We found the gate unguarded and unlocked. We slipped into

the grounds and loitered casually through the shrubbery toward the main buildings of the hotel. When some of the bodyguard spotted us, Chinky tore off a series of syllables that we were happy to accept as Cantonese. The guards were less certain; apparently Chinky's ancestors came only from the general vicinity of Canton. But each of us knew something of one or two dialects and we flattered and soothed the soldiers in everything from purest Mandarin to coolie Shanghai. We admired their beautiful uniforms and silk tassels; we said that we thought highly of the Kuomintang and revered the memory of Sun Yat-sen. We added that Russia, too, was an interesting country.

Soon all the idle soldiers had gathered around us, friendly and curious. For a quarter of an hour we worked obliquely to our point: Did they think it possible that we might get a glimpse of their splendid general? A great clucking followed, and it was agreed at last that this was unlikely. The Pine Tree Patrol countered: Perhaps the gentlemen would be kind enough to point out any famous persons who happened along? This request pleased the soldiers, and for ten minutes we reviewed a number of Chinese notables whose names meant nothing to us. Then Borodin appeared, crossing from one building to another, and one of the soldiers began to tell us who he was. I cut his explanation short as the Russian came near and said in a loud voice: "Of course I know Comrade Borodin." Borodin looked at us and I bowed. He jerked his head forward, grinned, and went on. The soldiers were impressed. A few minutes later a rather anxious-looking woman walked past. "Mme Sun Yat-sen," hissed the soldiers. She turned toward us and we bowed low. She smiled wanly and went on.

The bodyguard and the Pine Tree Patrol were probably a noisy combination, and more soldiers were constantly joining us. We had

been there perhaps an hour when the glass doors of a sun porch opposite us opened and a slight man in uniform stepped out, an aide beside him. The soldiers sucked in their breath and the grounds were still. The general spoke to his aide, who walked forward. The guard nearest us whispered that it might be a good idea for the foreign gentlemen to leave quickly.

The Pine Tree Patrol drew themselves up and bowed to the general. His hand flashed out toward us, and then he stepped back into the building. The aide bowed and we bowed. We moved toward the main gates, the aide slightly to our rear. At the gates the sentries snapped to salute. The aide returned the salute, and the Pine Tree Patrol gave the three-finger salute first to the aide and then to the sentries.

Had the general's sign been a friendly salute or a gesture of dismissal? "I think he smiled at us," said the most optimistic member of the Pine Tree Patrol as we paced alertly down the valley back to school.

WE MAY NOT CLIMB THE
HEAVENLY STEEPS

ROGER LEHR was a junior in the high school and I was a freshman when he came back to the Kuling American School in
the fall of 1926 after having spent a year in America. Since I still
roomed in the main building of the school instead of in one of the
cottages for older boys, and since my voice had not yet begun to
change, we moved in different spheres, speaking to each other perhaps once in two weeks. About the only thing that impressed me
was that he had brought back a pair of white leather soccer boots.
These boots attracted a good bit of attention because no one at the
school had ever owned a white pair, and only two or three boys
could boast even an ordinary pair from America. During the year
Roger had been away, his figure had filled out, and though he was
of no more than average height, his weight and his head of wavy
reddish hair gave him a bluff air of handsomeness that attracted the
girls without at the same time annoying the boys.

The first afternoon Roger failed to show up for soccer practice
none of us thought much about his cottagemates' report that he
had hurt his foot a few days before and wouldn't be able to play.
Most of us were pretty well bruised and hacked up during soccer
season, and it was not until two days later that Roger's friends discovered he hadn't even bothered to see the school nurse. That night

while Roger was undressing, he showed the wound on his foot to his cottagemates, and one of them noticed that a bright red streak had run up the length of Roger's leg from his foot to his groin. When Roger admitted that his whole leg ached a little and felt hot, two of the boys insisted that he go to the infirmary immediately. The nurse put him to bed and began to apply hot compresses to his foot.

Our first hint that Roger was seriously ill came the next day with a request from the nurse that everyone be quiet when going through the hall of the second floor, to which the infirmary, formerly on the fourth floor, had been moved that term. The room in which I was living was right next to the infirmary, so my roommates and I got into the habit of talking in whispers.

At first the news that Roger's life might be in danger stimulated most of the students and teachers, many of whom found reasons to tiptoe through the hall and put their fingers to their lips whenever they saw anyone else. Because there was a locked door between our sleeping porch and the infirmary, my roommates and I were constantly being asked what we heard, but we had to admit that we couldn't hear anything except the voices of the nurse and the school doctor, who had begun to make daily visits. And even when we heard their voices we couldn't make out anything more than an occasional word.

When the headmaster announced at morning chapel on the fourth day Roger had been in the infirmary that Roger had developed a serious case of blood poisoning, the news brought a change in the attitude of the school, tingeing it with a hint of hysteria, which was not calmed by the many special prayers that from this time on were said for Roger at regular times during the day. That afternoon my roommates and I saw three of Roger's cottagemates

being shown into the infirmary by the nurse. When they came out, one of them was crying openly. For the first time we suggested plainly to one another that Roger might be dying.

Just before we went up to study hall after supper that evening, we saw the nurse entering the infirmary with one of the high-school girls. At first we thought very little about this, supposing that she must be going in for something for herself, but when she failed to show up at her desk, I began to wonder if her absence had any connection with Roger. I wrote a note to one of my roommates and passed it to him when I went up to the front of the room to consult the *Webster's Unabridged.* He in turn wrote a note to the girl he was interested in and some minutes later he passed my desk on the way back to the *Britannica* and dropped me a note, which read, "Grace says that Roger has always been in love with Irene, but she really likes Curtis Sykes better."

Back in our room after study hall was over, we hurried to the locked door and listened. All we could hear at first was Roger's voice, and though we couldn't make out what he was saying, he seemed to be speaking in great excitement. We thought he might be delirious, until we heard Irene's voice answering him, but we could still make out no words and suddenly she broke into sobs. Then we heard a door open on the other side of the sickroom, followed by the sound of the nurse speaking. A few minutes later the door from the hall to the infirmary was opened and we saw Irene run past the open door of our dressing room, a handkerchief in her hand.

We slept uneasily that night, for throughout it a band of light shone from under the locked door. Every now and then we could hear the nurse and the doctor talking to each other. Sometimes Roger's voice broke in, and each time we heard him we sat up, trying to make out what he was saying.

The next morning we learned from my roommate's friend that Roger had asked to see Irene and that the doctor and nurse had decided he was so sick they ought to do whatever they could to make him feel better. Irene wouldn't say any more about it, but she spent a great deal of her time weeping and had been excused from her classes for the day, which was a Friday. The whole school was distracted, and two or three girls broke into tears during classes. At the close of study hall that night the headmaster came into the room and told us that Roger had died a few minutes earlier.

At lunch on Saturday the headmaster announced that after four o'clock Roger's body could be seen in the infirmary and that the funeral would be held Sunday afternoon. Although I had looked at more than one corpse during my life, the thought of looking at Roger revolted me and I determined not to go.

"He's dead," I said to my roommates. "Why can't they just leave him alone now?"

"But people will want to look at him," one of them said, and the other agreed.

"Well, I don't," I said.

"What's the matter?" the second boy asked. "Are you afraid?"

"No," I said. "I'm just not going."

By three-thirty the second-floor hall had begun to fill. Here and there a boy or girl was sobbing. At four o'clock the infirmary door was opened by the nurse and the students began to go in. I stayed in our dressing room, but another boy in my class, his eyes red, came in and said, "What's the matter with you? Somebody said you weren't going."

"No, I'm not," I said.

"What do you think people will say?" he asked. "You'll have everyone thinking you didn't like Roger."

"Oh, but I did," I said quickly. "I just don't want to see him dead."

My roommates came back and joined the other boy in urging me. "It wasn't bad at all," one of them said.

"I wasn't thinking about that," I insisted. "I just don't want to see him."

Another classmate came into the room. "I thought you liked Roger," he said. I gave up and walked out, the first of my classmates to have come into the room following me.

The line moved forward slowly. It went through the door to the infirmary, then into the room where Roger lay, past his bed, on into the dispensing room, where it turned back through a second door to the infirmary's short hallway, and then out the door it had first entered.

As we came into the sickroom, I saw that Roger had been laid out on a white hospital bed. Bouquets of wildflowers had been placed at either side of his head. A sheet came up to his waist. He had been dressed in his best blue serge suit. His head seemed to be thrown back and his skin was yellow. He had lost weight during his illness, and there was nothing about him that looked alive. The line shuffled past the bed, the girls weeping, some of them in gasping sobs, the boys snuffling.

I grew more and more angry as we went on, and by the time we were out in the hall again I wondered how much longer I could control myself. Two of the older boys stepped up to me. I thought I might hit out at them until I saw they were the tenor and bass of the boys' quartet, in which I sang soprano.

"The music teacher wants us," the tenor said. "We're going to sing at the funeral."

Without saying anything, I followed them to the music teacher's

room, where the boy who sang alto was waiting for us. The music teacher had opened four hymnbooks to a hymn she had chosen. She ran through the accompaniment on her piano while we read the words to ourselves.

"You'll sing just the first and last stanzas," she said. "Do any of you know it?"

None of us did. The opening stanza read:

> We may not climb the heavenly steeps
> To bring the Lord Christ down:
> In vain we search the lowest deeps,
> For Him no depths can drown.

We sang it through and it went fairly well. Then we went on to the last stanza:

> O Lord and Master of us all!
> Whate'er our name or sign,
> We own Thy sway, we hear Thy call,
> We test our lives by Thine.

"That's pretty good," the teacher said. "Of course at the cemetery you won't have any accompaniment, so John will have to give the pitch."

"Could I have a pitch pipe?" I asked.

"Oh, no," she said. "That wouldn't look right at a funeral. Let's try it again, without the piano this time."

We sang through the two stanzas.

When we had finished, I said, "I don't understand the hymn at all. What does it mean?"

The music teacher hesitated and then said, "Well, of course, it's not very clear, but it's a customary funeral hymn."

I felt relieved at first, and then more puzzled than before. If it

didn't mean anything, it was like looking at Roger's dead body. I turned to the other members of the quartet and asked, "Do you understand what the words mean?"

They shook their heads and looked embarrassed. The teacher broke in, saying, "Well, never mind, John. Just be sure you have the pitch."

"Yes, ma'am," I answered.

"And all of you be sure you have the words memorized. Take the hymnbooks with you. We'll practice once again tomorrow afternoon before we leave for the cemetery."

We filed out and I went back to my room.

The next morning, as we started out for church, we saw the coffin being brought to the school. It was made in European style and looked flimsy and cheap compared with the heavy, highly polished Chinese coffins most of us were accustomed to seeing. Its appearance troubled me and I said to my roommates, with whom I was walking, "I wonder why they didn't get a Chinese coffin. They really look better than that."

"Are you crazy?" one of them asked. "Who ever heard of being buried in a Chinese coffin? Something's the matter with you, anyway."

I said nothing and we walked the rest of the way in silence. The autumn day was bright and clear; here and there the leaves had begun to turn. A few very white clouds moved slowly across the sky. I felt depressed and deserted.

In the afternoon the other members of the quartet and I went through the two stanzas of the hymn unaccompanied a number of times in the music teacher's room. Then each of us recited the words to the music teacher to show that we had learned them, and after that we sang both stanzas twice.

As we left the music teacher's room, the boy who sang bass took hold of my arm and said, "Listen, you be sure to get the pitch right. If you don't, I'll kill you."

"I'll get it right," I said.

The whole school was gathered in front of the building when we came outside. In a few minutes six boys came from the infirmary carrying the coffin. The headmaster leading the way, we set out for the cemetery on a path that wound along the side of the mountain. Most of the girls were crying, many of the teachers were dabbing at their eyes, and under the warm autumn sunlight the procession seemed to be something with which I could have no possible connection. Just as the four of us in the quartet started to follow, I was seized by panic and ran back into one of the music-practice rooms on the first floor. I struck the opening note of the hymn on the piano. Humming it to myself, I ran out after the others.

"You get it right, see?" the bass said.

"I will," I said, and hummed the note again.

We walked slowly along the path. A slight breeze had sprung up and we could see that more clouds were moving in above the plains. I wondered if they might mean rain. The path rose gradually, so I could see the coffin being carried ahead of us. Whenever the sunlight struck it, the black unpolished wood looked dull and the brass studs glinting in the light seemed to me tawdry. Then the coffin disappeared around a bend, and when we ourselves reached this turning I saw that the boys carrying the coffin had set it down at a point where another path crossed the one we were on. We walked up to where the students had spread out in a circle around the coffin in time to hear the headmaster say, "Now we are going to give Roger his last look at the beautiful hills he knew so well."

I looked on, in disbelief at first, as one of the boys bent over the

coffin and began to unscrew the lid. I wanted to scream, to shout that this was an outrage, yet when I looked around me I saw that everyone was craning forward. I felt disgusted and tried to draw back, but the boy who sang bass was behind me and he grabbed my arms.

"Stand still!" he hissed.

At first I thought I would close my eyes, but I found that I couldn't. A sound sharper than a sigh came up from the group as the coffin lid was lifted off. Roger lay there looking shriveled and uncomfortable in his blue serge suit. His head lolled to one side and his voice box stuck up through the stretched skin of his throat. Irene, standing near the head of the coffin, broke into sobs. As if this were a signal, almost everyone wept a little or coughed or cleared his throat.

The headmaster said a prayer, but I found it impossible to bow my head and I stared straight ahead of me. The boy behind me had released my arms, and I moved them a little as the lid of the coffin was being screwed down. Once again we moved forward through the unreality of the autumn sunlight, which the clouds had not yet cut off.

In the cemetery the burial service was read at the graveside. The headmaster prayed and the minister of the church prayed. Then the four of us stepped to the head of the open grave. I cleared my throat and gave the pitch. As soon as I started to sing I knew I was sharp, but it seemed unimportant and I went on, my voice shrill and harsh as I sang the meaningless words out over the grave. I could hear the others following me, straining to reach their notes.

As we started the second stanza, the coffin was lowered into the grave, and I listened as if to someone else's voice as I sang out the final line. After a moment's pause we sang "Amen."

Just as we stopped, two coolies stepped up to the grave with shovels and began to throw in the earth. I looked down as the first clods hit the coffin, and thinking of Roger, with his head twisted a little to one side, I wanted to cry out. But Irene was standing near me sobbing dryly, and even the other members of the quartet had begun to sniffle. The wind that was bringing the clouds up from the valley floor had increased, and a few yellow leaves swirled over the nearby graves. But still the sunlight was bright and warm. As, dry-eyed and silent, I walked back to the school among all these persons who seemed to breathe out even in their sobs a vague satisfaction over what they had done, who seemed almost content with their sorrow, it was the sunlight and the deep blue of the autumn sky seen against the advancing clouds that bothered me and made me feel that I walked utterly, inescapably alone.

I DISCOVER THE WORLD

WHEN I RETURNED to Shanghai in December 1926 to spend the Christmas holidays with my family, I had no suspicion that I should not be going back to Kuling. Although there was a great deal of buzzing around about the civil war going on between the forces of Chiang Kai-shek, who had marched up from Canton the preceding summer, and the forces of the Peking government and the northern warlords, to anyone born and raised in China it was absurd to take all this too seriously. Certainly one would not expect it to interfere seriously with anything a foreigner might wish to do. Moreover, I had myself set eyes on Chiang Kai-shek and his immediate suite when they were in Kuling during the autumn, and had found him, for the few moments I had been allowed to gaze at him, a very mild-mannered and reasonable-looking man.

When we heard, therefore, that conditions were such that the Kuling School authorities felt it unlikely the school could be re-opened at the end of the vacation, I thought they were showing a very poor spirit about the whole affair. Having at last succeeded in establishing myself at the school, I was reluctant to abandon it and return to the Shanghai American School, where, if I would not be exactly a stranger, I should at least have to fit myself into my class once again. This would not be as bad as having to start all over

again in a new school, for I had entered the Shanghai American School in the first grade, and though my classmates had a habit of disappearing every now and then for a year or two in America or Hawaii or the Philippines, most of them returned in time and, after a few weeks of shyness on the part of everyone, were reaccepted into the class's normal life.

By the time the Shanghai school reopened, the Kuling school had announced definitely that it would be closed for some months, possibly more than a year. My sister returned to the Shanghai American School, where she was a boarder and a senior in high school, and a few days later the mission station at South Gate, where our house was, changed hands and found itself one morning in the possession of the Cantonese forces, or at least of an army planning to sell out to the Cantonese. So as soon as it became easy to move around again, I was sent off to the Shanghai American School, which had its grounds on Avenue Pétain in the French Concession, as a boarding pupil, my parents feeling it would be troublesome for me to make the trip daily. They were themselves beginning to wonder if it wouldn't be wise to abandon the mission for a time and seek shelter in the International Settlement.

Once at the school, where I started the second half of my freshman year in high school, I found a number of my Kuling schoolmates had made the change at the same time. There were, moreover, six students in the class who had been in it when I had left for Kuling three years before. These former acquaintances showed themselves willing to recognize me, and I felt that life would not be unendurable.

One thing, however, struck me at first as being very strange, and this was that at some time during the years I had been away, the Shanghai American School Troop of the Boy Scouts of America had become defunct. No one was quite sure how this had happened,

though one of the boys in my class, whom I had known for years, did remark, when he was telling me about it, "You know, there was always something about Shanghai that just didn't seem to fit very well with Scouting. Now the troop is gone, I can't say I miss it especially."

Though I was loath to agree with him, and for some weeks refused to let myself think that this, the first real ambition of my life, was so barren in its realization that it meant nothing to me to lose it, I finally had to admit I myself was very little affected by the lack of Scouting. Whatever dismay this caused me was soon forgotten, for I was confronted at this time with a number of urgent personal problems. My voice began to change with such rapidity that I found it impossible to recite in class without leaping an octave or two in the course of a single sentence. No longer could I carol along in my clear soprano; in fact, my voice seemed determined to move all the way down the scale and settle into a deep bass. At the same time I began to grow at a frightening rate, and the family agreed, after a number of serious conferences, that it was time for me to go into long trousers. I watched the encroachment on my chin and upper lip of a dark brown, which seemed to be more apparent to my eyes than to anyone else's, particularly my father's, when I suggested to him it was about time for me to own a razor.

Engrossing as all this was, I was still able to keep up with events in the city, among other things my parents' move into the International Settlement, where they and the rest of the South Gate station were accommodated in an office building on Peking Road. The building had just been completed and was still unfurnished, so the missionaries living there had to improvise their own arrangements, which gave the building the air of a camp. So much, in fact, had happened during the first weeks of the new term that no one had bothered

greatly in the middle of January about celebrating my fourteenth birthday. It was not until the members of the station were well settled in the building on Peking Road that one of my Courtesy Aunts realized she had passed me up that year. By coincidence, she was the same Courtesy Aunt who had accompanied me on my trip to the Kuling American School three years before, and it was left to her to put a symbolic end to my Kuling days and to show me how far I had advanced during the meantime.

I was as unconscious of this function as she was, for when she announced that she was going to take me to tea for a special birthday treat, I felt quite let down. I could imagine few things worse than having tea alone with this Courtesy Aunt. I was surprised even a Courtesy Aunt would feel under the circumstances that she was doing the right thing by me, when a handsome wristwatch or a substantial check would be so much better suited to the occasion. It was not until my Courtesy Aunt said, "Yes, I think I'll take you to the Palace Hotel for your birthday tea," that I felt the afternoon would not be an utterly disagreeable one.

I had never been inside the Palace Hotel, but this only emphasized for me the gravity of the event. Even in 1927 a number of new hotels were beginning to make the Palace Hotel and the Astor House look shabby, yet for anyone born in Shanghai none of these newer places could hope to displace the two older hotels in the life of the city. As far back as I could remember, the red and white front of the Palace Hotel on the Bund, which I had passed hundreds of times but had never entered, had stood in my mind for worldly elegance. I had already heard some of my friends speak of having tea at the Astor House or dining at the Palace Hotel, but though I felt myself to be as true a child of Shanghai as any of them, I had to confess that there was still this one thing lacking in my experience.

When my Courtesy Aunt and I entered the Palace Hotel tearoom from Nanking Road, I was troubled because my long trousers had not yet come from the tailor, but by the time we had been seated at a table beside a large plate-glass window overlooking Nanking Road, a table from which I could also look out through the windows facing the Bund and see the Whangpoo River, in which a number of foreign gunboats lay at anchor, I began to feel myself peculiarly at home. When a three-piece string ensemble, established on a platform in one corner of the narrow room, struck up the "Merry Widow Waltz," I savored the delight of being a part of this sophisticated scene.

My Courtesy Aunt, who was all too willing to take things out of my hands and do the ordering, was more than a little surprised by the way I began to take charge.

"I thought your mother said you'd never had tea at either the Palace or the Astor House, John," she said.

"I haven't," I answered, surprised myself that this occasion had about it an air that was both unusual and ordinary.

"Well, you're really doing very well," she said, and I appreciated the compliment, for she was one of my more worldly Courtesy Aunts and was quite fond of sampling Shanghai's simpler amusements.

"Thank you," I said.

As we drank our tea and ate our toast, I wondered why it was that to be sitting there in a window of the Palace Hotel, looking out over Nanking Road and the Bund, was such a familiar and such a comfortable sort of thing to be doing. My Courtesy Aunt and I carried on a rather ordinary conversation, which she attempted to base on my school experiences. As she asked me about my classes and what it had been like to change back from Kuling to Shanghai, I realized that these subjects tired me a little. When she said it was

too bad the Scout Troop had died out, I found that the whole business bored me. Even more surprising, I noticed when I spoke that my voice was remarkably well controlled, quite deep, and with a definite edge of adultness to it.

"Oh, Scouting was fun," I heard myself saying in a cool tone, "but of course you can't go on doing that sort of thing all your life."

"No, I don't suppose you can," my Courtesy Aunt said.

As we talked, I looked out of the window and watched the crowd of Chinese and foreigners walking along Nanking Road. Now and again someone would look up at us, and it seemed to me the most natural thing in the world to stare back with a look of weary tolerance and lofty condescension. The third or fourth time this happened, I began to sense that, although I had felt until now that the two centers of my life had been the mission station at South Gate and whatever school I was attending, there had been another focus of sensibility in my experience all the time. It was that middle area between the mission and the school, an area that I had passed through time and again since I was old enough to remember any-thing.

This realization pleased me very much, and even as I went on conversing with my Courtesy Aunt, I found myself silently examin-ing the features of this newly discovered world. It was a world, I recognized, that had its own laws and customs, just as did the world of the mission and the world of school. Some of these laws and customs I already knew, though I had never before thought much about them. The prospect of exploring this newfound yet familiar sphere was an enticing one.

I was polishing off an elaborate French pastry when I felt my Courtesy Aunt's hand brush my knee under the table, and I was

charmed with the instant recognition that she was passing me the money to pay for this treat. I took the bills and smiled faintly at her. She smiled back in what I took to be approval.

After I had tipped the waiter generously from the change he brought back, my Courtesy Aunt and I got up to go. We walked to the door, which was opened for us by a uniformed Chinese attendant, and as we stepped through the doorway the ensemble began to play "The Blue Danube." Then as I walked out into the street, I knew that though I might simply have come in from Nanking Road to have a birthday tea at the Palace Hotel with one of my Courtesy Aunts from the Presbyterian mission at South Gate, now that I was leaving the hotel I was stepping out not merely into Nanking Road but also The World.

THE SHANGHAILANDERS

PROBABLY Shanghai's reputation—and surely no one needs to be told what that is, or was, at least—grew out of the nature of the Shanghailanders. Your average Shanghailanders during the last fifty or sixty years were originally inoffensive Americans or Europeans who went out to Shanghai to make a living. In those innocent days, we Americans included the subjects of His Britannic Majesty in the general term "Europeans." Usually they succeeded amply in this, and one would have supposed that they would be content to live comfortably and not fret about Shanghai. But Shanghai usually proved too much for the Shanghailanders, and when they didn't find what they expected, they set about finding it. Something in the Shanghai air accentuated these persons' tastes and accelerated their speed in whatever direction they were taking. Shanghai offered them almost unlimited opportunities, and the idea of Shanghai became a grotesque spectacle of the Shanghailanders' own ambitions and desires, until the city grew into a gaudy concept of wickedness and individual license. Anyone wanting to search into the self-delusive elements of the Western world could have worked no richer ground than Shanghai's muddy flat on the banks of the Whangpoo.

Before I go any further, I must explain the exact meaning of "Shanghailander." I do not believe the word is listed in any diction-

ary, and I have no idea when it first came into use. Obviously, "Shanghaier" hardly conveyed the desired meaning when early expatriate residents were casting about for a word to describe themselves, and perhaps "Shanghailander" was as good as any one could hope for. At least it avoided the heavy humor of "Liverpudlian" and the coyness of "Angeleno." But the important thing is that everyone except those you would have expected called themselves Shanghailanders. After spending six months in the city you became a veteran Shanghailander. You could say without embarrassment, "I'm a Shanghailander," and no one would laugh at you. Yet those of us actually born in Shanghai never thought of calling ourselves Shanghailanders. If you asked us what we were, we would usually hesitate and then say, "Well, I was born in Shanghai," and let it go at that. If we were pressed and someone said, "Oh, you're a Shanghailander, are you?" we would, no matter how correctly reared, say with a sharp edge of scorn, "No, I said I was *born* in Shanghai." Often this was enough to break up a conversation and make a new enemy, but for anyone born in Shanghai it was better to make an enemy than to be taken for a Shanghailander. The greatest difficulty for persons born in Shanghai was to know *what* we really were. At times we were not certain we were anything at all except that we were definitely *not* Shanghailanders, and that if you could give us the choice of being anything in the world, a Shanghailander was absolutely the last thing we would choose.

Curiously, this distinction was not at all clear to the Shanghailanders themselves, and in their own Shanghailandish way they continued to think that they were identifying themselves with those of us who were born in the city. This made the situation more entertaining than it would have been had they realized they were

actually putting up a barrier against themselves. By the time I was old enough to understand what being a Shanghailander meant, few things gave me greater pleasure than to encounter one of a few years' standing who would say, "Of course, I don't know how you feel about it, because, after all, you're a *real* Shanghailander."

"Oh no," I would say, "*you're* the real one. You know, I was *born* in Shanghai."

"That's what I mean," the Shanghailander would say. "You really *are* one."

"You simply can't be a Shanghailander if you were *born* here," I would say, smiling coldly.

"What *is* a Shanghailander, then?"

And the one correct answer to that was: "Really, that's something only a Shanghailander should say."

So few of the Europeans and Americans living in the city had been born there that persons like my sister and me belonged to a small minority and could do little to counteract the reputation the Shanghailanders gave our city. Not that many of us would have done much about it, anyway, for it was not the nature of someone born in Shanghai to do much about anything. We usually just stood by and watched and made no comment unless we were with someone else born in Shanghai. It was the Shanghailanders who persisted in doing things. They organized the Country Club, which was British, the Columbia Country Club, which was American, and the *Cercle Sportif Français,* which was obvious. They formed a chapter of Rotary International and they talked about "the real China." They were proud that Shanghai boasted one of the many "longest bars in the world," that the city included the tallest building in Asia, that Frenchtown was governed by the most wealthy and corrupt colonial administration in the world, and even that the Sikh police-

men in the International Settlement were rivaled only by the Annamese policemen in the French Concession when it came to dealing out brutality to the Chinese. It was the Shanghailanders who shivered with joy at the evil of the city, who thrilled at being in one of the centers of the opium traffic and the white-slave trade, at living in the meeting place of the world's many navies, with its waterfront violence and crime.

I do not mean to suggest that all these things existed only in the minds of the Shanghailanders or that Shanghai was nothing more than a quaint little community set on the banks of the Whangpoo. But the great difference between the Shanghailanders and the rest of us was that they were always learning, they were always telling one another new bits of information, they were always discovering, exclaiming, being astonished by one more strange facet of "the mysterious East," whereas we—ah yes! we who were born in Shanghai—we *knew*, we had always known. We looked and we understood. We might be amused; we were never surprised.

Unfortunately, almost no one living in China understood the difference between the Shanghailanders and those of us born in the city. Thus it was that we were frequently hurt to learn that persons living in the interior felt we were quite as much victims as the Shanghailanders of a malady, nearly fatal to one's vision, that went by the name of "Shanghai Mind." To be a victim of Shanghai Mind was to believe that Shanghai was more important than all the rest of China lumped together, and of course it was a further sign of Shanghai Mind to think that all the rest of China *could* be lumped together. An advanced symptom of Shanghai Mind was to believe that you were in business in Shanghai because in some way or other you were "serving the cause of the real China" and not because you were interested in running up your own pile. To be accused of

suffering from Shanghai Mind was the ultimate insult that could be hurled at a person born in Shanghai.

It was because of all this, I think, that my sister, who was born in a private hospital on Rue Palikao in the French Concession, and I, who was born three years later in a residence on North Szechuen Road in the International Settlement, often felt that we wandered as strangers through our own city. Occasionally we would meet someone else who had been born in Shanghai, and when we did, a sense of ease immediately entered into our relations, no matter what the nationality or age of our acquaintance might be.

My sister and I endured more serious difficulties than most persons born in the city. We lived far outside the International Settlement and the French Concession in the self-contained world of the Presbyterian mission compound. We also attended the Shanghai American School from time to time, and here we moved in another separate world with its own values, some of them characteristic of Shanghai, most of them merely typical of any American school abroad. Though I was fourteen before I formulated in my own mind the character of the three worlds I lived in, I was aware even in my earliest youth that to go from South Gate into the Settlement or from the school into Frenchtown was to go from one atmosphere into another, though not necessarily an inferior atmosphere—at least not when thinking as one born in Shanghai rather than as a resident of the South Gate compound or a member of the Shanghai American School—but just a different one. This awareness brought embarrassments with it, for when we went into the international city, we might start out in perfect harmony with our parents or other members of the mission, but as soon as we stepped across the boundary into the Concession, our companions became in some degree Shanghailanders, and we

couldn't always be sure they would understand us, for we became nothing at all except more intensely ourselves.

My sister and I, furthermore, occasionally stumbled over a slight difference between the two of us, because she had lived in Shanghai for three and a half years before she left China to spend a year in the United States, whereas I had made my first Pacific crossing at the age of six months. Naturally, then, I was far more likely than she to slip carelessly from one world into another, and though I would have denied the charge vigorously, she may have felt at times that I was almost a Shanghailander myself in comparison with her, though not, surely, in comparison with a Shanghailander pure and simple, poor thing!

But perhaps I have been a little too hard on the Shanghailanders, considering that once or twice I came close to knowing how they felt. Shanghai was, after all, a lively city. There was plenty to see and plenty to do; and though I was certainly never truly shocked by any of its offerings, I had no objection to enjoying them. In a sense I showed myself something very close to a Shanghailander early in life. When I started to go to the Shanghai American School, my sister and I were unable to return home at noon, the school being too far away for this, so instead of carrying a lunch, we went to the Presbyterian mission press compound on North Szechuen Road, about half a mile south of the school, where we ate in the home of a Courtesy Aunt and Uncle with their children, our Courtesy Cousins. For a time some other Courtesy Cousins lived there, and one of the girls was almost the same age I was. We were members of the same grade. My sister and I and our Courtesy Cousins sometimes rode back to the press compound on a streetcar. My Courtesy Cousin and I liked to stand on the front platform behind and to one side of the motorman, and after the car started up, we put our

arms around each other. While the motorman tramped on his bell and laughed whenever he looked around, we indulged in a series of long, moist kisses. While this was going on, my Courtesy Cousin's American- and up-country-born relatives inside the car kept calling to us to stop and shouted, "Disgusting!" or, "Making ridiculous spectacles of yourselves!" through the door. My sister and the Shanghai-born Courtesy Cousins, meanwhile, looked at us without any special approval or even interest. Had I been a real Shanghailander, I would have kissed my Courtesy Cousin only in secret, but as one born in Shanghai, I enjoyed kissing her to the accompaniment of the motorman's bell, and I found that the noise of the bell and the motion of the car as it swung down North Szechuen Road made the experience, in itself a not too exciting time killer, quite pleasurable.

SAS I

WHEN A PERSON who has attended the Shanghai American School walks into a room full of non-SASites with Chinese connections, a hush comes over it for a few moments. Then whispers start up in the corner, like the first serpentine hissings of the fallen angels in *Paradise Lost,* and spread until someone screws up the courage to ask the newcomer, just to make certain: "Weren't you at SAS?" Every SASite knows the answer to that one. "Yes," he or she says, "and where were you?" It makes no difference what the answer is, whether the original questioner went to Kuling or Chefoo or Peking, and it makes no difference with what animation or pride this information is given; the SASite responds automatically with a flat "Oh," so flat an "Oh" that all pity, all compassion, have long since been wrung from it. The same sort of thing can happen in a group without Chinese connections. You can say to an SASite with all the confidence and aplomb in the world, "I was at Harvard," or "I went to the Sorbonne," or "I took a double first at Oxford," and he or she will still say "Oh" in such a way that even the double first is aware of having been found wanting.

I often feel mildly detached from the high feeling that runs in Chinese circles about SAS. Though I went to first grade there and graduated from high school there and am really more a part of the

school, as I shall show later, than anyone else who ever attended it, I did get three years of my schooling in China at the Kuling American School. Thus I can usually calm the non-SASite by saying, "Of course, I did go to SAS and graduated there, but I had three years at KAS and really thought it was an awfully decent place. Small, naturally, and cut off from the world, but with its own flavor." Yet even as I say this, in the hard core of my being as an SASite I cackle mirthlessly at the poor fool for being taken in.

Sometimes, as a person who went to Kuling, I look at myself as a son of the Shanghai American School and understand why others feel about us as they do. At Kuling I was a quite ordinary member of the student body, so when I catch a glimpse of myself as a member of SAS I am surprised to observe the offensive degree of superiority I exhibit. I notice that my lip curls, my nostrils narrow, my eyelids droop. Unfortunately this is no simple assumption of superiority; this is superiority itself, and a person who went to SAS can do nothing about it.

When I refer to myself as a son of the school, I am indulging in no mere trope. I should, perhaps, call myself *the* son of SAS. My father was lent by the Presbyterian mission to the school in order to start it, and I was born during the school's first academic year in the principal's residence at 171 North Szechuen Road. Not only was I born in the principal's residence; I was born on a school day just as the eight-o'clock bell rang. I feel sure that I have heard more ill-conceived jokes about my academic future than any other person alive. I wish I could say that all the prophecies I heard in my youth proved false, that I kicked over the traces at the age of fifteen and ran off with a circus fat lady. Alas, from the beginning, my destiny showed too plain to be cheated. When my playmates and I used to discuss the comparative merits of becoming a surgeon or a fireman,

I knew that the others might take themselves seriously, but for me it was only a game, that my professional life would be, as it has been, a matter of answering school bells—often, I regret to say, the eight-o'clock one.

Naturally, I can remember nothing of that first year, and, so far as I can gather from those then at the school, I made very little impression on anyone outside my immediate family. One or two students do recall that "the principal had a son that year," but that is as far as it goes. I have always regretted this, for if my father had given the school a holiday, even a half holiday, everyone would surely recall the day with delight.

Perhaps nothing so memorable as a half holiday saluted my birth because Father, on loan for only one year, did not think of himself as permanently connected with the school. The summer before, he had wisely prepared himself for the guidance of thirty to forty American boys and girls, not by brushing up his Hebrew, Greek, and Latin, but by practicing fancy diving at Mokanshan, the most popular summer resort in central China at that time, and by entering the tennis tournament. After returning to Shanghai he joined the American Company of the Shanghai Volunteer Corps as a private and won two prizes for marksmanship. One of these was a silver bowl covered with a chrysanthemum design, the other a loving cup supported by a tripod made of three miniature silver rifles. In later years these trophies gave such a military air to our sitting room at South Gate that innocents given to sneering at the impracticality and uselessness of missionaries often saw things in another light once they had visited us.

In preparing himself thus for the principalship of the Shanghai American School, my father showed excellent judgment, because no one who attends the school ever really needs an education. *That*

he or she enjoys by heredity and by right of attending the largest American school outside the United States and its possessions. All a member of SAS asks of the teachers is that they behave with discretion in public and show sufficient accomplishments not to let down the students.

During that first year at the school my father's task was no easy one, for missionary children made up almost the entire student body. Indeed, both his memories and those of his pupils center not on academic matters but on keeping things in line. One of my friends, who was then a boy of twelve, says that his most vivid recollection of the year, and the one that showed him what a sound man my father was, concerns a whaling he received when he had been caught buying food from a Chinese street vendor. In doing this he had, of course, broken the cardinal law of foreign life in China. You could, especially in Shanghai, break any one of the Ten Commandments and remain in society, but let yourself be caught buying food from a Chinese street vendor and your reputation vanished overnight. As a matter of cold fact you yourself were likely to vanish overnight too. Certainly in this instance my father's conduct was all that anyone could expect, and my friend has enjoyed a most successful career from that day on. Another friend recalls that he met a Japanese boy carrying an oil-paper umbrella one noon as he walked past the principal's residence. Just for sport he impishly jerked the umbrella down, only to hear a stern rapping on a window-pane above him. Looking up, he saw my father motioning him to come inside, where his hurried invention of the Japanese boy's having attacked him first received no credit whatsoever. He too was soundly thrashed, and he too has enjoyed a most successful career from that day on.

After this first year our family connection with the school was

carried on by one of Mother's aunts, who taught there for some years, but the rest of us left for a furlough year in America. When we returned to Shanghai the school had weathered its second year, and I think my parents went back to converting the heathen at South Gate with some relief. At least I never heard either of them express a wish to return to North Szechuen Road.

By the time I was myself ready, at five and a half, for the first grade, the school had grown. The first and second grades met in their own building on Dixwell Road, as did the third and fourth grades. I felt only a few of the uncertainties that a first grader is expected to experience his first day at school. I was prepared: I had been born in Shanghai; I was the son of the school; I had known my teacher, Miss Thomason, and the majority of my classmates for as long as I could remember. In fact I was almost confident that first day as I entered the First and Second Grades Building, carrying my pencil box and scratch pad under my arm and proudly wearing new steel-rimmed glasses on my nose. When Miss Thomason discovered that I was the only member of the class who could read and even write a little, and that I could count to a hundred and beyond, she proposed that I be put into the second grade. Luckily for me, my parents objected. During the rest of the year, while everyone tried to catch up with my advanced learning, I absorbed what the second grade was doing and found myself thoroughly prepared for it the next year. This, and no native cleverness, enabled me to stand fairly high in my class. Had I been started on a par with the others, I should have floundered; but the technique of keeping ahead, once mastered, has served me well ever since.

As early as the second or third week of school I heard the refrain that plagued me in one form or another for years. No matter what sort of misbehavior I indulged in, Miss Thomason would say with

sweet patience: "John, I wouldn't be surprised if Walter Hiltner or Joe McCracken did that, but you! You are the child of the school, you know. Your father was the first principal, and you were born right here on the grounds." Even this brought its reward, for it drove me early to purely mental misbehavior. While everyone else learned to count to a hundred and to spell "cat," "rat," and "dog," I did not throw spitballs or dabble in my inkwell. Instead, I sat at my desk with an intelligent expression on my face and let my mind range. What better use, I wonder now, could I have put it to?

Although I was sent to Kuling for the latter half of the first grade, I came back to SAS for the second and third grades. Perhaps I was not always a complete son of Shanghai. In second grade I fell in love with a girl whose chief attractions were two beautiful long blond braids. Her name was Virginia, and I decided to honor her with an invitation to my birthday party. That year my guests included, to my mother's amusement and my sister's disgust, all the boys in the second grade and Virginia. My sister sat at one end of the tea table, Virginia at the other, with me on her right. But this meant that another boy sat on Virginia's left, and she devoted most of her attention to him, while my sister was left to deal with what she has ever since described as "eight howling, snuffling, filthy little horrors, all grabbing for cake." This is a libel on my classmates, but I can understand her feeling. The day would have ended in complete failure, since I early saw that Virginia thought little of me, if my great-aunt hadn't given me a Pekingese bitch for my birthday. After tea, as we played games, I grew so angry with Virginia and my other classmates that I threw up everything I had eaten on the green rug of the sitting room. Pleased to find myself once more the center of attention, I was even more delighted when my new Pekingese bounded over, cleaned up the mess, and licked my face before Mother

or the amah or the boy could do anything about it. I have never felt, as the rest of the family still insists, that the party was a fiasco.

It was during this first period of attending the school that my sister and I ate tiffin with our Courtesy Cousins at the Presbyterian mission press compound about a mile south of the school on North Szechuen Road. By the time I entered the third grade the Courtesy Cousin I had been accustomed to embracing on the streetcar no longer lived in Shanghai, and after tiffin one of my male Courtesy Cousins, who was just a year older than I, would set out with me for the school. First we poked our heads in at the Japanese School just next to the press compound and made faces at anyone we saw. Then we might go on north of Dixwell Road to a small Chinese and Japanese shopping district, where we could buy candy or tops for a few coppers. After this we would stroll back to the school in good time for afternoon classes. One of the most unusual school fads I remember was the habit of taking Sen-Sen. Showing ourselves true children of Shanghai, we used it not to cover liquorish fumes but to breathe in each other's faces and inhale the flower-garden odor of Sen-Sen on someone else's breath.

At the press compound after school we rummaged in the press's trash barrel and came up with glorious long paper streamers trimmed from the tracts being readied for publication. For some time these streamers were coveted by everyone at school—and our Courtesy Cousins, my sister, and I enjoyed a spurt of popularity—for writing down columns of figures, starting with 1 and continuing until exhaustion on strip after strip. I think the school champion reached 50,000. My own numerals sprawled and I soon tired of the game, knowing that anybody could reach 1,000,000—everybody's secret goal—if he only kept at it long enough. I gave up my strips and spent my time hunting for exotic varieties of paper in the barrel.

These I generously sold to anyone for a few coppers above the rate we had established for plain white strips.

During third grade I picked up the only bits of academic knowledge my first three years at SAS gave me. Our teacher, a Miss Taylor, decided that we should get a sense of languages, so in addition to our biweekly Chinese and French lessons, we learned to number off for roll call in Latin, Greek, Hebrew, Japanese, German, and Russian. And by this time I had given up Virginia and fastened my attention on another blonde, who sat beside me during study periods. Once, while we were reading our geography lesson, she turned her blue eyes on me and said, "Can you imagine, the Arabs drink melted butter!" I have retained the information ever since.

Perhaps the SAS of those days sounds like an unsophisticated institution, but one memory comes back to show that it was no different then from what it was later. Shortly before our family left for its second furlough in America, Shanghai was flustered by a kidnapping scare. Kidnapping is one of the more respectable vocations in Shanghai, but an unusual number of Europeans were carried off in this epidemic. Because of this, Miss Taylor warned us all to be extremely careful while we were on the street, to walk three and four together, and to scream if anyone tried to force us into a car or carriage.

My Courtesy Cousin was warned in his class, too, but neither of us paid any attention, and the next day we went up north of Dixwell Road just as usual. As we came back to school Miss Taylor saw us strolling along North Szechuen Road and called us to her. When we reached her she scolded us for walking just two together and asked us if we didn't know there were kidnappers around. My Courtesy Cousin said blandly, "There's nothing to worry about with us, Miss Taylor. John speaks enough Chinese to get along."

"What difference would that make?" Miss Taylor inquired.

"We wouldn't *be* kidnapped, Miss Taylor," I said.

"How can you tell?" she demanded.

"Why," my Courtesy Cousin said, "maybe Robert Dollar and some of the others need to worry"—and he named two or three of our friends who were sons of businessmen—"but not us."

"And just why not?" Miss Taylor asked sharply, as if she suspected us of teasing her instead of telling her, as we were patiently trying to, the obvious truth.

"But," my Courtesy Cousin said wearily, "can't you see? If anyone tried to kidnap us, all John would have to do would be to tell him in Chinese that we're missionary children and he'd let us go right away."

It took me some years to understand why this perfectly rational observation made Miss Taylor so angry that she punished us for impertinence.

SAS II

IN THE AUTUMN of 1923 my sister and I returned to China from America with our parents in time for the opening of the Shanghai American School in its new buildings at 10 Avenue Pétain in Frenchtown. For three or four years the original North Szechuen Road site had grown less and less desirable as Hongkew and its environs became more and more a Japanese district while European and American development moved toward the west. Though it was still perfectly respectable to live in the older parts of the city, they grew crowded. The buildings on North Szechuen Road, put up in Shanghai's least lovely style of domestic architecture, had not been planned with the school in view, and suffered the further disadvantage of having very little open ground nearby for playing fields.

The school authorities decided to make the new plant a thoroughly American establishment. When my sister and I arrived at 10 Avenue Pétain one day in September to register with our classes and take up friendships interrupted for two years, we entered a red brick Georgian colonial administration building. Two other buildings had been completed, the girls' dormitory and the dining hall, both in Georgian colonial, each crowned—like the main building—with a small white cupola. A smaller building behind the dining hall housed many of the school servants, who didn't rate a cupola, and an old

residence in the northeast corner of the grounds was used by the first and second grades. Shanghai stands on a mud flat without a hill anywhere in sight. I am not sure that the architects took this into consideration when they made their plans, for from the first the three cupolas looked ridiculously inadequate, and many persons not familiar with the tradition in which the buildings were erected smiled at the sight of these three peeled radishes unsuccessfully challenging the great flat distances and the enormous Chinese sky.

The autumn rains made those first days at Avenue Pétain memorable by turning the school grounds into a sea of sticky yellow mud. To get to the administration building we had to cross part of this sea on duckboard. The first pieces of duckboard sank into the mud, and more duckboard was placed over them. Finally narrow planks were laid on top of the duckboard, but still the mud slowly engulfed the trails. Stories began to circulate in Shanghai of children who had fallen into the mud and been extricated only with the greatest difficulty. One or two were even rumored to have disappeared completely. At school we did nothing to counteract these reports, and though I think no one went in farther than his knees, an entire series of legends sprang up around those first days. (It is hardly necessary for me to say, I trust, that my sister and I walked over the duckboard and planks with perfect Presbyterian poise.) Once in the main building, a student was safe for the day, because the three buildings were connected by a colonnade that ran around three sides of what was later to be a turfed quadrangle. This colonnade was supposed to give shelter from the Shanghai weather, but here again something went wrong, for the Shanghai rains, which often sweep in almost parallel to the ground, sometimes made it necessary to walk outside the colonnade to get any protection.

Because of the mud, that opening week in 1923 became a land-

mark, and those of us who had lived through it smiled condescend-ingly on those who came to the school later. But this distinction, important as it was, could not compare with saying that one had gone to the original school. From this time on, we who had known the North Szechuen Road buildings grew fewer and fewer, until the others began to look on us almost as aborigines. We encouraged this attitude and reminisced at length on what it had been like to be at "the old school."

My second stay at SAS covered only one semester, at the end of which I went to Kuling, but this semester became a famous one, for during it three high-school boys, all boarders, stowed away on a U.S.-bound freighter. One of them knew how to operate a wireless set, so they planned to reveal themselves to the captain and then let this boy earn the trio's passage. None of the three had been born in Shanghai, I believe, and their simplicity probably came more from their up-country rearing than from anything else. The three boys scarcely waited until the freighter was out of the Whangpoo before they approached the captain. This man, having thoughtfully provided himself with a wireless operator, got in touch with the port authorities, and the three boys were soon on their way back up the Whangpoo on a pilot's tender. In the sixth grade, where this incident was thoroughly discussed, we were most interested in what might have happened had they concealed themselves for a full day. Even that seemed useless to us, for the freighter would still have been in the main shipping lanes and would have had little difficulty transferring the stowaways to a Shanghai-bound ship. We wondered, too, if the freighter called anywhere in Japan. We thought it likely that she would coal at Shimonoseki, and that would mean hiding for a number of days, because the Inland Sea would have to be passed, and Yokohama at least a day behind, before it would be at

all safe to appear. Even then it wouldn't have been difficult to get in touch with a Yokohama- or Shanghai-bound ship. That brought us to whether the freighter was to have called at Honolulu, but in the sixth grade when we got to this point we usually gave it up. As one of my friends, with whom I had started first grade at North Szechuen Road, said, "Those country guys are stupid."

Stupid or not, the three culprits enjoyed two or three weeks of notoriety, and even though the sixth grade had passed judgment, we looked at them with considerable respect. Had we been old enough to speak to them, we would have asked the question that troubled us most gravely: Why would anyone want to leave SAS? We couldn't believe that they would enjoy successful careers.

By the time we had exhausted this sensation we grade-school boys were hit by a craze for combing our hair in pompadours and keeping it back with the help of what we called "pomp caps." These caps, made from six triangles of alternating colored felt, could be purchased at a small store on the school grounds. Everyone who could afford to also bought a large black-and-gold jar of Stacomb and, after smearing the pink cream into his hair, settled his pomp cap over it. I discovered that a pompadour made me look even more depressing than usual, but a black-and-purple pomp cap at the store took my eye. The beauty of this lugubrious combination of colors seemed to be apparent only to me, but even so, I worried until I had saved enough money to buy it. When some of my classmates ridiculed me for choosing such a dingy pomp cap, I didn't mind, preferring to have them laugh at me for that rather than ask me why I wore a pomp cap while continuing to comb my hair as I always had.

About this time a chant of names fixed itself in my mind, a chant that still runs through it when I think of the school. Roll was called

in class each morning, and I can still hear it, starting with "Adamson, Black, Crawford, David, Espey, Huizinga . . ." A second and silent chant accompanied this roll, and it went "Mission Architects, Mission Architects, Presbyterian, Seventh-Day Baptist, Presbyterian, Baptist . . ." We knew who we were.

Although our Courtesy Cousins who had formerly lived in the press compound now lived on Route Winling, about a mile west of 10 Avenue Pétain, we no longer ate tiffin with them, because the school had at last worked out a scheme for giving day pupils the semblance of a hot meal. A small room off the main dining hall was reserved for those of us who brought lunches, and here we were served hot soup. At noon we rushed to this room, sat down at one of the two large round tables there, spread out our lunches, and waited for the soup. What lives in my memory and in the memory of everyone else ever closeted in that room is the character of the soup. As one who has eaten institutional food a good part of his life, I know better than to expect the personal attention of a cordon bleu at boarding school. But this soup, made from grease skimmings and bits of half-cooked vegetable, was impossible. It glistened in the bowls, it coated our tongues, it often brought on violent indigestion, and during the afternoon it rumbled distantly through our guts. The charge for this soup was not large, but it must have been pure profit for the Number One Boy. Very early we protested to our parents—not my sister and I alone, but everyone—and we all got the same sort of brush-off: "Don't be so finicky." "It's probably just good, hot, nourishing soup, dear." "I know the matron well, and she'd never dream of serving anything like the filth you describe." Day after day we brought back these reports and quoted them bitterly to each other.

Aside from the soup the three principal camps in that group

agreed on nothing. One was made up of Baptists who came from the Baptist College north of the city, another was made up of Episcopalians from St. John's University near Jessfield Park, and the third comprised the South Gate Presbyterians. A few meek and frightened business children ate with us, but they hadn't a chance. Though my sister and I were the only Presbyterians, I have never doubted that we held our own, and we were often backed up quietly by our Seventh-Day Baptist friends who lived at West Gate and were our nearest neighbors—an alliance that they must have privately thought even more unholy than we did.

No matter what subject came up, so long as it was not the nature of the soup, we fell upon it, debated, contradicted one another flatly, and shouted insults. No one supervised us, but a teacher from the main dining room would finally appear and demand less noise. I look back on those sessions as the most lively hours of intellectual activity I spent at the Shanghai American School. Beside them classroom discussions shriveled into inanity. Grounded in political maneuver and argumentation through a fairly thorough knowledge of the Old Testament and of mission meeting procedure, we spoke with authority and challenged with vigor. Our debates had nothing to do with religion. We simply felt that it must be impossible for Presbyterians, Baptists, and Episcopalians to agree. If we found ourselves so much as approaching an agreement, we backtracked, reversed our fields, clawed off on another tack, and confused the issue as blatantly and unscrupulously as I have my figures.

But we could always make peace. When a debate reached the point of breaking over from the intellectual into the physical arena, someone would bring up the soup, and on the soup we all agreed. Our voices rose, someone from the main dining room slammed the door on us to cut off our snarls, and we considered the horror of

the soup. Few of us any longer tried to eat it, but we threw our banana peelings and other trash into the bowls, half expecting to find them served up to us the next day.

Some months ago I met for the first time in years a schoolmate who had shared these lunches with us. One of the liveliest members of the St. John's group, she had often attacked the Presbyterian view with the skillful sophistry of her sect. She told me that she had been enjoying the published reconstruction of my Chinese childhood, but that there was one thing she was still waiting for. I cautiously asked what it might be, wondering if this was just another Episcopal flank attack. She looked at me with emotion still alive after all the years and said, "Perhaps it's not too late yet to get a little justice. The soup, the soup!"

UNDINE

I N 1923, when my sister entered the freshman class in the Shanghai American School and I started the sixth grade, our morning classes began at the same hour and we went to school together. But I got out of school an hour before she did in the afternoon, so I was on my own for the journey home. It was a devious, five-mile trip. I walked down Avenue Pétain to Route Pottier, which I followed to Avenue Joffre. At the corner of Avenue Joffre and Route de Say Zoong I boarded a No. 2 French Concession streetcar, which went down Avenue Joffre toward the main business district of Shanghai for two miles, jogged to the left, and then turned to the right into Rue du Consulat, which it followed to the French Bund. Here the car turned to the right again and went along the French Bund, ending up at the turnaround at Marché de l'Est. Often four or five cars would be making the turn, the motorman of each clanging his bell almost continuously as his car ground along slowly, paused to discharge its passengers and pick up others, and then started back down the French Bund on another run. At this turnaround I left the No. 2 car, walked through Fish Market Street to the site of the old East Gate of the Chinese city, and got on a streetcar that took me around to the South Gate, where I got off and walked through Mulberry Lane to the mission compound. On days when I was

particularly flush I might take a ricksha instead of a streetcar from East Gate. Infrequently, when I had either spent all my money or felt that I would enjoy the exercise, I might walk all the way from East Gate home. The walk was interesting enough, taking me past a number of shops and a lumberyard where coolies, chanting at their work, cut up logs with long two-man saws, but the road was crowded with beggars, some of them in genuinely wretched condition and others, as our cook frequently assured me, probably far wealthier than my father.

I had expected to be the only American school student to make the complete trip down Avenue Joffre to Marché de l'Est, for the car soon left the residential district. I was surprised when, on two afternoons during the first week of school, I noticed, from the third-class section where I was riding in order to save some of my carfare for sesame-seed candy, that a girl from my grade rode first class all the way to the end of the line. Then, instead of going through Fish Market Street as I did, she took a Chinese streetcar that went directly south into Nantao, running on up the waterfront on the Oue Maloo, the continuation of the French Bund into Chinese territory. I hadn't spoken to her, but I knew that her first name was Undine.

On Monday of the second week of school, when I reached the car stop at Avenue Joffre and Route de Say Zoong, Undine was there. When the car came I climbed on the first-class end and sat down across the aisle from her. By the time we had gone a mile all the other American school passengers had left the car. I crossed the aisle and spoke to Undine for the first time. "Do you mind if I sit with you?" I asked.

"Why, no," she said, "I think it will be nice."

"I didn't know anyone else lived near where I do," I said after I

had sat down beside her. "I saw you ride down to Marché de l'Est twice last week."

"Yes, I saw you, too," Undine said, surprising me. "Do you always ride third class?"

"When I'm alone I often do," I said. "It's cheaper, and as long as it isn't crowded it really doesn't make much difference. You get there in the same time, and it's fun to listen to the Chinese talking, especially when they think you can't understand."

"I don't know that much Chinese—just pidgin English," Undine said. "My mother doesn't like to have me ride third class. Really, she doesn't like to have me ride in streetcars at all, but right now we can't afford a car and chauffeur."

"We have a car," I said, "but my father does the driving and he doesn't have time to go to school and back."

"I see," Undine said.

Undine spoke somewhat odd English. It wasn't that she used words incorrectly but that she gave them a different intonation. She had a tendency to end every clause with an upward lilt, as if she were speaking French, and yet some of her pronunciations were British.

After the car turned at the French Bund I pointed out a British gunboat tied up to a buoy in midstream, and when we reached Marché de l'Est we said good-bye to each other.

As the semester went on, Undine and I got into the habit of meeting at the car stop of Avenue Joffre and riding together to the turnaround. At first we always rode first class, but later, on days when the car wasn't crowded, I was able to persuade Undine to ride third class. The first time she consented to do this she said, "I think my mother wouldn't mind since I have someone with me," which made me feel quite brave and gallant.

After a few weeks Undine and I would walk together from the school to Avenue Joffre and I would carry her books, but during the school hours we rarely spoke to each other, and no one thought of us as being a couple in the sense in which some of the other boys and girls in our class were couples. The few times our classmates tried to tease either of us we gave very little satisfaction. I was proud to be seen with Undine. She was better-looking in her own way than most of the other sixth-grade girls. Her hair was dark brown, bobbed short, and shingled, and she wore bangs. Her eyes were light bluish gray, and her features were both regular and delicate. Though she was slight she was not thin, and something in the way she walked, a lithe correctness of bearing, made the other girls seem gawky. Undine herself set the tone of our relationship. The first day we walked together from the school to the car stop we saw ahead of us another couple from the grade school, walking hand in hand. Undine sniffed and said, "Such silliness! There is time for all that when a person is older." Since I had already felt thankful that both my hands were full carrying her books and my own, I agreed, and the two of us felt very superior.

During our streetcar rides Undine and I learned a good bit about each other. I suppose that she learned more about me than I did about her, for I was always quite happy to babble on about my family and everything we did and everything I knew about America, a subject that especially interested Undine. One day I did learn that for a time Undine had gone to the French School. "But now Mother thinks it is better for me to go to the American School," she said. "It is probably more useful these days, you know." I nodded, though I wasn't sure that I understood. I also learned on this occasion that Undine was eleven and a half, and I told her that I was ten and three quarters. This seemed to

annoy her for a moment, but then she brightened and said, "You are really much taller than I am."

Undine and I had both been born in Shanghai, we discovered, but I was never able to get a consecutive story of her life. I gathered that the family consisted of her mother and her, but I was never certain whether her mother was a widow or a divorcee. Whenever we approached this subject Undine shied off, so I suspected that her father was still alive. Exactly where Undine and her mother lived puzzled me even more. Once, she mentioned that she could see the Whangpoo from her bedroom window, but she was always vague about just where their house was.

One day I offered to ride all the way home with her, but she laughed and said, "No, you mustn't do that. Our families don't know each other." I tried one Saturday afternoon to find Undine's house by myself. I started out by following the canal that went past our mission compound and down to the Whangpoo, where I turned north and walked along the Maloo on the waterfront. I knew that an oil company had a small compound near there, and I went past it and on beyond the Chinese Customs House, looking for places that might house foreigners. Undine had said that she lived in a compound, and I saw two or three gray brick houses built in the completely styleless architecture of most European buildings in Shanghai, each with its own wall and garden. I had no way of finding out which, if any, of these sheltered Undine and her mother—except possibly by asking someone, and I was too shy to do that; I gave up and walked back home. As my last effort to draw Undine out I said to her on the streetcar one day that my people lived in Chinese territory because they were missionaries but that I didn't see why anyone else would. "Oh, we haven't always lived there," Undine said. "Just since we have been without my father. And I don't think we'll stay there always."

Undine's interest in America grew so keen that for a time I thought she wanted to be as completely American as she could, and I tried to help her. Most of the girls at school wore tartan skirts and middy blouses, so for the first few weeks Undine, who usually came in a light silk dress, looked rather strange. Then one morning it seemed to me that she had at last decided to dress like the other girls. But that afternoon when we were riding home I realized that everything about her costume was wrong. Instead of the skirt's having one or two box pleats the whole thing was creased in tiny pleats, and the middy, instead of being made of cotton or linen, was an off-white silk. What was more, the knee-length socks she had put on in place of the silk stockings she had worn before were themselves dark-blue silk instead of ribbed cotton, and her patent leather shoes had straps that encircled her ankles instead of going across her insteps. I took all this in as discreetly as I could, and eventually I worked up the courage to say, "You know, Undine, you're always so interested in American things."

"Yes," she said. "I want to learn everything about America. Mother says it will probably be very useful."

"Well," I said, "in some ways the clothes you're wearing now aren't really any more American than the ones you wore at first."

"Oh, you have noticed them?" Undine asked, smiling at me.

"Yes," I said, feeling uncomfortable and wondering what I could say that wouldn't hurt her feelings.

"I am so happy," Undine said. "How do you like them?"

"Really," I said, "they're quite different from the other girls' things."

"Ah, I knew you would see the difference," Undine said, and laughed. "That is what being born in Shanghai and living here shows you, doesn't it?"

I was somewhat confused by this and said nothing. Undine looked around the car and, seeing that we were the only foreign passengers, she stepped out into the aisle and pirouetted twice. Her pleated skirt whirled out well above her knees, and I caught a glimpse of eyelet embroidery and red ribbons. She sat down again and pulled up her skirt. "I wear ribbons too," she said. "See? The girls at school, now—such clumsy skirts, and never any ribbons!"

Having shared a nursery with my sister until I was ten, I was more interested in the idea of someone I knew showing off like this on a streetcar than I was in the display itself.

Undine laughed again, ignoring the stares of the Chinese passengers, and said, "For me, everything American but clothes. Perhaps in New York, my mother says, it is different; but here, no American clothes."

By this time I had begun to understand that Undine's costume had been put together almost in the spirit of parody, and I couldn't deny that she looked far more interesting than the other girls. From then on I derived considerable entertainment keeping track of what Undine did to each fad that swept the sixth-grade girls. For a time some of them wore butterfly bows pinned in their hair with barrettes. After this fashion had spread to almost all the girls Undine appeared one morning with a bow of cerise silk riding on the top of her head, its wings reaching out at least four inches beyond her ears. She wore it throughout the day with great calm and pretended to be surprised whenever anyone commented on it.

Although I am sure that the autumn of 1923 in Shanghai was as humid and uncomfortable, and the early winter as raw and rainy, as ever, I find it hard to believe this when I remember my rides with Undine. As I think of them I see particularly the French Bund as it would be during the last mile of our trip, the sun striking the

yellow fronts of the godowns along the east side of the street, making them glow and sending some of their color out into the dust-filled air. The traffic would be made up largely of rickshas and bicycles and heavy man-drawn carts. Some of the godowns would be open. Coolies would carry out bales of cotton, or loads of stuff wrapped in straw matting, or boxes of tea, pausing as they came to the checker. Occasionally they lugged bars of silver bullion, chanting as they carried their loads. All this, and especially the heavy carts, slowed down the traffic, and the streetcar crept forward, the motorman tramping furiously on the bell. As the coolies shouted and swore, the musty odor of the godowns, mixed sometimes with spicy fragrances from the bales, filtered into the car. And through it all Undine and I watched the street and talked to each other about anything that came into our heads. We were especially interested in the silver bars, and whenever we saw them we speculated on how much each one was worth and how much it weighed. At the end of the line Undine and I got off, usually waiting for the car to complete the circle of the turnaround, even though that was really a waste of time, and then Undine boarded her Chinese streetcar and I walked through Fish Market Street to East Gate.

By late November the weather had grown chilly and I wore my mackinaw and woolen gloves to and from school. Undine wore gray leggings buttoned up the side, a gray overcoat with a fur collar, and a gray fur hat. At the turnaround the sellers of roasted chestnuts opened up their stalls for the winter, and when I had enough money I would buy some, wrapped in a pyramidal twist of coarse brown paper, and eat them as I walked to the East Gate, warming my hands on them as long as they lasted.

Toward the end of that month I learned that my parents had decided to send me away to boarding school in Kuling after the

Christmas holidays. I was not eager to go, and I delayed telling my classmates. I intended to tell Undine first, but I kept putting it off. We continued to ride together, talking, or sometimes doing our next day's arithmetic lesson, for Undine was not too strong in abstract mathematics, though she always showed a sound money sense.

It was in the second week of December, just before the Christmas vacation began, that Madge Brownlee, whom I had known even before we started in first grade together, said to me during our morning recess period, "I suppose you know that Undine's mother is a countess now, don't you?"

"A countess?" I asked, surprised.

"It was in the *North China Daily News*," Madge said. "She was married just last week."

"We take the *China Press*," I said.

I expected Undine to tell me about her mother that afternoon, but although she seemed to be a little abstracted as we rode along, she said nothing about her mother's remarrying. After giving her a number of openings that she failed to take advantage of, I didn't either. And Undine continued to be uncommunicative during the rest of the week. Nor did I tell her about leaving Shanghai and going to Kuling after the holidays. I was, of course, still curious about Undine's mother's being a countess. I was not sure whether it made Undine a countess too. I didn't think it did, but I thought it might make her something.

On the last day of school, after the car had turned into Rue du Consulat and shortly before it reached the French Bund, I said, "Madge Brownlee told me that your mother is a countess now."

Undine turned to look at me. "Yes," she said. "She is."

I hesitated for an instant and then said, "Well, I was wondering, does that make you—"

Undine interrupted me. "Oh, it doesn't make me anything—not really, that is," she said.

The car had turned onto the Bund and we had come to the first of the yellow godowns. A hand cart had stopped on the tracks, and the car slowed down.

"No," Undine said. "It doesn't make me anything really. But—" and she paused, wrinkling her forehead as if she were trying to find the exact words she needed. "But it means that I—well, that I can do better now, you know." Her hand fluttered out and rested on my left arm, the first time she had ever touched me.

Her tone, more than her words, told me she was apologizing, and I became aware that what Undine was actually saying was that she now could do better than to marry me, or if not me personally, anyone like me she might meet in Shanghai. I was startled for an instant, because I had never thought of marrying Undine at all.

Obviously Undine felt she hadn't made a good job of her explanation. Her hand went from my arm to my hand, and she said, "You know what I mean. I can do better now, not especially because I want to, but because—well, with Mother a countess I can—well, I mean, you know, America is very nice, but now Europe will be different for me."

"Yes, I suppose so," I said uncertainly. The car was picking up speed again, and the motorman was clanging his bell as we rode through the yellow glow reflected from the godowns. Although I had never before thought of marrying Undine, now that she had brought up the subject, I found the picture of marriage with her, as far as my mind could carry it, not unattractive.

Undine's hand gave mine a hint of pressure. "You don't mind?" she asked.

"Why, no," I said, not sure just what I should answer. "I think you're being very sensible."

"I thought you would," she said, smiling.

The car started to go around Marché de l'Est, and we stood up. For some reason it now seemed unnecessary for me to mention not coming back to school. I scarcely knew whether I should be pleased that Undine's mother was a countess or miffed because I had been rejected.

The car stopped and we got off. Undine hesitated. "I don't know if we'll see each other any more," she said. "We will be moving into Frenchtown as soon as we find a good house, and I won't go back to the American School, you know."

"No, I suppose not," I said.

Then I felt an impulse to make a gesture, to give Undine a present, since we would probably never meet again.

"Wait, Undine. Wait here a minute!" I said, and ran across to the corner of Fish Market Street, dodging among the rickshas and carts. I stopped in front of a stand where chestnuts were roasting over an earthenware charcoal-burner. I bought two of the paper-wrapped packages and ran back to Undine.

"Here," I said. "Here are some chestnuts—a sort of present, you know."

"Thank you," Undine said, smiling. She took a package and then she said, "Really, I don't think I should take them."

"Why not?" I asked. "You like them, don't you?"

"Oh, yes," she said, standing slim and elegant there in gray while the bustle of the Chinese street went on around us. "But now I think perhaps I shouldn't."

She put the little package back in my hand. Her car was coming, and when it stopped she got on, turning at the top of

the steps. "Good-bye, John," she said. "I didn't mean *truly better,* you know."

"Good-bye, Undine," I said. I tried to smile but found that I didn't feel like it.

The motorman clanged his bell and the car started off. We waved to each other and she was gone.

As I walked up Fish Market Street to the East Gate I didn't know for sure whether I was angry with Undine or sad at leaving her. I was too much a child of Shanghai to think that we would ever see each other again, and I derived what comfort I could from the discovery that with two packages of roasted chestnuts it wasn't any trick at all to keep both hands warm.

SAS III

I N FEBRUARY 1927 I reentered the Shanghai American School as a boarder. My sister had moved into the girls' dormitory three years before and had found this arrangement far more convenient than making the daily trip from the mission at South Gate and back.

Welcome as it was to avoid the streetcar trip, there was nothing very comfortable about the boys' living quarters of SAS at this time. A gymnasium was the only building that had been built since the school first moved to Avenue Pétain. Grass covered what had formerly been the sea of mud, though the large pond in the eastern part of the grounds remained undrained. An athletic field had been completed and tennis courts put in west of the dining hall. But the boys' dormitory continued to be nothing but the third floor of the administration and classroom building. The "rooms" we lived in consisted of partitions running out from the walls and two wardrobes that served as a fourth side of these cubicles. As a horsey classmate of mine remarked, our sleeping quarters strongly resembled box stalls.

Since three or four boys shared each of these rooms, privacy was impossible. A storage space opened off the rear of each cubicle, its entrance covered by a blue curtain. Here we put our luggage, what-

ever gear we weren't using at the time, and cast-off clothing. These spaces were connected by short tunnels, which made it possible to crawl from room to room along each side of the building without going out into the passageway marked off by the parallel rows of wardrobes. This feature of the building encouraged surprise raids, but the tunnels were so clogged with stuff that almost no one could make the trip quietly, and the surpriser himself was often welcomed with a basin of water in his face as he popped out from behind the curtain.

The most peculiar custom these storage spaces and the wardrobes led to was the Saturday-morning shoe fight. Almost everything else wore out in time, but old shoes lasted forever, and a dozen or so discarded pairs littered each storage space. After we had all passed Saturday-morning inspection (which meant that each room had been put in perfect order), rooms facing each other across the passage might agree to indulge in a shoe fight. All the old shoes were raked out of the storage space, and at a given signal hostilities opened. The wardrobes didn't reach the ceiling, leaving a three-foot open space above them, across which the shoes could be thrown. It was also perfectly fair to throw directly through the space between the wardrobes, but this meant exposing yourself to the enemy. It was safest to crouch close to the wardrobes in the corners of the partitions, then step back a pace, throw your shoe, and return to the wardrobe's protection. By following this strategy it was almost impossible to be hit by a shoe, and, in turn, it was almost impossible to hit anyone on the other side. Battles went on for two or three hours at a stretch. Dust rose in the hall. Truces could be arranged when so many shoes fell in the passageway that ammunition ran low. Anyone coming through the passage shouted for a safe conduct, and the contestants let him by. If a room scored three or four hits during a morning, the battle was considered violent.

If this entertainment sounds rather crude and too violent for a member of the Shanghai American School to enjoy, let me point out here that almost none of the boarders were natives of Shanghai. Most of them had been born up-country and had lived there during their early years. For the three and a half years I boarded at SAS the dormitory included only one other boy who had been born in the city. He was not a Presbyterian and could stick it out for only a year and a half. At times I felt that I was living among strangers, but so far as I know, I never showed this; and whenever my roommates and the fellows across the hall voted for a Saturday-morning shoe fight, I did my duty. Through all the shoe fights I took part in I was never hit once, but no one else seemed to notice this.

Perhaps the lighthearted way in which we fought this absurd show war influenced our attitude toward the actual civil war going on around us in 1927. Chiang Kai-shek's forces had marched up from the south. The Nanking Incident had just occurred. Rumor had it that the Chinese were going to attack the French Concession and the International Settlement and massacre the foreigners. Barbed-wire entanglements went up at all entrances from Chinese territory. The French strengthened their patrols and brought up Annamese troops. The Coldstream Guards landed and paraded up Nanking Road. The U.S. Marines were reinforced. Everyone took the situation seriously except the boarders at SAS, even though a few weeks before I moved into the dormitory stray bullets had whined across the quadrangle.

The principal and the teachers worked out something that they called, to everyone else's glee, Evacuation Drill, and shortly after I reentered the school we went through our first practice. When the fire bell rang three times everyone had to roll up his bedding and tie it in the Chinese manner, while the "room leader" picked up a

suitcase packed with pajamas, a change of clothes for everyone in the room, toothpaste, hair and tooth brushes, soap, and a few other essentials.

The principal hoped that we could complete Evacuation Drill in ten minutes, but he reckoned without the character of the SAS male boarders. Almost all of us believed the danger past, and many had refused to pack their suitcases correctly. The alarm sounded one morning as the whole school was dressing for breakfast. We bundled up our bedding, but with no intention of carrying it downstairs. Instead, we rushed to the windows at the end of the hall and threw out our bedding rolls with shouts of pleasure. The principal, standing directly below, had to jump under the colonnade for shelter. I don't know if he had originally intended checking our suitcases, but he did. Many were almost empty, but among the first rooms to be inspected was a conscientious group that had done everything according to instructions. Their toothpaste, combs, and brushes were smuggled down the line after they had been passed, and most of us got off with nothing more than a severe reprimand, which we were grateful for, since we began to worry after the squeezed-in tube of Colgate's had shown up for the fifth time. We never had to leave the school, but for months we spoke with delight of Evacuation Drill.

Once again the class roll went "Adamson, Black, Crawford, Davis, Espey...." As we advanced we acquired new posts, new responsibilities. We contributed to the school paper, we took part in various forms of student government. The boarders actually ran their own affairs in a limited way, and I was duly elected monitor and proctor. As monitor one had to stalk up and down the hall after lights-out, giving "points" to anyone caught talking. So many points a week and one's "privileges" were removed, which meant

that for the next week the offender could not leave the school grounds. A person who really enjoyed being monitor wore felt-soled slippers and sneaked up and down the hall, pretending to be going to the bathroom at one end when he was really starting right back down between the wardrobes. This sort of thing didn't appeal to me, and I always scuffled along and made plenty of noise. Whispering failed to attract my attention. I made a mistake here, of course, for I proved to be such a popular monitor that I was reelected time after time. In the end I had to buy some felt-soled slippers of my own, and for four weeks I handed out a record number of points. From that time on, my name was almost never put in nomination.

Life as an SAS boarder had its own flavor. The tradition of the school's missionary origin gave it its characteristic atmosphere, but outside, the city waited to be discovered. For the up-country boys it was probably more stimulating than for the rest of us to have all the naughtiness of the port just at hand. At any rate, those of us who had been born in Shanghai looked with alarm on occasion at the up-country boys, particularly at their habit of running in packs. One of their traditional amusements the last three years of high school was to visit one of the cheap downtown houses in groups of five or six. Most of them got all the sense of sin they wished just sitting in the parlor talking to the madam and looking at the girls. Why they enjoyed this the rest of us couldn't say. Anyone born in Shanghai preferred to be indiscreet without witnesses.

One of my closest friends and I worked out a far more characteristic pattern of Shanghai behavior between us. We walked up to the junction of Avenue Joffre and Route Ferguson to an excellent French pastry shop almost every school-day afternoon. At the shop we each bought a box of pastries to eat as we sauntered back to the school. Our up-country classmates were amused by this exercise of ours,

and many of them felt we were frightful sissies. But having been born in Shanghai, my friend and I knew that the less anyone discovered about you the better, and the wilder the misinterpretation your acquaintances put upon your character the stronger your position. This friend of mine and I had both been experimenting with tobacco for two months before we found each other out. Meanwhile, we had walked up to the pastry shop and back and had led the rest of our lives apart from one another.

Every third or fourth weekend I went home to South Gate, a change in atmosphere I always found invigorating. The only difficulty about it came from my parents' encouraging me to bring classmates home with me. I found it impossible to make them understand that there was little sense in escaping from the school if you insisted on bringing it home with you.

Life at the school continued, sometimes with strange overtones. I remember the shock some members of the junior and senior classes experienced at their annual party in 1929 to find themselves in one of Shanghai's more genteel night spots not, as they had been a few nights before, enjoying the drinks of the establishment and inspecting its fairly comprehensive floor show, but instead swilling fruit punch and indulging in a decorous waltz. (As a rigid Presbyterian I myself was not one of these, and I speak only at second hand.)

During the years since my first day in the first grade at North Szechuen Road I had gradually been allowed to forget my intensely personal connection with the school, but now this privacy was taken from me. A PTA sprang up at SAS, and shortly after my return in 1927 its president hit upon one of the most ingenious tortures I have ever endured. She remembered that I had been born in the school's first year and that my father had been the school's first principal. Once a term from that time on I was asked to attend an

afternoon meeting of the PTA. At a certain point in the program the president—whoever she was, for this became a tradition—would rise and say, "And now I think we would all like to have visible evidence of how the school has grown, how it has prospered and thrived since its earliest years. As many of you know, John Espey's father was the first principal, and John was born in the principal's residence at the old school on North Szechuen Road. I am going to ask him to stand up so we can all take a good look at him and see how things have changed." To a spatter of applause, I—always twenty-five to thirty pounds underweight and stooped, usually pale from an attack of asthma or a recurrence of the amoeba I had picked up when I was three and a half—would rise and bow. Just how much the spectators enjoyed this or what they thought of it I do not know. But I do know that only a member of SAS, and only one born in Shanghai, could have stood there savoring all the ludicrous irony of the situation, could have stood there, not just once, but term after term, and lived to write of it.

RAMÓN AND
THE NORTH AMERICAN ATTITUDES

I F RAMÓN HADN'T SAT beside me in English class his first day
at the Shanghai American School, I might not have got myself
tangled in his affairs. I was a junior in high school at the time, and
Ramón walked into the classroom that first day just as the second
bell rang. I was sitting at the back of the room, near the door, and
he dropped into the chair next to mine. At the end of the period I
introduced myself, and he told me that his father was a newly appointed consular official from one of the Latin American republics.
Ramón spoke with a slight accent, his English correct if not at all
idiomatic. He said that he felt more at home in French if he had
to speak a foreign language. I explained that my French wasn't too
good and observed that he was probably being sent to the American
School to perfect his English anyway. This, he said, was true, but he
was also being sent there to get what he called "the North American
attitudes," which his father thought would be useful to him later,
especially if he too went into government service.

At that time juniors and seniors in the Shanghai American School
were not required to attend study hall during their free periods,
and boarders were allowed to go to their rooms in the dormitory,
presumably to do their studying there. When I learned that Ramón
was a day student and that he had no class the next hour, I invited

him up to my room on the third floor of the main building. One of my two roommates owned a portable phonograph, and though we were not supposed to play it during class hours, we did. When a bath towel was stuffed into the sound box, only a thin trickle of music filtered through to us. I played several records for Ramón and discovered that that he was seventeen, not quite a year older than I was. He had curly black hair and his jowls already showed a fairly heavy beard. His arms were extraordinarily hairy, and he had about him a quality that I, who was at the time searching for precise words for everything, decided was "faun-like," probably because I was just then reading through Hawthorne. Among other things I learned that Ramón had been taught by tutors most of his life and that he considered his formal education virtually completed, though he thought it not unlikely that he would return to his own country eventually and enter a military school. After that his family connections should be good for an army commission—an excellent beginning, he gave me to understand, for almost any career. For my part I told Ramón that my father was a missionary and that I had been born in Shanghai but didn't expect to live there all my life.

Ramón and I found that we had identical schedules. We got into the habit of spending most of our free time together in my room, talking and listening to the Victrola.

It was during one of these conversations, when I had been telling Ramón about my family and what it was like to live in Shanghai, that he asked me, "And what about the girls, Juanito?"

"Oh, I really haven't much time for them right now," I said, not being involved at the time in a school romance. "It's more important for me to study, because I'll have to get into an American college."

Ramón looked at me in what I thought was a very stupid way and said, "You speak the truth, Juanito? You are beyond the girls?"

"Yes, for the time being at least," I said, and changed the record on the phonograph.

Against the reedy tones of a voice singing "That's My Weakness Now," Ramón said, "Ah, how I envy! You are then a *filosofo* in these matters?"

"What's that?" I asked, and then I understood. "Oh, you mean I'm a philosopher." I laughed. "Really, I don't know about that, but it seems to me you can waste an awful amount of time and energy on girls, and in the end they're all pretty much alike. Anyway, I'm not interested right now."

"Ah, Juanito, this is wonderful!" Ramón said. "You are like my father. He too is a *filosofo* with the girls now, he says, and it seems to be true. But you are the same age with me, and we can talk. You can advise me, because you are beyond it now." He paused for a moment, frowning. "But do you plan to marry?"

"Marry?" I said, surprised at the turn Ramón had given the conversation. "Why, I suppose so, eventually, but that won't be for years."

"And until then?" Ramón asked, spreading his hands.

"Oh, I don't know that it makes much difference," I said, shrugging my shoulders.

To my surprise, Ramón was almost overcome with admiration. As he talked on, the realization came to me, but very slowly, that Ramón and I had not been talking about the same thing at all; what Ramón had meant by "the girls" was not what I had meant.

For the moment the confusion we had plunged into entertained me, and I did nothing to clear it up. Later, each time I tried to explain to Ramón that he had really misunderstood me, he would double up with laughter as he rolled on the bed of one of my roommates. "You are so droll, so beautifully funny, Juanito," he

would say, laughing and drowning out the thin stream of music coming from the phonograph. "And you look so innocent, too!" he would exclaim. "If I did not know, I could almost believe. Ah, what an American attitude! What spiritual comedy!"

Unluckily, the very first time Ramón mentioned one of his problems to me, I responded with such glibness that I not only took him in but went a long way toward taking myself in, too. Ramón had been recounting a curious adventure and mentioned an address on Tibet Road.

"Tibet Road!" I said. "Why, Ramón, I don't think anyone but junior clerks, tourists, and newspapermen go to Tibet Road any more."

"You see!" Ramón exclaimed, delighted. "You know the city so much better. You are born here."

"Well, yes, of course," I said, seeing that I had got myself into a hole. "But, really, I don't know *everything* about the city."

"It is not important now, anyway," Ramón said. "Girls are one thing, but, as you yourself know, even with them there can be an end. Not that I am yet a *filosofo* like you. But still there is a monotony. I think I am ready now for my first grand passion."

"Oh?" I said cautiously.

"Yes," Ramón answered.

"Well," I said, gathering confidence, "if you're ready for a grand passion, I suppose you might as well go ahead and get on with it."

"Ah!" he said. "That is the problem. I don't know which one is to be the grand passion. You must help me."

"Which one?" I repeated, fearing Ramón had really got himself into a mess.

It appeared that he had two candidates in mind for this great experience and that he was unable to decide which should be the

recipient of his ardor. Having received a large part of my own emotional education from the standard English and American novels, I felt that this was a pretty cold-blooded way of considering a grand passion, but I had had enough experience of Shanghai life not to be taken utterly aback by it. So I urged Ramón to tell me more about his possible attachments.

Through a series of florid sentences I gathered that one of them, and perhaps the more convenient one from many points of view, was Dolores. Dolores was the wife of one of Ramón's father's underlings in the consulate. She was, Ramón assured me, a classic Latin type, with fine features, bluish-black hair, smooth shoulders, and generous endowments in all important respects. There would be no question, he felt, if he hadn't met Ursule at the French Club shortly after arriving in Shanghai.

"And just who is Ursule?" I asked.

Ursule turned out to be the widow of a minor official who had served in some capacity in the French Concession. A tall blonde, she enjoyed the distinction of possessing a pair of what Ramón insisted were purple eyes, though I accused him of exaggeration. In any case, Ursule was an exceptionally fashionable type, and "supple."

Struck by Ramón's use of such an odd and, for him, unusual word, I asked, "Where in the world did you pick that up?"

"The coach used it when we played basketball one afternoon," Ramón said, "and he explained it to me. As soon as I understood, I thought of Ursule." Seeing in my mind's eye Ramón on the gym floor struggling with a game he would certainly never play in later life and being transported at the thought of his supple blonde, I wondered what the coach, a somewhat YMCA-ish, cold-shower type, would make of Ramón's reaction.

"This is all very fine," I said, my practical Presbyterian nature

asserting itself, "but I should think that the measure of your success with either Dolores or Ursule might well decide which of them is to be your choice." This verbiage sounded absurd even to me, and I had to explain to Ramón more simply.

"Oh, my dear friend," he said, when I had made myself clear, "you really do not understand. There is no question of doubt either way."

"What makes you think that?" I asked.

"Why, they have already spoken their willingness."

"Spoken?" I said, as close to being startled at such matters as one born in Shanghai can be.

"Oh, yes, there is no question. I am invited."

"Really, then," I said, "I don't see what you're worrying about. They don't know each other, do they?"

"I think not," he said.

"Surely you are clever enough. I mean, why choose? Why can't you be happy with both of them?"

Ramón jumped up and thrust his hands out in front of him. "Oh, Juanito!" he exclaimed, as if shocked. "Really you are too cold. That is, I suppose, the North American attitude—*toujours pratique, n'est-ce pas?* Ah, yes, you are controlled, experienced, but I am not so advanced. And, truly, to have the grand passion, you know, I cannot have *two* first grand passions."

"Yes, I can see that," I said. "I suppose it really is a problem."

"You must help," Ramón pleaded. "You must advise."

"It's good of you to think I can," I said, "but there's nothing much I can do. After all, if your father gives you advice on such things and is, as you say, a *filosofo*, perhaps *he* can help you."

"Truly," Ramón said bitterly, "you are almost like what my father describes the English to be—so logical, so ice-like. No, no! Perhaps

you can ask *your* father about such a thing, and of course a father can advise on the girls, but with the grand passion—no, that is humiliating."

I had a hard time not smiling when I thought of what my own father's response would be to such a conversation, but I said soberly, "Well, Ramón, it's generous of you to confide in me this way, and of course I'll be glad to talk it all over with you."

"That is friendly," Ramón said, smiling. "That is what I want."

Ramón and I had many conversations on the subject that was troubling him. His grand passion, however, did not advance, for he was quite unable to make up his mind. No change in the situation occurred until one afternoon when he proposed that since there were both Dolores and Ursule to be considered and there were two of us, perhaps something could be arranged.

"We could begin by going to a *boîte*—how do you say—night-club?—sometime," Ramón suggested, "and then after meeting them both you could decide."

"My dear Ramón—" I began patiently, but he interrupted me.

"Ah, I was afraid you would not be interested. I cannot understand, but I do admire you."

"You are very kind," I said. "Anyway, I'm not in the habit of going to *boîtes*. Only round-the-world people and Shanghailanders go to *boîtes*."

Ramón shook his head and grinned. "You are too experienced," he said sadly. Unwilling to give up his plan entirely, he suggested a modification of it. He proposed to introduce both Dolores and Ursule to me, one at a time, in the cocktail lounge of the Astor House.

"Really, Ramón," I said, "it isn't that my family is prominent or anything like that, but we've lived in Shanghai so long that no

matter where I go downtown I'm practically certain to run into someone who knows me, and I think this might be difficult to explain at home."

"Then some small place," Ramón insisted. "After all, the city is big."

"That's true," I said.

"And surely it is not compromising to be seen with a man and a woman. It could not be more discreet."

"I suppose not," I said.

Ramón finally persuaded me that if we went to some small tea shop during the day, everything would be all right. We chose a little place on Avenue Joffre, a block or so down from the French Club. This shop, known as Olga's, served tea and first-rate French pastries.

Ramón arranged to meet Dolores the following Friday afternoon at the French Club. He and I set out from school together and rode in a taxi to Olga's, where Ramón dropped me and went on to the club. I took a table in a corner and ordered *babas au rhum* and tea for the three of us. In a few minutes, the taxi pulled up in front of the tea shop, and Ramón handed out Dolores. They came into the shop, and Ramón guided her to the table where I was sitting. I got up and bowed, and Dolores smiled at me. She was much as Ramón had described her to me, though she looked somewhat older than twenty-five. We all sat down, the tea was served, and Ramón and Dolores plunged into the *babas,* complimenting me on my taste. Since Dolores spoke almost no English and very little French, while I spoke no Spanish at all, this rendezvous, which I had looked upon as almost an assignation, proved a trifle dull. Ramón and Dolores chatted with each other, Dolores smiled at me from time to time, and now and again Ramón translated some remark of hers into English. Altogether I might just as well have been out for tea with

one of my Courtesy Aunts from the mission at South Gate, except that it was undeniably interesting to look at Ramón and Dolores and imagine them involved in a grand passion, something that would hardly have sprung to my mind in the company of a Courtesy Aunt.

After three quarters of an hour of this, we left Olga's. Ramón and Dolores walked back to the French Club, and I caught a bus to the school. Ramón had paid for everything, which was a relief to me, because he and Dolores had eaten a large number of *babas*.

Much to my surprise, Ramón turned up at the school early Saturday morning ecstatic over what he termed "the grand success" of our outing. Before he would let me speak he said, "Now before you have an opinion you must meet Ursule. And this afternoon we do the same with her. I have already arranged it."

"Where, this time?" I asked.

"But at Olga's, of course," he said. "Everything must be the same, to make the comparison fair."

"You have a truly English attitude about sportsmanship," I said, but Ramón refused to be led on.

That afternoon we went through the same routine. Instead of ordering *babas au rhum* again, I asked the waitress to bring us a tray of French pastries. This time it was the supple Ursule who was handed out of the taxi. Ramón and his companion spoke in French, and when I tried to say something in that language, Ramón scolded me. "It would not be fair," he insisted, to the bafflement of Ursule.

Ursule was charming, I decided, though she too looked a little older than I had expected, and her eyes could be called purple only by one on the brink of his first grand passion. Her suppleness I had little opportunity to judge. She worried me somewhat after a while, for now and then she let her voice shoot out of control in a rather distressing way. By the time we were ready to leave I felt that if

Ramón must have a grand passion immediately, he would probably do better with Dolores. Ursule, I decided on the basis of my sound Presbyterian training, looked as if she might prove skittish.

When Ramón came up to my room after English class on Monday, I felt adequately prepared to advise him. Once I had explained my choice he appeared to agree, but then he started to go over all of Ursule's merits and brought forward the argument that since he would probably not marry a Frenchwoman, perhaps it would be best to experience one for his first grand passion.

By the time he had considered all the angles of Ursule's nationality I had begun to weary of the whole business. "Really, Ramón," I said, "I have given you the best advice I can, and I don't see that I can do any more."

"Oh, I appreciate it very, very much," he said. "And I think you are perhaps right. But I must consider for a few days more. You still don't want to go four together? Each one thought you very charming, and they are most interested that you are an American. Everyone is interested nowadays in the North American attitudes, of course."

"No, no. That isn't for me."

Ramón shook his head. "Astonishing!" he said. "You make me feel so young."

Ramón spent most of the next few days away from school; so I didn't see him regularly. When he did mention Dolores and Ursule he sounded as undecided as before, and I began to think he had never been serious about his grand passion. On the Saturday three weeks after I had met Ursule, Ramón rode up to the school in a taxi and met me as I was coming out of the dining hall after breakfast. He drew me aside and said, "Ah, Juanito, it is all finished now."

"Finished?" I said. "Why, I didn't think it had even begun."

"You do not understand," he said. "I am leaving Shanghai."

"Oh, that's too bad," I said. "Has anything happened?"

"My father!" he said. I waited for him to go on. "You see, three nights ago my father and I are having dinner together, and after a little of the wine I decide to talk to him of my problem. I have already told you he is practical and a *filosofo,* just like you. And with the wine I forget in a way he is my father, and it is possible to speak of the grand passion."

"Yes," I said.

"Well, he says he too will look at the ladies for me and give me a decision. I think this is generous, and I tell him who they are. So last night he comes to me and says, 'Ramón, my dear boy, I think it is time for you to return home and begin a career.' "

Ramón's father sounded very sensible, I thought. "Perhaps he's right," I said. "Was that all?"

"Ah!" Ramón exclaimed. "You remember you have suggested to me, you who are so experienced, that I need not make a decision, that I can have two affairs at once?"

I nodded.

"Well, my father, as I have said, is like you. Yes, just like you, Juanito."

"You mean he wanted you to have two affairs?" I asked.

"No, no!" Ramón said. "*He* is now to have two affairs at once! It is truly extraordinary, and at his age, my friend!"

Before Ramón stepped back into the taxi he embraced me and we said good-bye. Then, tapping my chest for emphasis, he repeated, "Just like you, Juanito!" As the taxi drove off I sensed hitherto unsuspected powers swelling within me, and I began to consider myself with new interest and respect.

THE BUST OF JUNO

I N 1917 Miss Mable B. Jennings, teacher of classics at the Shanghai American School, presented a plaster-of-Paris bust of Juno to her senior Latin students as a trophy and unwittingly introduced to SAS what was to become the most important element of its life. Some SASites have been heard to say that SAS is not the repository of all knowledge; some have dared make fun of the white man's burden in China; some have even admitted openly that they considered a few elements of Chinese life not altogether bad; but to suggest that there is anything trivial about the Bust of Juno and the emotions it arouses is tantamount to saying that one has failed, and been failed by, SAS. If anyone gets even the hint of such a feeling from what I write, this will be through no conscious intention of mine, but because I received four years of my early education at the Kuling American School, one year at the John Nash Public School in Des Moines, and another at the John Fiske Public School in Chicago.

The seniors who became the Bust's first guardians passed it on to the incoming seniors at graduation, and for a couple of years this was all the tradition amounted to, and the Bust appeared only at senior class parties until the class of 1919 decided to display it to the public. This struck the junior class as something in the nature of sacrilege, and its members took possession of the Bust for themselves.

Angered, the seniors then fought the juniors to regain Juno, and the full-blown tradition was well on its way to establishment. Each year the graduating seniors gave the Bust to the next senior class, and each year the incoming juniors tried to take it away from the seniors.

Soon rules had to be drawn up to control the fighting over the Bust. Very early, the junior and senior girls were excluded from active competition, for they showed themselves prone to pulling hair and scratching. Since the boys did nothing worse then gouge and knee each other vigorously, the girls were plainly unfit, and all they could do from then on was stand by and scream encouragement. The class in possession of the Bust was expected to "show" it four or five times a year, meaning at first merely that the Bust was produced at a class party or an all-school event.

During a particularly bitter fight in 1927 the plaster Bust broke into a number of pieces. Though the seniors kept possession of them all, something had to be done. Luckily, the class had recently collected its dues and could afford to order a bronze Bust cast after the original. Whatever delicacy of feature may have been lost in the process, everyone felt the added strength all to the good.

Until 1927, despite many fierce battles, each succeeding senior class had kept the Bust, and each class's highest ambition was to be the first to capture it as juniors. As a member of the class of '30, consequently, I was as dismayed as all my classmates to learn in the fall of 1927 that the junior class, the class of '29, had got hold of the Bust during the summer. Two senior boys had decided to take it to the United States on a summer cruise. In mid-Pacific, Nancy McDaniel of the class of '29 caught sight of the Bust during one of its afternoon airings. At the first opportunity she searched the seniors' cabin and found the Bust. Knowing that she could never hope

to keep it by herself for the rest of the voyage, she very sensibly wrapped it up and placed it beyond recovery in the ship's mail.

The Bust returned to Shanghai on 1 September 1927, and we were afraid the juniors would keep it for the rest of the year, even though the seniors almost made off with it when it was shown at the annual Halloween party. The juniors, however, grew overconfident. In order to have the Bust readily available, they hid it in an old gravemound just next to the First and Second Grades Building. This grave belonged to a Chinese family that refused to let the coffin be moved except for an exorbitant fee, so the school just left it where it was. Part of the mound had fallen in, exposing one end of the coffin and a small cave beside it. One day a second grader, Townsend Brown, reached inside out of curiosity. Hauling out the Bust, he bore it off in triumph to show his friends. As it happened, the second grade was enjoying "supervised play" under the eye of some senior girls. Townsend Brown was immediately relieved of the Bust, which was then carted off to the house of one of the girls, from which it was later moved to a safe in the home of James Latimer.

One afternoon in December three seniors—Philip Bankhardt, Lewis Carson, and Floyd Marriott—brought the Bust to the dormitory and locked it in a trunk. Don Day, a junior, hid himself in the closet of their room and learned what they had done with Juno. Next morning during breakfast Don and two other juniors—Howard Baker and Harold Brown—opened the trunk with the help of a large key collection and carried the Bust off to the home of Robert Service, another junior.

In January 1928 some juniors took the Bust to the top of a water tower near the school and, concentrating on getting unusual snapshots of their prize, let it fall to the ground. Fortunately the bronze Bust escaped injury.

During May the Bust was lodged at the home of Merle Smith, and just escaped recapture by the seniors through being moved. The Smith house was ransacked, something that the parents of anyone whose class had the Bust and who lived in Shanghai had to accept in good spirit. Later in the same month the whole school was delighted when two seniors thought they saw Juno in a box some freshman girls were carrying across the quadrangle. The seniors dashed out of their class in Virgil, only to find that they had been hoaxed with a brick.

June 1928 brought a new problem in the history of the Bust, for with the juniors already in possession, it seemed impossible to have the official "presentation." Yet without it the one set battle of the year, between the incoming seniors and the incoming juniors, would be eliminated. A new rule was agreed upon, making it necessary for the juniors to return the Bust to the graduating seniors on the last day of school so that it could be publicly presented. This presentation was usually staged at night in the northeast corner of the quadrangle at the close of senior class-day ceremonies. The president of the graduating senior class handed the Bust to the president of the incoming senior class and then did his best to escape from the fight.

The battle of June 1928 was the first in which I took part, but I can't say I gave my class much help. The incoming seniors ran off with the Bust, leaving me and my classmates dismayed. But as members of the class of '30 we knew we had one thing in our favor; we were the first class at the school to be reared entirely in the tradition of the Bust. We had been first graders at the time of the original fight over the Bust in 1919. Consequently, I was not surprised to hear late in August that my classmate and fellow Presbyterian Scott Crawford, learning in Mokanshan that two seniors there for the summer had the Bust, had searched their houses for it and found

it. Knowing that his own family's house would be torn to pieces, he hid the Bust outdoors. When the holidays came to an end he sent one of the Crawford servants down the mountains a day ahead of the family with the Bust wrapped in his bedding roll. Later the Bust was sent to Shanghai and deposited in a bank vault.

The seniors, enraged, claimed all sorts of fouls, and feeling ran so high at the beginning of the school year that the Student Senate and the principal had to meet and draw up an entirely new set of rules. The most important points in this provided that the Bust could not be kept in a bank vault or placed in the mails, that the Bust could not be taken away from a showing by any means of public transportation or in a private car, that to be official a showing required a majority of the boys of the opposing class to be present, and that only members of the junior and senior classes could handle the Bust during a fight and getaway. The new rules also confirmed the unwritten tradition that frowned on hitting and slapping during fights, leaving us with such harmless tricks as full nelsons, scissors-, toe-, or strangleholds, and hammerlocks to fall back on. But the most brutal provision of all was the principal's insistence that the Bust could be shown only during the first and last quarters of the school year. The principal forced this through the Senate by threatening to retire the Bust to either the school's trophy case or the office vault, and backed up his demand by pointing out that at least half the year at SAS should be devoted to study. In the face of this the Senate had to yield, though many students felt it showed a dreadful lack of spirit in doing so and the principal a remarkable degree of obtuseness in insisting on the academic side of school life. A further provision made it impossible to show the Bust more than two times in each of the active quarters. During the other two quarters the class in possession was free to display the

Bust without threat of its being fought over—the Bust was then out of season.

During the first quarter of our junior year the Bust was shown twice, each time at noon in a window of the dining hall and in the hands of Charles Raven. At such showings tradition required the girls of the class in possession to sing:

> Where, oh where, is the Bust of Juno?
> Where, oh where, is the Bust of Juno?
> Where, oh where, is the Bust of Juno?
> Safe now in the junior class!

The second showing went wrong. The planned getaway did not come off when Bob Moffatt, to whom Raven had passed the Bust, was tackled immediately by some seniors. Soon all the junior and senior boys were fighting in front of the dining hall. After several minutes of sharp struggle Ralph Moller, a senior, carried the Bust to Harry Bernard, a sophomore and the school's ablest sprinter, who took it across the quadrangle and irresponsibly heaved it through the transom of one of the rooms in the new wing being added to the administration building. Moffatt climbed into the room through a window, followed by Howard Baker, a senior, who jumped on him as he picked up the Bust. Charles Raven, close behind Baker, pulled him off Moffatt, who ran to a window and passed the bust to Scott Crawford. Crawford tucked the Bust under his arm and got away through the front gate to the nearby fields, where he hid it.

I am ashamed to admit that all I did in this battle was of rather negative virtue. During the fracas in front of the dining hall I acted on the theory that if I could occupy a senior stronger and more vigorous than I, I should be doing all that could be expected of me.

Since at that time any other high-school boy was stronger than I, I simply reached into the pile and pulled out the first senior I got a grip on. He proved to be my friend Eugene Kazack, whose father worked in the Shanghai Customs, and for the rest of the battle I did nothing but keep Kazack from getting back into it. But I did perform one service for the class when the Bust had been rescued from the administration building. With a few other juniors and some seniors I reached the front gate just about the time Scott Crawford came cruising around the end of the building with the Bust. The first senior to notice him, Albert Nolting, was a sprinter of some powers. Just as Crawford went through the gate Nolting saw that he had the Bust and took out only to find himself on the ground, nailed, almost as much to his surprise as to my own, by a flying tackle I had never suspected myself capable of.

An editorial in the 6 November 1928 issue of the school paper contains this:

> The Juniors not being all together [sic] confident about the safety of the Bust were easily deceived into believing that the Seniors had found it. They appealed to Dr. Anderson on the gounds [sic] that the rules governing the Bust had been violated. Dr. Anderson requested that the Bust be handed over to him. The Juniors discovered then that the Seniors had not found the Bust so they went themselves to bring it back to Dr. Anderson. The Senate has taken over the question and is going to propose a solution of the question to Dr. Anderson.

A news story in the same issue of the paper contains this:

> Naturally all of the Juniors were in high spirits. However these received a considerable shock when it was reported that the Seniors had found the bust. This proved to be only a ruse on the

part of the Seniors, who hoped that the Juniors would go out to investigate.

What might have happened is a great question. All plans and thoughts were upset when Dr. Anderson demanded the bust on the grounds that certain of the rules had been broken. The bust was then brought in and is now in the office. What will happen is only a matter of conjecture.

The slight variants in these versions may come from the fact that the first was written by the paper's editor, Bob Barnett, a senior, and the second by the paper's news editor, John Espey, a junior.

The principal decided a number of rules had been broken by each side. The juniors kept the Bust, which had been out of our possession for one minute at the most. Another showing took place in the last quarter of the year in front of the senior English class. This time the getaway came off, only one senior, Halsey Wilbur, getting anywhere near Raven.

Why my class persisted in almost losing Juno I can't say, but we came close to doing so at the end of the year after we had given the Bust to the graduating seniors so they could give it back to us. On this occasion Harry Bernard, now an incoming junior, broke away from the man appointed to hold him and upset our plans. These had called for Crawford to take the Bust from Raven and run with it across the athletic field to the western border of the grounds, where Joe McCracken was waiting to receive it on the other side of the fence. The land here was taken up by a neglected Chinese cemetery, and when Joe discovered that Harry was over the fence and almost on him, he dodged about among the graves until he lost sight of Harry, and then hid the Bust in a mound that, like the one near the First and Second Grades Building, had collapsed at one end. Many graves in this cemetery were falling in, and since it was

already dark a thorough search would have been difficult. But the new juniors, suspecting that Joe hadn't got far, persisted in wandering through the graveyard. We, on the other hand, gave out that the Bust was once again safe in our hands and strolled off as unconcernedly as we could. At midnight Scott Crawford, Joe McCracken, Robert Moffatt, Robert Peterson, Walter Pettit, Charles Raven, Raymond Snell, and I returned to the graveyard. We had almost reached the grave in which Joe had hidden the Bust when about the same number of juniors jumped out from behind the nearby mounds, certainly a lightheaded maneuver on their part, for if they had been a little more patient they could have let us lead them to the Bust. As it was, we laughed raucously and assured them that we had come out because we knew they were there. Talking boisterously and pretending to go back to the dormitory, we left the graveyard, fooling, I imagine, no one.

We knew that when Harry Bernard gave up, the rest of them would go too. The Bernards' house, almost directly across the street from the new Masonic Temple at 178 Route Louis Dufour, lay within easy walking distance, so we went there. The Masons had seen fit to build a two-foot wall along the front of their lot, and we stretched out on the ground behind it to wait. We lay there for what seemed hours until Harry drove up in his car with another junior who lived near him. We heard them say good night and watched the other boy walk off to his house. Then we saw Harry's light go on and after a while go off. We got up quietly, sneaked off down Route Dufour, and in a few minutes rescued the Bust from the graveyard and escorted it to the McCracken house, east of the school on Avenue Pétain. Nothing that happened in my life afterward would ever quite come up to the feeling of masculine solidarity in that small gang as it stole along Shanghai's streets in the early morning.

The Bust's most popular function, especially during the two quarters it was out of season, was serving as a prop for snapshots. I have already noted that in January 1928 it fell from a water tower near the school. During the summer of 1929 a group of my classmates took the Bust to the top of the Foreign YMCA building on Bubbling Well Road opposite the Race Course and somehow managed to knock if off the roof, a fall of several stories. No one was brained on the sidewalk below, but, what was more important, Juno's head snapped off at the neck. My class was criticized severely for this, but after the two pieces were welded together, almost no trace of the accident remained.

During our senior year all showings of the Bust went off without a hitch. Near the end of the year I found myself saddled with the class presidency. So it fell to me to present the Bust, which we, the class of 1930, had kept for two years—the first class ever to make such a record—to the junior class president and then stand off with the rest of the senior men and watch the battle with a detached air. I have even forgotten who got the Bust in the fight, though I do remember that the junior president threatened to beat me up because the acting principal of the school changed the place of presentation from the northeast corner of the quadrangle to the center of the girls' hockey field. I went to the presentation well escorted by the senior brawn.

My class has come to delight in the minute or so the Bust was out of our possession. It makes our record even more remarkable than it would be without it, serving to accent our triumph, to show that we could lose the Bust and immediately recover it. Perhaps this is meaningless to a non-SASite. Indeed, much of what I have written about the Bust may appear meaningless and unnecessarily detailed, but only, I feel sure, to those who have had nothing to do with the school.

Once when I tried to explain the importance of the Bust of Juno to some Continental friends of mine, they insisted that it showed a surprising devotion—one not ordinarily found in American education in this century—to the classics. I am afraid they were mistaken. Equally faulty, I think, is the view of the few American and English friends I have tried to explain the tradition to, for they all attempt to demonstrate that it represents an astonishing survival in such an unsympathetic climate as China of the American male's mammary fixation.

Possibly one must be a member of SAS to sense the full significance of the Bust of Juno. As to the two theories I have mentioned, they can be disposed of easily. When the Bust was referred to in the SAS paper or the school annual, it was frequently called "Miss Juno."

JUST THE WAY THEY DO IT
IN THE STATES

O N STUDENT GOVERNMENT DAY in the spring of 1930 I acted as principal of the Shanghai American School. Each year on that day the teaching and administration of the school were turned over to the pupils. Our teachers said the experience would help us understand the American way of doing things, that it would develop in us feelings of self-reliance, and that it would be excellent preparation for life in an American college or university. Since then I have learned that these assertions were largely untrue, and I now suspect that Student Government Day existed simply to give the teachers a breather. Most of them left the school, and those that didn't stayed in their living quarters. Even the principal, who might have been expected to stand by in his office for emergencies, remained in his suite.

Customarily, everyone in the high school had a job on Student Government Day, because the number of students was small. When I was a freshman I taught my French class; when I was a sophomore I taught my Latin class; and when I was a junior I taught my English class. As a senior I would probably once more have taught my English class if almost all the senior boys had not been caught cheating on an examination shortly before Student Government Day. They were deprived of their prospective offices, and when it came to

appointing a principal for the occasion I was almost the only boy eligible.

Though I knew I should be flattered by the appointment, I felt very little one way or the other about it. Usually the student principal simply sat in the principal's office, gossiped with his student secretary, visited two or three classes, presided over a prearranged assembly program, and at four o'clock in the afternoon went to the teachers' sitting room, where he took tea with his "faculty." The real principal assured me beforehand that there would be almost nothing for me to do, and said that he had reserved for me a disciplinary case involving three boys in the third grade just so I would have something to make me feel useful. He said that I would have complete authority to act in the matter.

At eight o'clock on Student Government Day I went to the principal's office and greeted my "secretary," a senior girl whom I had known for years. Her parents were Episcopal missionaries. We talked for an hour or so, and then I said I supposed I might as well take care of the third-grade boys. I asked her to send for them. I had been told nothing about their offense and wondered what it could be.

When my secretary showed the boys into the office I tried to look solemn. They lined up and stared at me across my desk. "Now, you'll have to tell me what happened," I said, frowning. I nodded to the boy in the middle. "Tell me what you did."

Not until he started to speak did I realize that the boys were frightened, and that, far from having to maintain authority, I would have a hard time keeping them from breaking down. "You see, sir," the boy in the middle began, "we were going home for tiffin."

"When were you going home for tiffin?" I asked.

"About two weeks ago, and it was raining that day," he said.

"You mean this happened two weeks ago and you haven't been punished yet?" I asked.

"Yes, sir," the boy on the right said.

Then the boy in the middle continued. "It was raining and there were lots of puddles. So every time we came to a puddle we splashed through it."

"And got your feet wet," I said.

"Yes!" exclaimed the boy on the right, as if I had shown clairvoyant powers. "And when we got home—we all live near each other—our mothers were mad because we had to change our shoes and stockings." He stopped and stared at me.

"I don't wonder," I said, "but what does this have to do with the school?"

"Well," he said, "on the way back to the school after tiffin we splashed again." He stopped once more, and all three of them shifted uneasily, looking down at the floor and then peeking up at me.

"Weren't you wearing rubbers?" I asked.

"Yes," he said, "but some of the puddles were deep."

"I still don't see why I should do anything about it," I said. "Did anything else happen?"

"Our teacher found out we were all wet and sent us back home," the boy on the left said. "Our mothers called each other up, and next morning they sent a note to the principal telling him to punish us."

They all nodded and stared at me earnestly. The boy on the right began to sniffle. I was frightened by this and said, "Now, don't start bawling. Really, I think it's up to your mothers to attend to you. Nothing you did happened on the school grounds, and I think it's stupid to have kept you waiting this long." They looked at me hopefully, and the boy on the right stopped sniffling. "I know what," I said. "You tell your mothers this noon that the principal—that's

me for today, you see—has decided you have been punished enough, and that he thinks they have all neglected their duties as parents by trying to put this off on the school."

When this had sunk in, the boy on the right recovered himself completely.

"Now go on back to your room," I said.

"Thank you, sir," the boy on the left said.

"That's all right. Beat it."

"Don't you know who I am?" he asked.

"No," I said.

"I'm Bobby Alcott."

"Oh, so you're Wonky Alcott's little brother, are you?" Wonky was one of my classmates.

"Yes," he said, "but if I call him that he smacks me."

"And a good thing too, I imagine," I said. "I was sure you couldn't be a missionary kid, but I guess my parents know yours."

"I guess they do. Say"—he grinned impudently—"when the teacher sent us back home, we splashed that time too."

"Oh, go away," I said.

As soon as my secretary had let the three boys out, she said she thought I would probably get into trouble.

"Well, I was given absolute authority," I said, "so I don't see what anyone can say. Anyway, I think it's disgusting to keep them waiting all this time, especially for something their parents should have attended to in the first place."

"I know," she said, "but that's how it is with these wretched business families."

"That's right," I observed. "My folks would have beaten the devil out of me and called it a day."

"Mine too," she said. "How about a cup of tea?"

"How do you think we can get tea here?"

"Oh, the principal's secretary—the real one, you know—has an electric thing in her desk. She showed it to me yesterday. And there's a box of arrowroot biscuits too."

"Sounds like a good idea," I said. "Perhaps I ought to visit some classes, though."

"You can do that after assembly. The tea's almost ready now. I'll bring it right in."

She went out and soon came back with two cups of black tea and a box of Huntley & Palmer's arrowroot biscuits. "This isn't bad, is it?" she asked.

"No, it's fine," I said. "But I don't suppose the principal gets it every day."

We chatted on. Both of us had been going to the Shanghai American School off and on for a number of years, and we were reminiscing over a scandal that had occurred while we were in the third grade when we realized that someone was knocking gently on the door of the office.

My secretary got up and opened the door. M. Netchkov, the Russian pianist who was to play for the assembly, stood there. I jumped up and shook hands with him while my secretary tried to gather up the cups and the arrowroot biscuits as if this were the sort of thing that happened every day.

M. Netchkov was obviously puzzled at being greeted by a youth who had been drinking tea in the principal's office. "I play for the school," he said. "The headmaster?"

"Ah, M. Netchkov," I said, "this is Student Government Day, when the students run the school instead of the teachers."

M. Netchkov looked horrified. "Revolution everywhere!" he exclaimed.

"It really doesn't mean a thing, M. Netchkov," I said. "We do it one day a year. It's supposed to be good training for leadership and all that sort of thing, you know, and the teachers say that every high school in America has a day like this each year. Do sit down, sir."

He sat down on the edge of the chair I had indicated, and I sat down behind the desk. "Really, it doesn't make any difference to you," I said. "I'll present you to the school at assembly, and of course we're all looking forward to hearing you play." I smiled hopefully at him.

He smiled back. "Student Governing Day, you call it?"

"Government," I said. "Student Government. I know it probably sounds foolish to you. It sounds foolish to me too, frankly, but many of the teachers have just left America, you know, and don't understand Shanghai very well."

We talked for some time, and I thought I was doing a splendid job of putting M. Netchkov at his ease when my secretary knocked on the door leading into the main office and came in.

"Excuse me, M. Netchkov," she said, and then turned to me. "Something awfully funny is going on. There are seven Japanese students out in the hall, and I can't understand what they want. They're wearing the uniform of Futan University, and one of them keeps saying, 'Play assembly, play chapel.' "

"Well, I don't know what they're doing here," I said, "unless they have heard that M. Netchkov is to play, and want to hear him. That wouldn't be at all surprising."

M. Netchkov rose and bowed at this, and I excused myself. In the hall, as my secretary had said, stood seven Japanese students in uniform. As I approached them they bowed without giving any sign of surprise that the principal should be so young. I bowed in return, and, remembering what little I knew of Japanese manners, I almost

beat them to the second bow, when we all went down lower than before, and as soon as I could I bent over almost double in a third bow, thinking to myself that I was doing a perfectly wonderful job and that the principal himself surely couldn't have done so well.

Then I abandoned my Japanese manners, having exhausted them, and stepped forward, holding out my hand. The one who was evidently their leader stepped forward, and we clasped hands violently.

"It's charming, perfectly charming of you to come," I said. "We are so happy."

He hissed politely and said, "We play assembly. We play band assembly."

"Oh, it's not a band," I said. "It's M. Netchkov who is going to play the piano for us."

"Yes," he said, "Futan University Harmonica Band play assembly." He turned to the other six, and at a signal they all drew harmonicas from the pockets of their dark-blue uniforms and raised them to their lips. Their leader, smiling, saluted me, and I, in complete confusion, raised my right hand in the three-finger Scout salute and returned their courtesy.

"Well, it's charming anyway," I said feebly, sensing disaster, "that you have a harmonica band. I don't know that you'll get many pointers from M. Netchkov's playing, but perhaps you will."

The leader's face went blank, and he said, "Harmonica band play assembly."

As he said this a sickening awareness came over me that these seven students had come to play their harmonicas at the school assembly. Who had invited them, what they were going to play, I had no idea, but there they were, harmonicas in hand.

"Charming," I said again, inanely. "Won't you sit down here?" I indicated a long bench in the hall. "I'll be back in a few minutes."

They bowed and I bowed. I bowed again, backing away, and they bowed again, and by the third bow I was in the doorway to the office. Smiling brilliantly at the seven Futan students, I closed the door. M. Netchkov looked up as I came in. "Excuse me, M. Netchkov," I said. "I have to make a phone call from the main office."

My secretary was waiting in the main office. "Get me the principal's suite," I said. "This is hideous. Those Japanese from Futan think they are the program for today. They must have the wrong week. They are a harmonica band."

"I've never heard of such a thing," she said.

"Neither have I."

Once the connection was made, I almost yelled into the phone to the principal. "Why, I guess I did invite them," he said after I had explained the situation to him. "Yes, come to think of it, I did, and for today too. After all, they should fill in the time nicely."

"But what about M. Netchkov?" I demanded.

"Oh dear," he said. "I'd forgotten about him. Perhaps he won't show up."

"He's already here," I said. "And it's about three minutes before assembly time."

"That's right, it is," he said. "I can see that it is by my watch."

I didn't care what he could see; I knew only that I had on my hands representatives of the two touchiest groups in Shanghai, the White Russians and the Japanese. "Well, John," the principal said, "it will be very good experience for you. It's a problem you'll have to solve as well as you can. Remember, you *are* the principal today."

"I know," I said, "but I didn't get mixed up and arrange for two programs."

"Now, now," he said in painfully tolerant tones, "don't feel that

way about it. Think of it as a challenge. It's wonderful training for your life in America."

He hung up before I could point out that it was most unlikely I would ever have to cope in America with a Russian virtuoso and a Japanese harmonica band.

The bell for assembly rang and I rushed back to M. Netchkov. "M. Netchkov," I said, "something perfectly ghastly has happened. The Japanese students out there were asked by mistake to play on the program today, and I really don't know what I can do. I can't send them away—you know how unreasonable the Shanghai Japanese can be."

"Yes, yes," he said, and I suspected he hadn't understood.

"Anyway," I went on, "I wonder if you would mind playing just twenty minutes or so. Then the Japanese can play for the next twenty minutes."

M. Netchkov was beginning to understand. "They play what?" he asked.

"Harmonicas," I said. As I pronounced the word I wondered how the music would sound. But M. Netchkov was still in the dark. "I do not know the Japanese instruments," he said, "but will be interesting."

"Oh, I'm sure it will be interesting," I said, not having time to explain that the harmonica was not a Japanese instrument. We went out into the hall. The harmonica band sprang to attention and bowed. "M. Netchkov, the Futan University Harmonica Band," I said. "The Futan University Band, M. Netchkov, the distinguished pianist."

The band hissed politely and M. Netchkov nodded. As he did so, I thought of the Russo-Japanese War and wondered how we would ever get through the program.

The student body quieted when it saw the unusual group I led on to the stage. I asked the harmonica band to sit at one of the two library tables behind the rostrum, and M. Netchkov at the other. After making a few routine announcements I said, "We are all pleased, I am sure, to be able to hear M. Netchkov, the distinguished Russian pianist who so often plays with the Shanghai Municipal Orchestra. M. Netchkov will be happy to announce what he has chosen to play."

M. Netchkov rose to a polite spatter of applause and went to the grand piano. In somewhat curt tones he said, "I play two Chopin preludes," and sat down at the instrument. After rippling through the two preludes he seemed to be somewhat warmed by the music and the enthusiastic response of the assembly. He smiled at the students and asked, "What would you hear?"

Of course someone shouted, "Rachmaninoff's Prelude in C-Sharp Minor."

M. Netchkov beamed. I wasn't sure how long the prelude would last, but he had already crashed into the opening chords, so I sat back in my chair trying to look calm. I glanced over at the Japanese and saw that their leader was sitting stiffly, a blank expression on his face, and that one member of the band was polishing his harmonica on his sleeve.

At the close of the Rachmaninoff prelude everyone applauded loudly. M. Netchkov rose and bowed. I got up and went over to him and grasped his hand, afraid that he might forget himself and play an encore. When the applause died down I thanked M. Netchkov and showed him back to his seat. Then I took a deep breath and turned to the student body. "And now," I said, "we have a most unusual treat. The Harmonica Band of Futan University has generously consented to give us a few numbers."

Fortunately, the students of the Shanghai American School were well trained, and the rustle following my announcement could easily have been interpreted as pleased surprise. At the mention of their university the band members had sprung to their feet. They stepped in front of the piano. I asked the leader if he cared to have me announce their numbers, but he smiled at me without saying anything. So I retired and sat down beside M. Netchkov.

Then the leader announced in a loud voice, "American song," and gave a signal. The others raised their harmonicas, and as the leader dropped his arm the most alarming burst of sound I have ever heard broke out. The whole student body stiffened, and it was a few moments before I discovered that the harmonica band was doing what it could to "It Came upon a Midnight Clear." As I recognized the tune I foresaw difficulties at its close. I felt sure that most of the students would not applaud a hymn, but I was certain the Futan students wouldn't understand if they were not applauded. I looked down at the front seats, where the seniors sat, and, staring at my best friends, I put my hands together and gently went through the motions of clapping. Two or three of them understood, and when the hymn ended, even to the extent of a long-drawn-out and discordant amen, I raised my hands high and clapped furiously. Slowly the entire school joined in. M. Netchkov murmured, "*Extraordinaire! Extraordinaire!*"

So far as I know, Larry Adler had not been heard of in Shanghai in 1930. I am sure Larry Adler can do a lot of things that the Futan University Harmonica Band could not do, but I strongly suspect that the reverse is also true. I have forgotten the complete program by the harmonica band, but at one point I was roused from my stupefaction when the leader shouted, "American march," and they launched into "Marching through Georgia." More than one mem-

ber of the school belonged to a Southern family, and the Civil War—at least we didn't call it the War Between the States—was a subject we treated gingerly. I looked beseechingly at a girl in my class who belonged to a First Family of Virginia when I began to applaud at the end of this selection, but I think the whole school was so benumbed by this time that nothing really mattered. M. Netchkov had collapsed limply beside me, but I could still hear him whisper *Extraordinaire!* from time to time.

We listened to "The Little Brown Jug," "The Eton Boating Song," "Solomon Levi," and what seemed to me dozens of other numbers. It was impossible to stop the band. As soon as the applause for a piece began to die down, the leader would shout, "English tune," or "American song," and off they would go again. I felt that nothing more could happen when, following one number, the leader hissed to the others. Then he announced, "Russian song." The seven of them wheeled toward M. Netchkov, who looked at them glassy-eyed. They bowed and M. Netchkov managed to rise from his chair and fall back. The band faced front again and started to wail and whine through "The Song of the Volga Boatmen." M. Netchkov gasped. I looked at him imploringly, but he had closed his eyes and for all I knew had fainted dead away.

Just as "The Song of the Volga Boatmen" ended, the electric bell in the hall rang. I jumped up and shook hands with the leader of the band and thanked him. We bowed and bowed, and the students began to leave. Though they had behaved handsomely up to this point, they began to break down and laugh as they left. "You make us happy, very happy, you see," I said to the members of the harmonica band.

"We come back," their leader said.

"I'm sure you'll come back," I said, trying not to laugh hysteri-

cally. "I'm sure you'll come back, year after year. Charming, perfectly charming."

We bowed again and again. M. Netchkov, apparently quite overcome, remained seated. I bowed the harmonica band out into the hall and said, "You *must* come back. Next year the school would be glad to hear you at one assembly a week if it can be arranged. You must call up the principal about it."

At last they left and, turning back to M. Netchkov, I went up to him and shook his hand. "M. Netchkov, I'm terribly sorry," I said. "I had nothing to do with this, you know."

There wasn't much life left in M. Netchkov. He looked at me dazedly and said, "I thought you have said Japanese instruments."

"I must have been mistaken," I said, feeling that this was no time for explanations.

"Yes," he said. "And the last piece. They play that for *me!*" I couldn't tell if M. Netchkov was going to be insulted or amused, but all he said in the end was: "Student Governing Day. Very interesting—the whole world is in anarchy." I hadn't the heart to correct him as I led him gently to the school gates.

By early afternoon I had nearly forgotten about the third-grade boys. They hadn't made a deep impression on me, and after assembly the day had been passing as uneventfully as the principal had said it would. I was sitting in my office, hoping that I would continue to have nothing to do and thinking of asking my secretary to brew some more tea, when she came in.

"It's Rick—" she began, and then corrected herself. "I mean it's Mr. Richard Petchum. He's outside here."

"Don't try to be funny," I said.

She had no time to answer, for a stocky, black-haired man of middle height shoved past her and said to me, "Say, what's going

on? I came to see the principal. My kid Jacky ran away from home day before yesterday and didn't come back."

"How do you do?" I said automatically, and held out my hand. He looked surprised but shook hands with me, and my secretary went out and shut the door behind her.

Something I had never expected to do was shake hands with Rick Petchum, who was one of Shanghai's small-time racketeers. He owned a couple of cheap restaurants, which were said to be nothing but fronts for his dealings in opium and anything else that came along. Although he was still married to his first wife, an American woman, he was reported at that time to be infatuated with a Japanese girl.

"Where's the principal?" he asked.

"This is Student Government Day, Mr. Petchum," I said. "For today, *I* am the principal of the school. I don't know if your son is here or not."

Rick seemed puzzled but interested. He wanted to know about Student Government Day, so I explained it to him as well as I could. "Everyone in America does this," I concluded sweepingly.

"We didn't in Chicago when I was a kid," he said.

"Oh, are you from Chicago?" I asked. "I lived in Chicago for a year myself. My father and mother were both doing graduate work at the university, so we lived fairly near it. My sister and I rather liked Chicago. We used to go through the old empty buildings left from the fair, and in winter we learned to skate on a flooded section of the midway."

Rick Petchum looked doubtful, as if he didn't recognize his hometown from my description. "Say, now," he said abruptly. "About my boy Jacky. He's in the third grade, and he really ought to come home."

"The third grade!" I exclaimed. "But where could he be? Two nights alone in the city! We must call the police." The thought of an eight- or nine-year-old missing that long in Shanghai frightened me. "Listen," I went on. "A British cousin of my father's is married to an inspector in the Municipal Police. I think I ought to call him right away." I mentioned this man's name, which was known throughout Shanghai.

"Oh, we don't need a policeman," Rick said hastily.

"But your son's lost," I said. "Why, he might even have been kidnapped."

"No, he hasn't been kidnapped," Rick said, so positively that I felt he must be certain of it.

"But where can he be?" I asked. "You know, I was born in Shanghai, but I'd hate to think of being lost in the city for two days at that age, even with my sister along."

"Jacky's not really lost. If you call in a kid from the third grade called Bobby Alcott, he'll tell us where he is."

"Bobby Alcott? You mean you *know* the Alcotts?" I asked. There was, I reflected, no telling what connections an oil-company family might have.

"No, no," Rick said. "How would I know the Alcotts? But Jacky runs away to the Alcotts' whenever I beat him up real hard."

"Did you beat him up two days ago?"

"Yeah. I guess I didn't know how hard I hit him."

My missionary heritage asserted itself. "Why did you beat him, Mr. Petchum?" I demanded.

"Oh, I guess I had a hangover."

"I don't blame Jacky for running away," I said, somewhat to my own surprise.

Rick Petchum rubbed his head. "I suppose not, but, hell, he

ought to come home now," he said. "Just call the Alcott kid in and I'll talk to him about it."

"Mr. Petchum," I said, "*I* am the principal of the Shanghai American School today, and *I'll* talk to Bobby Alcott." Even as I spoke I was shocked, not only by what I was saying, but by my voice, which seemed to have changed into one of decided authority. And, what was even more curious, the voice, though not my own, had a familiar ring to it, which I couldn't place.

Rick looked surprised. "Well, if you feel that way about it—" he said.

I interrupted him. "I do feel that way about it," I said in my new but oddly familiar voice. "Just wait here till I come back."

I walked down the hall to the third-grade room, still wondering what had happened to me. When I called Bobby Alcott out of class he grinned and followed me into the hall. We sat down on a bench near the school's trophy case.

"Is Jacky Petchum staying at your house?" I asked him.

"Yes," he said, "but he didn't come to school today. He's all black and blue, and anyway he was afraid his father would come for him."

"His father's here now," I said.

"He is?" Bobby gave a worried glance down the hall.

"Yes, and he wants Jacky to go home."

"I don't think Jacky wants to."

"Say, your people don't really know Rick Petchum, do they?" I asked.

Bobby gave me a disgusted look. "Of course not," he said. "My father works for Standard Oil."

"That's what I mean," I said, not intending to be put down by a third grader. "What's Jacky Petchum like?"

For a few moments Bobby was silent, as if making up his mind whether to answer me. Then he said, "He's all right. He's nice. But his father's always beating him up. And then. . . ." He paused.

"Then what?" I asked.

"Well, I'm not supposed to know this at home, but there's always some woman up at their place, and Jacky's mother is always away. It's a Japanese now, and sometimes Jacky doesn't get anything to eat at home because the servants keep leaving. His father beats up the Japanese girl too, sometimes."

"Yes," I said, "I've heard about that. I think if it's all right with your mother for Jacky to stay there awhile, I'll tell his father he isn't coming home right away."

"Gee, can you do that?" Bobby asked.

"Of course," I said, pleased to show off. "I'll tell him anything I want to." Once again I was surprised to hear my new voice.

Bobby looked doubtful, but he said, "Say, I told my mother what you'd said when I went home for tiffin today, and you know what?"

"What?"

"At first she didn't believe me, but then I told her it wasn't the regular principal, it was a senior on Student Government Day."

"What did she say to that?"

"She asked me who it was, and I said it was you, and she laughed and laughed. Then she said, 'Oh, that's just like a crazy damn missionary kid.'" Bobby edged down the bench and watched to see whether I would laugh or be angry.

I looked at him and then heard my new voice say in a kindly way, "My dear boy, your mother's language is only to be expected from an oil family. She didn't try to punish you?"

"No, she didn't," Bobby said. "She laughed so much I think she's forgotten all about everything else."

"Good," I said. "The whole thing was ridiculous anyway. If any of you business kids amount to anything, it'll be a miracle. Now go on back to your room and I'll talk to Jacky's father."

When I got back to the principal's office I said to Rick, "Your son is at the Alcotts', Mr. Petchum. He's black and blue all over and he doesn't want to come home. Nor do I see why he should."

"The Alcotts are high-class folks, you know," Rick said, as if this somehow excused him for having beaten Jacky.

"I suppose they are, in a way," I answered. "Bobby says Jacky doesn't want to come home. I don't see that the school can do anything for you, but I must say, Mr. Petchum, that beating up your son just because you don't feel well seems utterly absurd to me." As I said this I knew at last why my voice sounded so familiar. It was exactly like my father's when he was preaching a sermon. I also realized that I had just tossed my head to one side and back a little, one of my father's characteristic gestures when making a particularly telling point. But I hadn't much time to think about this discovery, for my father's voice was speaking again. "And when it comes to ideas of discipline, Mr. Petchum, Mrs. Alcott's aren't. . . ." My father's voice faded out, apparently remembering that whatever Mrs. Alcott's ideas of discipline might be, they were probably a lot better than Rick Petchum's.

"If I could see the principal . . ." Rick said. He ran his right hand over his hair in what seemed a rather menacing gesture, and I wondered if he was going to force the issue. For a moment I thought of putting through a call for help to the principal's suite. Then I remembered the look of alarm with which Rick had greeted the name of the police inspector, my relative by marriage, and I was pleased to hear my father's voice say, "My dear Mr. Petchum, *I* am the principal of the Shanghai American School today."

"Yes, I know," he said. He stared at me a moment and then began to laugh, as if he found me and the whole situation somewhat amusing. "I've enjoyed this. I really have," he said. "It's quite an idea, this Student Government. Nothing like good American ideas. Maybe Jacky'll be principal when he's in high school."

"Maybe he will be, if he isn't beaten to death meanwhile," I was terrified to hear my father's voice say.

"Oh, he isn't hurt bad," Rick said, still looking amused.

"There can be hurts other than physical ones," my father's voice declaimed resonantly, to my horror.

"Well, say, I guess I've got to go now," Rick said, looking a little less happy. "And, say, any time you want to be fixed up with anything, you let me know."

"I was born in Shanghai," a voice that seemed to be a blend of my father's and my own said haughtily.

"Oh, well, then . . ." Rick said, waving his hand at me and chuckling. He looked at me closely and laughed again, shrugging his shoulders. "Thanks anyway. I guess Jacky'll be back one of these days. And I can always send the Alcotts a present, can't I?"

"Yes, you can," I said to his back as he went through the door.

I waited four or five minutes before going out to suggest to my secretary that we close the office and join the rest of the "faculty" for tea in the teachers' sitting room. When I did go and speak to her at last, it was with almost as much regret as relief that I found my father's voice had left me.

THE THREE WORLDS

WHEN I WAS A BOARDER at the Shanghai American School, I tried at times to get in touch by telephone with my father at the mission. In those days the entire mission station was served by a single telephone in the gatehouse of the Boys' School compound. This should have made things simple enough, since Father taught at the Boys' School, but in actual experience it didn't help at all, and my frustrations gave me a lasting telephone phobia. I would ring central from the school and give the mission number, Central 1850, being careful to say "One-eight-five-naught," and not "One-eight-five-oh," because if one said "oh" to a telephone operator in Shanghai that was just what the girls would say right back. This part of the process was not too difficult, requiring no more than three or four repetitions. Afterward, I would wait for some time while the operator rang the Boys' School gatehouse. Eventually, the Chinese gatekeeper would answer, shouting the standard Chinese Shanghai telephone salute, a loud, nasal "Waanh" into the mouthpiece. I would shout back my own "Waanh" and he would ask in Chinese, "Where are you?" I would say, also in Chinese, that I was at the Flowery Flag School, and ask where he was. He would say he was at the Pure Heart School, and who was I. I would tell him who I was, and would he please be good enough either to call my father to the telephone or take a message for him.

At this point the fun, from the gatekeeper's point of view, would begin. Having grasped who was speaking and knowing that my Chinese was far from fluent, he would ask me to repeat four or five times who I was, where I was, and what I wanted. When he ran out of questions, he would announce in cold and precise tones that he had no intention whatsoever of calling my father, that he doubted my being the person I said I was, that he wondered what in the world my father was doing in China, that he was not interested in doing a thing for me if I *was* who I said I was, and that he would be glad to tell me just what he thought of both me and my father. Once more I would ask him to call my father to the phone or take a message for him, and the gatekeeper would ask me if I hadn't understood what he had said. Again I would ask him to tell my father I wished to speak to him, and the gatekeeper would begin with great clarity to say what he thought of me, of my father, and of foreigners in general.

I find it hard to believe that I let myself in for this conversation more than two or three times—and I doubt that I did—but in my memory it lives as an endlessly repeated performance. I do know that no matter how many times it took place I never once succeeded in reaching my father by phone at the mission. Whenever I was at South Gate myself and went into the Boys' School, this gatekeeper nodded coldly to me and I nodded coldly to him. And whenever I spoke to my parents about my trouble with the phone, explaining why I hadn't called up instead of coming all the way out to South Gate to deliver a message, I was told that my Chinese was so poor that I couldn't possibly understand what the gatekeeper was saying, that he had probably been telling me Father was out, or that he hadn't, perhaps, really understood a word I had said to him, my Chinese being so faulty. This was not altogether true; the gatekeeper

used quite a few phrases that I suspected my parents were ignorant of, but I felt it best after all not to go into this.

Whether the entire telephone system in Shanghai was inefficient or whether my experiences with the Boys' School gatekeeper so unnerved me that I was unable to use the instrument properly, I cannot say, but I found that even an ordinary call from the school to the Settlement, or from Frenchtown to the school, usually led to confusion. Persons I telephoned failed—refused, it seemed to me—to understand me. They insisted that my voice, if it really *was* my voice, sounded cold, flat, and dead, and I began to believe that to establish communication among my three worlds I myself had actually to move from one sphere into another.

I have no wish to strain the symbol. In spite of my ineptness I must have put through a few successful telephone calls, but at that time everything I did seemed only to point up the cleavages between the three areas of my life. Although I did my best not to confuse the three worlds of mission, school, and city, at times I failed to keep them far enough apart. Nothing really serious ever happened, but I came closest to a genuine clash late in my Shanghai life, when I should have been skillful enough to avoid completely even the risk of conflict. By this time I had started to build up a small collection of books, and since my funds were limited I found the Modern Library a convenient series on which to concentrate. I think it is fashionable now to shake one's head and sniff in disgust at the first mention of the Modern Library's old imitation leather bindings. Perhaps the everyday smells of Shanghai were so strong that they had dulled my nose, or perhaps the Oriental air worked a change upon those bindings, for I never found them at all disagreeable to smell or to handle, and the volumes I still have on my shelves do not get sticky or mold

or melt or break out in cancerous growths or do any of the other horrid things reported of them.

I bought most of my books at the China American Book Company's store on Nanking Road. On my way home to South Gate weekends, I often spent a couple of hours browsing here, and though I was repeatedly tempted by items fresh from the presses of London or New York, I usually compromised on another Modern Library volume, preferably bound in blue. And though I cannot claim to have missed many meals in order to feed my mind, I did forgo a number of movies and snacks, wondering all the time if I could ever save enough to buy a four-volume set of Borzoi books that I coveted as much for its Dwiggins design as for its contents.

In the Modern Library I started with Conrad Aiken's *Modern American Poetry* and went on to *A Portrait of the Artist as a Young Man.* Later I bought *Sons and Lovers,* and near the end of my last year at SAS, when the seniors chose *The Importance of Being Earnest* as their class play and I found myself cast in the role of Algernon, I was delighted to find that it gave me an excuse to buy *Salome and Other Plays.* That any of this literary exploration should have led me into trouble seems strange when I recall the careful way in which we pruned *The Importance of Being Earnest* to make it acceptable to the audience of missionary and Shanghai business families we expected to attend our performance. Under our prudent eyes all of Oscar Wilde's lines were passed and approved except for the loose remark tossed out by Jack Worthing when Miss Prism claims the portmanteau checked in Gower Street Station. At this point Worthing turns to her with a passionate cry of "Mother!" We thought this moderately funny and wanted to keep it in the play, but after careful discussion among ourselves and with the teacher coaching us, who was himself the son of missionaries, we realized that the

naughty implications would prove too racy for our Shanghai audience and we reluctantly slashed the line.

When I remember that we had sense enough to do this, I wonder why I was so foolish as to confuse the world of the city and the quite different world of the school. Near the end of the school year a girl in the junior class asked me if I couldn't give her something interesting and "modern" to read, preferably fiction. She had, she assured me, exhausted the school library, and I could understand this, for I had long ranged beyond its somewhat severe confines. Having thought over the titles of the twenty-odd books I owned, I asked, "Have you ever read any D. H. Lawrence?"

"I've never even heard of him," she said.

I suggested that she might like to read *Sons and Lovers*. She thought she might, and I lent her the book.

A couple of days later I heard indirectly that the girl no longer had the book. Apparently some passages of it had puzzled her—I should have said earlier that she was not Shanghai-born—and she had gone to consult the wife of the acting principal. This good woman assured her that she and her husband had once started to read that very novel and, finding it appallingly immoral and nasty, had pitched it into the fire. The girl, saved from contamination, had departed, leaving my copy of *Sons and Lovers* in the hands of the acting principal's wife.

I wondered how the blue binding would react to fire. Not having been officially notified that the girl no longer had the book, I sat tight, waiting for the punishment I felt sure would come. Perhaps I was lucky to have run afoul of only an acting principal. I may also have been lucky in that most of the senior boys, as I have noted elsewhere, had been caught cheating in an exam a few weeks before. Ordinarily, my crime of confusing the worlds of school and city

would have been far more serious than anything as understandable as cheating, but with the class about to graduate, at least one boy *had* to come through with a clean record and fairly decent grades in order to be a candidate for the annual Rotary Bursary, a substantial cash prize given by the Shanghai chapter of Rotary International to "the most outstanding boy" of the graduating class. The winner was expected to stand high in scholarship and "character," to take part in athletics, and to be a "leader." I was almost the only candidate left for this honor, and the acting principal and his wife may have decided to keep my name clear. A week or so after I heard that my book had been confiscated, the girl returned it to me, mumbling a few words about having found it somewhat dull. This may sound a rather stringent judgment of Lawrence's work, and a surprising one, though it would not have sounded nearly so surprising had it come from a person born in Shanghai. On looking the book over, I found that two leaves near the end had been crumpled with what must have been some fierceness. Just who had done this, or why, I couldn't guess, but the pages are badly marred to this day. There are no passages in them that I should have thought alarming to anyone, but as a Shanghai native I may be biased.

In spite of my obtuseness on this occasion, I used to take pleasure in my awareness of the three worlds, and never more than when I could move from one world to a second and from the second to the third in a single day. This happened most frequently on the Fridays that I went home to South Gate for the weekend. Leaving the school for the city was to leave a world of slightly artificial and self-conscious values, most of them based on American models, for a more fluid sphere. Although in Frenchtown the underlying tone was French, and in the International Settlement British, the city retained a largeness that let me slip into it and forget that I was

anywhere but in Shanghai. As long as I was alone in this world and met no one from either of the other two, I could be pretty much whatever I wanted to be.

At first I was usually overcome by comfortable languor as I relaxed after leaving the school world on Avenue Pétain. If I were the only person from SAS on the bus that left from the corner of the grounds at Route Dufour, I would sprawl in the back seat and look forward to the ride downtown. If I were not alone I knew that I must wait to enter the world of the city. But when I was alone I sank into this new world with some relief as the bus crisscrossed its way down through Frenchtown to Avenue Edward VII, where I got off. Here I had to choose among several attractions. I could go to Nanking Road and look at books, I could attend a movie, or I could walk down Kiangse Road to the edge of the Chinese city and continue directly to South Gate. Usually I spent some time in the Settlement, often doing nothing but wander through the streets, enjoying my anonymity but ready to return instantly to either of the two other worlds if I met anyone I knew who insisted on carrying his world with him. Perhaps this was why I frequently went to the cinema, for once I stepped inside the darkened hall no one could question the world I lived in.

Eventually it would be time for the rest of the trip. This continued through the city, but now the definitely Chinese part of it. Though it was a world apart from the international sections, it bore far more resemblance to them than to the school or the mission. I plunged from a busy, bustling life into a busier and more bustling one, from a life in which people had enough leisure and money to keep up appearances and maintain a degree of privacy to a life in which no one cared about appearances and only the very wealthy could hide from the public eye.

This intensification was made more vivid if I was in a hurry to get home, for then I left the bus at the corner of Rue du Consulat and Rue Palikao and walked south toward the Chinese city. On this walk I dived abruptly into a completely Chinese atmosphere. If I made the trip in spring when a basket fair was held outside South Gate, I would have to shove my way through a solid press of persons, all chattering and bargaining, before I could get home. At any time of year, if I walked along in the dusk, I would be flattered and disturbed by the invitations of the amahs soliciting for highly painted prostitutes who stood back from the street in shadowed doorways.

An entirely different route was possible if I went all the way from Avenue Pétain to South Gate by bicycle. The transition to the Chinese section was as definite as an electric shock when I left the pavements of Frenchtown for the Chinese cobblestones. But whatever direction I came from, as soon as I came within the mission walls I knew once more just where I stood. In the school, values might be a trifle artificial, to say one thing and mean another; in the city, life might appear relaxed and indifferent; but in the mission I knew no doubt, no hesitation. The answers were written, the rules established. I had only to act upon them, to speak the words already given. I was often relieved to enter this world, to know for certain what meant what. Yet it was impossible to bring any other world into it, as impossible as it was to bring any one of my three worlds into another. Instead of blending, they grew more and more distinct and unyielding, drew farther and farther apart, until I came to see that if they were ever to meet, it would not be in Shanghai itself but only in the person who knew them all and took them with him when he left.

When I stepped to the front of the platform on Commencement

Day at the Shanghai American School one June afternoon in 1930 to receive the Rotary Bursary, I knew that many persons present thought me an astonishingly feeble winner compared with the boys who had received it in former years. These had been fine upstanding athletes of impeccable appearance. Certainly everyone in the audience except my parents and the other Presbyterians wondered how I could be thought in any way to meet the standards set up by the committee on awards. It did not occur to me at the time, but I have occasionally felt since that if some of these Shanghailanders had known about *Sons and Lovers* they might not have judged me so harshly. They might even have felt that I possessed qualifications beyond those of a number of my predecessors.

DEPARTURES

M Y GRADUATION from the Shanghai American School in June
of 1930 coincided with the beginning of my father's sabbatical year. My parents felt that I needed to take a year off between
high school and college, and when I discovered that they had no
objection to my splitting this time between Europe, where I could
presumably strengthen both my French and my lungs, and the
States, where I would be spending at least the next four years, I
happily agreed with them. The Passion Play at Oberammergau was
scheduled for this summer, and playing on my mother's wish to see
it as well as her dislike of ocean travel because of seasickness, I
pointed out that the voyage through the Suez Canal would be hot
as well as time-consuming, but we could avoid it altogether by taking
the Trans-Siberian Express to Moscow and on through Warsaw to
Berlin. This was something I very much wanted to experience, having discovered, though not in any classroom, the great Russian novelists during my last two years of high school. I felt that actually
seeing Moscow as well as experiencing what I believed would be
day after day of travel across open tundra and wilderness would
somehow deepen my understanding.

All this took a little persuasion, especially to win Father's approval. He had never been sure that he approved of the Passion Play

spectacle, and he had no particular interest in visiting a Godless Russia. In addition, because the United States had not yet recognized the Soviet regime, Americans wishing to cross Siberia bought their tickets on faith in Shanghai and then took passage to the port of Dairen, the site of the nearest Russian consulate. After obtaining their visas they entrained on the Sino-Japanese Railway to Harbin and Mukden and eventually proceeded to Manchouli on the Mongolian border where they boarded the Express.

Getting a visa, we were assured, was a mere formality. This inconvenience was simply the Russians' way of pointing out to Americans that it was about time for their government to recognize the Soviet Union. In the end, I succeeded in winning my parents over to my plan.

Our voyage up to Dairen went smoothly. At the Soviet Consulate, a subordinate official handed each of us a long form to be filled out in triplicate. It contained questions of whether we had ever borne arms against the Russian people, or been convicted of illegal activity in a court of law, or changed our citizenship, and I can't remember what else, except that the list of queries was a long one.

Mother finished first and was ushered in to be interviewed briefly by the Consul himself. Shortly after she came out, having told me that this official's English was rather weak, I was shown in. The Consul ran his eye over my application and asked me what my plans were after reaching Europe. I said that I was hoping to live with a French-speaking family for a time before going on to an American university. He promptly switched to French, putting me at a disadvantage, but I managed to get out adequate replies and he wished me well, handing my passport over to a secretary for stamping.

Father, carrying his and Mother's passport, went in next. I told Mother that I had had to get along on my French, and showed her

my visa. We tried to make out words in the Cyrillic alphabet and then sat waiting for Father to appear. After at least a quarter of an hour had gone by we began to wonder what was taking him so long.

"Surely your father isn't so rash as to bring up any questions about religion," Mother said anxiously.

"I wouldn't think so," I said, "but you never can tell."

In my memory we waited for at least an hour, but it was probably no more than another fifteen minutes. When Father did appear with the Consul, they both looked haggard. Father was holding the passport still open, so I could see the visa, and that was a relief.

The Consul conducted Father over to us as if he were delivering him into our care, saying that he hoped we would have a pleasant journey, though he spoke without much confidence.

"I'll explain when we're back in the hotel," Father said, cutting off our questions as we left the building.

We finally learned that as he was filling out his application form Father remembered getting a parking ticket in downtown Chicago in the winter of 1923–24—he was not certain of the month—while I was having my sinuses irrigated by a doctor who had assured us that this would cure me of asthma. Father had parked our Model T Ford sedan in a no-parking zone that had been neglected for so long that all the red paint on the curb had worn off. This was the first ticket Father had ever received. Instead of paying the fine he went to court to defend himself and explain why he couldn't know that he had parked his car illegally. The judge was sympathetic, but on learning that there was a no-parking sign posted some thirty feet away on a utility pole, he reluctantly enforced the law with a minimal fine.

Consequently, when Father came to the question of being convicted in a court of law he, being a stickler for truth and the written

word, had indicated that he had been. The Consul had been surprised by Father's admission and had asked him to explain. The Consul had been clearly skeptical of Father's claiming to own an automobile, but what particularly worried him was that all this incomprehensible lunacy, involving a judge and a court and a missionary claiming to have owned a private automobile, had taken place in Chicago, well known in 1930 as a smuggling center for illegal alcohol, not to mention other, more serious crimes.

When Father assured him that he had lived in Chicago for the better part of a year in order to attend the University of Chicago, the Consul had grown increasingly skeptical. Hadn't Father already attended a university? Well, yes, Father had said, he held more than one university degree, but he had wanted to keep informed on recent developments in psychological theory.

What the Consul made of that I have no idea, but apparently what had puzzled him most was Father's claim, as a missionary, to have owned an automobile; for he not only thought that strange but believed that anyone who owned an automobile would certainly not be subject to the discipline of what Father claimed was a court set up to deal entirely with such matters.

As he had escorted Father to where Mother and I had risen from our chairs, the Consul, I suspected, had felt he was turning over for safekeeping an essentially mad, but probably harmless, victim of capitalism.

At Manchouli, we found the Express waiting for us. Though Presbyterians felt an obligation to travel first class, we had decided that what was known as "soft class"—between "de luxe" and "hard class"—would be acceptable, and we settled into our compartment. The seats were upholstered with plain cloth as apart from the plush of "de luxe" and the bare wood of "hard." Having been warned of

the expense of eating in the single, always crowded diner, we had supplied ourselves with several cases of canned goods and a small spirit lamp for heating.

Even before the Express moved out of the station, I felt that I had left China behind. I also suspected that it would be a long time before I returned and that even then it would not be for anything permanent and certainly not as a minister or missionary. I hadn't yet worked up the courage to tell this to Mother, who would probably not have minded, or Father, who would certainly have been seriously disturbed.

Once on the move, as I looked out over the open slopes of grazing land for the remainder of that day and all of the next, I silently prided myself on having prepared for this in my reading. This was exactly the Siberia I had visualized, especially in the evening light, which lasted at least until ten o'clock. I could imagine serving out years of exile in this empty land that would be snow-covered during its short winter days.

Complete betrayal faced me as I woke the following morning. The empty rolling slopes had disappeared. We were traveling through heavily wooded areas from time to time, crossing rivers that could obviously be harnessed for electric power, and the railway stations where we stopped briefly were crowded with people apparently waiting for local transport. Only later was I to learn of the dispossession of their land that had brought this about.

But if my views had suffered a rapid change, Father's feelings about Russia, which had certainly been reinforced by the Consul in Dairen, were undergoing a gradual shift. Quite a number of Soviet army officers were on the Express, as well as what were probably middle-level bureaucrats. Many of them carried pocket chess sets, and Father, a keen player, found himself gradually incorporated

into this international brotherhood. He would return to our compartment from time to time, reporting enthusiastically on matches he had either observed or played in.

"You know," he would remark, "though I can't understand what they're saying, it's obvious that they're splendid fellows—frank and open. I can't really believe that they aren't in their own way regular God-fearing people."

A daylong tour of Moscow only confirmed him in this view when our official tourist guide led us to a chapel inside the Kremlin where we witnessed a Greek Orthodox service. "What a lot of misinformation we've been given about Russia," Father said as we went out to look at Lenin's tomb. Mother and I murmured a few noncommittal syllables, careful to say nothing about the fact that this service had obviously been a feature of our "tour."

A few days out of Manchouli I had come down with an attack of asthma, so I did little sightseeing until it was time to leave Munich for Oberammergau. Just what Father's reactions were to this pageant I couldn't tell, because at the very first meal we ate at the hostel where we were staying, Father ran into an old colleague of *his* father's, a Dr. Gerwig. Dr. Gerwig had lost his only child—a son—in an air-force training accident shortly after America entered the First World War. He was traveling with a pleasant middle-aged woman whom he introduced as his housekeeper, assuring us she was of great assistance to him when he traveled.

As one born in Shanghai, I found it startling that both Mother and Father apparently swallowed whole Dr. Gerwig's version of this relationship. Sneaking a look that evening at the hostel's registry, I found that Dr. Gerwig and his companion were registered in the same room, but I saw no reason to pass this information along to my parents. What was more important, Dr. Gerwig had connections

with a number of persons in Switzerland and thoroughly approved of my plan of spending some time there. He felt certain that he could arrange something, insisting that I looked exactly like his lost son, Percy, when Percy was my age.

This lucky encounter seemed to take most of Father's attention away from the Passion Play itself, which we reverently attended. I could tell, glancing at him from time to time, that this unplanned meeting with Dr. Gerwig had thrown him back to his own youth, moving him to relive the past.

Only on our final day did he come out of this sufficiently to make a single remark about the production. He had been one of the first missionaries to commission a Chinese artist to recreate major Biblical scenes in traditional Chinese style, producing a number of scrolls that he used in his teaching. This had shocked the more conservative members of the mission, who did not hesitate to voice their disapproval, but when the scrolls proved to be effective teaching devices they grudgingly admitted their usefulness, though still expressing their belief that "Jesus couldn't have looked like *that!*" It must have been with these memories in mind that Father made the only pronouncement I can remember on the hours we had spent watching the story unfold. "It's interesting to think of all that happening in Bavaria, isn't it?" he said.

In Switzerland, armed with a letter of introduction from Dr. Gerwig, we called on Percy A. Scholes, who was later to publish *The Puritans and Music in England and New England* as well as *The Oxford Companion to Music.* Mr.—later Dr.—Scholes lived in Chamby-sur-Montreux, and like Dr. Gerwig, he heartily approved of my spending some months in the mountains, even in this particular area, where he had many connections. Mrs. Scholes served us tea on their balcony overlooking Lake Geneva, and when we left,

her husband assured us that by the time we reached London he would have word waiting about arrangements for my return to Switzerland.

After stays in Geneva and Paris we reached London. Percy Scholes had made tentative arrangements for me to live with a French-speaking family in nearby Corsier-sur-Vevey. In *Two Schools of Thought: Some Tales of Learning and Romance,* cowritten with Carolyn See, I have already recorded my brief first visit to Oxford with my parents, a visit that eventually led to my applying for candidacy as a Rhodes Scholar.

A few days later we boarded the *Bremen* in Southampton, and after crossing the English Channel, I waved good-bye to my parents that afternoon from dockside in Cherbourg as the liner headed out for New York.

Certainly my French was strengthened in Corsier-sur-Vevey, and I even undertook some Alpine climbing with the older three of the six sons of the Gardiol household, which also included a much treasured daughter. Though I kept in touch with the family for years, and visited them in the winter of 1936–37, I hardly expected the village of Corsier-sur-Vevey ever to attract any international attention. But on the death of Charlie Chaplin in 1977 there was my "Swiss hometown" in the headlines.

Back in the States, I joined my family in Wooster, Ohio, where my sister was a graduating senior at the College of Wooster, which had been Father's college as well as his sister's, our Aunt Clara. Father now drove a Model A Ford, and I accompanied him on a number of jaunts that he enjoyed finding reasons to take, going as far east as New York on one occasion and on another as far south as Asheville, North Carolina.

During this period I decided that Wooster had been privileged

to educate more than its share of our family, a conclusion reinforced by learning how to shovel snow from the sidewalk in the morning and how to bank the furnace fire at night.

The following summer, our entire family drove across the American continent. Once again an attack of asthma changed the direction of my life, with everyone agreeing that I should spend my college years in southern California. I have never regretted my choice of Occidental, which boasted a remarkably varied, if small, Department of English. I can still shout every syllable of our traditional cheer of *Io Triumphe!* and I tend to choke up a little over the Savoyard doggerel of the school's anthem, *Occidental Glorious!*

My chapters of *Two Schools of Thought* record the major miracle of my winning a Rhodes Scholarship and a partial record of my three years there as a member of Merton College.

As I have said in my Introduction, I began my teaching career at Occidental, and eventually achieved print with *Minor Heresies.* By the time it had gone through six printings, Father had almost persuaded himself that it was *his* work, ironically enough when I considered my basic intention in writing it and my convictions concerning the entire mission movement.

But I had found at least one of my voices, and while Father was chiding some of his colleagues for their lack of a sense of humor I was already at work on what was to become *Tales out of School.* I benefited from a first-reading agreement with *The New Yorker,* with Katharine White as my editor. I learned a great deal from Mrs. White, though I did have an occasional conflict over some of the magazine's taboos.

Only after the publication of *Tales out of School* did I run into any difficulties. I had planned my third series of reminiscences to deal with International Shanghai, *The Other City,* as apart from the

South Gate mission, which was the City of (a Presbyterian) God. My experiences in International Shanghai were not particularly lurid, but when "Ramón and the North American Attitudes" came out in *The New Yorker,* my parents let me know that I was embarrassing them in the eyes of their friends by revealing that I had had tea with Ramón and his two candidates in an establishment on Avenue Joffre. They pointedly failed to mention the *babas au rhum.*

On the defense, I said, "You know, neither of you had ever heard of *The New Yorker* until I began to appear in it."

They nodded.

"None of your friends would know I had anything in *The New Yorker* unless *somebody* told them, which *I* would certainly never do."

"Yes, that's true," Mother said.

I felt I had scored. But at that point Father threw back his head and "*Nevertheless,* John!" rang out in his most emphatic pulpit voice.

I scarcely hesitated before I said, "Yes, Father, I'll see what I can do about it."

During that moment of hesitation, though I knew what I would say, I had time to realize that I was answering not as an American being obedient to his father, but as a Chinese son of the house knowing he should not bring shame upon it or in any way lead to either of his parents' loss of face.

Thus it was that, for me, my third book lacked much of what I had wanted to write about, such as the parallels of mission and outpost-of-Empire attitudes as well as their contradictions. Obviously I couldn't say what I wished to and remain a loyal Chinese son as long as my parents were living.

Family concerns contributed to the delay of getting around to what I did have to say. I also felt that, just as I should not injure

my parents, I should probably wait until there was no one left of their generation connected with the mission to feel hurt by what I might write. Some persons, however, might claim that the delay was caused by sheer laziness.

In addition to this, I had carefully avoided mention of a dark side of our family inheritance, and I wanted to be able to write openly about it—as I have in my third published novel, *Winter Return*, which is autobiographical in part, though not an autobiography—but not until the reminiscent pieces had been completed.

Finally I had no excuse left. *Strong Drink, Strong Language,* my fourth collection of reminiscences, came out in 1990—a mere forty years after the publication of *The Other City.* This clearly shows that I am only in part Chinese; for if I were completely Chinese I would have waited for a tidier figure to elapse, something humbly brief in the scheme of things, at the very least a half century.

Designer: Barbara Jellow
Compositor: Maryland Composition Co., Inc.
Text: 11/15.5 Adobe Garamond
Display: Adobe Garamond
Printer: Maple Vail Book Mfg. Group
Binder: Maple Vail Book Mfg. Group